The Kingdom of Mist and Blood

AMANDA J STEVENS

Contents

I dedicate this book to my high school English teacher Mrs. Susan Marie McClellan. She told me my senior year that I was born to be an author. She was that one teacher who changed my world when I had her first semester of my freshman year, and after that first class I made sure I was taking at least one of her classes each semester throughout my high school years. I found a love of reading, writing, and even problem solving. She encouraged me to step outside my comfort zones and I got into her public speaking classes. She got my novice poems published and throughout my adulthood I think of her often, especially through my long journey of writing this book. This is my thank you, Mrs. McClellan, for being an unbelievable teacher and inspiring a youth to push herself and manifest her dreams!

And, to my loving and encouraging husband, Zachary. To our four beautiful, little monsters, I love you more than you'll ever know. My precious bloodline, may you continue to grow in grace and beauty so that you can make your dreams come true with just a little bit of elbow grease. ~xoxo~Mum

"Deep into that darkness peering, long I stood there, wondering, fearing, doubting, dreaming dreams no mortal ever dared to dream before"

"Words have no power to impress the mind without the exquisite horror of their reality"

~Edgar Allan Poe

Prologue

I wander through the forest, leaving behind the town and my home. It is raining, and I am cold and wet from the storm. It's so dark, black as the scariest night. I have lost everything. My mother is gone, taken from me. Two men from our village, those horrible monstrous men, they came for me. They burned our home and hurt my mother when they couldn't find me. My mother protected me, and then a different stranger came... a stranger with strange eyes and skin. That creature came to save us.

Forever I walk through the endless night until I trip on the root of a large willow tree and my small five-year-old body falls to the ground. I curl up tight into a little ball in the thick mud. Memories flash when I close my eyes, and my brain replays them over and over, torturing me.

I hid. I hid up high in the rafters of my home, right where Momma told me to. She told me not to leave my spot, to stay hidden and not come to her. She told me in her rush to conceal me that it was so important for me to stay hidden and quiet 'til the men had gone.

Alone and exhausted, haunted by the last few hours, I hug myself tight and begin to cry. I try to recall what happened and how I ended up here. I am cold, wet, alone in the dark and without my mother. Surrounded in darkness, surrounded by the deepest of darkness. I know the evils of the forest lay in wait; this is where nightmares are born.

A wolf howls into the darkness—something nears. Its feet crunch against the forest floor.

CHAPTER ONE

The Human World

My mother can hear them coming long before I can, but now I hear them, howling into the night and yelling my mother's name. We hear their drunken voices getting ever closer to our home. A heavy fist slams against our door.

The one at the door is the evilest man in our village. He makes bad things happen. Momma hides me as the banging continues.

A splintering crack pierces our once peaceful evening, and the door frame and wooden bolt cave. Our door crashes inward as I hurry to get positioned in my safe and hidden spot way up high. Up in the rafters, I settle myself in the joints of the big beams.

A large man emerges from our broken doorway and yells for Momma. He begins to destroy anything within his reach, his even uglier companion close behind him.

"Amanda!" the first man slurs. "Princess and Guardian of Hell! Where are you, woman?" His deep voice is a throaty growl.

The pretty dress Momma was making for one of the little girls in our village is finished and hanging in its place. He rips and tears it to shreds. Momma's needle machine that she made herself to help her sew faster is hammered into tiny pieces by the thinner ugly man's fists.

The big man calls out, "Amanda! Show yourself."

"Here, Gregory," she whispers, stepping from the shadows and into his path. "How is it that I can help you this evening?" Momma lowers her head in submission to the man before her.

"You birthed a monstrous beast! Don't lie, woman, we've seen it." Spit flies from his mouth. His breath reeks of stale ale. She backs away from the two men until she is trapped in a corner.

The evil Gregory hits her hard across her beautiful face, but she does not cry out. Just a single tear escapes and runs down her soft cheek. The thinner man grabs her long raven hair and pulls her head back violently. She finds my face in the shadows of the rafters and looks into my eyes. Her eyes are bright green and telling me everything will be okay, to stay where I am and how much she loves me.

"Lord, woman, your skin changes and deepens in color by the day, you know." Gregory examines her head to toe then whispers to her in a voice like silk, "You were once so pale-skinned with gorgeous emerald eyes. Beautiful!" He burps into her face. "Every man in this village dreamed of owning your beauty and claiming it for his own. Look at you now—your skin turns a sickly hue of green. Is it because of that child? The child you chose to bear? Do tell me, woman, what creature from the forest came and raped you that night? Killed your unlucky betrothed the night before your wedding and left you to rot amongst us? The villagers whisper it's because of you these curses—droughts, famine, and sickness—have spread. It is all because of you and that child. It's your fault! You should have done yourself a favor and killed yourself. Letting a beast take you, let alone birth its spawn!" The big man hits her again, hard across her face. I want to go to Momma, help her to be able to run away.

"Run, Momma, run," I say to myself. "Why don't you run?"

Her eyes, her wonderful, loving eyes tell me to stay and plead to me, *Hush, my baby, hush. Soon they will go.*

"Where is the demon child, woman?" Gregory yells at her. "Tell me now! Where? The demon's life needs to end and if you cannot stomach it then I'll do it my damn self!"

Momma says nothing. The two men have her held down on her knees. She is looking at me, seeing only me. Her eyes brim with her love and joy of me. I can feel their power filling me with her love, yet the pain and anguish these men are causing her is starting to show. Her eyes dim their brightness of green and turn dull. She smiles at me and mouths, *I love you, my baby, shhhh.*

"Tell me," Gregory growls into her ear with gritted teeth, pulling a dagger from his work belt. "Where is the demon child?" He slices Momma's arm with the sharp blade.

I hiss loudly from my safe perch and get into a hunched pouncing position. Momma's eyes scold me, and I freeze. My hiss makes the ugly man jump. He frantically looks in every direction. I am still hidden, hidden from their angry eyes in the comfort of the shadows.

The big man doesn't seem to notice. He smiles. His pupils dilate, growing black and evil. My hiss did not even startle him. This is just a game to him, and he's going to make my mother pay.

"Tell me." He stares her down, playing with his knife, catching the light from a hanging brazier. "Where is the child?"

He waits but a moment before slicing into her arm, deeper this time. Fat, crimson red droplets form and run down her arm. Momma blinks and smiles her sweet smile to me. She looks at the big scary man and whispers something, but I cannot hear, nor can he.

"Speak up, woman!"

But Momma speaks so quietly, he leans in towards her mouth. Her words and voice are strained. Closer he leans.

Momma spits in his eye and slams her own head into Gregory's, hard, but only on his jaw. He curses her, smacks her again hard across her beautiful face and then sinks the blade into Momma's shoulder. He drags it down to her breast. I whimper but she stays still, just looking at me with her loving eyes.

"Where?" he screams in frustration, and with that Momma turns her sweet smile on Gregory. Without a second thought he slices his sharp knife across her throat. The thinner ugly man gapes at Gregory and lets go of Momma's soft raven hair and she falls... her delicate body falls to the floor.

"We weren't supposed to kill her, Greg!" the thin ugly one says, cursing at him. "What the hell have you done? She's still favored by most of the villagers—we'll be hanged for this!"

"So we make it look like an accident," Gregory says with a shrug, "and no one will be the wiser. Let's start a fire." He grins as wickedly as a raging psychopath and slowly he picks up one of our candles. Both men throw everything in the room into a pile before our fireplace. Gregory lights the fabrics of Momma's projects. He destroys Momma's long sewing table and throws the pieces into the growing flame. Pleased as the fire grows, they make to leave.

"This will surely kill the demon child. We've freed the village of the curses this woman brought to her people!"

Gregory takes a moment for one last look to find me before he steps through the broken door and leaves.

I climb down from my spot and slowly crawl towards Momma.

"Ouch! It is hot! Momma? Please, Momma, get up," I whimper in her ear and nuzzle my face against hers. She is very still and hardly a breath comes from her lips. I lay beside her, afraid. It is getting hotter and the smoke is choking me.

"MOMMA, PLEASE!" I scream, tugging on her hand.

There is a tremendous crash from the back of our home and a man appears. He is different from the other men—his skin is green like mine, dark emerald green. In fact, he looks a lot like me. His eyes are ferocious and purple, ears tipped at the top just like mine and lips set in a grim line. I crouch protectively over my mother and hiss wildly at this strange man. Claws grow long from my fingertips, and this scares me. I swat at the stranger with my newfound sharp curved claws as he comes near.

"Hush, my son, my sweet Merek." He reaches out and caresses my cheek. "I mean neither of you harm. Please let me look at her!" He steps closer.

"Son?" I say to myself, deciphering the word and meaning. Where did he come from? Why have I not seen him, and why didn't he come to Momma when she needed him most? I adjust my stance, trying to look more menacing. I hiss fiercely and swat at him again.

The word *father* repeats like a whisper within my mind. Momma said he would come for us one day. That my father was incredibly special and loved us both more than breath itself. My thoughts are all tangled, and the fire is building. I whimper again as the heat draws closer to me and Momma.

He crouches down beside us. He's not so scary now that he's at my height. Maybe he's here to help. He looks from me to Momma and back to me. A brief smile comes to his lips upon looking deep into my eyes, but the smile quickly turns to a deep frown when he glances at the fire coming so near.

"There may still be time. Please, my son, let me try to help her."

He raises a hand and reaches for my face, but I snap my teeth at him in warning. He pulls his hand away from me and instead rests it against Momma's wrist.

"You see! Feel right here! Her pulse. It is weak and slight, but her heart still beats. I need to act now."

Without giving me a chance to feel Momma's wrist, he gently pushes past me. Leaning down by Momma's throat, he begins licking her wound. I hiss loudly at him and hit the man as hard as I can. My fisted hand meets his side and instead of sinking into his flesh and causing him pain, my tiny hand abruptly stops as if hitting stone. I pull my hand back and cradle it. I can only watch in horror as he bites down hard on her shoulder and neck, then licks the wound across her throat. That's when I see it—Momma's deep cut is healing under this creature's tongue. When he's satisfied that her wound is fully closed and no longer bleeding, he picks up Momma and cradles her in his arms.

"My brave one, my love," he says to her, and kisses her lips so gently. He stands and orders me to climb up onto his back.

I hesitate. I don't trust him. He stares down at me, a stranger, and I'm helpless to protect my mother who's nearly lifeless in his arms. He adjusts Momma's small limp frame into the crook of one arm with little effort and reaches down to take my little hand in his. Nervous, I accept. His hand is big, warm, and welcoming, and with that he lifts me in one fluid motion and slings me to his shoulders.

"Hang on tight. Do not let go! I need to get you two out of here before we all perish."

I wrap my arms around his neck and rest my head on his shoulder. My cheek is flush with his skin and I hear his voice from within my mind. He is singing to me, gently. A warm gentle feeling creeps through me as he sings, and I relax into the curve of his neck.

He jumps with amazing agility, dodging falling rafters and shielding us from the hot flames. He enters the next room, frantically looking for an escape. His melody still soothes me. His gentle song becomes louder but more soothing in my ears and I relax against him again.

The rafter above us gives way and falls—it's going to crush us. With my scream in his ear, he jumps out of its path, springing up to an exposed beam and landing with such perfect balance and ease it's as if Momma and I weigh nothing at all.

"Shield your eyes, son!" he grunts.

I close them tightly and reach down with one hand to cover Momma's eyes too. I hear glass shatter as he kicks out a small window, but it's too tiny for the three of us to fit through. He begins kicking again and again at the wood wall encasing the window. The beam below his feet cracks loudly in protest and he stops.

"Merek!" he screams. "You must crawl through. Come, my boy, give me your hand!" He steadies me as I wiggle through the tiny window. I fit, but how will he and Momma fit through? How will he get through the opening? It is so small, just barely big enough for me.

"Merek! Jump! You must jump to the ground below—"

The beam breaks. Our fingers unravel. I reach back through the window and look down. They fall, fall to the floor below covered in flames. They are nowhere. I cannot see them. Where are they?

"Momma!" I scream, looking feverishly at the space below filled with tall flames where they should have fallen. There is nothing but flames. "Momma!"

"Merek, jump! You must jump!" I hear his voice within my mind. "We are safe! Jump down then come to the other side of the house." I look down. It's so far, I'm too afraid. "Merek, JUMP NOW!" his urgent voice rings within my ears.

My little legs bend and spring, the small landing that was beneath my feet now ablaze with flames. I arch through the air and reach for the tree beside our home. My fingers grasp a branch.

"I caught the tree! I caught the tree!" I cry, elated that I caught it. My body swings up and I quickly slip, losing my grip, and then I'm falling again, screaming as I accelerate toward the ground. My instinct takes over and my small little body twists, one hand grabbing another branch. My body rotates up and over and my feet land hard on the branch. I am safe and perfectly balanced with the ground just a small leap away. I let all my breath out at once.

"Momma!" I leap down from my branch and take off running around the house to the other side. Rounding the corner, my whole body tingling with adrenaline, my one urgent need to find Momma lending me speed, I look up and see in the window the man and Momma! He looks down at me with pride and a huge smile spreads across his lips.

The flames behind them grow bigger and brighter. I can see each of their faces illuminated in dancing flames. Momma looks weak and she's slipping away from me.

"Stand back, Merek!" With that he jumps and lands like a feather upon his feet. "Follow me," he commands. Still cradling Momma, he takes my hand in his and we run toward the Forest of Wedgemore.

We are indeed running straight for the forest. The forest is forbidden. Momma made me promise to never enter. The forbidden Forest of Wedgemore is bewitched and calls to small children like me and they are never seen again. Even grown men that venture too far into its woods lose their way in the frightening mist. Blinded and confused, they are never able to return. These lost ones wander forever lost, forever roaming. You can hear their calls when the moon is at its fullest, those soulless cries of pleading from something that is no longer quite human. It is a very scary place, a place of nightmares.

I pull back against him. Sensing my fear, his melody fills my ears. I become hypnotized by his beautiful song. My resistance against his hand weakens as my body sways in time to the rhythm of his song. He slings me up onto his back and I hold tight as he leads us into the deep, dark, forbidden, and haunting wood.

I hear Momma stir and whimper. Her body straightens and tightens. He rests me on my feet and lets me kiss her forehead.

"Your mother is strong, Merek, but we must make haste. I need to get her to my home. Can you be a big help and run with me? Take my hand."

Hearing my mother's whimper of pain still ringing in my ears, I know she lives. Energized and holding his hand tight, I begin to run with him. Her life fills me and surrounds me. It pushes me and I run faster, so much faster than I have ever run before.

After a long time, the man slows, and we come to a small shack of a house. It is so dark here; I blink several times.

"Let your Goblin eyes adjust, my son, do you see now?" he asks.

I relax and close my eyes and a strange sensation pulls at them. I blink and refocus and it is as if I am looking through new eyes. A shimmering green glow covers everything and illuminates the woods where there was no light before. Now I can see every log, stone, bug, and animal perfectly. A beautiful green shimmering world lies before me.

CHAPTER TWO

My Father

After having run for a long time, Momma lets out a strange painful scream. The man cradling her rushes for the shack of a house that just before was shrouded in shadows by the darkest of night. Now it is lit by a shimmering green glow by my new sight. I follow closely behind as we enter the house.

He lays her gently on a simple bed of stuffed hay and feathers. Lifting her head, he places a soft feathery pillow and lays her against it. He reaches for a tattered blanket to cover her. I see her loving face, but she is sweating with a fever.

"Merek, there is a small stream just outside a few paces away. Take this bowl and bring back water," instructs the man.

I take the bowl and run out the door but abruptly stop just outside, afraid of the deep darkness and shrouded shadows that begin to swallow me whole.

"Use your Goblin sight," his voice calls within my head.

I close my eyes, and upon reopening them the shimmering green world returns to me. Up in the trees, the leaves and branches are dancing in the slight breeze in shades of green I have never seen before. Peeking around the corner of the house, I spy an old wooden fence falling apart on one end, but no sign of the stream.

I notice a tall pillar of stone diagonal from the corner of the house and approach it. There are deep carvings in the stone, a deep emerald color with twinkling gold. Absently I trace a symbol with my fingers, and it shimmers. It makes me smile as the shimmering makes my fingers tingle, and I wiggle my fingers as gold light dances off them.

Momma screams from inside the small home and a panic takes hold of me. I listen hard and hear the trickling of water. I follow the sound of trickling water until I reach the small stream. I sink the bowl to the bottom. The water is freezing cold and bites at my fingers. I race back and enter the home of this strange creature of a man... is he really my father?

"Good boy!" he says as I approach. My eyes are blurred and fuzzy. "In the cupboard by the door you will find a cloth. Bring it to me."

I blink in the dim glow of the single lit candle. Reopening my eyes, the shimmer of green light softens and disappears, replaced by the light of the candle. Carefully and gently, I place the bowl so as not to spill it and search for the cloth. I hand it to him.

"Your mother is succumbing to my venom, and we need to soothe her fever." He rips her dress at the chest and peels the materials back and away from her, exposing her nakedness. I hiss at him and jump up, crouching over her protectively.

"You are a good boy, my son, ever trying to protect your mother. I am very proud of you, but you must trust me now and let me work. You may sit here beside her head and keep the cloth cool against her forehead. Like this." He dips the cloth into the cold water and wrings it out, placing it against her head. A sigh escapes my mother's lips. I do as I'm told like he shows me but continue to watch him intently.

"Ah! I see!" he exclaims as he rips through her satin underdress, exposing more of my mother. I hiss again. "You see, my boy, you must have bitten her while you were still reliant upon her milk! You have given her your venom already!" He claps his hand over his face in disbelief. "So that is why this woman is so strong!"

I look down and see many scars, crescent moon shaped teeth marks and bites all along and across both her breasts. Tears fill my eyes and spill down my face, and my chest heaves.

"No, my boy. Do not cry!" A warm hand touches my cheek. "This is good. Unexpected, but good. Your bites have helped in saving her, my child." I glance up at his face and he meets my runny eyes with a gentle gaze, but I still don't understand and I'm so confused.

"Yes, Merek, you are my son. My own flesh and blood," he tells me proudly.

I look down at Momma's face and dip the cloth again into the cold water. Concentrating on wiping her face, "My father?" I say, just barely a whisper. "She told me one day, *one day* he would come for us." My pain turns to anger, and I shout, "But why not 'til now when we were left unprotected?" He must not truly love us and that's why he left, a voice says within my mind. My brain begins to hurt trying to understand this man.

I hear his voice within my mind. "It pains me to have stayed away from you two." He looks down at Momma with longing and love and reaches for my hand. Instantly our minds become one. His voice echoes within my mind, "Let me show you. Turn your gaze and see my memory. You are still here, safe beside your mother, but able to see my memories."

I turn away from him toward what should be the wall of his home, but instead find the structure gone. The space there is hazy and full of drifting, thick mist. Straining my eyes, the mist swirls and dissipates. My vision clears, and I see a place before my time in his memory. I realize I am looking out through his eyes. I blink twice and the images sharpen.

Glancing around, I see my father is at the edge of a wood. He's hidden up high and concealed by the tree's foliage. Peeking through the leaves, I see my mother! Younger and so beautiful, she is working in a garden, picking and weeding as she sways and moves. From her lips I hear the same beautiful, soothing melody the man was singing to me earlier to calm me when we were escaping my burning home. She sings with her wondrous voice and I feel entranced.

"Yes, Merek, that's your Momma," Father whispers to me through the vision. "This is when I first had the courage to speak with her. Watch and listen to my memories. It is my hope that after you see, you may better understand."

Suddenly an older man enters the yard with a loud thunderous voice and calls to my mother. She runs to him, calling him Papa. The door of a nearby cottage opens and in the door a woman appears and the three embrace in a hug. I feel a longing deep in my belly, a powerful longing, yet somehow I know it isn't mine but belongs to my father... his name is Drake. He wants to touch her, to hold her.

"Your mother's name is Amanda," he whispers to me. I watch through his eyes as a man approaches my momma. "That is her father, Merek, your grandfather," my father explains to me.

My grandfather starts running towards my mother, his arms waving with great excitement, and with a flourish he proclaims that Amanda is to be married to a boy in town named Caelen. His parents are rich; they have many cattle, sheep, chickens, and pigs to trade to

Amanda's parents. Amanda's motherclaps and kisses her daughter with pride. Yet Amanda's face is sad and scared.

I hear my father's voice tell me that she is fifteen years of age—she is considered a young woman. Amanda's father proclaims the wedding will be in two full moons from tonight's moon. That he, himself, and Caelen's father will begin building their new home across town. Her father says the home will be built on land Caelen's father owns, close to the Forest of Wedgemore. Amanda cringes in fear in her father's arms. He chuckles but soothes her and kisses her forehead and tells her they will build a mighty wall against the tree line to protect her new home from the dangers of the forest.

Amanda's mother reaches for her hand and explains that they must set to work on her wedding gown. She instructs Amanda to go and wash in the river, handing her a basket with towels and soap and ordering her to return with haste. Amanda reluctantly turns away from her excited parents and sets down her satchel of freshly picked food, heading towards the far edge of her father's land to the river.

Drake's body begins to follow Amanda, high up walking on the branches, his presence masked by the thick foliage. He continues leaping from branch to branch, feather light and quiet.

Drake looks upon Amanda looking at herself. She gazes at her reflection in the river's cascading flow and tears fall from her cheeks. Why does she cry? Drake continues to watch from high up in a tree, covered and hidden by its leaves. He steps further out on the branch for a better view and it cracks and startles Amanda below. She wipes her eyes with her dirt-covered hands, smearing her beautiful face.

"Who's there?" Amanda's voice calls out. "Come out and show yourself!" she shouts. "It is not polite to peek on a helpless maiden such as myself!" Amanda reaches behind her for a large rock, arming herself.

Drake jumps and lands on the ground below. He slowly walks out from the shadows cast by the foliage and into the sun. Amanda shrieks in fear. She stumbles backward and lands upon her bottom.

"Please don't run! I promise not to hurt you." Drake speaks quietly. Amanda turns slowly back to him, her eyes wary and body trembling.

"Who—who are you?" she asks tentatively.

"My name is Drake, Amanda," he says in a low and gentle voice, fiddling with his fingers.

She stares at him. "How do you know my name?" She examines every inch of him, taking in all his details.

He stammers, making my mother giggle infectiously. Amanda slowly and cautiously moves back to the river and begins washing and rinsing her hands and face. Drake's longing to touch her soft raven hair, her pale skin, returns. He sits on a rock at the river's edge just a little closer to her. He watches hypnotized as she washes her arms and dabs at her neck with the cool water.

"I know you, too," she whispers, looking up at him, "but not your name. I have seen you before, while I sleep and in my dreams. I did not recognize you at first."

Drake's face contorts in confusion. Amanda begins to sing the lovely melody again and Drake becomes paralyzed, entranced by her voice. She rises from the riverbed and moves slowly towards the strange but familiar creature before her.

"You are somehow different than my visions of you, yet you are more beautiful. Forgive me but, you see, in my dreams you were always in the shadows." She sits beside him on the rock.

Drake sighs. "Let me begin by telling you a tale. I am made of a Goblin and Elf, the creation of a long-ago forbidden love. My mother was a pureblood Elf, my father a pureblood Goblin." Amanda jumps at the word and pales. "My kind, Gelfin, is exceedingly rare. I am the only one that I know of. Through time my being has become more accepted, per se, and I have grown powerful in my own way. I am the perfect blend of Elf and Goblin lineages, though our Elders were cross when I was born into the world, as the Realms are not supposed to mix. We are to stay separate, never to breed with one another. The Elders have strictly enforced this law and forbidden the mating of different species out of fear for what future species might be bred. A contract was made between the different Realms. The purebloods—Humans, Elves, Goblins, the Werewolves, Fae folk, and so on—all signed the contract and now stay within their own Realms." Drake pauses to see if Amanda understands. "I overheard your kind has sold you," he says sadly. "You are to be married off to someone you do not love." With a sigh, he goes on. "The Moon Goddess was once supposed to show us our true mates, but the Elders overruled her power because of their fear of mixing the species. This forest," he glances back over his shoulder, "is what borders all our lands, keeping us apart. It was difficult for me to find you, Amanda. I am sure that as time has passed, the humans have knowledge of all the rest of the species only from what they hear from your legends, stories, or folklore. I believe those stories are meant to frighten you of the others." He sighs again. "So the problem now is that we are not allowed in each other's Realms, though my dreams led me to you and you say you have dreamt of me. The Moon Goddess must have chosen us as mates. Can you feel it? A pulling, a longing to be near me?" He steadies himself for her reaction. "Why would the Moon Goddess allow our meeting? She knows the creatures no longer want her interference in mating. Or could this be the work of the Mother leading me to find you?"

"The Mother? Moon Goddess? I don't understand," Amanda whispers. "Who are they?"

Drake's eyes widen in surprise. "How do you have no knowledge of either?" He sighs heavily. "Perhaps a story for another time. Two very important beings, one of Creation and the other the Goddess of Love. Has your species truly forgotten its own origins?"

"A Gelfin!" Amanda says, ignoring his questions, eager for him to answer her own. She questions the sound of it. "Gelfin?" she muses, deep in thought. "I thought Goblins were evil... hideous, tortured, deformed creatures. Elves are of course beautiful, sacred and extremely powerful, but I have never heard of a Gelfin," she says flatly. He crumbles at her words.

"Yet..." She reaches slowly and tucks the blonde lock of hair hiding his face behind his ear. "You are quite handsome and shy. So you do not wish to eat me then, like a Goblin no doubt would?" she teases, turning to face him more and brushing her fingers against his face, tracing his jawline. My father melts and leans into her hand.

"No. I long to be with you, that what's so confusing. I feel that you are my mate. No, never would I ever *eat* you, Amanda," he tells her seriously, shivering at the thought. "Is that what your people think of Goblins? A Vampire perhaps, but not a Goblin! We do not eat your kind. By the light! Really? Those are some scary stories of lore you have!" He smirks at her. "A unicorn perhaps, if one happened to stumble upon a human, might eat it."

"A unicorn? Really?" Amanda gapes at him.

Drake laughs out loud. "No, I was just poking fun. They are magnificent beasts. Honorable and very noble steeds." The laughter in his eyes turns to gentle love. "When did your dreams of me start?"

"Two full moons ago," she answers.

"Aye, me too, but I only just found you one full moon ago." He blushes, his green cheeks turning a darker emerald, as he admits to spying on her.

"I have always dreamed things before they happen. It frightens my mother and father. I am forbidden to speak of it." She quickly clasps her hand over her mouth. "You mustn't tell a soul! In this village you could be hanged as a witch if anyone knew. I suppose we have that in common."

"Why would your people kill a Witch, your own healers? Who helps when you are ill, then?" he asks. "You don't smell like a Witch, so I do not believe you are one." He rubs his chin in thought.

"You have the green skin, but blonde hair and ah! OH!" She breathes in deep and stares dreamily as she turns his face toward her fully. "You have purple eyes!" She again pushes back the unruly soft golden hair behind his ear. "Your skin is soft and smooth, green but no hideous scars or boils. Your hair is wild and unkempt but smooth and no snakes or hideous poisonous creatures lurk within. White teeth, not black with rot. Your hands are like mine." She puts her palm and fingers flush against his. At the touch, an electric wave pulses through her body and she quickly withdraws her hand.

"Wow." She examines her hand. There is no pain, no marks left. She stares at the Gelfin before her in awe as he examines his own hand. "Did you feel that?" she asks.

"Yes!" He stares at her. He has never felt anything like it before. "Mating between my people can be strong. It makes the two connected and attached to one another. A unique and complex union occurs when the right two are paired. It is rarer to see the marks that would tattoo the pair in a perfect pattern that always complete and compliment the other when near each other. It is a beautiful visual representation that the two are mated, but so exceedingly rare."

Again, Amanda touches his cheek, this time a slighter pulse erupting from her fingertips through her body. She traces his jaw down to his shoulder, her fingers continuing to trace down, meeting at the intimate spot on his sternum just next to his heart. Drake's body is wild within, senses overwhelmed. He moans against her touch, his mind spinning.

Something powerful and strong *shoots* through her. She grabs both his hands and places them over her own heart and his. It feels like a sonic boom. She joins their hands again, palm to palm, and laces her fingers through his. A black ribbon dances along the skin of their fingers up and around their wrists, mirrored in each other's skin as it stretches and grows. Drake's head cranes up; his eyes flash wide, turning from their beautiful hue of purple to huge black ink orbs. This human is his mate, and her intoxicating scent grows stronger. This explains his dreams—it was the mate bond calling them to be together.

Drake raises his right hand with hers still interlocked and touches her cheek, leaning in to kiss her slowly, gently, yet deeply and possessively. He pulls her into his lap and closer against his chest. Amanda accepts his kiss and adds her passion to his. With their bodies locked together in a tight embrace, the ribbon tattoo snakes around each face, neck, arm, hand, torso, abdomen, leg, and foot. A beautiful swirling of black sinks deep into their skin, forming a bond unbreakable between the two. Drake sinks his teeth into her neck, and Amanda screams with pleasure from his bite.

***

I look away from my father's memory vision and back at my parents, here in this time.

"Yes, Merek, I love her very much." I hear his voice from within my mind and I look at Momma, sick with fever as my father tends to her.

"What..." My sight is blurry, and my head feels slow. "What happened? I felt and saw everything through you and your eyes as if it were me," I stammer, still confused.

"I mind-shared with you. I just showed you a piece of our past to prove to you that I mean neither of you harm. I deeply love you both so much. More than you will know. My son, my Merek," he breathes with a sigh and reaches for me.

I crawl to him and he lifts me into his lap.

"Why did you leave us? Where did you go? What happened to the boy that was to be married to Momma? *Why did you leave us?*" I shout the last as tears prick my eyes.

His hand touches mine once more and through time I am sent to another of my father's memories.

CHAPTER THREE

Memories

I watch my father's vision memories play before me. I watch as Momma's mother scrubs and washes and scrubs some more until Momma's skin is raw, desperately trying to wash away the intricate beautiful black ribbon tattoo that now marks my mother's entire body. How her parents fear the strange boy by the riverside my mother tells them about. How she pleads with them, hysterical, that she cannot and will not marry the boy from the town, that her true mate came to her from the forest. How her brothers are ordered to guard over her every minute of each day so that she will not seek out the strange green boy. I watch as my mother creeps from her house each night once her family is fast asleep to meet my father by the river. I witness their relationship bloom and blossom. They tell each other every detail about their young lives.

One night my mother is full of fear and dread. She runs as fast as she can to the river to find Drake and tell him of her vision.

"They will not stop this marriage, Drake, and I had a horrible nightmare," she shrieks, on the edge of hysteria, as she reaches for my father's arm. She studies his face intently. Something is off about him, different somehow. Exasperated and frustrated, she cannot put her finger on it, and continues, "You kill him, Drake! You kill him!" Her voice is harsh with the strain of running. Tears build in her eyes.

Drake holds her tight and soothes her by running his fingers through her hair. "Who, my love? What is it? What did you see?" he asks as calm as he can, praying that she doesn't sense that he is indeed not the Drake she has come to know. He came with a purpose, he came determined, but seeing her, holding her, he cannot do it. He steadies himself.

"The boy from the town, the one my father forces me to wed. He attacks me the night before our wedding, brings me to the home where we're supposed to live—tries to touch me—rips my dress! You come through the window and knock him away from me, but he hits you hard across the jaw, he breaks the bone! You two fight like mad men." My mother sobs. "You pull a knife from your side, a wooden hand carved blade with runes and a curved blade of white stone, and... and you pierce his heart and lay him upon the wedding bed that we are to share where he bleeds and bleeds until there is no life left in his eyes."

Drake pulls away from her and his eyes widen. He lets out his held breath and reaches with one hand for something at his side. "Did the blade look like this?"

My mother gasps and starts to shake. "We have to run away."

He shakes his head. "I cannot take you to my people, Amanda. I told you, I'm not even supposed to be here, let alone near your kind. My people signed a treaty many, many lifetimes ago promising to stay away. We will be taken away from each other, my father the King will no doubt kill you as soon as he discovers you, or—" he stops, and a shudder runs through him "—or he will claim you as his own," Drake explains with bile rising in his throat.

"King," she whispers hoarsely. "You're their Prince?" She whimpers. "Is there no place where we can be in peace, just you and me? A place in-between our lands?"

"The forest!" he cries out with hope. "The forest lays between our lands. It will be a hard life, Amanda. There are creatures and the mist to contend with, and we will only have ourselves to build a home and truly little protection from what calls those woods their home." Drake pales and sighs heavily. "It's a place to start, a difficult and hard path. If you choose me, you will have to give up everything you have ever known here. Anyone who discovers us will be in their right to slaughter us." His knees buckle out of fear for his beloved. He would gladly die if need be to spare her. She is now his only reason for breathing. His body, heart, and soul belong to her.

"The Forest of Wedgemore." Amanda pales. She bites her lower lip. "If it is the only path that leads us together, then we must. I cannot lose you, Drake, I love you. I can barely breathe when we are separated! Without you I would have no life. You are my everything."

Tears stream from my mother's eyes. My father relaxes and holds her tightly as she clings and tries to climb into his arms. He scoops her up and lifts her high above his head and spins her.

"I love you and I will give you everything that I can, Amanda. I promise to protect you at all costs, to care for you and honor you." He whispers this into the night and gently puts her down, setting her bare feet back upon the earth, and kisses her deeply. "I promise we will be happy."

***

The memories of my father blur and he touches my face and smiles. "That was the night your mother and I made you, Merek." His smile fades, and he looks sad. Father dips the cloth in the cold bowl of water and puts it back to Momma's forehead, then pulls my small body closer to him.

"When your mother left my side that night to return home, I told her that I would leave for two nights and return for her on the third sunrise. She begged me not to go, scared that I wouldn't return for her in time, but I left to find a safe place within the woods, a place where we would be protected and sheltered while we started to build a new life. I knew this book," he says, pulling it from a hidden bottom cupboard inside the table by the bed. "It would help us. This book is incredibly special, enormously powerful, and full of my mother Elgeeva's magic and knowledge. This is her Grimoire. She handed it down to me.

"My plan was to meet the morning before the wedding at the riverside. I walked a great length before I found what I was looking for, a small opening to a cave with caverns throughout. I gathered wood and stones for a fire inside one of the caverns. I started my walk back to your mother when the sun rose on the third day. I remembered her vision then, her nightmare of the boy. When I left, she was so hysterical that it was hard to leave her behind, but it is not safe in this forest. I could not risk her safety before I could find somewhere safe for us. I began to run, since according to her vision it would happen that night. It had been three days of searching. I ran and ran, trying to go faster and faster. I reached the river just as the night turned dark. I ran to her home and peered through the small windows. It was empty and dark. My mind raced, and I cursed myself for not listening to her. I frantically tried to remember the details of her dream. I heard faint music in the distance.

"A celebration! In the center of her village, a celebration for the soon to be married pair. I ran through the dark towards the town. Her voice kept replaying in my mind: 'he touches me.'

"I dug deeper and ran harder. No one would ever touch her but me. A large building with massive double doors was alight and filled with music. I ran to one side of the biggest building of the town and peered through the windows and found her.

"When I saw your mother, it took my breath away; she was dressed in an elegant gown of navy-blue satin with a crown of wild-flowers atop her beautiful raven silk hair. The dress highlighted her small frame, showing off her curves that only I had seen, the night we gave our bodies to one another, but now her body was on full display to all. A possessive growl erupted from deep in my chest.

"I watched, hypnotized. She was a goddess of beauty dancing happily with her youngest sister, each spinning and twirling the other. I smiled to see her so happy. The song ended, Amanda and her sister kissed each other's cheeks, and a big burly man stood before the crowd and proclaimed in a loud booming voice, 'The next song will be for the engaged!' Cheers rose from the crowd of people. 'They will share this last dance before leaving us and our company to go and see the new home that has been built and finished for them!' The crowd reacted with tender murmurings and then abruptly booed the speaker for it being the last dance with the soon-to-be-married couple. The man laughed a full belly laugh and continued. 'My son Caelan will escort his bride to their future home and spend the remaining few hours together alone dreaming of their future.'

"'Shouldn't the children be chaperoned? They could get themselves in trouble,' a large and voluptuous woman shouted with a laugh while pushing up her breasts and giving her chest a shake. The men whooped and cheered, clanking their glasses with the men beside them, and burst into a fit of laughter. Amanda turned pale and looked as though she would be sick. Her eldest sister whispered in her ear and Amanda began breathing deeply and slowly while her elder sister stroked her back and glared at the woman jiggling her chest. The other women about the room made an array of disgusted faces.

"Amanda's mother stood and said sternly, 'I'm sure the children will behave themselves this the night before their wedding. I am sure my future son-in-law will keep his hands well to himself and be respectful of his bride. He has not yet said the sacred words promising himself to my daughter when they are wed.' She flashed a stern look at Caelan, who looked same in age to myself, but I was already one hundred years of age, the boy about twenty.

"Caelan was a mirror image of his father, just as tall, just as large and strong. The smirk on his face as he took your mother's hand and led her to the dance floor... I had to fight back my urge to charge him then and there. She was still looking ill and extremely nervous as he led them into an intimate dance. The musicians played a slow and sultry tune, and Caelan spun her in a gentle circle around his body before pulling her into him. I fought against my jealousy with anger building in my chest as I watched him dip and sway her across the floor. They were speaking now but I could not hear through the glass pane and the loud conversations. I focused on her lips and her face. She was not enjoying herself, she looked pale and was trembling, and I could practically feel her thumping heart and the fear coming off her in waves as she clumsily fought to follow the steps of the dance.

"The music seemed to go on forever. Finally, it began to die. Caelan pulled her to him, looking into her eyes for the first time since beginning the dance, and seemed to notice her distress. He kissed her hand and bowed to her as the music ended. The crowd cooed at them and gently clapped as the couple left the floor and headed for the large double doors of the building. I moved to see them exit into the night. Amanda released his hand as he closed the door and began to breathe more rapidly.

"'Ahh,' he breathed in, 'it's much cooler out here. Beautiful night, is it not?' Caelan asked.

"Catching her breath and with a small, strained voice, she said, 'Yes, lovely truly and easier to breathe.' She turned away from him, closing her eyes, trying to center and calm herself.

"'Have I already taken your breath away? What a pleasurable compliment, thank you, Amanda,' Caelan replied with a bow. 'I am looking forward to when you will take my breath away when I see you tomorrow in your wedding gown.' His cheeks flushed as Amanda turned around to look at him.

"'Ah, yes, the dress is my mother's masterpiece,' she said flatly.

"'Oh, but the dress will be nothing compared to the beautiful woman who wears it.' He bowed again to her and offered his arm. 'Shall we? Will you walk with me so that I may show you our new home?' Amanda hesitantly placed her small hand on his arm, looking nervously all around them.

"'Amanda, is something wrong? Did you see something? Come closer to me and I will protect and escort you. I will from this day forward always be your protector, Amanda.' He smiled at her and took her chin between his free fingers and sweetly kissed her cheek. Amanda smelled the ale on his breath and did not reply. She stared ahead of her toward the pathway that led from the center of town to her new home.

"I followed closely behind them, staying in the shadows. Your mother was on edge, constantly looking left and right, searching for something. What was frightening her? I know she sensed me. I could feel it was helping to calm her, yet she was on high alert. I desperately tried to recall her dream and what she said. Caelan talked endlessly while they walked, unaware of Amanda's search for something in the woods along the path.

"'I am so looking forward to seeing your reaction to the house, Amanda. I helped in building it. My father and I worked long hours, days, weeks to finish it in time. Spent a small fortune.' He chuckled, then coughed. 'But it is strong and sound. I do look forward to watching you till the earth for your beautiful flower and vegetable gardens. I promise to always have flowers for you upon my return home.' Caelan kissed her hand.

"Amanda paused her frantic search about them to look at him. 'Caelan,' she said softly, 'that is extremely sweet and kind of you. Thank you.' She sighed heavily. 'I'm sorry Caelan, I just... we don't know each other, we've hardly spent any time together to even pretend to understand, let alone know each other. With the wedding already here, tomorrow—' she started to hyperventilate '—I'm sorry, but to be honest, my stomach is sick and in terrible knots.'

"Caelan stopped and turned Amanda to meet his eyes. 'Really? Goodness, here I thought I was nervous.' He dropped to one knee, took each of her small hands in his large hands and looked right into her eyes. 'I promise to earn your love. I promise to make you happy even if that means my sorrow. I will protect you and keep you. I promise to give you my everything until your heart is full. All I ask is for you to try and find it somewhere deep inside you to love me in return.'

"He proclaimed those lies loudly to her and the night, a wicked grin taking hold on his face, and when he had finished spun on his knee away from her and plucked a wildflower growing along the path. He stood and kissed its petals one by one and offered it to her. I choked back a growl and held onto the tree rooting me in my place, my fingertips digging into the bark 'til they all bled. He reeked of vileness;

his scent was louder than his words. He courted and flattered her, but I could smell it and saw the lust in his eye. He was planning on taking her once they reached that house. I almost leapt from the trees to slice him in half, scoop her into my arms and carry her away, away from the evil, vile man that would bleed out upon the dirt and filth of the road where he belonged. Amanda took the flower and smiled.

"'Amanda, my betrothed, kiss the center of the flower, a promise to each other here and now to love each other more than we can possibly think of.' Caelan's speech was slurred. She nervously and frantically searched, eyes darting all around them.

"'Please can you try to love me?' he whispered.

"'Caelan, I... I don't know what to say,' she choked, eyes darting. She lifted the flower's bloom to her lips.

"Elated, he lifted her up by the waist, high up in the air, and twirled her around and around. She gripped his shoulders and winced in pain at his grip and his lack of balance, but she nervously laughed, unsure of what else to do.

"'I swear and promise to make you laugh just like this every day of our lives. Your laugh! It fills me full! How have I become so lucky to call you wife?' Caelan screamed with delight into the night. 'Come, run with me. We are nearly there! Wait, close your eyes, I will guide you.' He pulled her along with her eyes wide open, fearing they would surely trip and fall.

"'Caelan, slow down, I can't, the stones are hurting my bare feet!' she shrieked as he dragged her. Quickly he scooped her up in his arms and ran. 'Caelan! I am not yet your wife! Put me down!'

"'Keep those beautiful eyes closed! Almost there, Amanda!' he laughed with excitement.

"I wrenched myself away from my hiding place behind the tree and raced after them. I caught up in time to hear Amanda gasp at the sight of her future home all lit up with softly burning torches. Her arms went wide and then she pressed her fingers to her lips in delight.

"'Oh Caelan, it's beautiful!' she cried. At her words he scooped her up again and carried her through the door.

"I ran to the house and peered through the pane glass, my eyes following them through the rooms as Caelan explained each one and how he built it. He clumsily carried her up the narrow staircase while I climbed the side of the house. I could hear the thumping of his shoulder against the wall, drunk and unbalanced as he was, and I swore he'd surely break her neck if he fell. I cursed myself again for not attacking him along the road.

"There was a long hallway and they entered one of three doors furthest from me. He showed her three small rooms, each for their future children, and I felt my stomach flip and had to hold back the urge to vomit. Then he led her to a fourth door. A large, elegant bedroom opened wide to her—it was the biggest room in a house she had ever seen. The only furniture in the room was a large bed with elegant linens and thick decorative fabric for the bed curtains. She was so busy staring wide-eyed at the bed, she did not see him approaching her from behind. He placed the front of his body flush against her backside, pulling her back flush to his chest, then spun her to face him.

"'Caelan, this is very wonderful, beautiful. I am just a bit overwhelmed. We should go now—our fathers will be waiting for our return.'

"'I hand carved this bed. Alone! I made it just for us. Look, see here, I've even carved your tattoo into the wood.' He pulled up her sleeve, exposing her arm, revealing the black ribbon weaving around her skin that now matched the crude carving in the wood of the bed. The same symbols and vining ribbon of our love, not his, *mine*. Amanda paled and pulled her sleeve back down.

"He reached out to her as her knees buckled. He caught her and laid her gently upon the bed.

"'Your mother traced this line in your skin, said it appeared upon you the night your father told you of our wedding. That these marks were made from your love of me! I carved them into our bed, being so careful to match the tracings.' He pulled her sleeve back up to stare at the intricate ribboning and placed a soft kiss on her inside wrist.

"'I also paid a small fortune to your father just to claim your hand. This sweet delicate hand to be all mine.' A wicked grin unfolded on his face. 'No other man may touch what's mine! I made sure I was the highest bidder at your auction. Believe me, every man in this fucking village placed a bid for you.' Anger exploded through him and he gripped her wrist tightly, causing her to wince in pain. He sharply spun her back, holding her in place, her back against his chest, restraining her.

"'You are mine, will always be mine, and no man will ever touch you, do you understand?' he screamed at her, spinning her yet again to forcefully kiss her soft trembling lips. Her body went limp in his arms, her eyes rolled back into her skull. He laid her gently on the bed, bruises forming on her wrists. 'Wake up!' he roared in her face, smacking her across the check. She did not wake. I watched in horror as her nightmare in detail started to play before me.

"Caelan began by touching her face and found the courage to roam along her unconscious body. I broke through the glass pane window, startling him. His eyes widened, taking in the sight of me. The sharp claws, my glowing eyes. He looked down and I followed his gaze as his trousers dampened while he pissed himself. I smirked, but I didn't intimidate him enough as the next thing I knew he leaped from her and connected his fist to my jaw—something cracked. I turned away from him, wincing with the pain. He tackled me and we began crashing into the walls and throwing each other into furniture. I grabbed the back of his head, fist full of his greasy hair, and slammed it against the headboard, once, twice, 'til the wood cracked and splintered.

"Caelan howled in agony but recovered quickly. He reached out to the elegant curtain and began to wrap it around my throat. He pulled the cloth tight. I released his head, trying to grip at the fabric at my throat, but it lifted me off the floor. His teeth were gritted and blood dripped from his forehead down his eyes and stained his bared teeth. My throat constricted. I tried grasping for a breath, but he pulled it tighter and grinned as he lifted my body higher. My weight began to rip the silk fabric and I fell to the floor. He charged at me and I kicked out with my foot, hitting him square in the ribs, and I heard the delicious sound of a few of them breaking. He staggered back gasping and spitting blood at me. Amanda woke and began screaming.

"'Amanda, stay back!' Caelan and I shouted in unison. Caelan glared to me in complete confusion at how I could possibly know her name.

"'Drake, your knife!' she shrieked. It was too late. Caelan had already freed the blade and was aiming for my ribs. I grabbed his wrist and turned the blade. His momentum forced the blade into his own heart. His face was that of shock, brief discomfort, then changed to confusion as he stared down at the hilt. He breathed one last gurgled breath before his head fell back. Still holding his body upright, I dragged him to the bed and laid him upon it.

"'There is not much time. There is more to my vision that I haven't told you.' Amanda's voice was hoarse and frantic. 'Your father is coming, Drake. You will disappear before me and without me. Oh his face, his monstrous face and wicked grin when he takes you.'

"'What, wait, no—' I reached for her and gave her one last kiss.

"'Drake, I'm with child. Your child: you name him,' she whispered to me with tears streaming down her cheeks.

"'Merek' we said together.

"'He's almost here and you'll be gone.' Amanda sobbed as she frantically kissed my lips hungrily. She was pouring her soul into that kiss.

"'I'll come back for you, I promise.' I took her face in my hand, smearing Caelan's blood across her cheek. 'No matter what, I'll come—'

"That's when I felt the presence of the Goblin King, my father. Just as in her dream. A strong arm wrapped around my guts, a fierce hand clutched at my face, yanking me away. He had materialized from behind me. Your mother shrieked and I knew my father's evil but breathtakingly beautiful face must have materialized over my left shoulder as he rested his chin upon me.

"'Well, well. What, pray tell, has happened here?' His pristine sculpted face contorted in disgust. *Tssk tssk*-ing, the evil face of an angel tilted left and right. 'Drake, the blood of the boy is all over you, and the female's scent is so entangled with yours.' He inhaled deeply through his flared nostrils. Black orbs penetrated from within his eye sockets. His face was pure beauty even when full of rage, like that of a god. 'Where does her scent in fact end and where does yours begin, my dear boy?' Spit flew from full, luscious lips. The Goblin King relaxed his grip on my throat, just enough for me to take a small, ragged breath.

"'She is my mate, Father,' I growled, twisting and groping at the hand gripping my throat. It raised me higher, my feet no longer touching the floor. 'Father!' I choked out. 'Mate... bond...life...'" My vision tunneled, darkened. Amanda gasped and began to sob. She dropped to her knees before the terrifying, beautiful creature.

"'Please, my Lord, my King,' she whimpered, but he spat and, *tssk*-tilting his head to one side, glared at the female before him.

"'*I am not your King!*" he screamed at her, his black eyes like fire, his claws drawing my blood. She flinched, and the Goblin King blew a hot gale of air out his nostrils. In a heavy, pained voice, he said, 'I love my son.' He *tssk*ed again and tilted his evil, gorgeous face to the left and right. 'But this relationship is an abomination. My bastard son, my only heir, my only son—' He gripped me by the back of the neck, shook me violently and hissed into my face, covering me in spit '—chose a human for a mate, punishable by death.' He slowed his speech, making sure each word sank into her. *Tssk, tssk,* the same tilt of his head left then right. 'I love my son, but he will pay dearly for his crimes.' He looked to the female and licked his lips.

"Amanda trembled at the sight of his wicked and beautiful face, and the two of us slowly disappeared right in front of her as his voice trailed behind, haunting her, squeezing her heart with pure fear.

"'Such a specimen,' it came, breathy and heated. 'Lovely and full of fire. I see his obsession with you, dear one.'

"His moans of pleasure echoed sickly in her ears as she lowered her face to the floor, sobbing from the absence, pain, and loss, the unimaginable fear that voice instilled in her. And there was nothing I could do."

In my father's lap, Momma stirs. She whimpers in pain. My father dampens the cloth and puts it back to her forehead. He sends me a memory vision. My sight is blurry, as if traveling through a murky past, 'til at long last it comes into focus.

My father is locked in a cage of black and silver bars. He is in the center of an enormous arena, surrounded by creatures dressed in long, dark blue robes, hoods blocking their faces from my father's sight. They look down upon him. The room is large and intimidating, supported by tall stone pillars with beautiful intricate designs. Row upon row of large stones that serve as steps and seats encircle my father. A large, black marbled balcony high above painted to resemble the purest, darkest night sky holds seven more creatures in dark red robes, also hooded.

A haunting chanting begins. Each creature dressed in dark blue hums in unison as they stand. Fear and desperation seep through my father as he pulls against the bars of the cage. The chanting abruptly stops, all eyes on my father in the cage. The creatures in dark blue remove the hooded cloaks to reveal their faces. Each has a different hue of green skin and all have pointed ears and variously colored eyes. Once all are seated again, the seven in the marbled balcony stand and pull back their hoods. Six retake their seats, eyeing my father with disgust, while one remains standing.

With a loud booming voice amplified for all to hear, he bellows, "Drake, son of our beloved Goblin King and High Lord Molag. You are brought before this council and your people for crimes you have committed against the Species' Treaty. You allowed yourself to be seen by two humans, one of which you have murdered. Its blood is still on you." There is a collective gasp from the audience. "You have exposed yourself and your people to the inferior human species. Do you understand the charges?"

Within the cage my father is full of despair and replies in a whisper.

"Yes, I understand."

The creatures surrounding him stand in an uproar, some angry, others with scared expressions. Some even try to plead for Drake's life.

"*Silence.*"

The loud, booming voice causes every creature to jump. A creature in black robes appears from behind the ones in red. Every creature bows their head.

"Drake, my son and *PRINCE* to our people, you have been charged and will be punished." The Goblin King's face appears sad and sullen. "You are banished from our village to the Forest of Wedgemore's northern border, where you will mine the dangerous poisonous caves for the precious stones our people hold dear and sacred. There you will be the furthest from the human world but will still be close to our border just at the edge of our lands. The mist that plagues the forest is at its most concentrated there, especially within the caves themselves. If you do not succumb to the mind-crippling insanity of the mists and if you harvest three tons of the precious stones, then will you be redeemed, and your crimes paid back to your people. I pray you will keep your mind sound, that you will indeed succeed in your mining and not be lost to the mist. Only then may you be able to return to your people."

Molag disappears from the balcony and reappears kneeling in front of the cage of his son. He reaches in to hold Drake's face and whispers, "Damn you for what you have done, foolish child. Listen to me—be safe, be well, be strong, be the fighter I know you to be and promise to survive the mist and return to your home."

Drake nods and slowly disappears from within the cage, transported to a cavernous cave with spiked rock and uneven ground with the mist swirling around him. Where it touches his skin, it leaves welts and blistering burns. Drake rips the bottom edge of his shirt and ties it around his head, protecting his mouth and nose against the thick purple and blueish hue of the swirling mist. He falls to his knees and screams. Three tons, an impossible feat. Tears streaming, fists shaking and gritting his teeth, he vows to stay alive and sane, to return to her and the babe that grows within her womb.

He takes a deep breath to gather his courage and begins his tedious work of mining for the impossibly rare stone. He smiles as his thoughts drift to her soft, beautiful, and luscious lips, knowing one day he will indeed feel them once more. He just has to pick himself up and literally bury himself in the work ahead.

My father's memory vision clears, and he is holding me in his arms. Cradling me, silently weeping.

CHAPTER FOUR

Losing Them

My father continues to hold me and rocks me gently. I reach up to touch his face, acknowledging his struggles to find Momma and me. I'm overcome with grief for what my father and mother had to endure because of their love of each other and me. I reach out and wrap my small arms around his neck, hugging him as tight as I can.

My father shifts suddenly, tension and fear radiating from his body and into mine through our embrace.

"Oh, no, not now! Merek, you must hide." He picks me up off his lap, standing quickly while holding me close. "Up here, there you go, hold on tight." My father quickly scans the room and his hand swiftly moves in a rhythmic whirl. Small linens float up into the air, wrapping my father's book, and the small table drawer pops open. The wrapped book floats inside and the drawer quickly closes.

"The book is very important, Merek. You must touch it at least once every day—the book is very special—it will teach you everything you need to know—understand? You must touch that book every day!" he says frantically. "My father, the King of our people, comes for me, Merek. Stay hidden! Everything will be okay! The book, Merek—you have to do this. It will show and tell you how to keep the runes and if you do it right... *No one will ever find you.*" He choked on a sob. "Not even me," he whispered so low I almost didn't hear.

Father kisses my forehead, each of my palms, and turns away from me to throw blankets over Momma, covering and hiding her. "The Goblin King has come to take me away and back to my people. You must stay right here, hidden. Make no noise. If he takes me, I will come back for you, I promise. Just stay here in this house, care for your mother, remember the book! Promise? The house is protected by runes, symbols upon the stone cairns I have made at the north, east, south, and west points surrounding the house. Protect them. As long as they are standing, the magic will keep you safe within the house—the lost ones cannot cross its boundaries. Do you understand, Merek?" He kisses my small feet and I nod.

There is a knock on the door that causes both of us to jump.

"Merek, hush now," he whispers, touching my cheek. The door flings open to reveal a tall and large creature dressed in black robes, cloaked and hooded. It steps inside.

"Ah, here you are Drake, our Prince. I see you have not succumbed to the insanity of the mist. I must say I was concerned when I could not find you along the northern border. It has been quite tricky—" The creature pauses and examines the room about him and sneers "—trying to find you, my boy. How did you find your way out of the cavernous mountains and through the mist to this particular spot, to this? I apologize—we really did send you off to the caves with nothing, didn't we? No matter. It is a humble home, one built in a hurry." The creature removes his hood, stepping further into the room, looking around at the meager shelter and studying my father. Drake falls to his knees and bows low, low to the floor.

The evil creature chuckles. "Drake, rise. I am your father. You humor me—do not bow so deeply." He laughs harder. "You have redeemed yourself and paid for your crimes. I've come to take you home, my boy," he boasts, slapping my father on the back. "Our people and lands are very proud of you indeed. We now have many... precious..." Molag stops abruptly and sniffs the air. "... many of the precious stones that you have mined for us."

Molag inhales deeper and anger flashes across his monstrous face. He strides past and shoves my father aside to pull back the blankets that cover Momma. His rage simmers as his gaze falls on her. Momma is so beautiful while she sleeps. Her skin has now taken on a darker hue of green. She's changing. Her tattoos have darkened, her wounds have sealed themselves, but she is still sweating with fever.

"Rise, damn you!" Molag bellows to his son. "Here I come to return you home and I find this! The human girl! She is sick and struck with fever. Many wounds, I see, healed—and now her skin darkens in green. And marked!" he spits through gritted teeth, ripping father's shirt off him to see the mirroring marks. "YOUR venom is responsible for her healing and changing." He smacks my father hard. "Damn you, what have you done? It is *forbidden*!" He grabs my father by the throat and lifts him high up in the air.

"I—she is my MATE!" my father growls back, coughing as his throat is crushed.

"Do you think I'm daft? I can see with my own eyes the connection between you, but you know our laws," Molag spits.

"She was dying, my King. I followed the sound of our mate bond ringing through my veins and found her. I found my way through the mist and past the creatures of the wood to find her, even through your magic. Yes, *your* magic that contained me in that forsaken land. I have magic of my own. I'm stronger than you'd like to believe!" He strains for his voice to be heard. Molag drops him to the floor.

"Now I have no choice but to take both of you back with me, unless of course you take pity on this weak creature and allow me to kill her final and true. Oh, but no! Damn you, my lovesick son," he spits. "You will be whipped for this. You, my only living heir. Pathetic! I will have you stripped of your royalty. You cause me so much sorrow and pain. Why must you disobey? I don't give a rat's shit if this sack of bones is your mate. Learn to control yourself! I will whip you myself while all our people watch your suffering. Your childish decisions try my patience!" he hisses in my father's face.

"You have no idea how strong the mate bond is!" Drake screams. "You have no true mate of your own! The Moon Goddess never blessed you with one! You hypocrite! But what of your collected wives, *father*?"

Molag slaps him hard across his mouth, drawing blood at the corner. Molag grins as he licks the blood from the back of his hand. His eyes dilate, rapidly turning to huge orbs of black despair. Drake stands shocked, completely still, watching his father, knowing just what information that small amount of blood has given him. Drake panics.

From my hiding place, I let out a loud hiss. The black robed creature stands before me, reaches up and grabs hold of the back of my neck, and hisses in my face.

"Papa!" I scream.

"No, my Lord, you came for me. I will return with you and you can have your revenge on me, but leave her here with our son. It is not her fault. I beg you—leave her here. Leave her!"

"She'll die! She'll die if left here alone, Drake. I'm sure you don't wish that suffering upon her since you won't allow me to kill her myself. This will ensure her continued breath. Maybe I just should, *hmmm...*" He scratches his chin. "No, the girl will come with us. I will decide her fate, whether death or perhaps claiming her as my property." He purrs violently in my father's ear. "Do you think so much of the strength of your bond that she will find it in her weak heart to forgive you, my dear son? Forgive the pain you have now sentenced her to?" He laughs and licks his lips, eyes tracing over my mother. "It would be a lovely treasure to own such a creature. Her beauty would most definitely compliment my other wives, don't you think so, Drake?" He grins.

I am ripped from the creature's grasp and cradled safely against my father's chest, surrounded by strong loving arms. He kisses my hair and then slings me onto his back, where I wrap my arms around his neck and hide my face from the horrifying creature standing in utter shock before us.

"*Do. Not. Touch. My. Son!*" my father barks through clenched teeth, his body poised and tensed for a fight. "I love them, and they are MINE!" he screams.

The King's face falls with sadness. "I will punish you myself, Drake. I will display you before our people and make an example of you. Then I'll claim your mate as mine and burn this little atrocity as a warning to all, burn him upon a stake, the fire so big it will choke our village for weeks. What you have bred will not live past the full moon!"

"Leave me," Papa begs. "Return to our people with the belief that your son, their Prince, succumbed to the insanity of the mist and was lost to the forest. Tell them you arrived too late to retrieve me, your beloved son, from the horrors in the darkness."

"Oh no, Drake, their favoritism will not protect you! The three of you will come with me and be displayed to the council. You will be made an example of what will happen to those who disobey me! You and your son will die, Drake, and your mate will watch it all and then be made mine." Molag smiles at my father.

Drake backs away, closer to the open window. Just as the King lifts his hand, my Papa throws me from him, through the window and out into the night.

"Run, Merek, run!" he shouts, and then all is quiet, he is gone.

I run, as fast as my little legs will carry me. I run until eventually I trip. For a long time I'm on the ground curled in a ball, wet, covered with mud, until I find shelter from the biting rain in a hole in the trunk of a giant willow tree. I am so cold. Wet and alone, I curl into a small ball and let the tears come.

Everything has been taken from me. I am lost and alone in the cursed and scary Forest of Wedgemore. I know the evils of the forest lay in wait. This is where nightmares are born.

A wolf howls into the darkness—something nears. Its feet crunch against the forest floor.

CHAPTER FIVE

The Forest of Wedgemore

15 years later

I awake abruptly, dazed and confused by my nightmare, and blink against the brightness of the rising sun. It is early, the sun just rising over the trees. I reach for my father's book, palm up and hand outstretched. The book lifts into the air and into my waiting hand. It springs open.

"Strange," I mumble.

Another new page. I gaze at it, puzzled. It is only an image of some place here in the forest. In it, Brice and I are backed against an edge, a border of some kind unseen in the picture, but I feel its presence pulse in my body. It is most definitely a wall of some kind, disguised. It looks as though we are both poised for a fight.

Huh. It is a small image, and the other half of it, the part that shows what Brice and I are looking at, is blurred by shadow. Something stands, no, *many* somethings are standing before us where the image will not let me see. I blink to my Goblin sight for a closer look.

While I study the image, Brice, my wolf companion, tangles his legs with mine in a long stretch. We're curled together on some ratty cushions on the floor in the small home that was once my father's. Both lost and alone in the Forest of Wedgemore, Brice and I found each other that night when everything was taken from me. He was only a pup—and so was I—in the hollow of a willow tree in the deepest of the blackest, scariest of nights. We found each other taking shelter and kept each other warm while the biting rain stormed and hailed down. Over the many years, he's become my closest friend, filling that lonely void.

I push him off me while he moans from deep within his throat, reluctantly waking beside me. Burying my face in his soft fur, I breathe in his wonderful scent and tickle his sides. Brice kicks me away, stands, stretches, yawns, and sits, looking at me with annoyance.

"Well, Brice, breakfast?"

He snorts in agreement and we exit the house. Together we visit each of the stone pillars with the ancient rune writings that surround the house. Carefully gazing over each and inspecting them, I whisper the spells to fix a certain placement stone that has shifted, just as the book has taught me to do over the years.

We begin our walk toward the stream near the house. From my father's satchel I pull out a flask and fill it with the cold, clean running water. I take a needed sip as Brice laps away at the stream. A songbird sings not too far away, and the squirrels squabble and chase each other. Brice has his eyes on the dancing squirrels and goes off in hunt of his little prey.

Following the birdsong, I spy a nest and begin to climb. Mother bird is close by. She begins screeching at me, fluffing her feathers and jumping up and down. I speak a prayer to her of thanks and take two of the three eggs. Carefully I place them in the front pocket of my satchel and climb down, headed along a well-worn path to the berry patch to collect fresh berries. Filling my small bowl, I place it in the bottom of my pack, being mindful not to spill or squish them.

It is a beautiful morning, warm, and all around me everything is full of life and in bloom. While I walk along, I hear the rush of stumbling feet, crunching in the undergrowth. I freeze and listen, quickly scanning the area around me. Brice is nowhere to be seen and I am alone.

I see movement between the trees and crouch down. There is a creature, what once was a man from the human village, tall, skinny, and sickly. His skin is molten, rotting, and obvious chunks of flesh are missing and exposing the bones beneath. He continues to stumble through the woods. Little hair is left atop his head, and his clothes have long since been ripped away. His hands are bare, feet bleeding. The creature stops and smells the air. He changes direction slowly and is on a path straight toward me. I see his vacant eyes darting around until at last he sees me.

"Brice!" I call as I break out into a run. "Brice!"

I hear his howl from up ahead and run for him. He meets me happily, prancing with four squirrels dangling from his mouth. I take his catch and cram them in my satchel.

"Run, there's another one, just behind me!"

Brice senses my panic and we run zigzag and away from our home so as not to lead the lost one there. Lost ones are humans from my old village that ventured too far from the boundaries of that world, and not just humans, but other creatures that inhabit this world. Each ventured into the woods for who knows what, becoming lost in the mist. Lost much like me, only they have been driven mad and insane from breathing large quantities of the toxic mist.

He is close behind us now. I grab a fistful of Brice's fur and reach up for a tree branch to swing us up. Quickly and silently, we climb the tree. The sickly man is below us, searching, listening, smelling. I press my finger to my lips. Brice has learned over the years just how important this signal is. We had many close situations when we were young and were still learning the dangers of this place. When he was still a pup, he would howl and bark, giving away our hiding spot. Now he sits quietly, always smelling with his powerful nose, searching for the best way to navigate through the upper tree branches and away from the danger below. Together we silently leap from tree to tree using the long branches.

The creature below leaves. We watch his form disappear in the distance until we can no longer see it. I nod at Brice—it is safe to climb down.

The lost ones that roam here are no longer themselves. Whether once humans or creatures from the other boundaries, they are no longer what they were. Driven mad by the mist, they are stuck here, never finding their way back home and remaining permanently changed into these wretched creatures that hunt this land for their next meal. My father's book has taught me well—of the Lost Ones, of the other Realms that surround the forest, of the witches, vampires, werewolves, Fae, and humans.

When I was still young and small, a female lost one found me. Still not fully understanding these creatures, I ventured too close, and she grabbed me and started biting my arm. Fortunately, she no longer had teeth. Frustrated at her inability to break my flesh and eat, she gripped me tighter. She held me in a vice grip with unbelievable strength for hours, dragging me all over and circling around and around, constantly stopping to try a different area of my body to gum on until finally exhaustion took over and she fell against a nearby tree, her skin scraping down the bark. She whimpered at me, still trying to bite into my arm but only able to gum me. She sobbed and shook me hard and then continued to try and get my fingers.

For hours after she first tried biting me, I was paralyzed with fear of her, but at that moment I felt so deeply sorry for her. Her words no longer made sense, babbled like an infant, and she yelled a deafening shriek at me, but her speech was more like grunting and clicking noises. I pulled my fingers from her mouth and leaped away before she could grab and try for my toes. I held up my finger, signaling her to wait, and she gazed blankly at me with bloodshot eyes. Pulling berries from my bag, I dumped my bowl out on the ground in front of her. She did not reach for them, just stared at me vacantly.

I picked up one of the berries and shoved it in her mouth. Her dead stare changed to lively excitement and awe and she immediately copied me, carefully grasping a berry between her fingers and tossing it in her ruined maw. She ate every one of the berries. Fingers and face stained in juice, she accepted my outstretched hand and followed after me to the berry bushes. She happily sat and plucked the bright blue and purple berries one by one from the bottom of the bush. I left her there and that is where she stayed. Each day I greeted her, and she left me alone, content with the berries. Although her mind was not there, I pretended as the days went on that we were friends.

Brice did not care for her and stayed away but I approached her, spoke to her as I picked berries of my own, told her all about my day. Each day before I departed, I kissed her forehead and told her to keep herself safe. Each evening I tucked the wayward strands of her hair behind her ears and told her I'd be back in the morning. Then one day when I went to get my berries, I found her being eaten by another of these creatures. Brice and I hid and watched in horror as the other lost one, a huge gangly thing so ravaged by time and loss that its yellowed bones were visible between gaps in the rotten flesh, clamped its mouth on her and raked her with its gray fingernails. I wanted to help her, but this creature was much too big and engrossed in her flesh. His eyes were too focused, unlike hers.

He is the one that scares me the most, more than the others I've seen. The others are thin and sickly, whereas he is tall and strong. The biggest and "healthiest" I have seen, his skin still resembles human flesh, not molten and rotting. He smashed her head against a rock again and again until her skull cracked open. Blood sloshed everywhere as he dug inside her skull to satisfy his hunger. I almost fainted before Brice wedged himself underneath me and quickly jostled my body in place across his back. He found the courage and strength to walk away quietly and ensure that the creature would not see or follow us. For days after I felt like I was among the living dead myself. I had nightmares, waking to my own screaming, while Brice nuzzled my face to calm me. I did not eat for three longs days, refusing and pushing away what Brice would bring into the house for me. It was a hard lesson learned as to what these creatures were capable of doing. We have kept our distance ever since.

Back on the forest floor, I follow the stream that is fed by the giant pond beyond the house. Brice and I walk in companiable silence until we reach the water. Brice loves the pond. He loves to swim and chase the fish. I set down my satchel and remove my newly made shorts, giving them another look over; I have done a fine job at sewing them. I smile despite myself—how proud my mother would be of them! The son of a seamstress, I am so grateful to be able to make my own clothes. I quickly frown with a deep longing for my mother.

I place the shorts on top of my satchel and look at Brice. An unspoken countdown and we are off and running, leaping with a splash into the water. We swim, and I welcome the cool water cleaning me. I dive deep to the murky bottom and kick off, shooting myself straight up to the surface. Wiping the water from my eyes, I find Brice with a large bass in his mouth.

"Good boy!" I call to him and take the dead fish from his mouth.

I swim for shore and place the fish beside my bag. Over by the large oak I grab my spear, the tip whittled sharp with a jagged black edge. I meander past the giant oak with its wide, glinting minty green leaves, its trunk smooth with age, polished by the winds and rain. My feet sink into the warm sand of the beach, the rushing of the falls in my ears as I get closer to the small mountain of dry warm rocks that towers over the pond. I begin my climb. The falls is where the river spills over and feeds the pond. It is peaceful here, in this space. A special safe haven in the gruesome forest in which it is hidden. A place where Brice and I can relax, let our guard down, ease the anxiety of survival.

I gaze down into the water when I reach the top. The stones are slippery here with a mossy algae coating them. In the small, relatively calm pool of water at the top, little minnows dart between my ankles. The water below casts a brightness from the shine of the sun, and it's hard to see through the glare across the water. I close my eyes and reopen them to see with Goblin sight. With the glare gone, the water is crystal clear.

Deep down in the water I see a fish with its silvery shimmer and throw my spear. It pierces the fish, which floats to the top. Brice retrieves the spear and paddles back to shore with it. I dive into the pond from the rocks above and glide through the cool cleansing water.

Dripping wet, I put my shorts back on and take the fish off my spear, returning it to lean against the oak tree. We head for home and I collect fallen limbs along the way to feed the fireplace. As we near the house, Brice runs ahead of me and sits waiting for me by the door. I pet his wet fur.

"Shake, Brice, shake."

He shakes his fur out, sending fat water droplets everywhere. I pass him a wide branch which he takes in his mouth and I open the door, glancing around at the cairns closest to the door that my father once created. They're smeared with black gooey ink. All are erect, all are intact. Each stone is in its place. I place some of the wood on my fire and stack up the remaining pieces, including the piece Brice carries in, now slobbery and wet.

I pour some water from my flask into the black cauldron and hang it close to the fire to warm, then begin skinning the squirrels and descaling the fish. From my satchel I take out the berries and pop a handful in my mouth. Once the squirrels are stripped of their skins, I carefully hang the furs to dry near the fire. Later they can be made into clothing.

The cauldron is starting to bubble. Brice has already been snacking most of the morning on other critters I know he crossed, and I give him a side eye when his stomach growls. I laugh, tossing the catch into the cauldron, cracking the eggs to the side, their yolks glistening. I set the table the same as always, with the one wooden plate and spoon that I whittled years ago.

"Today we eat like kings, Brice! It was a good day indeed."

I bow my head to him in thanks for helping catch our food. He bows back at me and purrs as we feast together in silence.

I sit and lean into my wolf companion, who is splayed in front of the fire. I work the skins of the squirrels, scraping and cleaning them and hooking them into a ring I made to stretch and dry them. When finished, I run my fingers through Brice's thick fur and begin to feel sleepy now that the sun is setting. I get up and go to the small table beside our bed and pull one of books from the bottom shelf. There are only three books to choose from. The first is smaller with a faded hard cover, the second is thick and old, and the third is tall and slim with a golden cover.

The smaller, hard book is one from the human village and I practice reading it every night. I read out loud to Brice so he can hear the story too. I long for a different book. Anything other than this story of a brother and sister who fall down only to break their stupid crowns.

The thick and old book is my pa's. I cannot read all of it yet—instead the book speaks to me. A friendly female voice emits from it and that voice teaches me my lessons every day. The cover of the book reminds me of a thick animal hide. Its pages smell musty and old, and the whole book is feather light considering its size, but the pages are un-rippable. It feels *wrong* in some way. Almost like the book itself is alive. When I touch the book, I can feel its longing and sense that it is lost just like me, wanting to be back somewhere, perhaps with its true owner. Yet somehow a happiness fills the book when I touch it and I promised my pa to touch it every day.

In the margins are my pa's messy doodled symbols and little strange images that he added after the book was originally made and that make no sense. They must be ancient runes of the Witches, but I cannot understand them. One page in the book is so perplexing; the words and phrases literally race about the page. Constantly moving, they never hold still long enough for me to read. Sometimes, for fun, I try and pin a word down with my finger. It vibrates so rapidly it makes my finger itch.

Instead of reading it, I listen to its whispers. It makes me recite different languages: Human, Wiccan, Goblin, Elf, Vampire, and even

Giant. I am not sure of the book's proper title, but it is incredibly old. Besides the languages, over the years it has also taught me all about the different Realms outside the forest. I have learned their histories, the creatures that reside in the Realms, their culture and folklore. The book knows so much—the origins of each creature, like the first vampire and how it came to be, the first witch, werewolf, and centaur—the book contains everything! Each creature is fascinating, and all were created by "The Mother." So the deity is called in each of the Realms and languages: the Mother of Creation.

At times I feel like the book is trying to tell me something, like it's holding back on the information it gives me, something other than what the lessons are teaching me. Like a secret, or a burden? I sense that the book knows how urgent it is for me to know. There's a feeling of dread, of responsibility. Of war?

Honestly, the book's emotions are so confusing and exhausting that I have no idea what it is trying to tell me. The most important page, the one the book flips open to and makes me recite over and over again, has dark red lettering that seems to hum. It is titled 'the bloodline prophecy.'

When the Realms are torn and separate, a great evil divides.

The Moon Goddess and the Mother are long since lost.

Two souls will be transformed.

One male, One female blood given and split. Rebirth of the kins, unknown powers and abilities.

The Souls: mated and destined to find what once was lost. A new beginning must be made.

I do not really understand it, but the book makes me say the little poem every day.

I look at the book and sometimes when I look at or touch it, it glows. Come to think of it, it glows more brightly now than in past times. I blink. Reopening my eyes to use my Goblin sight, I see something move and ripple inside the book.

Hesitantly, I reach out my palm. The book obeys and comes to me. It gently floats through the air and opens itself upon my waiting palm to a new page I have never seen before. I feel its meaning and sigh. It is a sketch my father has drawn of a mighty wolf. I fall in love with this new page as it looks so much like Brice. The stance of the creature, its fur all tussled and those eyes, just like Brice's.

The page glows bright green and words dance across it. It has never done that before. The book bounces and falls from my hand, still open to the page, and the words dance and race beautifully across and around the page.

I reach out a finger and try to pin a word down. Instead of the book whispering to me, an electric bolt zaps my finger. I quickly snap the book closed, annoyed yet again at the infuriating book.

I am neither shocked nor surprised as the book whirls, twirls, and whips through the house in a tantrum. It spills my flask of water and begins dumping sand from its pages, piling it up around me at an alarming rate. As the sand is already up to my neck, the book threatening to drown me in it, the hovering book plows into the side of my head. Sometimes I swear the book finds it funny just to cause me pain.

"Alright already! Lesson learned! I won't snap you closed anymore, but did you have to zap me?" I try to throw my hands up in surrender as the sand is swallowing me but then it slowly disappears.

I notice Brice looking at me with a concerned, puzzled look, shaking the extra sand from his fur. I replace my pa's book on the shelf a bit more forcefully than required and growl at it. I take the slim golden book instead and lean my back across Brice's stomach while he curls himself around me so he too can see the pictures in the book while I read to him. Another of Pa's gifts, it is a small version of the old thick book. There are few words in this one and it is always changing as new pages are added. The pictures themselves move: they are like twenty second memories that come to life on the pages. They are full of pictures of all sorts of creatures, snapshots of the outside world. Sometimes even my mum and my pa are in the pictures. I study those pages for hours when my parents show up. I long to be a part of this harrowing adventure they seem to be on, but the book has been quiet for weeks now.

The first page is of a female humanish form, and she radiates power. She is aglow with a bright yellow light—so beautiful. She has long, cascading silver hair that rests at the small of her back, a crown of red and golden flowers atop her head like a halo. She has wide hips, a large chest, and is barefoot. Her gown is like a sheer second skin of ivory with twisting hues of ocean blue. She smiles and waves at me lovingly. My pa's voice whispers her name:

"Emira."

The second page is of a noble-looking male and an equally beautiful female, skin ghostly white, lips as red as shining rubies. They are embracing each other, smiling at one another, long sharp canines peeking through their wide smiles.

Pa's voice whispers, "This is Vladimir and Lottie. Vampires!"

The next page is of two small-statured females fluttering up and down with beautiful glistening wings. They are holding hands, and each blows me a kiss, giggling.

"Gwendolyn and Sorcha," Pa whispers.

Turning the page, I am greeted by two large faces. The male smiles and winks. The female's eyes are so kind, and her smile seems to go for miles.

"Agrok and Esurg, Giants!" Pa exclaims.

The page after is of a king and queen. Glinting crowns adorn their heads and the female waves and bows her head to me.

"King Conway and his Queen Opal. Elves," Pa states.

Four creatures are on the next page, and they seem to be sharing a joke and are laughing. Two males and two females wave at me.

"John, Rebecca, Giles, and Susanna. Witches," says Pa's voice.

Then a male and female stand before me, a big bright beautiful moon behind them. At first they look like normal humans but the next second they turn into wolves. I love this picture the most! It fascinates me to watch the two creatures change from one form to the other and back as they laugh with me.

"Xander and Nikilaus, Alpha and Luna. Werewolves," Pa whispers.

Then a lovely female and male warrior stare back at me. I can see their mouths moving but hear nothing. I can't make out what they are trying to say. Then the female glows and smiles at me. Her eyes always lock on mine.

"Elgeeva and Azlocke. Your grandmother and her partner," Pa's voice says.

After these, pictures of my parents started appearing in the book. In the beginning, my parents looked tired, weary. Mum appeared to have been beaten and bruised yet she still smiled. I saw her surrounded by five familiar women. New friends of hers, perhaps.

Pa's voice states, "Amanda with Gwendolyn, Lottie, Opal, Nikilaus, and Nuala."

My favorite image of Pa is him battling a soldier dressed head to toe in gleaming silver armor, a huge smile on his face while dueling since he was winning. One day a picture appeared of Mum and Pa together, embracing. My heart filled with joy, and I longed to join them, but no new pictures have come from the book, so I flip through the ones that I have.

"To bed, then?" I ask Brice as the fire begins to die down. Brice nods in agreement and he and I curl up in the simple bed made by my father long ago. I cover us with our bear skin blanket and I nuzzle my head against his, laying on my back as the memory of this particular bear flickers through my mind. Brice has always been so brave and strong, always protecting me from another danger here in the forest.

We had met the bear along one of our worn paths in search of food. The bear, also in search of his next meal, charged at us. Brice charged back, darting quickly to a tree and kicking his legs off the trunk and onto the back of the bear. He sank his teeth into the beast's neck and it stood on its hind feet, reaching and twisting, trying to get the great wolf off its back. Brice swiftly snapped its neck. The bear crumpled to all fours before finally lying flat. Brice held his jaw locked upon the animal for a long while, making sure no breath came from it.

It took me all that day to skin the beast and collect its meat for the both of us to eat. Brice helped me drag it off the path and into the woods where we left the rest of it. I stretched and dried its fur to make our blanket. The extra chunks of meat I sank in the stream to keep cold and fresh. We ate like kings for well over a full moon 'til the next.

I smile at my friend, who cuddles up closer to me as he drifts off to sleep. Pictures frozen in time of my past with Brice play before me like a kaleidoscope in fast forward. Finding Brice curled in a hollow of a tree trunk, whimpering, alone and scared. Our first finding of the pond and how we swam all that day. I watch as our bodies grow little by little, running, racing, playing, and wrestling in the mud. Surviving the Forest of Wedgemore, a brotherly bond formed between us. Our survival both physically and mentally depended so much on having each other, and I am so grateful to have Brice as my companion, my brother. Our only family, we rely on each other for food, warmth, and safety.

Suddenly my picturesque memories change course and turn into a horrible nightmare.

CHAPTER SIX

A Decision Made

Dark images dance before me in slow motion. I watch as my grandfather the Goblin King waves his hand and my mother, father, and he himself disappear. I cry out, "Momma!"

I feel something nuzzle my face. "Mother?" I call out as something wet licks my cheek. It's dark, black as night. Where am I? "Who's there?" I demand as I hear breathing.

"Merek." Something wet licks my nose. "It's me, I'm here." And I feel something soft rub into my cheek.

I still cannot see. It's black as dark and dark as black. I close my eyes and reopen them with my Goblin sight. The familiar green shimmering glow brings sight to my eyes. I am in my father's house. Brice is beside me, but I see no other. I scan the room again.

"Who's there? Show yourself!" I say more firmly, looking around the small room for the source of the voice.

"Merek, be calm, my friend. It is just I. You were having a nightmare, so I woke you."

Again I look for the voice but see no one. It's just Brice and me. Brice nuzzles my face and paws gently at my hand.

"Brice, someone is here," I whisper to my friend. "Sniff them out, be careful. I'm going to reach for my knife."

"Oh Merek, I wish you could understand me. Hear me! There is only you and I here," Brice whispers gently from within his mind as he stands and stretches and begins his futile search of our small home. I look to the wolf beside me and Brice stares back at me.

"Brice? Can you hear me?" I whisper inside my head.

"YES!" he roars, his voice ringing between my ears.

I grab my head—I must still be dreaming. I must be dreaming, yes. I shake my head for good measure and pinch myself. Brice sniffs my hand. "Ouch. Okay, so I'm awake? Brice?"

"Yes!" he answers. "I'm not sure how, but I could see into your dream, Merek, and knew I needed to wake you." He nuzzles my face again.

I must have hit my head in my sleep. This cannot be possible. Yes, I must have hit my head. Brice snorts loudly at me and shakes his head. I am so tired; really tired. I sit back down hard upon the bed and then fall into it, back into a deep sleep.

I wake with the rising sun shining in through the window of my father's home, hot, sticky, and quite tangled up with my wolfish friend. I stretch, roll, and bury my face into Brice's fur and tickle his sides. He kicks me away, hops off the small bed, stretches, yawns, and sits looking at me.

"So, what will we do today, Brice? A walk? A swim?" I ask my friend and rise from the bed, stretching once more.

"Let's go for a walk today, Merek," a voice rings between my ears.

I hunch and stiffen. I scan the small room in search of the voice.

"Oh, not again." I hear Brice snort and huff. "Come off it, Merek." He paws at me. "It's me, Brice!"

I jump back in shock and trip, falling back onto the bed. I quickly right myself and then kneel before my friend, searching his eyes.

"How can I hear you?" I whisper.

"Maybe it was your father's book. You were holding it and looking at it last night." Brice looks me deep in the eyes. Just then my father's book leaps from its keeping place and opens. It is an image of Brice, the page that zapped my finger last night. Then the pages shuffle, landing on the image of Brice and I somewhere in the forest, a place I do not recognize but whose image is familiar. It's the edge of something important but unseen. Again I try with Goblin sight to see into the blurred edges of the image and this time I see something new. We are indeed at the edge, the edge of the forest that leads back to the human village. The village is at our backs and we are surrounded by many lost ones. I throw the book from me.

Brice breaks the silence, already knowing what I have just seen. "A walk, then. Shall we go now?"

I nod in agreement.

We walk together for a long while without speaking. I realize we have walked so far that I no longer recognize anything around us. As I try to get my bearings, Brice and I both freeze at the sounds of twigs snapping. We quickly glance in every direction, but I can see nothing. I grab a fistful of Brice's fur and swing him up onto the branch of a nearby tree. Silently we climb and separate. Toward the top of the tree, we scan below for the source of the footsteps.

Brice calls to me from within my mind and I make my way over to the other side of the tree to sit next to him. We look down upon a lost one. This one is new to us, not yet fully driven mad from the insanity of the mist. He is still clothed, but dazed and dangerous all the same. We sit in silence and wait until it ventures off and away from us.

"It is time to find our way, Merek," Brice says to me as we sit on our perch up in the tree.

"Find our way where?" I ask Brice, but I already know his answer. Brice looks me deep in the eyes and nods his head. To find our way to the border of the forest and back into the human world.

It is not the first time that thought has come to me. It's something I've thought about for a very long time. I have contemplated going many times, but there is nothing there for me. Everything I once knew is gone, taken from me, and only hate lives in that place. The humans couldn't accept me as a child, let alone now, a green mixed breed of human, goblin, and elf. I have always decided against going, so why go now?

"You were only five when you found me, Merek, I just a pup and both scared and alone. You and I have grown, and fifteen years have passed. Merek, I hear a strange voice, barely a whisper, but I think it's your father trying to tell us something. It feels like a warning that something is coming for us. Finding the border and crossing into the human realm is the message, his urgency that it will be safer there, for a time. Something is happening, or perhaps somebodies are venturing too close. Whatever it is, your father does not believe we can withstand it. He promises safety in the other Realm." He pauses.

"You hear my father, Brice? Why does he not speak to me? Why now? We live happily here—we have kept each other safe all these years, haven't we? The human world is unforgiving toward me and will be toward you. Your size alone would frighten them. They'd just want to hunt you down. You're longer than I am tall, Brice, your legs taller than mine. The humans would see you as a prize to either tame or slaughter." I vent this in anger, in fear, holding back tears as the memory of that horrible night starts like it always does, a silent picture show playing in my brain that I cannot shut off.

"*We must go.* There is something in your father's voice full of fear and panic that there is a new great danger in the forest we have not yet faced. I think it best if we make our way back home, pack for the journey ahead, prepare."

"How can you be sure it is my father who speaks to you, Brice?" I pause, then ask, "Is he well? He is not coming for me, then?" I look to Brice in despair.

"It is hard for me to hear him, but he urges us in haste. He is very weak, Merek. We must go."

I stand and turn away from my friend. How can this be, how can we just go? This is our home, a life we know and have survived in. I cannot leave! The thought of leaving pains me and makes my stomach turn. Brice comes from behind me and pushes his big head between my ankles, hoisting me up onto his back. I press myself against his big, strong back and hug my friend, crying into his fur.

"I'm scared, Brice. My memories of the human world are of hiding, hate, and anguish. How can I possibly return?"

The graceful mighty wolf makes his way, in the tops of the trees, branch to branch with me still upon his back. I feel him begin our descent down from the safety of the tree and trot off for our small home.

"I do not know, but we will have each other this time."

Once home I pack my satchel with our favorite picture book and the berries and edible leaves we still have left. I take my dagger and fill the flask with the stream's clean flowing water. I look warily at my friend and again he takes me up onto his back. Slowly we head along a worn path, away from the safety of our small home.

My father's home. The one he made for all of us, himself, my mum, and I. But only I have ever known this as home. It was meant to be for the three of us.

I look back one last time, cast one last look upon the small shack of stones. It may be the last time I will ever see it. A feeling of forgetting fills my core and flops my stomach. I cannot place it and it nags at me. When I look back again toward our home, I realize Brice has walked faster than I had thought, and the little cottage, the only place I've ever truly called home, has disappeared among the trees.

CHAPTER SEVEN

Journey to the Border

I let Brice carry me for a while. I bury my face into the comfort of his fur, panic wreaking havoc upon my body, causing me to vomit every now and again. Brice stops while I empty my stomach yet again. Tears uncontrollably stream down my face until finally my body heaves from pain one last time. I lay upon my friend as he walks us away from the only happiness, only home I ever knew and into an unknown, unwelcoming world. I breathe in deeply, inhaling Brice's wondrous scent of earth and pine. Slowly my body begins to calm. As long as I have him, as long as we are together, we can overcome whatever threatens us in our future. It is because of Brice, his friendship, companionship, and his love for me that I have survived this long. As long as I have him, I repeat to myself, I will be okay. I sit myself upright upon his back and have a look around at our current surroundings.

The trees grow thick and compact here, and Brice weaves between the trunks. This part of the forest looks untouched and old, foliage so bright and green, birds signing, small critters darting out of the way only to study us and follow our path, trying to determine if we are threatening. The light is muted on the forest floor, blocked out by the impressive canopy above us. Colorful birds perched on branches track us with beady black eyes, heads cocked to the side. Bright red and orange fungi grow large and florally, protruding from the trunks at ground level. A breeze rustles the canopy of leaves above.

"Do you know the way, Brice?" I scan around us once more. "Where are we, my friend? You have carried us a long way from home already!" I realize the sun is setting, and we have indeed traveled very far.

"Your father guides me this way. We have traveled for most of this day and now I need rest. You are much bigger and heavier now, my friend, than you once were," he says shyly to me.

"Yes, let's rest."

I look again at our situation and see a large cave opening, high above us in the rocks. "There, do you see it, Brice? A cave. Let us have a look, make sure that something does not call this cave home."

Brice nods as I slide off his back. He trots away and leaps rock to rock and scouts out the entrance of the cave. As I begin to climb up, I hear his voice telling me to wait at the entrance.

"All clear," I hear Brice call. "I smell nothing from within the cave; it's empty and pretty dark in there. The entrance doesn't let in much light. You should gather wood and build a fire before the sun sets."

I stand before the mouth of the cave and close my eyes to reopen them with my Goblin sight. I search the cave for signs of anything living within. Brice is close beside me, sniffing and smelling with his powerful nose. The opening of the cave narrows and I am not sure Brice can squeeze through. He answers my unspoken question and does a graceful tiptoeing maneuver through.

"Nothing here, Merek," he shouts within my mind. I shake my head against the echoing of his voice and begin collecting twigs, sticks, and logs to start a fire. After several trips outside the cave to gather wood for the night, Brice helps pull together the two large shrubs growing on either side of the cave opening and I use long vines to tie them closer together, forming a makeshift door. We both retreat into the dark mouth of the cave and I begin starting a fire.

Brice pulls and tugs at the bear skin blanket to make us a bed for the night. Once he's straightened it to his liking, he curls up on the end nearest my small fire. The warm sun has long since set and the night chill starts to creep into our cave.

I shimmy through the narrow opening to check the back of the cave once more. I hear the hypnotic pitter-pattering of rain now and all I can hear is the falling water. I feel a bit better because of the highness of the opening of our cave, the large shrubs now blocking the entrance, and the little fire's light that doesn't reach the opening. I breathe a heavy sigh. Maybe we will be safe tonight, maybe nothing will find us while we sleep. My stomach knots at the thought of a lost one finding us. As far as I can see, the back is blocked, and the front entrance is the only way out.

I make my way back to Brice, deciding to have a thorough search through the back end of the cave to make sure there is no second opening. Brice is nearing sleep and his light snoring has started. Poor beast, he carried me all this way, wherever we are. I tip-toe by him so as not to disturb his slumber and blink my eyes, switching to my Goblin green shimmering sight. I notice a large crack at the back of the cave. I thought it was a solid wall of rock but, switching sights, I see it and squeeze through the narrow opening between its walls. I get stuck for a moment, then I turn myself sideways and shuffle down the corridor of rock to find myself in another much larger opening. This cavern is luminescent, dimly light but bright all at once. Examining the walls of the cave, I notice millions of tiny slug-like creatures pulsating with a blueish, purplish light. It is damp here; the enormous cavern is drenchingly humid.

I blink away my Goblin sight and inhale sharply at the beauty around me. The ceiling is covered in spikes, long and slender as if trying to reach the floor below them, and they too are covered with the glowing slugs. Glistening in the floor, a still mirror image of what is above, is a pool as wide as the cavern itself with a stone path laid in the center before me. I take a gentle step onto the first stone, testing its balance and hold in the earth. I make my way slowly and carefully so as not to make a sound to the middle of the cavernous room. My eyes catch a prism of light beneath the water. Cautiously I kneel on the stone step and carefully slide my fingers into the water. It is so warm and so clear. I reach my hand deeper into the water and retrieve a sparkling stone.

It is a magnificent stone—it looks as though made of glass, nestled in the palm of my hand. Holding the stone up into the light of the slugs, a rainbow of dots fills the cavern. I play with the stone, turning it in my fingertips against the light and making the rainbow dance. I pocket my new treasure and continue along the stone path.

Nearest the stone path it's very shallow on either side, but it quickly drops off away from the center path into a deep, dark royal blue depth. At the back of this cavern is a mighty wall of rock covered in slugs pulsating their light as they wiggle their way along their path.

A small black hole along the wall just off the center from the stone path catches my eye. Nearing the hole, it appears larger than I first noticed, as none of the light-giving slugs are near it. The creatures give this hole in the rock a wide berth, giving the impression that they fear it. I step into the warm shallow water and make my way towards the hole. It is truly smaller in size up close but the hollow of it is so dark. Switching to my Goblin sight, I bend down and have a look inside.

I scream from fright and push back and away from the out-stretched skeletal bony hand trying to grasp my shirt. I fall backward into the deep royal blue water. I feel like I am being flipped upside down and pulled farther below the water's surface. Kicking hard and swimming with all my might, my eyes search for the surface for a gulp of air. I only see the cavern's ceiling above, not knowing just how far I am falling into the water. Something from the deep grabs and pulls at my ankle, carrying me further down and away from the surface as I involuntarily scream.

I watch as the last of my air forms large bubbles and floats towards the surface, silenced by the water around me. I chance a look down at my ankle, struggling for clear sight in the watery darkness, but nothing is there. I kick with the energy I have left and reach for the far-off surface. I feel surrounded by a thick muck instead of what should be water. It's no use. I am stuck in this thick substance and not able to take a breath.

A musical voice fills my head.

"Child, child?" a voice sings to me. My body continues to sink further down into the deep dark muck of this pool where surely I will die alone, swallowed up by the cavern.

"Child, breathe," the voice coaxes, but my mind knows that I'll surely drown if I do, inhaling only water, not air.

"Open your eyes and see me, see what I have done for you," the voice sings.

I gaze in fright at a creature I have never seen before through the wall of a large air pocket. I find myself standing on a massive boulder covered with shellfish. I suck in a long deep breath, and my body bends and begins a violent coughing fit.

Once my body calms and I can breathe normally, I chance another glance at the creature that waits for me on the other side of my delicate air bubble wall. It appears to be female with long white hair flowing about her in the water. In a white skull face with deep sockets where eyes should have been instead glows an iridescent blue and purplish light. Black markings of twirling patterns and flowers cover its bony face. Pearl white dagger teeth glisten in the little light here, displaying a devilish permanent and deathly smile. Her body of bones is marked with black swirls that lead to one long fin-shaped tail.

"Ah, such a handsome boy you have grown to be. A lethal creature created of a Royal Gelfin and a fragile human. If only your grandfather knew just how important you are to all of us, I am sure he would have killed you when he discovered you that night." She pauses and a chill runs down my spine.

"Luckily for us, we keep our precious secrets. He knows not of your prophecy. He turned away from you, thinking such a tiny help-less creature could not survive on its own, but we knew you would. We knew the wolf would keep you safe. We have waited so exceptionally long for you, dear child," the creature sings to me. I feel my body calm further and cannot help but stare at her. My heart pulls with a recognition of familiarity. Deep within the marrow of my bones, somehow, I know her, love her, and would honor her.

"Dear child, your path is still long ahead and you will learn along the way. As for I..." She pauses. "Your time to free me is here. Your body is still weak and unlearned of your potential power and only I can begin its awakening. Your grandfather imprisoned me here long before your birth. I have remained here, stuck in this forsaken cavern, for too long now. My subjects desperately need me, but I knew you would come for me. Without me, your path will not begin, the future will not be changed, our people will continue to die." She says this to me quietly and her words are so sad.

"I was once a Goddess of creation. My name is Emira, one of the last of my people. Your people call me Mother." She smiles her skeletal grin wider at me. "Your grandfather is my great grandchild and fears me above all else. I was one of many beings made to breed a new species to save our dying races. Your grandfather despises his mixed blood for being un-pure, but he certainly relishes the power it brings him," she says angrily. "My kind began to discover what would happen. We would soon be overthrown by our beloved children. Your grandfather killed many of my kind but was not powerful enough to slaughter me. Enraged that he could not harm me, he imprisoned me here, long, long ago, hoping time would all but swallow my memory whole. But there live a few who still know of me, pray to me, and search for me, for I am the Mother and your true Queen."

Entranced, I listen and hang on each of her beautiful words. I long to be closer to her—my body grows warm and my eyesight blurs. My heart pounds in my chest, a sign of extreme danger, and yet I beg to touch the creature, to have her hold me.

"Yes, child. That is right, trust in me. Trust in me," she whispers, and I inch closer to the wall of my delicate air bubble, closer to her. "Now will you help me, child?" she whispers again, and I nod to her. "I need blood from you, and you need blood from me, to show my love for you and, as you are one of my creatures, my good faith that I mean you no harm." She draws closer to my bubble. "I'll let you drink first from me," she whispers even quieter.

I search the skull face before me, just inches away from the watery side of wall. "In this form, I cannot withstand the air you breathe. It tortures me in this form and will slowly kill me. I will just place my hand inside for you." The wall of the bubble ripples but holds tight.

I look at her offered bony hand and back up a bit further, out of her reach. Her hands have long white claws, razor sharp, where fingernails should have been.

"Do not fear me, child, sweet child. I will do you no harm. I have waited so long for you, waited for this, for my freedom. Please, child, come and bite the bone of my hand. Feel my life source flow into your mouth and into your body, making you stronger, more powerful, and share in my magic and my ancient knowledge."

Slowly I take a step toward her. She reaches a bit further into my bubble, offering her hand once again to me. I study her bony face, looking deep into her eye sockets that glow more intensely of blue and purple. Tremblingly I reach out my hand for hers. I take the small hand in my own, turning it over and back but very confused.

"Yes, just bite with your sharp teeth to puncture the bone and drink. Please, child, hurry, the air burns my bones," she says so quickly.

I look back down at her small, seemly, fragile bony hand. How is it even held together, no ligaments, no tendons connected to knit the bones together? I notice in the low lighting that the bone is turning red. I grab her hand and hold her tight, pulling the arm in a bit more through the bubble, and bite into the bigger of the bones in her arm. I feel her bone give way to my teeth and a warm liquid drips into my mouth. It tastes sweet and of salty water, warm and tingling down my throat. It feels wonderful. My Goblin sight takes over and my sight sharpens in the low light. Warmth floods my body.

My whole body thrums and pulses. I feel overwhelmingly happy and light, powerful and strong, until the pain begins coursing through my body, shaking me violently. I suck harder, flooding my mouth with her delicious liquid. It brings every cell in my body to life with excruciating pain. I see memories of the past flash before my eyes. Too quickly they race through my brain, each image fading into another too quickly to be able to make any sense of it. I grip the bony arm tighter.

Such anguish runs through me that I feel I can no longer live with such loss. There is pain and the devastation of battles and wars, of lovers and loving so intensely. So many different, beautiful, and horrifying creations of creatures. Utter betrayal. Then with a hum I feel her magics, spells, creations, and knowledge flood my system. I suck in through my nose a huge lungful of air. Pure light, happiness, and joy overtake me. I see a small, beautiful baby wrapped in silk linens smiling back at me. My eyes fill with tears at the pure joy of that child, at what is felt for the beautiful baby before me. It is me. She loves me.

"Child, stop now," she says sternly, and tries pulling her arm back through the bubble wall and away from me. I hold her tighter and suck more deeply. I desperately try to recall the image of the baby, swallowing the sweet and salty treat that she has offered me. I cannot stop; it is much too good. It feels more wonderful than anything I have ever felt before. She is mine now; I will never let her go. I will drink from her forever, until my last breath. To drink her knowledge, power, history, love... Every essence of her is in me, most of it so confusing but somehow clear as well, and I understand. I crouch over her arm protectively while I continue my drink.

"STOP!" her voice bellows and she yanks with all her might and reaches through the bubble with her other hand for one of my arms. I hold fast, solid like the boulder I am standing upon. She in turn pulls her skull face and upper bony body through my bubble wall. It ripples dangerously but holds strong.

"Fine, then, if you won't let me go, I won't numb my bite first. Brace yourself, child. This will be painful!"

My eyes widen but I refuse to let go. She then sinks her dagger pearl teeth into my arm and sucks at me much more quickly. I let out a deep growl from my throat and take one last long suck before letting go. Her bite causes extreme pain that electrifies my whole being, yet she holds me tight and still. The blue and purple in her eye sockets glow even brighter and her grip tightens even more. Fear takes over me as she drinks fast, hard, long gulps of me. She will surely drink me dry. I could not stop, how will she? Panic takes over as I pull and pull my arm back and away from her, and then she releases me.

"*I am Emira, I am the Mother,*" her voice screams within my head. "I will see you again, my dear child. Keep the stone in your pocket safe. Remember these words: *when the time comes, throw the stone into any water and dive down and into the deep. A choice you will have to make.* Keep it safe, keep it close, keep it hidden, for when you have need of me or to save a life."

She begins to disappear before me, her deep glowing blue and purplish eyes staring deep into my soul. "Remember these words!" her hysterical voice screams. There are burning flashes of light and so much pain, and my body is thrown backward and crumples against something hard as stone.

***

I sit bolt upright, panting. Drenched in wetness, I cradle my arm. The sun's early morning light creeps its way into the cavern. I search about the open room to find only Brice curled up next to me, waking with my fright.

My arm burns and bleeds. I lick at the wounds that punctured my skin. The bleeding slowly stops, and the burning begins to fade. Brice nuzzles my face and looks up at me with concern.

"*When the time comes, throw the stone into any water and dive down and into the deep. A choice you will have to make. Keep it safe, keep it close, keep it hidden, for when you have need of me or to save a life. Remember...*" a voice sings from deep within me. I reach into my pocket and there in my hand is the glass stone. I hold it in the light and rainbow dots of light fill the cavern.

I blink against the bright morning light and bury my face into Brice's thick and soft fur. I tickle his sides and he kicks at me to push me away. He stretches, yawns, stands, and sits back down, looking at me.

"Ready to leave, Brice?" I ask my friend, wanting to be far away from this cave. He nods, and I pack up. Once outside the cave, I look around us and nothing is familiar. "Which way, Brice?"

He begins to sniff the air with his powerful nose and sweeps this way and that. Finally, he stops and cocks his head in the direction of his reasoning.

"That way?" I ask, pointing. He nods to me and we begin our walk.

We walk for miles. The sun is now high in the sky and our stomachs begin to growl with hunger. Brice stops and sniffs again and follows the scent to a large and plentiful blueberry bush.

"Good boy." I rub behind one of his ears and he leans into my massage. We eat ourselves full of berries. My lips are dyed purple from the juice of the berries, and he snorts with laughter at me. I pick more and stash a supply of the berries away in my pack and head out for our long walk, once again searching for the border between the Forest of Wedgemore and the human Realm.

I am strangely comforted by the new knowledge, power, and strength that flows through me. I feel it tingle in my veins as we continue, knowing we are on the correct path to wherever it is my pa's voice leads us.

CHAPTER EIGHT

The Border

We walk well into the day without rest. My legs and back have been screaming in protest to stop for a long time, so I finally decide to listen and sit abruptly. Brice also crumples to the ground and lays upon his side to rest.

We are not able to rest long before we hear the crackling of sticks under feet, which only means one thing: a lost one is stumbling around close to our resting place. Brice and I make our way up the nearest tree to the highest point to get away from it and continue our rest while we wait for it to venture off and away from us. Searching the ground below, I finally spot it. What once was a man is now naked like all the others, skinny and sickly. It sits at the base of our hiding tree.

"Great, this may take a while," I whisper. We won't be able to make our way back down the tree and continue on our journey to the human border, not while the lost one is there. I decide to take advantage of the situation and settle back against the tree trunk for a snooze.

I notice Brice smelling the air and a concerned look flashes in his eyes. I am just about to question him when I see two more lost ones walking toward our tree and to the lost creature below. Both were once women, their clothes tattered and torn.

"They know we're up here, Merek!" Brice calls to me within my mind. "They're looking for us. They've come with a purpose."

I give Brice a concerned look. Lost ones have no purpose, no rational thought. They just roam around in search of food, void of reasoning. They never travel together, usually dining on whichever one of them is weakest.

"Can you hear their thoughts, Brice?" I ask.

He shakeshis head. "I can smell it in their scent," he answers.

"Most likely we will have to witness a blood bath. Looks like we are going to be stuck in this tree awhile. Let's use this time and rest," I say, so sure that the three creatures below will soon begin trying to conquer each other's flesh. Instead, I watch and listen in horror as the three begin a series of grunts and groans at one another. They are communicating. Stranger still, I listen intently and without knowing how, I can understand what they are saying. A chaos of chaotic voices speaks,

"Wheres..."

"Kills, kills it!"

"Finds its, maims it."

"Kills, kills, kills!"

The multiple voices are haunting, stacked and layered on top of one another as they are.

I look to Brice in bewilderment and am about to tell him of their conversation when Brice's nose catches a new scent. Fear takes over my friend, and he inches closer to me.

"We are near the border, Merek. They are here to stop us from crossing it. Your grandfather is nearly upon us." His words race through my mind. "He comes this way. Get on my back—we have to leave here. We are close to the border; I can feel it!"

Without questioning him, I climb upon his back. I peer down to the creatures below, who now stare at Brice and me. They have discovered us. A cold wind blows, so cold that it sinks deep into my bones and causes both Brice and I to shiver. A murky blue mist seeps out of the surrounding trees and encircles the three creatures below. The blue mist is humming. It begins as a low tone I barely notice but grows louder and stronger. Brice is growing more nervous by the second. Something is very wrong. The blue mist swirls around and up into the faces of the creatures below.

Each inhales it deeply. Each creature bends, rattled with coughing fits. Then, as if on command, the three look up to us in unison. They growl a horrid noise. Their faces turn a shade of violent red, mouths opening and elongating. An ear-piercing scream erupts from the open mouths. I lay my chest upon Brice's back and clamp both hands over my ears as he winces against the painful noise.

Within seconds, the three have leapt at the tree and have already climbed halfway up to us with newfound claws, climbing faster and faster. They have nearly reached our branch when Brice gets a running start and leaps away from the branch and into a neighboring tree. It is a sizable distance and my mind races at the feat he accomplishes as Brice is able to leap and land soundly.

Brice moves along the branches further away while I glance back at the three now standing where we had just been. I have never seen a lost one act the way these three do. Nor have they ever been able to climb the trees.

I watch as one of the female creatures surveys her surroundings, and, just like Brice, runs along the branch and jumps. Her body contours and flips in the space between the branches. She has not leaped with enough strength, and she is not going to make it. She begins to fall, fear riddled all over her face. I can see the sadness in her eyes as she reaches out for anything to stop herself from falling but grasps at only air and lets out an ungodly cry of frustration and pain combined. She lands on the ground below in a horrible heap of twisted and bent limbs. Staring at her, through a transparent patch in the mist, I make sure she does not move and that she at least will no longer be a threat. It is just two against two now.

Brice continues leaping from branch to branch. I hold on tighter, both hands full of his fur and my thighs squeezing his sides. I watch as the other two creatures cock their heads side to side like disoriented insects, looking down at the ground and whimpering at their companion's crumpled body. Brice pauses and follows my gaze to the remaining creatures in the neighboring tree, their faces again turning violent red, mouths elongated impossibly long as they unhinge their jaws, the dark opening revealing sharp and gnarly teeth. They bellow a horrid, painful, and vomit-inducing sound. Brice crouches down before he begins to race straight down the trunk of the tree. I grip at him more and hold on with all my might as we reach the forest floor in an accelerated sprint.

Somehow both creatures are already at our heels, reaching out to grab at Brice's tail. I lean into Brice, wrap my arms around the beast's massive neck, and loosen my grip on his hind legs. He runs faster and faster as I let go of my hold on his sides altogether and center myself upon him, relaxing and letting my body move as he moves, hindering his movements less. He can run, stronger and harder, putting distance between us and the two creatures. Soon I am no longer able to see them, even using my Goblin sight. We have lost them, they are not following, and I heave a sigh of relief.

I begin to realize just how fluid and one Brice and I have become since he started running. It is as if I'm part of him, both bodies fueling the run, each comfortable and empowered in our escape as our bodies blend into one, a single creature.

I feel myself running, my heart rate elevated, our feet pounding the ground. My sight is his sight. Completely in awe, both Brice and I silently acknowledge the change in our bodies morphing into the one. It is easy and comforting, powerful and strong. We run like this long into the day before finally we both are fatigued. We slow our pace and feel our bodies coming undone and separate once again. We fall to the ground, each spent of our energy, completely depleted. We lay beside each other and begin dragging the evergreen boughs that have fallen to the forest floor to cover our bodies and scent. Once fully covered and camouflaged, I reach out to my dear friend. I hold his paw in my hand. Each of us asks the unspoken question of *how?* before we succumb and drift off to sleep.

***

I am wakened by my nuzzling friend. I reach for him and bury my face into his soft fur, inhaling deeply his scent and tickling his sides. He kicks me away and we unbury ourselves from our makeshift hideaway of evergreens. Brice yawns, sits, and looks to me.

I look back into the eyes of my friend and smile at him, but my smile is quickly replaced by a frown. His eyes are wide, staring at something behind me. My stomach is turning, a strange pulling sensation, and I stumble as I try to rise to my feet. Brice nips at me in warning of whatever it is behind me, but if I do not back away from where I stand then the nausea of the pulling sensation will surely make me vomit. My mind fuzzes and my eyes blur. Brice tugs at my shorts, pulling me closer to him and closer to whatever it is that is causing the pulling sensation. It makes my stomach turn violently. Brice begins a low, deep growling, and I turn to face what he is seeing only to find nothing.

"Brice?" I whisper within my head as it too begins to spin.

"The lost ones, about a mile off. You must pass through the border. Walk in a straight path behind me. Fight the sickness! It is the mist that divides the human world and the forest. Go, now!" he urges.

I fall to my knees, weakened and dizzy. "Not without you. Help me to walk. Let's cross now, together," I plead with Brice.

"Do you see the strange blue mist? It is guiding the lost ones right to us, look! The mist followed us, creating a path right to us." He sniffs the air. "It's the two from yesterday plus more, many more. There is a whole pack of them. You must go *now*! Walk through the border and cross—it is just there through those trees. Can you see the open field beyond the tree line? I will hold them off. Merek, go!" His eager voice rings within my head and he pushes me still further back toward the border.

"Merek!" he shouts at me.

I feel the pull again and my vision goes dark. White lights dance across the forest wherever I look, and a buzzing like a swarm of bees is in my ears. My chest feels heavy and it's as if I'm moving in slow motion, each step backward against Brice's urgent shoves lasting a lifetime. I stumble and follow the pulling sensation to the trees where Brice has pointed me.

At first I see no field, only the thickness of trees, impossible to pass through. I blink and see with Goblin sight a thick and murky grey mist swirling and dancing between the trees. My vision strengthens against the milky pea-soup mist; there is an open field with long golden grass dancing in a wind and glistening in bright sunlight. I blink again and the vision is gone, leaving a mirage of thick trees and endless forest. The now invisible mist is causing me to feel this sickness. It is stopping me like a thick murky shield, preventing me from passing through. The mist fills me with fear. My body trembles and all I want to do is turn and run away.

No wonder the lost ones can never find their way home. They cannot see the world just beyond the mist. The abrupt sickness and crippling fear that soaks into every pore is almost enough for me to think twice about passing through it.

Brice is now leaning into me, pushing me back into the false boundary and through the mist border, his broad body in front of me, protecting me from what is coming. More of the bone-chilling blue mist is in front of us, as well as a pack of lost ones... and something else. I sense a more powerful creature with them, but I am unable to focus with Brice pushing me back into the grey sickening mist. I stumble and see the tall golden grass swaying in a breeze. There are flowers, so many flowers.

"Brice! The border is here. Do we just walk through? I'm so sick and confused, my brain is swimming and spinning."

I follow the gaze of my friend. We are surrounded by ten lost ones in a semicircle. Their heads are cocked to the side, staring at Brice and me. Brice sits back in front of me, blocking my body. I reach to him and grab a fistful of his soft fur and hold tightly. Brice growls and snaps his jaws in warning.

As one, the lost ones' naked skins turn violent red, mouths and eyes grow wide and then they let out a deafening scream. A haunted and tortured sound escapes their lips, causing me to fall to my knees and cover my ears. It blurs my eyes with tears. Brice shakes his mighty head and whines against the screaming. He backs up into me and slowly we back up together, step by step, inching closer to the border. When the screams stop, the blue mist swirls and pulls tightly together, forming an intricate, tall and wide door. I marvel at the beauty of the incredibly old, decoratively carved wood. The door opens and the insoluble mist takes shape, transforming into a black hooded cloaked figure. My scalp prickles and the hair all over my skin stands to attention as fear runs deep through my body.

The figure steps through the opening and stands before the line of insane lost ones. With both hands the creature pushes back its hood. There before me and definitely the source of what is compelling the insane pack behind him is my grandfather, the Goblin King Molag. The lost ones rock with impatience, tilting their heads from one side to the other and back again, enlarged black vacant eyes searching and ready to pounce, mouths elongated and snapping. This is the image I saw in my father's book.

The book!

Holy hell, my stomach curls in on itself. I left his book behind. I only grabbed the moving picture album. My mind races. *I left his book behind*. How *stupid* of me! I scramble to think of what to do now as my father's warning becomes reality, but it's too late. I can't think, can't breathe. My knees shake as my grandfather looms before me, a cold dread fixing me to the spot. I couldn't run if I tried.

My grandfather lifts one hand. The lost ones are hushed, swaying back and forth, quiet and in some sort of a trance, humming a soft, sweet sound. It causes goosebumps to ripple across my skin. Brice backs into me, urging me back, but I am frozen to the spot I stand. Brice then takes a protective stance in front of me and glares into the eyes of my grandfather.

A realization sweeps through me. My grandfather controls the mist. It is his creation, his power that is now fueling the lost ones. He has the lost ones under his complete control.

"My, how you've grown," his voice hisses through his teeth. Brice growls low and deep. Grandfather laughs deeply. "I assume I need no introduction." He smiles at me and bows with enthusiasm, then look up quickly mid-bow. "Ah, yes, you do recall who I am! Alas, you must know that I cannot allow you to leave the forest today, my dear boy," he states flatly. "You must return with me now. You will come with me to my home, to the Kingdom of—" He pauses to find the correct words "—*our* people," he coos to me. "There are two very excited and expectant someones who wish to see and be reunited with you, Merek."

My heart instantly burns with longing as I know he speaks of my parents. I try to take a step towards the creature that is my grandfather but Brice shoves me roughly back.

"Merek, this is a dangerous creature, and he lies," Brice whispers within our minds. "Your parents are not in that kingdom. Go, now, cross the border!"

"Oh, so Brice is your name, brave one." Brice growls at my grandfather. "Let's see how brave you are against *me*."

Instead of an attack from the Goblin King, it is Brice that whips around to snap at my face. I stumble backwards at his sudden attack and again he snaps at me, backing me further away from the Goblin King and closer to the border.

"You! Mother of Light, you fowl, overgrown, insolent mutt!"

With a twist of his hand, my grandfather causes Brice to crumple before me and writhe in pain.

Tears prick my eyes as I reach for my friend to try and comfort him. I glare at the evil creature before me. I grab a fistful of Brice's fur and drag his seizing body, inching us closer to the edge. Another wave of my grandfather's hand and Brice howls in pain, his body getting heavier and heavier, writhing and wriggling beneath my grip. I can feel it, the edge is pressing into my back now. I feel it sucking me into it, the sickness spinning my vision. The lost ones have now come much closer, closing in, tightening their semicircle around us. Eyes wide and black, skin violent red and mouths hanging open, poised to jump. Brice becomes too heavy to drag. Why is he so heavy? I'm dragging him hard against the earth, leaving a small trench where his body once was. It is like trying to drag a boulder.

I look into the eyes of my friend and through his pain I see him there, strong and brave. Tears run down my face as another seizing fit crumples his body. This evil creature, my grandfather, is causing him so much pain. I tighten my grip in his soft fur and his eyes focus on mine. I look deep into his. His last wish is to see me safely through the border and away from the King.

Brice kicks me hard one last time and I begin to fall away from him, losing my precious grip on my friend. The border sucks me into its clutches, crushing and squeezing all the air from my lungs. Time slows and I find myself in a nothingless void. It's as if I'm stuck between worlds, in a whirlwind of chaos.

My body contorts, flipping over and over, until I am abruptly spit out on the other side. My limbs flail as I try to regain my balance. I have been thrown with such a force into the long green and golden grass that it leaves me choking without breath, a handful of Brice's fur in my fist, but no Brice. My head swims as I roll over and lay there coughing and gasping for air, a loud buzzing in my ears. I scream out with no breath in my lungs. No sound comes from my lips, but I call for Brice anyway.

I wait and wait, pace and pace along the edge for hours. Days turn into nights, waiting for my Brice to come, unable to see through to the forest side, not even with my Goblin sight. Frantically pacing and searching at the edge. Screaming with all my might, calling to him, pleading for him to come to me. Three days and nights of no sleep, just sitting, waiting, listening, pacing. Night falls again. I close my eyes and reopen them with my Goblin sight, scanning and searching the edge of the meadow and forest. No creature stirs here, not even birds. I begin again on my well-worn path along the meadow's tall grass. I trip from exhaustion and fall to the earth, succumbing to fatigue and grief. The sleep is unwelcome that takes a strong hold of me, and I dream.

***

I see her sitting there at her table, sewing a small dress colored of pink and white silk. I crawl under her table and watch her feet work the peddles up and down. When her feet stop, her beautiful face appears and smiles at me under the table. I fall back in a fit of giggles from the surprise. She gets up from her chair and grabs my legs, pulling me from under the table. She lifts me by my ankles until we are nose to nose. I laugh out loud harder. She spins my little body into her arms and tickles my belly. Nose to nose, we nuzzle and laugh.

"Bedtime, Merek."

She hugs me tightly and carries me up the stairs to our bed. She lays me down and I roll and roll all over the bed. Momma laughs. She pulls up my shirt and tickles my belly with her mouth, making a funny noise. I squeal and laugh.

"Come, Merek, under the covers now." She pats the bed. I crawl to my spot while she changes into a night dress and climbs in beside me. She sings a song and brushes her fingers through my hair. I suck on my two fingers and as she sings and brushes my hair. I drift off to sleep, safe, warm, and cuddled by Momma.

I wake abruptly, sweaty and drenching wet. Where am I? I am in a meadow and the sun is setting through rainclouds. How long have I been asleep? I search for Brice but fail and the painful memory returns. I stand and shiver. I turn away from the edge of the meadow and forest and walk through the long, tall golden grass, not knowing where I am going.

The meadow proves to be large and vast. I walk until the moon is high, just barely seen through the raining clouds. When I finally reach the other edge of the meadow, I see a small house and large barn standing before me. It is dark, cold, and I'm wet. I need shelter from the stinging rain and cold. I dare not head for the house but instead creep into the barn.

It is so dark, I close my eyes. I hear the rustle of animals, nervous and scared of me. I open my eyes and see with green shimmering light the many pigs, sheep, and cows. My stomach growls loudly with hunger, which frightens the animals further. I hush and soothe them, telling them I mean no harm to any of them but that I am in need of shelter from a cold and rainy night. A smaller cow in a back stall *moos* to me and calls me to her.

"Come, young one." I hear her soothing voice within my mind and stumble to follow her voice. Her pen is the smallest of the stalls and she is half the size of the other cows. "My youngling died just after his birth. I am full of milk and it is causing me much pain. I offer you my milk and my stall for sleep in trade for not harming my fellows."

Her thought envelops me. I bow low and very deep to the wonderful creature before me to show her my utmost respect and gratitude. She nods and I unlatch her door and enter. She lays down upon her side and I fall beside her.

My mind swims from fatigue, hunger, and grief. My muscles will move no more. I lay spent upon the hay of the barn floor.

The sweet cow takes pity upon me and nuzzles me closer with her soft face, urging me to drink my fill. Her milk is warm and creamy. It fills my mouth and I drink hungrily. The fatty milk coats my throat and begins to warm me from the inside out. When I have drunk my fill and have eased her fullness, she nuzzles into me and I fall heavily into a deep and warm sleep. She begins tossing hay, covering me in it, and settles closer to keep my body warm and out of sight while I sleep so deeply.

CHAPTER NINE

Rowan

I awake to weeping and the morning sunshine.

Where am I? Oh, right, the barn and the sweet cow beside me is urging my silence. I pet her tenderly, then slowly and very quietly uncover myself from the makeshift hay bed.

The weeping continues near the entrance of the barn and I venture a peek at the source. It is a girl, her back to me. My curiosity takes over, for the human creature, she is intriguing. She is perched upon the door of a horse's stall. I look above me to the shadowed beams and rafters. I allow my claws to grow from my fingertips and jump, arms stretched out, reaching for the beam high above, carefully and quietly pulling my body up and out of the light. Squatting upon the beam, I look down to the sweet cow, who shakes her head at me and *moos* in disagreement.

I frown at her and press my finger to my lips, shushing her. I stand and balance myself on the beam, making my way closer toward the entrance of the barn, still hidden by dark shadows and out of sight, quiet as a mouse, moving quickly. The girl continues her weeping, tears running down her face. Why does she cry? Where did she come from? I need a better viewing spot, and my mind races. Fascinated by her, I dodge and weave through the support beams up in the rafters.

She pets the horse's long nose and rubs her cheek against his face and hugs his neck. When she pulls away from the beast, I gasp as I gaze upon her face. My intake of breath startles her, and she tears her gaze from the gentle old horse in search of the noise. I freeze. The horse neighs at me loudly. Hidden in the darkness way up high where the sun's rays cannot yet reach, I watch hypnotized as she studies her surroundings.

Her hair is auburn in the bright sunlight, with delicate flowing waves of loose curls that frame a slender face. Skin as white as cotton freshly picked, so soft and smooth like silk. Cheeks freckled, with lips the color of a deep blood red. Her eyes are a bottomless and muted blue-green, covered in long black lashes.

My heart begins to pound against my chest as I gaze upon her beauty. My body is on high alert and wired, longing to touch her soft skin. Her dress is simple cotton dyed the color of evergreen, and it appears to be getting too small for her since it clings to her body and I see each curve. She's thin but has well defined small muscles—she seems fragile yet strong. So strangely beautiful, like nothing I have ever seen, with long bare legs draped so delicately as she sits. I see a pair of tenderly soft feet. She looks to be the same age as me.

She reaches for the old horse's face and nuzzles it for comfort. I feel a tightening in my heart as I wish and long to hold her, to stop her tears and kiss them away. Skinny, long fingers brush through the horse's mane and I sigh at watching her gentle touch, just wanting to have each of her perfect fingertips touching my own.

Again, the girl flinches at my heavy sigh, still holding the horse and running her fingers through his mane. Then I hear the sweetest, most joyous, most beautiful sound that has ever blessed my ears escape from her lips—she giggles.

A voice like the brightness of berries in my mouth proclaims, "Winston, I do believe we are not alone in this barn." The horse stamps its front hooves upon the ground and bounces its great head up and down, agreeing with her.

"Traitor!" I whisper to the old horse. I freeze as best I can with a pounding heart that I am sure she can clearly hear. She gently wipes away her tears and jumps down from the door. I watch her sway around the hay bales below as she makes her way to the back of the barn, to the sweet small cow. She peeks into each stall as she walks by, no doubt in search of me. Does this girl know nothing of danger or fear? Yet with her head held high she continues her search.

"Are you still here, then? Come out, come out wherever you are," her voice sings to me. She moves tendrils of loose curls away from her face and stands still in the middle of the open barn, frowning. "Hello?" she whispers as tears erupt. Her hands cover her face and she quietly sobs. She begins walking again and stops at the sweet cow's stall. Gently she pets her head, tears streaming down her beautiful face.

"I'm so sorry, sweet Bella, I'm sorry I could not save your baby calf." She hugs the small cow's head. "If Pa had been here, he would have known just what to do." She bends, hugging the cow's head, and cries into her neck.

I can hear the sweet cow *mooing* at her, trying to calm the girl. The cow tries so very hard to communicate that the death of her calf was not the girl's fault. She continues to *moo* quietly to the girl and gums at her, trying to comfort her from her grief.

"She says," I pause, hesitant, "she knows it is not your fault and that you helped her immensely. She says without you, she would have died, too." I whisper this from my hiding place, longing to hug her and save her from her grief and pain. "What is your name?" I ask.

"Rowan," she smiles, still hugging the small cow. "Rowan Paige. And yours?" She scrunches her nose to the air in front of her as a result of not being able to find me.

"Merek," I blurt out, a little too high-pitched. "My name is Merek." I sigh in embarrassment at myself.

Rowan giggles and mouths, "Mm air ek. That's a funny name!" and bends in a fit of laughing and giggling. I huff loudly at her teasing and pout.

"Oh! I am sorry, Mm air ek! It's just a very uniq—*handsome* name. I have never heard it before." She proclaims this high to the rafters and bites her finger. From somewhere deep down within my belly, a new series of muscles clench tightly at the sight of her.

"Humph, where are you anyway? It's not very polite of you to hide away and sneak up on me!" she says grumpily.

"If I come down, will you promise me not to, not to…" I hesitate; I cannot show myself to her! She is human! She will run screaming, and I am sure her father and older brothers will be running at me with pitchforks.

"I've gathered for myself you mean me no harm," she calls out to me, "or else you would have already tried before now. You must not be a thief or else my flock would already be gone and nothing from my home is missing. I am guessing," she pauses, deep in thought, biting her finger again, "that you're not from around here and you are very much alone. A traveler from a distant land maybe, lost? By the sound of your voice, you are youngish, maybe close to my age? I am nineteen, how old are you?"

"I mean no one any harm. I believe I am twenty years old and I am lost. I got separated from my companion so yes, I'm alone. The small cow in the back—you called her Bella—took pity on me last night. She allowed me to share her hay bed," I say a little too sadly. "I am not from anywhere near here, nor do I know why I've come to be here. The only thing I have taken is the cow's offered milk. I hadn't eaten for days."

She scans the barn again in search of my voice. She looks sad again, tears at her eyes.

"Are you still hungry?" she asks, then continues, "Well, I am alone, too. Ma and Pa have left, my baby brother too." She sniffs. It pains me to see her sadness.

"You are alone? No brothers or sisters to watch after you?"

She begins to cry even more. "I am the only one left, but I can care for myself and I have." She wipes away her tears.

"I am starving. Will you promise to close your eyes until I say you can open them?" I'm unsure of her and what I could possibly be thinking. It is as though I cannot control myself being near her. I need to be closer to her, but I should be running away.

"Yes," she pouts from behind her hands.

"Closed tight, no peeking! You promise?" I make my way along the beam directly above her and pause my descent when I see her peeking.

"Oh, hurry up then, I don't understand why I have to close my eyes..." she begins. I let go and jump, landing so close, just in front of her; quiet as a feather landing upon the ground. My movement causes a gentle breeze that blows her hair away from her face. My nostrils flare and I breathe in deep her scent. Coconuts. My stomach twists and pulls, my heart races faster, and a heat floods my body.

"Ah, not yet!" I yell, panicked, and put one of my hands over hers to ensure no peeking.

At the first touch of her hand, sparks fly beneath my skin. Electricity shouts and erupts throughout my body, clenching muscles tight deep down in my belly. Each of our breaths hitches at realizing how close we are to each other.

She breathes in deeply, inhaling my scent, and I can feel the excitement within her. Her hands slightly tremble, and her heart begins to race but soon relaxes. I could have sworn that maybe she too felt an electric shock when my hand touched hers. I did feel it; I continue to feel it, a strangle pulsing electrical current weaving between us. Not painful, it feels...

Wonderful.

"You make my skin tingle," she whispers.

I let out my held breath. "Rowan, I am very different from you." I pause as she places her other hand over mine, covering her eyes, causing more of that current to erupt and flow through my body. She gently pulls my hand away from hers. I suck in as much air as I can, panic washing over me. I brace myself for her scream. I stare at her eyelids, which she still has closed. She takes one of my hands and places it palm-side against her check. She leans into my hand and I relish her touch. There is a warm and beautiful current flowing between us.

"You have big, strong, and warm hands," she whispers to me and holds up both our hands, her eyes still closed tight. I look at her small delicate hands, calloused from working the farm. I touch each of her fingertips with my own, my green skin against her pale cream.

"Please place my hands on your face," she says with a smile, and I do, taking her small wrists. But I pause before her fingers touch my skin. My body tenses. "I promise, I will keep my eyes closed 'til you are ready, but this way I'll be able to see you through my hands." She giggles, and butterflies soar in my stomach. I place her wiggling fingers upon each cheek and let go. I tense as she begins to trace my features. She traces her fingertips over my nose, then my lips, one thumb running along my bottom lip. She moves up to my eyes and I close them, so she can trace the lids with her fingers. Then she moves on to my hair, and I reopen my eyes to watch her facial expressions.

"You have long hair, oh, with curls!" She smiles with her eyes closed like she promised and traces each ear up to the pointed tip. My eyes dart to hers, expecting to see hers wide with fear. Yet hers are still closed. I find a puzzled look upon her beautiful face, and it causes me to smirk. She moves down either side of my jaw to the point of my chin, down each side of my neck, and holds my shoulders.

"You are *very* tall," she giggles again. The butterflies flip in my belly and I look down to see she is standing on her tiptoes to reach. She moves her hands down my arms and back up again.

"You're strong, too! I really could use your help with all I am responsible to do around here." She continues down my chest and places each small hand upon my hips, where she stops and my eyes flash to hers.

"Wait!" I say before she opens her eyes. I place my palm back on her cheek, studying our skin color contrasts. Green against white. I wipe away her recent tears and gaze at her beautiful face. I hold one of her hands, her small in my large, my deep green against light. I reach for her auburn hair with its never-ending waves and curls.

"May I see you now?" she asks. "I have a good idea from my fingers but want to see with my eyes." She smiles and holds up both hands, wiggling her finger at me.

"You're not afraid of me?" I ask shyly.

"No, I am not. Why should I be?"

"Because I am nothing like you. I am not even fully human!" I stammer out.

"I'm not afraid!" she says sternly.

"Okay, then. Open your eyes."

She nods and with the one hand still entangled in mine takes it back to her cheek and leans into my palm and blinks. I know how this will end. She is going to look at me full of fear and run.

Her gaze starts down at my bare feet, so I wiggle my toes. She laughs but does not leap away from my green shade of skin. Her eyes go to my chest. I close my eyes for what I know is coming: her screams. Instead I hear her gasp.

"Please don't run away, please don't run away," I repeat over and over and hold her hands tight and make her look into my eyes. Her mouth drops open and she stares deep. I realize my hand is still at her face and I trace my thumb over the bone beneath her cheek. I wait, looking back at her, waiting for her to speak.

"You have crystal blue eyes." She blinks and studies me for a long while, saying nothing else. She looks deep into my eyes as if searching for something and then embraces me in a tight hug. I melt into her tiny frame, bending to hug her back.

"I've waited so long for you, Merek, so many years have gone. So many years alone. The woman that comes to me in my sleep kept promising me of your arrival. I thought I'd go insane with all the waiting and loneliness." Her words are so pained.

Confused, I pull away and investigate her face.

"Will you keep me, Merek? Will you stay like she said you would?" she asks, again searching my soul through my eyes.

"How could I ever leave you, Rowan, now that I have found you? I do not think I could ever go anywhere without you!" I realize the truth within my words. "Who is this woman, who comes to you in your sleep and told you of me?" I ask.

"I do not know her. Well, I do know her. She comforts me when I need it, she loves me very much, but she can only come to me when I'm sleeping and that frustrates the both of us." She pauses. "Merek, come with me. I have food. You can eat and drink." My stomach growls at the mention of food and I let her lead me away from the barn. She stops abruptly at the door to the small home and turns to face me, blocking my entrance.

"Merek, now it is your turn to promise not to scream." She pauses and my eyes flash wide. "You mustn't be afraid, understand?" She looks to me for assurance.

What could this tiny creature possibly do to scare me? Though now I am curious. What could she be hiding away in the small home? She squeezes my hand for my answer.

"I promise not to scream."

"Nor will you run from me and leave me alone again?" she adds.

"Promise."

She takes my hand and opens the door. She leads me into a small kitchen with a large hearth at the back wall.

"You are hungry. We will eat first and then I will show you!" Rowan sits me down at a small table. "We have carrots." She smiles at me; it is so infectious that I smile back. She tugs open a cupboard door, grabs carrots, bread, and mashed berries. She opens another cupboard and takes out a chunk of dried and herbed meat. She lays the items before me and hands me a carrot. I bite into it and she smiles again. She brings back a sharp blade and slices will-nilly at the meat. She cuts the bread and piles the meat slices in the middle, adding the mashed berries on top. I finish my carrot and she hands me the pile of bread, meat, and berries. I look at it and give it a sniff.

"It's a sandwich, try it." She begins to make herself the same but a much smaller portion.

"Sandiwitch," I repeat, and she bursts out laughing.

"Oh!" She jumps up, startling me, and goes in search of two glasses and pours a white liquid into each. "Fresh milk from Bella, to drink." I take the glass from her.

I wait and watch her take a bite of her 'sandiwitch' then copy her, taking a bite for myself.

It is so heavenly good! She watches with a grimace as I devour the concoction she built and starts to make me another. I take it eagerly from her and stuff my face, gulping down the milk.

"I've never seen someone eat so fast in all my life!" she exclaims. "Are you still hungry? This is cheese, and crackers. Take the knife like this." And she trims off the top layer, revealing a white and creamy center, and spreads that across the cracker and eats it. "Here, you try." She hands me the knife and brings me black berries on a vine.

"These are grapes. They grow out back along the trellis. You may eat them all, we can pick more later." She plucks a few off and pops one into her mouth.

I dig into the cheese and spread it like she did over the hard cracker and take a bite. It smells horrible yet tastes delicious. While she finishes her sandiwitch, I eat every grape and half of the cheese and crackers.

"Thank you, I was starving!" I say, leaning back into my chair, belly full.

"Come." She pulls me up. I grab another carrot as she takes me into another room. "This is the sitting room." I see another fireplace on the back wall, two soft chairs facing it. There is also a large box near the fireplace with a handle of sorts on top. I wonder what that is. Rowan tugs at me and leads me up small and steep steps. Reaching the top, we are in the middle of a narrow hallway with two doors at either end. She tugs me to one end and opens a small door and walks in. I duck my head and enter. It is a small room, about as long as I am tall with only a bed pushed up against the wall. A thick blanket stuffed with feathers rests upon the bed.

"This is my room!" she says happily. "Come." And she pulls me back into the hall, causing my head to hit the top frame of her door.

"Oh! I am so sorry. You really are very tall, aren't you?" She pauses. "Does it hurt much?"

"No, I'm fine," I say, and let her continue pulling me down the narrow hall. I follow behind her as there is not room enough to walk beside her. She stops a few steps from the open door and turns to me. She takes her free hand and pushes back the hair that has fallen in my eyes. I melt at her touch.

"Promise?" she asks.

"Hmm?"

"Promise you won't scream and run?" she asks again.

"Promise."

Becoming a little nervous, she slowly opens the door and enters the room, still holding my hand. I enter the room and what is left of the carrot hanging from my mouth drops and hits the floor. Her grip tightens on my hand, and my breath is knocked away from me. Rowan reluctantly releases my hand, carefully making her way around a large bed to sit in a small chair.

The room is white and meticulously clean. A big window with its shutters thrown open lets in a gentle breeze that billows the curtains gently inward. The room smells of fresh flowers and lemons.

"Come, beside me, CAREFUL!" she yells at me. "Do not disturb the bed, please."

I twist my body and shuffle sideways by the foot of the bed, my back pressed hard against the wall, trying to stay as far away from the bed as possible. I look to Rowan, who sits, beautiful, in the chair beside the bed as I ever so slowly slide my way toward her.

"Good morning, Ma," Rowan whispers. "We have a guest. This is Merek, Mama." And she looks up and smiles at me. I give her a small smile and my heart fills with sadness.

There are three skeleton bodies in the bed. Fresh flowers are everywhere, covering the entire perimeter of the bed, carefully placed and tucked in-between bones. I reach Rowan's side and kneel.

"Merek, this is Mama." She gently strokes one of the forearm bones of what once was her mother. "That is Pa. He won't leave Ma's side. And this beautiful baby boy is Timmy, my brother." Rowan stands from her chair and gently and carefully leans against the bed, and on tiptoes and stretching she places sweet gentle kisses and rubs the tiny bone skull of her baby brother.

Each skeleton has been covered here and there with beautiful wildflower blossoms, picked with patience and love from the meadow outside. Each eye socket has its own beautiful flower resting in it. Their bones have been bleached white from the passing of time and the sunlight that streams in through the big window. I stare at the family before me, trying to absorb the situation. Three skeletons lay before me. I rub a hand over my face, my heart aching for her loss and the obvious dedication she has in protecting and preserving their environment.

"Merek, will you stay with me? Forever?" Rowan asks this in a whisper as she gazes lovingly on her family.

I turn her chair slowly and pull her gaze from her mother's skeleton, and she looks deep into my eyes. I reach for her face and pull her into me and hug her. She begins to cry again, and I feel her tears run down my neck. I pull her face up toward mine and wipe away her tears.

"Can I keep you?" she whispers with a hiccup.

I nod very slowly and hug her tighter. I glance back at the skeletons. Something is strange. These three have fanged teeth, whereas Rowan does not. The shape of their skulls is different as well, shaped more like my own, a long and narrow structure, unlike Rowan's round face. There are long pointed claws on each of the fingers much like my claws. If Rowan is human, then the three were not related to her. They are not the same species. These creatures are like me. Something pulls in my gut and clouds my mind, and I pull Rowan away just enough to investigate her face. I tip her chin up, lift the left corner of her lip. Her teeth are different from theirs.

"You had me at first sight of you, Rowan. I am yours to keep if that is your wish." I say this softly and hug her again. I lead her away from the room. Gazing back, I nod my head to the skeleton family and whisper to myself and to the three of them, "I know your secret and that you kept it from her. I won't tell her for a while, but one day she needs to know, and I promise to watch over her." I bring Rowan back down the steep stairs and into the sitting room and sit her down in one of the soft chairs.

"Rowan, what happened to your parents?" I ask carefully.

"Mama was bleeding a lot while Timmy was coming out of her and continued bleeding after he was out. I wrapped him in a blanket and brought him down here like Pa told me to. Pa stayed with Ma. I sat with Timmy here and warmed him by the fire and cuddled him, but he did not move, he did not take a breath. He and I stayed here all night; I fell asleep with him in my arms. In the morning when I woke, Timmy was still nested in my arms. I took him back upstairs. Ma and Pa would not wake up, they would not answer me, not even when I shook them. I placed Timmy beside Ma in the middle close to her and Pa. But—" tears stream down her face "—they never woke up."

"Rowan, how old were you when this happened?" Judging by the lack of decay and only the bones left behind, I know it must have been years. I gently caress her cheek.

"I was six years old."

My mouth drops. She has survived alone for thirteen years. How has she survived alone for thirteen years? How have I survived *fifteen* alone?

I hug her tighter. "Can I keep you, Rowan?" I whisper gently.

She pulls away, looks deep into my eyes, and nods.

CHAPTER TEN

A New Life

"Rowan," I call. I am crouched in the tall grass of the meadow. "Rowan!" I tease again.

I know right where she is, even without her giggling giving herself away. I crawl through the grass with stealth and pounce, catching her from behind in my arms and dragging us both to the ground. She screams with delight and laughs as I pull her down and roll us over each other, over and over again in the long grass. I lay flat on my back with Rowan beside me. I close my eyes and bask in the warm late spring sun. It has now been three quarters of a year that has passed since I found Rowan. We have become the best of friends and welcome company for each other.

My start at farm life was rough and hard. I knew nothing of farming, but Rowan has taught me well. Together we hayed this field with the push blades her father invented to cut it all and used his device that collects the cut hay. The push blade machine is easy enough to use; it has a seat with foot pedals attached to a handle to steer with, which is also attached to long oval containers that hold several long, sharp metal blades. Its length is twice my height.

The collecting machine is slightly more complex as it runs off steam. We had to constantly keep refilling the machine with cold water from the nearby pond to keep it moving. Many fork-like prong fingers extend from the bottom on a similar long oval-shaped housing unit. As the machine moves forward along a track system, the prong fingers spear the ground and comb backward, forcing the cut grass into a boxy container. Once full, Rowan and I pull one lever to flatten it from the top and push another lever to compress the sides, forming a cube of hay that Rowan ties off with twine.

Rowan taught me how to care for each animal in the barn. I make sure they all have hay for eating and enough water, and I clean their stalls and milk the small sweet cow Bella. We collect eggs from the chickens each morning. I taught Rowan how to track deer and bear at the edge of the woods; I made a bow with arrows and taught her how to use them. I showed her how to skin and clean the animal, and she taught me how to dry and hang the meat using herbs and flowers to keep the meat fresh. I work the skins to stretch and dry them out, to prepare them for making new clothes, even neat things she calls shoes and of course bedding for our bed. We each took turns chopping and stacking wood, placing it in the barn for the coming winter to keep the kitchen and sitting room fireplaces going for warmth and cooking. We spent many winter nights sitting in front of the fire talking and telling each other about our lives.

I laugh at the memory of showing Rowan my photo book. I remember how she jumped in fright when she heard my pa's voice come from the book. She soon fell in love with the book's moving pictures. Every night we watch the creatures that fill its pages: moving snapshots of Emira in her glowing beauty; of Lottie and Vladmir in their embrace, smiling at one other with their sharp teeth; of Xander and Nikilaus changing from their human forms to their werewolf forms; of the witches Rebecca, John, Susannah, and Giles laughing; of King Conway and his Queen Opal; the moving images of my parents together.

Two new pages have been added to the book since I found Rowan. The first is of Brice, seated with his head held high. He looks so handsome and regal. The second page is of Rowan. She faces away, then her picture moves and she turns toward me as if I called her name, her arms outstretched as if to embrace me in one of her warm hugs.

I feel so grateful to have remembered to grab this book. Unfortunately, I left behind the other book, the one I promised my pa to touch every day, the old ancient tome that taught me my lessons. I miss having it near me. I still cannot believe I left it behind.

One of our nightly routines involves Rowan reading to me from her own little collection and teaching me how to read the words and recognize them before falling asleep.

Rowan props up on her elbow and gazes at me. Here in the middle of the meadow a gentle breeze blows her auburn hair. She inches closer to me and I smile. I never knew how much one could genuinely appreciate another being, this human who makes me smile, laugh, and enjoys having me be her company. My heart sinks as I think of Brice and I find myself sitting up and looking toward the direction of the forest, hoping to catch a glimpse of him. Rowan traces her fingers along my crested brow. She frowns at my sad face and looks up to follow my gaze.

Resting her head on my shoulder, she asks softly, "Would you like to go and walk along the edge of the meadow again? Maybe today will be the day we find him, Merek."

I lean my cheek against the top of her head. "No, not today, Rowan. I just miss him. I do not understand why he didn't just follow me to the other side. It's been too long. I can only assume my grandfather did something to him." I breathe out and she can hear the pain that I am trying to hide from her.

She looks up into my eyes. Hers shine beautifully. I remember her birthday and my mind flashes back to that day, right when the winter was at its coldest. I had woken early and gone and picked as many winter berries as I could find. I filled the pail full of sweet Bella's milk and took the five eggs from the chickens, being so careful not to wake the creatures for fear they would wake Rowan. I cooked a wondrous breakfast for her birthday as a gift. I woke her gently and served her while she stayed in bed. I presented her with a pan-cakie and egg 'sandiwitch' covered in a berry sauce. I smile at my memory of the day she turned twenty and the look on her face as I served her in bed.

Rowan touches my cheek and pushes my hair away from my eyes, bringing me back from my reverie. She inches closer and I pull her into a hug as we lay there in the middle of the meadow and I sigh with happiness. She grabs either side of my face with her small hands and rubs her nose against mine, then leans her forehead into mine. Before I can realize what she's up to, she gently and softly presses her lips against mine.

My eyes flash wide. I pull away slightly and cock my head to the side, quite confused. Mother of Light! My body goes into overdrive whenever she is near me, the feelings that rush through me confuse me. What do these feelings mean? I know that I hate when she is away from me, even just inches: my body always wants her skin flush against mine. I quickly pull her against me again. A tight knot forms deep and low in my belly. My body wants my lips on hers, wants to hold her tighter. My body craves to touch more than just her arm or face.

"What was that?" I ask. She has never done that before. A memory of my father embracing my mother in that way comes to mind. I remember he felt love, that they were... what was the term? Mates? Rowan blushes and her pale cheeks turn red. Her reaction puzzles me further.

"It was but a kiss, Merek. It's what you do when you love someone," she whispers. "My ma and pa would steal a kiss whenever they could, and Pa would always spin Ma when he would see her." She sighs.

"Oh," I breathe out. A tightening deep in my belly continues to pull and form a hard knot. It stirs between my legs. It shoots a need through me. A need for something I do not know, but it is screaming for me to kiss her.

"It's a way to show a special someone that you love them and only them." She pauses and seems a bit upset. "I think it's time for me to give you another haircut." She pulls at a long curl in front of my face and pushes it back.

"Love?" I ask in a whisper. "Is that your word for Mate?"

She frowns at me but gets to her feet and turns toward the house, not waiting for me. Confused at the knot forming in my belly and with my heart pounding, I realize I am still sitting when she calls back over her shoulder, "Are you coming already? The sun will be setting soon anyway." She says this to me gruffly. I quickly stand and jog after her. I want to reach out and touch her when I catch up, but I decide not to and walk along behind her.

When we enter the kitchen I ask, "Would you like some tea, Rowan?" as I grab the kettle. That always soothes her when she is upset and, by her scent, she is upset.

"No thank you, Merek. Come sit."

She shoves the stool at me with her foot and opens a drawer, fetching the sharp scissors. I sit and she sets to work pulling at my hair in sections between her fingers. As my hair falls to the floor, I can't help but think of her kiss. She's never done that before. It was soft and gentle. I trace my lips with my fingers, trying to recall the sensation. I can still smell her delicious scent of earth, grass, and flowers, of Rowan, the sweetest, most perfect smell, coconuts and a refreshing breeze. My eyes close as the sensation flows through me again.

Rowan is at my ear, cutting away. She is so close and again I breathe deep her scent, so strong and floral as it fills my nose. She grips my chin and slowly turns my face side to side. I feel a warmth radiating from within her; I can hear and feel the thumping of her heart. As she lets go of my chin, her thumb grazes across my bottom lip.

My eyes open wide with my Goblin sight; the shimmering green glow dances all around Rowan, with waves of blue and silver rippling against the green. It pulses and sways, encircling her body, and I feel a pull again, stronger this time and deeper within my belly.

I hear her gasp as something has surprised her, then a sharp cry of pain. My nostrils are assaulted at once by Rowan's heated scent mixed with her blood. Instantly I reach out, gripping her bleeding finger, and bring it to my mouth. I suck, and her blood fills my mouth, a warm tingling blanketing my tongue. Her heartbeat increases as she tries to pull her finger from me. With my other hand I grab her hip and tug her into me, holding her tight. Her delicious scent envelopes me, her blood coating my tongue, a tingling blanket and then... fear. Strong and full of fear, Rowan's heart hammers and finally my ears hear her pleading.

"Merek! Merek, let go! Please stop, Merek, can you hear me? What is wrong with your eyes? Why are you sucking my finger? Merek!

Let go!" she yells at me, her whole body squirming to be free of my hold.

Just before I let her go, a last drop of her blood coats my tongue and that is when I see her, in Rowan's memory. Just a drop of blood flashes me into Rowan's past.

Rowan is in a small village, in a market holding her mother's hand, when she spots a creature hooded and cloaked at the outside edge of the market. Rowan makes eye contact with the creature as her mother releases her hand and the creature races toward her, grabbing Rowan, picking her up and running with her. Rowan's vision has slowed, the humans and the world around her slowed in motion. Each human's step is so painfully slow it is like they are almost completely frozen. The creature sets her down behind a small building and pulls back their hooded cloak. I gasp at the memory of my mother's face. Still she has her long raven black hair, her loving green eyes, but her skin is no longer a milky pale hue of green but instead an evergreen, deep, forest green, her black tattoo marking still intact.

"Here you are, child, finally I have found you! Oh, sweet Rowan, you beautiful child," my mother's sweet voice calls to Rowan. She turns her face to hers, away from the slow-moving humans in the marketplace.

"Please, child, listen to my words. I will only be able to come to you after this meeting in your dreams. I will comfort you when you are alone. He will one day find you and you will lead him home to me. You will grow into a brave and courageous young woman. The path laid before you is long, dangerous, and full of uncertainty. I promise to always be with you—just close your eyes and search deep inside yourself to find me. Oh my dear child, I am so happy I found you. You are our everything and I will keep you safe and hidden."

She places a small trinket around Rowan's neck. "He will find you; be patient and call to me when you need me. Stay strong, stay safe, stay hidden—until we meet again!" My mother picks up the small girl, bracing her within her arms, her small head nestled into my mother's neck, and rushes through the market with such speed and looks deep into Rowan's eyes. "Do you understand, child?"

Rowan is young, maybe three, maybe four. She is confused by my mother's words, but I can feel the recognition of the words run deep and strong. She nods her head. My mother picks her back up and covers her face with the hooded cloak. When she turns, she somehow looks right at me. My mother's face lights up with happiness and she smiles.

"Merek!" she breathes.

She reaches her hand out to touch me, but her face falls in misery; her outreached hand pulls back then wraps around Rowan as she cradles her, hugging her tight. She whispers, "Bring him back to me, please," and steps through me, the shadow I am in this memory, whisking Rowan back to her mother's side.

As Rowan watches my mother run off away from the market, from the humans, and from the world around her, time speeds back up to its normal way.

"Merek!" Rowan screams.

Her fear has stopped. I am no longer holding her, and her fear has turned to concern for me. I blink and shake my head; she is kneeling before me.

"Merek! Your eyes! What's happened?" she screams with hysteria at me. I blink and refocus.

"Rowan? What is wrong, what's happened?" I ask, shaken by Rowan's memory. Her scent, strong, earthy, and floral, still clouds my mind.

"Your eyes, Merek, they were large orbs and black as night! It startled me, and you won't let me go." She heaves with relief that I am talking.

"I didn't mean to frighten you. You were bleeding and I didn't realize my eyes changed with my Goblin sight."

I shake my head again, trying to analyze Rowan's memory of my mother through Rowan's scent, lingering thick and heavy, clouding my judgement.

"Goblin sight?" she questions.

"Yes, I have sight like the way you see the world as well as my Goblin sight, which lets me see things in a different way," I explain.

"Oh." She pauses. "You looked to be in a trance of some kind. I thought you were going to be ill," she whispers.

I eye her pale hands and take them gently in mine to examine her finger. A small cut is already healing and as we watch it scars and disappears. Then a tiny spark from the tip of her finger shoots out at me.

It jolts me backward a bit, unharmed, but surprises us both.

"Wow, how did I do that?" she laughs nervously out loud, looking at her finger again. I inch forward, but nothing happens.

She gets up and goes into the sitting room, plopping herself in the small chair before the fire. I place three small logs on the fire. These spring nights often cool off and the fire is still welcome warmth. I fill the kettle with water and hang it over the fire, bringing back a small plate and a wooden cup with one of Rowan's tea bags in the bottom. I carved two cups and the small plates for Rowan's birthday. The wood I used has different pigments throughout, and I also carved an intricate swirling pattern into the wood. She loved them so much when I presented them to her. She smiles at me as I hand her the cup.

"Rowan, tell me of the creature you saw in the market."

I pour hot water into her cup. She looks up at me in surprise, then she sighs.

"She is the woman that comes to my dreams. I met her when I was very young, maybe when I was six? It was when Ma and Pa were still here with me. Ma took me to the market for the first time, and I saw her there. She seemed frightened and scared, but she was so gentle with me. She somehow knew that I would end up alone and she has kept her promise to be there for me while I sleep. She told me that one day 'he' would come and that he would find me. She never did tell me 'his' name." She slowly trails off and then says, startled, "Merek, another woman saw the woman come to the town that day. She saw us together when no one else had. An old woman, she had once been a renowned midwife here in this village, but after the disappearance of her own only daughter she, well, she went quite mad." Rowan pales a bit. "My ma told me that the old woman had resorted to begging for food and shelter, that no one from the village would request her skills as people claimed she talked in riddles. She spoke to me of Goblins and other fearsome creatures that took her daughter and dragged her away and into the forest. She just kept repeating over and over, 'I knew she survived the fire; I know she got out.' She repeated the phrase in a whisper, like she was trying to convince herself that she was right. It was quite sad really.

"She questioned me about the woman she saw with me; she wanted to know if her grandson was still alive. Ma stopped bringing me to the market after that, but I did return with her once many months later. The elderly woman was there waiting for her. She approached me, grabbing me hard on the shoulders, shaking me and demanding answers. The woman made Ma extremely nervous. She was just overly excited, she kept telling my ma that she had indeed seen me with her daughter, and that I had spoken with her. That I had the answers she was so desperate for. She was frantic that I bring her to her daughter. She shook me harder and began screaming for her daughter to return, but she never came. Three of the village men took her away. Ma told me later that the old woman died that evening.

"The woman who comes to me, the creature in my dreams—" Rowan smiles at me "—she is so happy now, her face bright and glowing, but I have not been able to hear her words. Since you have come, I see her lips moving but no sound comes from them. I dreamt of her last night. She seems so distant now, somehow farther away. She was scared, Merek, and finally last night I was able hear her but only barely. She says that you need to go back for the book. Her words were rushed and muffled like being underwater but that is what I think she said; she says it's almost time for us to leave." Rowan's voice drops to a whisper with tears in her eyes. "She says we must go back, Merek, into the forest! It's very important that we go. We have to get the book. I have never left my home." A tear spills down her cheek.

"We are not going," I say flatly.

She looks at me, shocked. "We must, Merek. She is very scared, and *we* are a part of something that's supposed to help everyone."

"Help who, Rowan? Brice tells me my father is telling us to leave and I left. I left already, Rowan! And now I have lost my best friend because of it. I have been here all this time, why now? My mother is telling you! Telling *you*, not me, for *me* to return! For a book! We are not leaving. Ha, my grandfather, the evil Goblin King, I am sure is lying in wait for me to cross back into the forest, waiting just to kill me or take me prisoner like he did my parents and Brice. He has taken everything from me! *Everything*!" I spit at her angrily, my chest heaving. A tight pain in my heart knocks me to my knees. My father's strange book, I can feel it calling to me. A chill runs down my spine, full of dread and bitter cold.

"Wait! Your mother?" Rowan whispers, and lets the tears fall along with her cup and tea. She hides her face behind her hands and sobs. "How can the woman be your mother? The old woman said her daughter disappeared over fifty years ago and that was... but that would make you well over fifty years old, Merek, but you said you're only twenty. You surely don't look old—" She cries softly, unable to finish her sentence.

"I don't understand!" I get up and then kneel in front of her, pulling her hands from her face. "Why didn't you tell me this earlier, when you woke?" I ask softly.

"Because I don't know what's happening! I don't want to leave, but we have to. I can *feel* the book—it's calling to me, too, you know! Plus, I didn't know what you would say or how you would feel about it!" she cries back at me.

"When did she say we need to leave?"

"The day after tomorrow. Early morning, before sunrise, we must cross the border. The woman, er, your *mother*, said that would be the safest time." She gulps after her words, holding back the bile rising in her throat, her eyes wide with fear.

"So it will be, then," I breathe out heavily.

I kiss her cheek gently, but Rowan's remark of the timeline of when she met my mother in the market and the old woman speaking to her... how could fifty years have passed in the human world when it was only fifteen years ago that my parents were taken from me?

CHAPTER ELEVEN

An Unexpected Reunion

We talk late into the night.

I recall everything from my painful past, trying to piece together an impossible timeline of events. Questioning how my mother had found Rowan. Understanding that the old woman from the village, who must have been my grandmother, was the woman I saw in my father's memory. How Rowan had learned from her parents that the old woman had died during that cold winter. About Brice and I journeying to the border to leave the forest as my father told us to do. How I came to the farm's barn, alone and without Brice. What could have possibly happened to him to prevent him from crossing through? Why didn't the pack of lost ones and my grandfather the Goblin King follow me through the border? So, so many questions and no answers.

I warn Rowan about the forest, the horrible nightmarish creatures within it, and the animals, too. I admit that I do not fully know my way back to my father's home in the woods. Where in the forest would we be upon crossing through? It was Brice that had been the one leading us on our way. How easy it is to get lost, and how Rowan thinks she can handle being in the woods. Will she succumb to the sickening mist that has turned so many humans into dazed, confused, and survival-driven crazed beings? If we do manage to find our way to my father's house and retrieve the book, what are we to do after? My mum has not given instructions to Rowan for after. Are we to return to the human world or stay within the forest?

All the uncertainties, the unknowns, and dangers... We will always need to stay alert. I make her swear and promise to listen to me without hesitation or it could mean our deaths.

We spend all the next day preparing to leave and return to the Forest of Wedgemore. We pack the few clothing items we have along with blankets. Rowan gathers and packs all the food she can fit into her mother's market basket. Together we open the barn stalls and turn all the animals out into the meadow. All but two leave us, the old gentle horse and sweet Bella the small cow. Each wants to accompany us on our journey into the forest, the gentle horse promising to help carry Rowan and our packs, sweet Bella wanting to provide us with her milk. I warn them of the dangers of the forest, but they still want to stay by our sides and make the journey with us. Rowan spends time saying goodbye to her skeletal family and covering them in a fresh blanket of flowers.

We make our way through the long grass of the meadow, beneath the full moon. We stand at the edge of the meadow near the tree line of the forest. It is two hours yet before sunrise, still pitch black. A gentle breeze sways the long grass with crickets singing to each other. An owl hoots from within the woods. All seems calm, quiet.

My heart pounds within my chest and at my temples. Goose-bumps rise all over my body, and a cold chill runs down my spine. Rowan reaches for my hand. A flash of a vision plays before me of the last time I stood here. Alone, full of pain, and at a complete loss without my wolf companion.

We stand beneath the full moon's light hand in hand. I look to Rowan, trying to read her face, her thoughts. How can this creature before me be so brave? I smile at her tender, determined, brave face as she tries and fails to see through the dark gloom of the tree line and grips my hand tighter. She takes a step toward the boundary line. I pull back against her.

"Can you feel the pull, Rowan?" I ask as my stomach flips.

"Feel what?" she whispers back.

"Your stomach—is it flipping over and making you feel sick?" I ask again.

"No," she replies, but seems to analyze her body quickly and says, "I feel fine. Maybe a little cold from the breeze that's blowing."

"I feel it and remember it!" I groan, clutching my stomach with my free hand. "I wonder if it will feel the same to walk through it from this side as it did when I crossed months ago, and it spat me out the other side," I think out loud as my face pales.

"Should we just, um, cross now or wait for the sunrise?" Rowan whispers so quietly, petting the gentle old horse and looking over her shoulder for Bella, who nods at her.

"I am not sure. My mother told you sunrise, correct?" I question her, even though I already know the answer since we have gone over her dream so many times.

"Yes, sunrise." She pulls her shawl down over her shoulders and clutches it tighter.

I close my eyes and take a deep breath and wait, listening for any sound that comes from beyond the tree line. I reopen them with my Goblin sight, half expecting to see my grandfather waiting for me on the other side. Instead I find that the sun is already just beginning to rise on the other side. Nothing moves, no sounds come from the other side. No footsteps crunching through the forest floor. I blink and with human sight find myself in darkness with the moon's pale light pooling around us.

"The sun is beginning to rise already on the other side. I think it's time to cross." I gulp down the fear and uncertainty that remains within me. I need to keep my mind clear and alert. I need to relax so that I can rely on and feel my senses. Rowan grips my hand tighter.

"How can the sun be rising on the other side? I see only darkness beyond the tree line. How can there be light when it is so very dark?" She pauses. "Time must be different between the Realms and forest." I shrug in response. "Do you suppose your mother meant sunrise time on the other side or this side?" she asks, confused.

"I suppose we should just cross now," I sigh, "before I lose my nerve." And with that I grip Rowan's hand tighter this time and step forward, but Rowan pulls me back.

"I... are you... is it safe? Is the other side clear?" She turns and looks behind us, silently saying one last goodbye. She closes her eyes and faces me. "You promise to watch me closely for signs that I might change into... one of those lost things? You will do what is necessary if I do, you promise me you'll leave me there to retrieve the book? Hopefully to find me again before it's too late and try to change me back?" She paces a few steps back and forth, still gripping my hand.

"I won't leave you, Rowan, let's just go. I'm ready."

Together, hand tight in hand, we step forward, the gentle horse and the sweet cow following behind. The pull of the border constricts my belly one last time before walking through. I close my eyes and brace myself at the oncoming sickness and tormenting chaos of being thrown about, holding tighter to Rowan's hand, waiting, but it doesn't come. At the sound of Rowan sharp inhale and gasping coughs, my eyes fly open with Goblin sight, scanning the area.

"Lord have mercy, what was that! I'm soaked to the bone!" Rowan releases my hand and shakes out her arms, wiping down her face. "It was like being stuck in a rising, crashing wave. I thought we'd be ripped apart!"

Strange, I am dry, but she looks like someone has thrown her into water and she rose out of it disheveled, her hair matted to her face.

"Oh, the sun is rising! It's... it's beautiful here!" she exclaims, and we listen to the sounds of the forest waking. "But ouch, my hand, Merek, loosen your grip!" And she begins wringing out her clothes.

I blink and rescan our surroundings with my human sight, still finding no threat.

Still scanning around, I say, "Actually, coming back through was much easier than last time." I take in the beauty of the forest, the sunlight pooling along the forest floor, glinting off the trees' leafy canopy. The normal sounds of chirping birds, the wind rustling the leaves, and the croaking of the frogs... I feel like I am finally home. I have missed the forest even if I pretended not to. It is my home. I take in its beauty and scent. Home. I am home. Soon I will be back in my father's small shack of a house.

My stomach calms and I begin leading the way. At least the way I think Brice and I came. I made sure to enter the border where I had come through it so I could retrace our steps here. I turn to check on Rowan. I drop her hand and gasp—she is indeed soaked to the bone and bloody hell! She's changed! I blink and look again. I gape at her and close my eyes to clear both sights.

She slowly spins in place, taking in the sight around us, warm trickling light filtering through the canopy above. "I don't think I've ever seen trees so tall and wide, and the mossy floor... I feel like I could just lay here forever. I can't believe this is your home. It's not haunting... it's magical... What is it, Merek? Why are you staring at me that way?" she whispers, anxiety seeping into her voice. She searches all around her, looking for the danger. "What is it?" Her voice is shrill and scared.

"It's you! Rowan!"

I take in her changing appearance. Her skin tone darkens to a slight hint of greenish bronze. Her hair becomes white as snow and grows long, hanging below her waist. Her jawline becomes more etched like mine but softer. Her lips begin to pinken in color, changing from the red they had been, becoming fuller, swollen maybe? Her eyes search my features, and I sigh with pleasure upon gazing into them—bright slate grey with speckles of blue. I dreamily gaze at her while she continues to slowly, subtly change, committing each new feature to memory until fear contorts her pristine features, and she notices the changes.

"Rowan, your hair." My voice comes out breathy and heated. I gently pull a tendril of white curls forward for her to see.

She yelps and begins staring at her hands. "My fingers!" she shrieks. They indeed are growing longer and thinner. She turns her hands this way and that, she lifts her dress and stares at her naked feet and legs.

"Am I greenish-brown?" she yells, horrified.

"Only slightly, just maybe a hue. But your eyes!" I hold my breath; they shape into almonds and grow bluer, bigger speckles mixing perfectly into the gray and silver! She was stunningly beautiful as a human in the human Realm, I could never imagine she could become lovelier.

After a time, her features settle and she opens her mouth slightly, her tongue exploring new fanged teeth. We are able to find a small creek where she can properly take in her new appearance.

"Do you suppose all humans change like this? When they cross the boundary?" she asks, admiring her newness.

"I don't know, but why did I not change when I crossed into your world? Why didn't I look more..." I pause for the right word but settle with "human? Do I look different at all to you than I did before?" I quietly glance into the creek and find my same reflection.

"No," she giggles.

"I have a gut feeling, Rowan. I don't think you were actually ever human." I remember the skeletal family blanketed in flowers. Her new features match that of the family.

We leave the creek and walk all morning. Now the sun is high overhead. Rowan begins to skip merrily along, and watching her is so infectious I find myself skipping alone beside her. It isn't until my legs ache that I take in our surroundings. This part of the forest is unfamiliar and I cannot recognize anything from my journey before. We have been traveling for a long while and I slow to a walk and then stop. Rowan's hand pulls against my outstretched arm, stopping her, and she turns questioningly to me.

"What's the matter Merek, weren't we having fun?" she coos at me.

I frown at her. "Yes, but we traveled far and I do not recognize this area. I need a moment to try and get a sense of direction." I take a deep breath; the air feels strange, thin. I'm hungry since we have not eaten. Rowan begins humming and I shut my eyes, my brow crinkling together, trying to concentrate against her humming and dancing about. A beautiful melody fills my ears as she begins to sing, and her voice, so soft, grows louder as she continues to dance. I feel relaxed, calm even, given the fact that we might be slightly lost. My body sighs in delight and ease... until I recognize that melody, and my body freezes, goosebumps erupting over every inch of my skin, the hair standing up, and my eyes fly open. I hear no sounds around us, no birds, no chattering of squirrels, no wind. The only sound emanating is from Rowan—her singing and prancing about. She sings the beautiful haunting melody, she smiles at me and sings louder, and I'm frozen stiff and a chill runs down through my body, deep into my bones.

"Rowan?" Still she hums, sings and dances. "Rowan!" I shout at her. She stops abruptly in front of me but continues to hum just above a whisper. It has been years since I first heard the beautiful song, but how could Rowan know it?

"Rowan." I take her hand and place her palm flat against my chest, so that she can feel my racing heart. "Where did you learn that song?" My voice is broken, holding back tears.

"I hear her singing... in here." She points to her temple as she continues to hum the melody.

I reach for her face but Rowan steps back away from me and begins to hum louder now, swinging and swaying. I reach for her again. Her eyes close as my fingers touch her face, my fingertips touch her *sweet* face, then something takes hold of me. I feel myself pulled into Rowan's thoughts as her eyes grow larger into black orbs. My sight blurs, and I feel dazed. I am no longer quite within my own body, yet I can still feel my body before Rowan, hands holding each side of her face, standing, seeing her and into her mind.

I try to focus, but my vision blurs; everything is fuzzy and all I can hear is a buzzing. My vision begins to clear. I can make out a woman dressed in green robes, her back toward me a few paces away. Long raven-colored hair blows in a breeze. My vision clears further, and a slender frame fills my sight as she turns toward me. She is singing, singing that beautiful song, and begins to walk toward me. I'm relaxed and at perfect ease and I sway to her song. She reaches her hand out for my cheek. I close my eyes to clear my tears and inhale a choking breath. I can just barely, ever so slightly feel her palm against my face. I look into crystal blue eyes and notice a faint scar at the base of her throat. She cups my cheek and I lean into her hand.

"Merek." Her lips move but I can barely hear her now, she sounds so far away. "Merek, I love you, my sweet, loving boy, Merek."

I feel myself being pulled backwards. She no longer touches my cheek. She stands there, arms reaching out for me, tears in her eyes.

"Mum!" I yell, and I thrust my arms out to her, trying to fight the pulling against me. "Mum! No, wait, Mum!" I take a step toward her, grabbing, desperately trying for a hold on her, but grasp nothing but air. I can't breathe, I feel like I'm choking, and my vision blurs.

"Merek!" I can hardly hear Rowan screaming. Her voice and her face are so far away and I feel like I'm trapped underwater.

"Merek!" Her voice echoes and bounces off the walls of my skull. "Merek!"

She is shaking me. I see fear etched into her face. I choke and cough, but everything is making me so dizzy. I let out my held, hitched up breath and gasp for fresh air, stumbling backward. Rowan grabs at me, pulling me forward and closer to her. I see her face, her lips forming each syllable of my name, "Mm air ek!" I hear her clearly.

"Rowan." I shake my head and instantly regret it as my brain pounds and throbs within my skull. "What, what is it?" I ask, trying to regain my balance.

"Look!" she shrieks, her voice hysterical as she points behind me. She grabs me and forces me to spin around. "It's the biggest wolf I've ever seen!"

"Mother of Light!" I whisper hoarsely, still dazed, and gaze at the wolf just yards in front of me. It slowly makes its way closer to us. I lift my gaze from the creature and carefully up at the trees above, searching for a branch. Rowan is clawing at my back, pressed tightly against me. I back up just a few steps and she mirrors my steps. Reaching up to my shoulder, I grab her hand, pulling her in front of and facing me.

"Reach up and hold on tight, don't let go!" and with that I grab her waist, hoist her up and throw her into the air above, silently hoping she sees the branch high above her. She shrieks as she flies into the air but thankfully she sees and grabs hold with arms and legs wrapping around the branch, maneuvering herself to lay atop it, while the wolf lunges at me and I charge at it, confusing it and leaping in a flip over its head and body. The wolf skids to a stop upon the slippery, leafy forest floor. I adjust my stance, ready for an attack. The wolf glares up at Rowan then quickly back at me. I glare right back. It's large, with a silvery grey coat and big brown eyes. His head low, he snarls at me, drool dripping from his jaw, teeth snapping. The sun glints down through the tree canopy above and into one big brown eye, and I see something familiar. Something deep in my heart sings brightly. My heart races, but no, the fur is different, the wrong color, this animal is bigger and older than him.

There! Right there, I see it, in his other eye. His head dips low again and he growls deep, deep within his throat. I relax my body, let the fight and defense melt away from me, and drop to my knees. I close my eyes and outstretch my arms. Rowan shrieks from somewhere high above, causing the wolf to wince at the pitch and go into a more aggressive stance. I place one finger before my lips, trying to shush Rowan, and move forward toward the wolf, still upon my knees. Rowan whimpers as I continue my slow kneeling walk, arms now stretched out wide to either side, my eyes never breaking contact with his. Slowly I move, and the great wolf snorts and snaps, eyes completely upon me. His growl stops and his eyes are now puzzled and confused.

"Brice?" I whisper.

The wolf's giant head lifts. I continue my slow walk, now one hand reached out toward the wolf's muzzle.

"Brice?" I repeat softly, but he snaps his jaws, tongue sticking in and out, lips curled over his teeth, then growls at me one last time. I drop my arms and jump up to stand. "*Sit!*" I yell. I hold up my outstretched hand. Without pause, the mighty creature sits.

"*Brice!*" I scream, and race the short space between us. The now tame animal sits before me with its enormous tail wagging behind him. I wrap my arms around the girth of his neck. I bury my face in his fur and breathe deep; it's him, his scent, my Brice. Tears stream down my face as I instantly sob into his soft and wondrous fur. His giant head knocks me to the ground. I laugh out loud and cry even harder as he licks my face and nudges my whole body with his big nose, tail wagging furiously.

"Merek!" he shouts within my mind. It rings loud and clear. "My friend, my brother..."

"Brice!" I tickle his ribs and we roll and tackle each other, rolling and rolling, my laughter and his barks. I pin the mighty beast on his back beneath me. "Brice," I sigh, hugging him as his body twitches back and forth with excitement. I climb up him and bring my forehead to his and then our minds blur together.

I see his memories flash before me, from when he kicked me through the border. Molag the evil Goblin King continuing his torture, Brice's fur whitening from the pain, and that pain sinks deep within my bones. I see Brice rear up and bite, holding tight onto the wrist and arm of my grandfather with his mouth, the blood welling up and trickling down and between his teeth. Molag screams. The pack of lost ones scattering into the wood, and the evil King waving his free hand and disappearing, leaving Brice heaving, beaten and alone, writhing in pain. Brice wandering for so long, pacing for miles and miles, lost along the border within the forest, trying to find me, to find a way through the border. Trying to survive, alone and wounded. I feel his hungry belly, the cold of the winter's storms, hiding high up in the trees away from the lost ones. Until here and now, he never stopped looking for me, waiting for me to return. Patrolling the woods, watching, listening for signs of me.

I open my eyes and gaze upon my dearest friend as our mindshare separates and I hug him more fiercely as he nuzzles me. We hear a small cough and look up.

"Um, hi." Rowan gives a little wave. She is still wrapped around the branch and clinging to it tightly. I stand and with Brice walk so that I am directly below her.

"Let go, Rowan, and fall. I'll catch you!" I adjust my stance and ready myself to catch her.

"What!" she says, horrified.

"It's okay, Rowan, jump down. I'll explain everything."

She's still frightened and now looking slightly green... well, greener than she has already become. I notice Brice circling and pacing beneath her, looking up at her. I shake my head at him to stop so he sits still, looking up and panting.

"I'm too high, Merek," she whispers, looking faint.

"Just loosen your grip and let yourself roll off the branch. I'm right here. I promise, I will catch you," I coo gently to her, trying to relax her. She lets out a long breath and inhales quickly. Her limbs hesitantly, slowly, and jerkily release their death hold upon the branch, I hear her heart beat *thump, thump, thump, thump* and!—she faints.

Her body goes limp and slips off the branch. Within seconds she's in my arms cradled safely. I kiss her forehead.

Her eyes flutter and she screams. Brice is now sniffing her hair. She wraps her arms around my neck, flinging her body up and around onto my back, clinging with legs wrapped around my waist. Her heart races, *thump, thump, thump, thump*. I reach for her hand and kiss the back of it, hoping it will help to calm her.

"Rowan, this is Brice," I say calmly. Brice circles around us sniffing the air while Rowan watches his every move. He sits once he reaches my front again. Brice makes a whimpering noise and stretches his big head toward our hands. He nudges his forehead against us. Rowan stiffens at his touch. I gently put her down and steady her on her feet. Still holding her hand, I place our hands upon Brice's soft fur.

"Brice, this is Rowan." I nod my head at him. Through our mind connection, I say, "Rowan is overwhelmed—move slowly 'til she calms." He winks back at me.

Rowan gently and tentatively runs her fingers through Brice's fur, twirling them and petting him. Brice sits very still but gives her more access to his face, and she looks deep into his big eyes—and then giggles. She leans into his forehead and rubs hers against his and says, "Brr ice." After a moment she giggles again. Brice's scent turns shy and he looks away from me, leans into Rowan, and gives her a purring sound as he leans against her body. I laugh out loud at the sound of him and he snorts at me. He half circles around Rowan and nudges his head between her ankles. Swiftly and gently he lifts her up and she slides down his neck and rests upon his back. She lies against him, wrapping her arms around his neck, and he begins to walk away from me. I laugh again more to myself and follow his lead before remembering the gentle old horse and cow.

I stop and turn—both are hiding poorly behind shrubs, shaking and wide-eyed. I whistle to them and they slowly make their way to me. I pet each of them and reassure them that they are safe. The horse, the cow, and I bring up the rear. I hear Rowan giggling. She is now sitting upon Brice, riding proud upon the beast's back, and she keeps looking back at me every now and again. Brice pauses and turns as Rowan laughs out loud, both staring at me, their eyes alight with amusement and happiness. All I can do is grin. My family, a family of my own.

"Rowan can hear me, too, Merek. I've just told her about the first time you heard me speak." He snorts with laughter through our connection and I *humph* at him and frown deeply.

Mother of Light, it's going to be a long night. Brice chortles deeply.

CHAPTER TWELVE

Along the Path

I wake to warm sunshine on my face. I'm high up in a tree upon a thick, wide branch. I realize that I am alone; no Brice and no Rowan. I sit up quickly and lean to look down the tree to the forest floor. I do not see them. Surely Brice would have alerted me had Rowan fallen from the branch. Where is he?

Just then I hear Rowan shriek with laughter and the reassuring rustling of the forest floor giving away their footsteps. I heave a breath of relief and begin to climb down.

I gaze out and around me, trying to spot them. Brice is in a clearing a few yards off. He's bouncing up and down on his front paws, snorting. Rowan chortles from somewhere hidden beyond the shrubs. I laugh to myself as I find they are playing hide-and-go-seek, Rowan's favorite game. I check on the gentle horse and cow and find them nibbling at the tall grass near our sleeping tree. I rub each of them down while they eat, then start loading up the gentle horse with our packs. I feel a small hand on my shoulder and turn.

"You're awake!" Rowan smiles at me and I hand her one of the biscuit breads she made before we left and bite into mine as she too takes a large bite.

"Can I have the..." she starts to say with her mouth full, but I hand her the jar of honey before she can finish. "And the..." I reach in and hand her my flask filled with water. She sighs happily at how I know what she wants.

"Share it, will you!" I call to her as she walks away from me and back to Brice, no doubt to share her morning breakfast with him. As I catch up to them, I find Brice laying in front of Rowan, sneaking licks of honey from the glass jar. I sit with them and take the honey from Brice, dipping my biscuit into the jar and savoring the bite.

"Did you sleep well, Rowan?" I ask after swallowing and re-dipping into the honey.

"Yes! I never thought you could sleep so high up in a tree! I had the most wonderful dreams!" she replies.

"We've spent our fair share of nights up in a tree, right, Brice?" I nudge him and he nods with a sigh. "What did you dream?"

"Your mother showed me our day today. I cannot wait 'til we reach the big pond!" She takes her last bite. "We will have a safe journey through the forest today. Nothing knows we are here yet."

"Oh! Well, we should still stay on guard just in case." I pause. "A pond, you say? Is it near a small house made of stone?"

"No, your mother says we are still three days yet from the book. Tomorrow will not be a good day to travel. We are to stay in the cave on the other side of the pond—a waterfall hides it—all day and night, then it will be clear to travel the next morning. She gave strict orders and we are to listen. We must stay in the cave."

My face pales at her words. I hope she is referring to a different cave than the one Brice and I stayed in. I look down and turn my wrist so my hand is palm up and examine the crescent moon scars on either side where the boned fish woman bit me. I wonder if Emira has been freed or not. My wrist tingles slightly with pain and I feel the glass stone reach out to me, hidden in a deep pocket of my satchel, and a memory of the voice comes to me:

"When the time comes, throw the stone into any water and dive down and into the deep. A choice you will have to make. Keep it safe, keep it close, keep it hidden, for when you have need of me or to save a life."

My body shivers as I hear her voice sing the riddle. I still don't understand it. What is the rhythm about? 'A life.' Is that Rowan's? My mother's? *A choice you will have to make...* I shake my head and let the memory pass.

A rustling of leaves makes me leap to my feet. Brice's tail begins wagging as his stomach growls. Squirrel.

"Go, find what you can and eat. We will need to leave soon." I nod at Brice and he silently stalks off in search of his meal.

Rowan and I finish our small snack and get the horse and cow ready to travel again. I share our water with each of the animals.

"A pond, you say. That will be helpful to refill our water containers. This is the last of our water." I sigh and look to Rowan.

"Yes, she promised we will come upon a pond at the base of a small mountain. Together you and Brice will catch ten fat fish and the cave should be located across the pond, behind the falls. We will have to swim to reach it." She pauses. "Brice catches six, by the way." And she starts chuckling at me, teasing. I *harrumph* at her and frown.

"We'll see about that!" I whisper to myself, and she laughs even harder. I whistle for Brice and he pops out ahead of us on the trail.

"Brice, it's that way, I believe." She points in a direction off the worn path we have been following and into the thickest part of the woods. Brice sniffs in that direction, then bobs his head up and down in agreement. He paws at me and I let him drink the rest of the water.

"I am quite certain this is the correct path," Rowan repeats to Brice and I. "Going that way will only take longer if we stick to the path. This way cuts the time in half, and was your mother's preferred path for our journey today." She folds her arms and stares at Brice. He lets out his breath and trots beside her; he kneels and she hoists herself up onto his back.

Through our connection I whisper, "How does she know which way to go?" Brice snorts at me, but it is Rowan who replies through Brice and I's connection, startling us both.

"Your mother pointed the way." She folds her arms again, her eyebrows creased together at me. Dumbfounded, I shrug at her and begin following along behind them with the horse and cow at my side.

We walk for miles, the sun high above us, midday. It is hot, sticky hot, and we have no water left. Along the way I find the perfect stick to make into a spear, long and thick. I extend my thumb claw and begin whittling the end into a sharp point as we all amble along slowly, dripping with sweat. Brice is panting heavily, still carrying Rowan and leading the way, the horse and cow with me bringing up the rear. The hotter it gets, the more Rowan's scent fills my nose. I inhale deeply, drinking her in. She has braided and tied her hair up high on her head. Her cotton white dress is damp. I breathe out, trying to clear my nose, and try concentrating on our surroundings, listening, blinking in and out with Goblin sight at the path around us. Each time I get my senses to focus, her scent drifts back to me.

Suddenly Rowan claps and surprises me. She slides down off Brice and sprints. I run to catch up to all of them and then smell it—water, fresh, cool water.

We race through the tree line and across a sandy beach, each crashing into the water and drinking thirstily. I blink my eyes to my Goblin sight and search the pond for any dangers below the water's surface. I see only fish, and a large smile comes to my face. There is a waterfall spilling down and over the tall rocks, filling the pond. Bright and colorful flowers cling to the rock wall, their roots deep in cracks and crevices of the stone. I see darkness, a small opening at the water's edge to the right of the waterfall. I blink and with Goblin sight see an entrance to the cave from Rowan's dream.

Rowan returns to the beach and steps out of her cotton dress and lets down her hair. It ripples down her back. My cheeks burn, and I look away from her as she turns to face me to re-enter the water.

"Come swim with me, Merek!"

She dives into the pond, swimming through the water, popping up in the middle. My heart races. I've never seen Rowan without her dress. A thick strip of cloth wraps her torso and a separate piece covers her lower half. Her back is long and narrow. My stomach clenches and pulls.

"Come swim, Merek," she calls from the middle of the pond.

She dives down and heads closer to the waterfall. I step out of my shorts, run, and dive into the cool crystal-clear water.

The cool water feels divine, cooling my body from the heat of the day. I kick hard and spin my body, gliding and cutting through the water. I can see Rowan just ahead of me, her pale skin reflecting under the water. I surface for breath, kicking hard to break the surface, and dive again, trying to catch up. I find a pair of legs standing on a boulder beneath the water and a small hand reaching out to me. I take her hand and let her pull me to her and onto the rock. Quickly I shut my eyes against her nakedness. She pulls me into an embrace. I rest my check against the top of her head and feel her laugh. When I open my eyes,

I find Brice popping up and down, splashing his paws as he paddles along, enjoying his swim.

Rowan releases her hold of me and I reluctantly let her go. She stands beside me, the water up to the base of her neck. She walks along the flat rock into the falls, placing her back and head against the stone, letting the water rush down her face. The sun's light is muted by the tall rock wall of the falls in the alcove we're in. I walk around to the right, testing the length of the rock we are standing upon, to the entrance of the cave. I stub my toes on a rock, causing me to fall forward into the water, but feel more stones. Blinking, I see there are stone steps leading up, hidden under the water. I glance back at Rowan, who still has her head against the stone, letting the water rush over her, eyes closed. I quickly walk up the steps and see that the opening is quite large but hidden well behind the falling water.

With my other sight I scan its depth. It's not too large and the back half is surprisingly dry. I can see Rowan still leaning against the rock, water trickling down her beautiful face. My heart begins to race again. I sit near her inside the cave and admire her. I inch closer to her. Something deep within me wants to just lean into and ever so gently press my lips to hers.

A fish flies and hits me in the back of the head. Looking back, I discover Brice dripping wet with a mouthful of fish.

His head cocks to one side, staring at me, puzzled. I crinkle my brows at him and rub the back of my head. I turn back and find Rowan unmoved.

"Five!" I hear Brice from within our connection. He gives me a satisfied look. "I'm ahead!" he snorts proudly at me.

Out of the corner of my eye, I see Rowan move away from the falls. I back up into the cave.

"We'll see," I retort to Brice and break into a full run.

At the edge of the cave from behind the falls, I leap through the water and dive, leaving Brice with his mouth hanging open, causing him to drop his fish. Breaking through the falling water, I turn and look at Rowan. I give her a full toothy mouth grin as she screams, surprised to find me coming through the other side of the falls and diving into the water. Just as easily, I snare a fish between my teeth and resurface, mouth full of the slippery silver fish, grinning ear to ear. Rowan erupts with merriment at the sight of me and begins clapping at my catch. Brice sticks his giant head through the falling water and snorts at me.

He disappears only to reemerge barreling through the water, all four of his limbs flailing with an enormous open jaw smile and tongue hanging out, crashing into the water. He creates a wall of water that crashes over my head. Rowan laughs harder at this then dives down deep into the water. I sink down into the water and watch her swim, her eyes wide and searching. She finds a fish and swims after it. The fish stays just barely out of her reach. I can see that she needs to surface for a breath of air, but that is when I see it: a tiny spark of a flash of light jumps from her outstretched fingertip and zaps the fish before her. She smiles, triumphant, grabbing the fish, and begins swimming up. Mystified, I kick off the bottom and resurface before she does. She pops up with the slippery fish in her mouth, smiling ear to ear.

"How did you do that?" I call to her, swimming closer.

"Do what?" she mouths around the fish. "I got one!" She holds it up high in her hand, waving it over her head.

"You..." I pause, not even sure at what I have seen. "You... zapped the fish?" I question even myself.

She blushes and gives a shy beam. "Yeah, I'm not really sure how I do it. It just happens when I think about it. It was really helpful in the winter getting the fire going in the sitting room. I'm sorry I wasn't honest with you when you asked about it before, but my mother warned me never to show it in front of others. Not everyone has this ability. She said it was important to keep it quiet, to myself."

She begins to swim away from me, heading back for the sunken boulder beneath the waterfall. I grab her hand and pull her back to face me.

"Try doing it to me," I say, reflecting. She has done something similar before. "It's strange, but now that I think about it, every time you've touched me I've always felt a tingling at your touch," I say to her.

She blushes again, this time a deeper shade of red, then extends her hand and touches my cheek. Each fingertip zings a gentle tickle against my skin. My eyes go wide as I stare at her.

She smiles shyly. "Every time I touch you, my whole body zings and tingles, so I just thought..." Her cheeks burn red again and then she coughs at her admission. "I didn't realize you could feel it too, but I'm never thinking about the electric light when I touch you. I just get butterflies in my belly and thought it was just my stomach doing flips." She gives me another shy smile and swims off toward Brice, adding her catch to his.

"Brice won, by the way—he caught fifteen!" she calls over her shoulder. "Plus your fish and mine, we should have plenty to eat later."

"You said he'd only catch six," I remind her.

"The future is not always set in stone," she explains. "It depends on someone's choices, or if they decide on different path at the time of my vision. Seems Brice wanted to showboat and beat his own number," she laughs.

Brice, hearing his name and that someone finally noticed his hard work, holds his head high and paddles in circles around Rowan, purring at her.

While Brice and Rowan continue to swim and play in the water, I go over to check on the horse and cow. Each has found a deep shaded spot within the tree line and is snoozing when I get to them. I know it is later now into the day and ask the animals if I can help them swim across to the entrance of the cave.

"Night will come soon," I whisper to them. "You'll be better protected in the cave. The sound of the falls is louder inside, and I might not hear if you're in trouble. The woods aren't safe at night, there's always something lurking. I'd feel better if you were with us and not out here in the open."

They both look at me as if I've lost my mind to ask that they swim. I collect the bags and baskets from Winston the horse and hold them up over my head, paddling slowly back across the pond. I turn back and find sweet Bella bravely wading into the water.

I send her a silent message to wish her luck at swimming and that I'll return to her once I get the packs across. She snorts and nods at me while she walks deeper into the water. Brice comes up alongside her when her hooves no longer reach the pond floor and helps Bella keep her snout above water. I meet them at the sunken steps leading up and into the cave and help guide her feet. I look up and find Rowan pulling on the horse's reins, trying to lead him into the water. I hear his silent plea to just be left alone but Rowan is not giving up.

"It might not be safe here for you, like Merek told you. He knows these woods. Please, swim with me to the cave," she urges the horse.

Winston rears up on his back legs to pull back on Rowan. Brice has snuck behind the old horse and gives a deep, loud growl. The horse spooks and sprints into the water, dragging Rowan still holding on his reins as she stumbles into the water. She swims ahead of Winston, pulling him along, and Brice paddles next to him to help keep his head above the surface. Once in the cave, Winston stamps his hooves and snorts loudly and angrily at all of us. He refuses to look at any of us and goes and plops his butt down toward the back of the cave. He gives a mighty shake, sending water in every direction, and then just looks pitiful, a freakishly large drowned rat.

The three of us gather logs and sticks from the tree line and carefully swim them across 'til we have enough wood to last at least two days. I make a ring from round smooth rocks and pile on the sticks and branches, and it is Rowan with her electrified fingertips that gets the fire going.

We cook and share the fish between us all, each enjoying mouthfuls of the flaky white fish while we eat in silence. Rowan and I squat near each other with a small pile of fish before us, carefully grabbing at the hot chunks of flesh to keep from burning our fingers. Brice gulps down his pile, not at all concerned with the temperature as his are raw.

After eating, Rowan throws the fish remnants into the fire.

"To cover the smells, hopefully," she explains. "We wouldn't want an unexpected visitor tonight."

She finishes her task and then sits on the edge of the cave entrance with her feet in the water, watching the sun set and disappear behind the tree line from behind the falling water.

I sit down quietly beside her and we watch the sky turn from yellows to oranges, deep red to pink, and as clouds change from blue to purple then black until the moon is high. It blankets everything in a white glow. I want so badly to reach out and take her hand, but I do not. I internally fight with myself as to why I have not yet done so, and then my stomach fills with butterflies.

I watch the sky but mostly I like gazing at her. But I turn quickly back to the sky when she tries glancing at me. I'm not sure what has changed in me. Rowan has become my best friend. I trust her completely. Why am I now being so shy in her presence? Her admission of her whole-body tingling and zinging at touching me makes me feel warm and loopy. For this reason, I begin to smile and cannot help but smile 'til my cheeks begin to get sore.

I finally build up my courage (or just get over myself) to take my best friend's hand, enjoying the dark sky, when she breaks the silence and I pull my hand back.

"Merek." She takes a deep breath. "Something will soon happen to me and it will make us unable to leave here tomorrow. I feel it coming." She is silent a moment. "I just wish I knew what was going to happen. It's frustrating not knowing." She pauses and gathers her courage. "Whatever happens, I know it will be briefly painful and more like a long sleep that I am unable to wake from, but it angers me that you and Brice will be stuck here having to watch over me. Ugh! Of all the things, I don't need to be watched!" She sounds furious but softens her voice and continues, "I suppose if I must, I must. But before whatever happens comes, let's swim again. We won't be able to tomorrow."

I frown at her, not sure how to respond. 'Something will happen'—she talked of this earlier. I use my Goblin sight and gaze into the woods about us.

"You'll swim with me, won't you? I'm going to undress," she whispers. My stomach pulls and my cheeks heat and I close my eyes.

"Okay, Merek. Now your turn."

She stands beside me completely naked, no bands of cloth covering her chest or between her legs. My whole being melts and feels like mush as I gaze upon her moonlit skin. She reaches out her hand for mine with a small, shy smile. I cannot even move my body; I'm paralyzed. She lowers her arm, backs into the cave, and runs leaping through the falling water.

"Come swim with me," she calls over her shoulder, swimming out toward the middle of the pond. I swallow the lump in my throat and slide out of my shorts and enter the lukewarm water. I swim to follow and find her sitting on a submerged rock. She starts re-braiding her hair and looks at me.

"Come sit," she beckons.

I obey, finding and feeling the rock where she sits. I distance myself from where she sits, seeing her shyness with the full moon. I do not wish to intrude upon her.

Yet she inches along the rock and sits right next to me and places her hand upon my leg. She tangles her ankles around mine, effectively tickling me, causing me to let out a nervous chuckle. Her fingers tingle where she touches; a heat blooms within my whole body, spreading fast and wide, and my heart races and pounds.

Mother of Light, it is happening again. My body goes into overdrive when she gets so close to me. Her hand takes mine and places it flat against her chest.

"Is your heart pounding as hard as mine?" she questions.

I nod, gazing out toward the cave. From within my mind, I hear Brice sleepily say, "She wants to mate with you. It explains both of your scents and erratic behavior toward each other. I noticed it right away when we were reunited. Why haven't you, Merek?"

"Mating?" I ask him.

"You've chosen each other as your life partner, or mates. If you choose her, then you will consummate, making a soul promise, and become one another's one and only partner. I do hope she decides yes. To be honest, she has been very indecisive and conflicted; she has no idea how to tell you! She is a loaded bottle ready to burst with the feelings that have been in her for a while now, but even she cannot hide her scent when she looks at you. I do believe she is in heat. You can hide your scent better, but as I can see into your mind, I know those same confusing feelings coursing through your body are running rampant in hers. Though, Rowan may not ultimately choose you, if she does not think you are a strong enough partner. I do wish you both luck; she has a fiery spirt, that one! Goodnight, Merek. I'll leave you two to it then." Brice closes the connection before I can even fully understand what he has said.

Mating? My heart races harder. What does that mean?

"Brice! Explain—what am I supposed to do? What does she expect from me?"

My head begins to swirl, but Brice has closed the connection. This is what my parents had done. It is forbidden for creatures of different species to mate. It is for that reason my parents were taken from me. We cannot... we can only be good friends...

"BRICE!"

"Merek?" Rowan whispers.

My hand is still placed against her chest. I can still feel the rhythmic thumping of her heart beneath my fingertips. "Look at me?" Her voice is so low, heated and breathy.

"Brice," I urgently call out in my mind. "What you said, mating, that's what my parents did. That's what created me. It's forbidden, Brice. That's why my father was taken from us. That is what took them both from me!"

I realize painfully I do truly love Rowan. I yell within my head, I just scream. Is she going to ask me to move our friendship into something different? The memory of her kiss back in the field, the feel of her soft lips against mine... My stomach pulls and knots. A low purr escapes my throat. I can smell her; her scent is intensified. It's wafting off her strongly like an aura. My nostrils flare as I breathe her scent deeply. My body grows hot, my hand still resting against her upper chest, my brain wanting my hands to touch and explore every inch of her.

I shake my head and move my hand back to my side, my fingertips digging painfully into the stone beneath me. Suddenly I am full of worry and panic. I cannot let myself do what my brain and body are screaming at me to do.

I stand. I walk away along the rock as it dips further into the water. I leave her there alone and unsure and I instantly regret it. It drives a pain deep into my gut.

"What's wrong?" she calls softly. I feel her reach out to me, touching my shoulder.

"I cannot do what you want of me."

I don't turn around to face her. She inhales sharply and I sense her straighten up, making herself as tall as she can.

"You do not love me, then?" she croaks out, holding back her tears.

"I'm completely infatuated with you, Rowan, everything about you!" I yell and turn to her. "But I don't understand all this." My hands swirls in front of my body. I jab at my heart, then head. "I just—Mother of Light! I love you. I do! But we cannot, we *cannot* love each other!" I whisper this, defeated, and hear her sigh then feel her hands on my shoulders. I open my eyes and find her staring into mine.

Instantly I am lost in them. I have to fight this, fight the throbbing, elongating hardness between my legs. I have to stay strong and look away.

UGH! I take her wrists and hold them away from my body.

Her eyes narrow in frustration. She leaps forward, her body gently crashing into my chest, her lips upon mine. I wrap my arms around her and hold her so tight. I suck at her lower lip and she gasps in surprise. When her mouth opens, my tongue greedily twists and twirls to explore her sweet mouth. She hums and my head clouds in lust. I pull away from her and set her on her feet away from me. I regret it and my body screams.

"Mine!" I bark at her, holding her arms by her sides. I shake my head and step back. "Wait! Rowan, no, back up," I shout. I shake my head again. "We cannot be that way, you and me. The creatures of this world will come for us if we are. They will kill us, Rowan! *This*," I point at her dreamily wanton expression and then at myself. Mother of Light help me! Her scent is even stronger and thicker, deliciously coating my insides. "*This*! This is what took my parents away from me," I choke out before my animal instincts kick in full force. My arms reach out to her, pull her flush against my chest again. "Mine!" I bark out again. "NO!" I set her back down on the rock beneath us and back away further.

"You cannot help who your heart chooses, Merek," she whispers back at me.

"Yes, you can! We are friends. That is what we will be—friends! MINE!" I clap my hand over my mouth and close my eyes. *No, no, NO!* My body is fighting against my heart and brain and I am losing.

"No, *you* listen!" she yells at me, jabbing her finger hard against my chest. "I chose you! If you don't choose me back because there is nothing in your heart for me, then fine! Say that! Do not tell me that we cannot be together because you are you and I am me! Human, Gelfin, Goblin, I *don't* care! Love is love and I will fight for it!" she shouts at me.

I cup her face in my hands.

"It's too dangerous. We both could die. You—" I pause, feeling completely overwhelmed, wanting to tell her how I much I truly love her, what my body wants to do with her, but I will seal her fate if I do.

"You could die, and the King, my wicked grandfather, would ensure our deaths in a public square!" I search her eyes.

She pushes my hair from my face and gazes into my eyes, searching so deeply for something in mine, and then pushes against the bottom of the rock and jumps, wrapping herself round me, legs wrapped around my waist, her arms locked around my neck, and she kisses me. She holds me like that for a long time. I slowly relax into her hold. Then I kiss her back, filling that kiss with all my passion.

I sit down with Rowan tangled around me. When she whispers

"Mine!" she laughs softly and smiles at me.

She adjusts her position against me and straddles my lap. Before I can figure out where she is going, her body lowers over mine and I enter her body. She hisses against a popping feeling as she lowers her body too fast and I am pushed further in. She holds very still, holding her breath, her face scrunched in slight pain. Her nails dig into my skin.

She holds still. Heat courses through my body at the experience. All the world falls away from me. An animalistic urge comes over me; my senses heighten. I can feel every inch of her warmth around me, soft as velvet. I hold her in my arms so still, not wanting to move. I can feel her inner walls clenching and swallowing more of me. *Hold still*, I whisper to myself, and feel a comforting calm of being with Rowan. It is euphoric and I hold still.

"Merek?" Rowan whispers, and relaxes against me. Her eyes glow, her face perfectly lit in the moon's glow. She lifts her body slightly, her inner walls sliding against me, then slowly she lowers herself again.

I can feel my eyes change into long orbs of black, the Goblin, the animal side of me taking control, instinct-driven. Rowan's head dips back, her neck exposed to me. I thrust deep inside her once, twice, three times then bite down upon her neck. She cries out, pleasure-filled throaty breaths waving out of her. I drink from her greedily 'til her body goes limp in my hold. I hold her, frozen in that place and time. This time, this moment, I commit to memory—this perfect moment, forever burned in passion of my Rowan. My eyes blink; my body relaxes.

"Rowan?" I whisper, lifting her off me to cradle her in my arms. Her eyes are closed and she does not answer me. "Rowan?"

I shake her shoulders gently and kiss her forehead, but receive no answer. I lift her and carefully carry her back to the cave, gently laying her on the floor beside the fire. Her skin is hot with fever.

"It is your venom, Merek," Brice whispers, stepping toward us on soft paws, alert by my side. "She will change, be stronger than before. It will take at least a day for her to recover." Brice rubs his cheek against mine. "Sleep now. Lay beside her and pull her body against yours. It will help her fever stay low and your touch will help soothe her through the process. I'll take first watch. Sleep, Merek."

Brice pads away toward the entrance, still as a statue, gazing out at the unknown, watching for signs of danger. My head swims, my vision turns black, and I fall beside Rowan in a deep sleep.

CHAPTER THIRTEEN

Dreams and Visions (Part One)

"Run, Merek, run!" I hear my pa shout.

My eyes are blurry, and I blink to clear them. My mother lays sick in my father's bed. He throws me from him and through the little open window out into the night, but just before I pass through the window, everything freezes. My evil grandfather stands before me about to wave his hand.

I am unseen. I realize it is just a dream of shadows that have once been. I reach out to my pa to touch his arm. His other hand clasps over mine, causing me to look up at him.

We vanish from my pa's shack of a house. I recognize the village where my pa is from. We are in the ancient theater where my pa was judged once before. There within the familiar cage is my pa. He is reaching for a limp hand that hangs from a decorative carved stone. I follow his outreached hand and see my mum, laid upon her back atop a huge stone table. Her eyes are closed but I watch her chest rise and fall. She sleeps. The dress I remember her wearing is gone, replaced with one so sheer, an almost see-through cream satin gown. It has a high neck collar reaching the top of her ears, her hair long and black cascading around her beautiful face. I bend and kiss her cheek.

She is warm and solid, not dreamlike at all. Confusion takes hold of me. This may be my only chance to touch her once again. I slide my arm beneath her back and draw her into a bone-crushing hug.

"Mum," I sigh, and breathe in her pure scent, her smell so familiar that my eyes fill with tears. "Mum," I say louder, "please wake, I've missed you."

A loud clack of metal hitting stone reverberates throughout the chamber and I look up. We are surrounded once again by creatures above us looking down, hidden beneath long and hooded navy robes. The council members too are above us but seated, gazing down and pulling back their hoods all at once. I lay my mother back against the stone table where she continues to sleep and return to my ghostly, misted pa. He is kneeling inside the cage. I try to reach through the bars, but they prevent me from touching him.

He looks up at the council, his face tired and so full of worry. I know that worry is not for himself but for his love that lays so close, just out of his reach. He too has been stripped of his clothes. A rich, thick fabric is tied at his waste and pools down and onto the floor. His back is covered in deep cut marks. Fresh blood still trickles from the wounds. His face turns to me and one eye is so black and swollen I cannot help thinking he'll never see from it again.

He continues to look at me. I know I am only a shadow in this vision, but then, in the midst of his obvious pain and agony, he smiles at me. I quickly turn to check over my shoulder to see who has made him smile. There is nothing behind me but a wall of decorative stone.

I snap my head back to face my father and leap to my feet. He lifts a horribly broken finger to his lips.

"This is one of my memories, Merek. Listen carefully. Watch every detail and learn from this." His voice is hoarse and just a whisper. "We are alive and trying to find you. After you witness this, you must retrieve the book. It's beyond important: you will need it."

A loud clang again reverberates through the chamber and sets my teeth on edge and sends a chill down my spine.

A black cloaked figure emerges from behind the council members, strides forward to the front of the balcony, and looks down. I know before he even pulls back his hood that it is my grandfather, Molag, the ruler of all, filled of pure evil. The Goblin King.

"My dear son," he snaps, "let us just see what this pathetic half-breed you have created will now think of you! You survived the whipping and the stoning at our village's center for all to bear witness. It's no surprise that your body is strong, but will you survive *her* judgement?" he spits at my father. "Will she still love you, dear one?" His booming voice shakes the stone around us.

My father straightens and stands as tall as he can make himself. His raw wounds stretch from his moving and begin to bleed again. Members in the audience whimper at the sight of him, wishing they could only help. He gathers all his strength and holds his head high. He looks up to glare into the eyes of his maker.

The crowd of navy blue robes stands and cheers, proud of the man in the cage, defiant as he is. The roar encourages my father, empowering his soul.

"SILENCE!" screams Molag.

The navy blue robes hush and sit immediately. Molag tilts his head from one side to the other, never breaking eye contact with my father, his son, below, caged like an animal. The council members shift nervously in their seats. Even from down here I too feel the unhinged, wild energy wafting from the Goblin King. My father stares back and smiles up at his father.

Molag waves a hand and my mother's body is lifted into the air, arms and legs spread wide, suspended for all to see and bound by invisible restraints that cause her limbs to quiver. Her head hangs down, lolling from side to side from the movement of her body being stretched tight. Her head is raised, her eyes begin to blink, she wakes from a deep sleep.

I rush to try to help her, but she is too high above the table of decorative stone and is held there. She does not see or feel me below her. She focuses on her hands and turns them over and back again. What once was pale white skin now glows light emerald with swirling marks etched deep into the skin. She cranes her head and looks down. My pa's hand reaches out to her. My mum gasps softly as she tries to focus new eyes, never-used orbs of black searching my father's pain-filled features.

"Drake!" her thoughts shout, and her body spasms against the hold of the restraints. "My love, my love?" Her voice is shrill and panicked. "What has happened? What is this? Why are you in a giant bird cage?" Her voice is hysterical. She stares at my father for a long while, trying to focus. "Where is Merek?" Her voice is now taught and tight, full of fear.

"Amanda, oh my sweet love, listen to me, look at me! Only me! No, Amanda, do not look away just yet. My eyes only, my love, look at me and hear me. I was too late, Amanda. I did what was necessary to save you. Do you remember the fire?" he asks softly.

My mother's face contorts, trying to remember. Confusion washes over her perfect face and I kneel before my parents, longing to reach out to them, to reunite our family. My mother tries to extend her hand once towards my father.

"Drake, where! Where is our son?" she screams, fighting against the hold.

"Amanda, we are in the village of my people. The Goblin Village," he says slowly, and my mother's face pales. "No, my eyes, Amanda! We are in the great hall and I will be judged. My eyes, Amanda, please, my love, I only did it to save you. I could not let you die," he whispers.

"What are you trying to tell me? Are we in danger? Where is my son? If we are in your village..." My father stares at her face, forcing her to not break his eye contact. "If we are in your village, we are in grave danger," she whispers to him. "Drake? What do we do? Where is Merek?" She breathes out a breath, gripped in fear, barely able to whisper.

I stand on tiptoes upon the decorative stone table and try in vain to touch her feet to get her attention. To my surprise, she looks down at me.

"Listen, watch, learn!" she mouths to me.

I jump in surprise and when I look back at her, her eyes are even bigger, blacker. Her body violently spasms and somehow she is released from the invisible hold and laid with grace beside me upon the table.

A loud clang of metal against stone reverberates once again through the chamber. A flash of silver whizzes by my face and sinks its sharp blade into my mother's scar upon her shoulder. It passes through her. The blade has no effect on her; it is the phantom memory of a knife once held to her throat. Layers of the past seep together, my head cramps, trying to focus on this current time, in their past.

She climbs off the rock and rushes to my father's cage. My mother presses her body against the cage, reaching in and grabbing hold of Drake, pulling him closer to her.

"Do you love me, my heart?" my pa questions her.

"Always," she whispers.

A loud clang sounds, and the King speaks. "Amanda, you are no longer in your Human world, you are here in mine and I am the ruler of all." She at last looks up. She places her back to my pa's front, her small back pressed against his cage, gripping his hand. She slowly looks around her. A sea of navy blue robes murmurs in approval at my mother as she scans the assembly before her. Some of them, she sees, are nodding to her or winking at her. Each creature pulls back their hood, revealing their faces, each a different shade of green or emerald, purple, smoky grey, deep tan, and even some with wings. She swallows hard and presses further back into my pa's cage, the bars digging into her. She at last tilts her head back to be able to gaze up even higher to where the voice has come from, the council balcony. I take hold of my mother's free hand and grip her tightly and turn to face my grandfather. I stand tall and proud alongside my parents.

Even Molag lets out a hiss when he gazes at her, for I assume this is the first time he has seen her face since her transition. Now half-human, half-Goblin.

"Your beauty surprises even me," he chuckles, and I feel my father flinch. "Even though you are—" he swallows "—a half—" he coughs and gags as if it sickens him to even speak it "—a half breed." His head shakes with disgust. "It is difficult to visualize. This is proof, my subjects. This is why we do not mate outside of our kind. This female creature before us is a danger to us. We do not even know her full power or what destruction she may be capable of to our kind."

"Half! Half of what?" my mum's voice sings. She once again examines her hands closely in front of her face. Elongated fingers, green arms. She releases my pa's hand and mine. She hugs herself tightly. She spins and gazes at my father. She catches her reflection in my pa's one good eye, wide and black. She too sees her own black orb eyes. She reaches for my father's tortured face and kisses him deeply. Pure love and passion emanate from around them. A bright white light dances from between them and encircles them.

"No! Stop! I will not have it!" screams my grandfather from above. Navy blue robes stand and begin to run for the nearest exit. Metal against stone clangs and shakes the chamber. My parents continue with their embrace and shared kiss.

"You, Amanda, will become my property. Seize her now! Take him to the tower to rot."

Red robes race forward and grab at my mother. She holds my father more tightly while hands pry at my father's grip around her waist. Their lips still hold together; the white light flashes out, filling the chamber. Red robes jump and start backing away.

"Grab the female and take her to my chamber, NOW!" Molag howls, and another clang hits the giant cage. It flings my mother away from my father, sending her up and over the stone table where her body crumples. Her head hits the stone floor and a small pool of blood begins trickling away from her. Red robes scoop up my mother's limp body and carry her off.

My father screams, "NO, *NO!*"

In a smoky haze, Molag stands beside the cage, no longer upon his perch in the council area. A red robe approaches.

"Take him from my sight!" Molag growls. "Wait!" He pauses. "Drake, you frustrate me so! You survived me whipping you 'til my strength weakened. Still you held yourself against that pole, chained up and stretched as if the might of two powerful Goblins had no effect upon you. You dared challenge me just now, here in front of our people in your weakened state. And the female completely forgave you for the hideous abomination of a creature you turned her into," he screams in anger. "The bond between you is incredibly strong, and as legend has it, a bond that strong can have its downfall. Your suffering will be my revenge. I will torture her, and you will feel it all. Her pain will become your pain. Her longing for you will become your longing. Her torture, yours to endure. That..." He inspects his finger nails, "That will be most rewarding punishment to watch!"

Molag's words are full of evil and he licks his lips as he stares my father down. "I bet it will kill you to feel her responses at my touching her, claiming your mate Amanda for myself, making her mine, contorting your bond when I perhaps could impregnate the creature. Although... an Old Prophecy did claim, so I've read, that a demon will be spawned from my loins." He rubs his stubbly chin. "Perhaps my seed in her will create that demon and I will have it unleashed upon you while I watch as it kills you!" He smirks to himself. "I will enjoy torturing her, Drake, and I know you will feel every bit of her pain!" He smiles deeply at his son.

My father had fallen to his knees long ago. His stomach rolls, lurching as his father speaks these words, fear of what would become of Amanda crippling him.

"Not so strong now, are you?" my grandfather spits. He points at the hooded red robe and then points to my father. "To the tower with him. Chain him, strip him, and *for the Mother of Light* do not feed him!" Molag turns and walks away from me and my father. "Time to welcome the new lady to my kingdom!" He claps and disappears.

I hang my head and walk through the bars to my father's side. I am only a shadow in this past. He lays upon the stone floor, silently gazing at the ceiling. At first, I am unsure if he has perished and is laying there dead. I notice the hooded red robe pacing on the other side of the cage.

Father places his arm over his eyes and bursts out crying. His whole body shakes, a scream bubbles up through the tears, mucus sticks in his throat. I reach for his arm to pull it away from his eyes when suddenly he pulls it away and the scream turns more into a growl. He sits up. I too scream alongside his growl, frustrated that I am unable to do anything but witness. I'm helpless in that I cannot change what I'm seeing, what has already happened in the distant past.

I realize my father is now quiet and crawling toward the door of the cage. He looks back at me and smiles. "Watch, learn!" he whispers. I stare at him, knowing somehow that he speaks directly to me. But how? This place is so frustrating! I let out a strangled, huffed, and aggravated growl.

The red robe, still hooded, is pacing faster, and my father hisses. The red robe stops and kneels against the door of the cage and my father rips the hood back. It is a woman, much smaller than the robe would have suggested. My father sighs and she gently touches his hurt cheek.

"Gwendolyn," he whispers.

She places a finger over her lips and pulls something from under the robe and waves it. I watch as my father shrinks, smaller and smaller. The female rests her hand upon the stone floor and my father crawls into her waiting palm.

"I've got you now, my Prince! Azlocke, let's get him out of here!"

She gently passes his small body to the waiting palm of a male, hooded, his face obscure. She waves her hand over my father slowly. He lays back in the male's palm and sleeps.

"Please try to rest, it will be a long journey." She gently closes the male's fingers up and over his small sleeping body, then she watches as the male disappears into the shadows, and she turns on her heel, cape billowing as she exits the chamber.

I am left in an empty chamber with my mouth hanging open. I shake my head and press my palms into my eyes. What is happening, *how* are they communicating with me? *Listen, watch, learn...* What, *what* is the point of these visions? To torture me? Never to be able to be reunited with my parents except in their memories? I scream at the empty room and then I am pulled from the giant cage and into a lavish room.

A handful of females surround my mum. I know these women. I have seen them before, in my pa's book of moving photos. Each one of them looks very worried, expect one. They stand at mum's feet. One gazes upon my mother with distain. I believe her name is Nuala.

The woman at her head is whispering a chant. My mum's head has stopped bleeding, and her eyes are fluttering. The other women help her sit up and prop her up with pillows. She stares at them as they all stand before her. Each one is smiling ear to ear, expect the one that one looks bored and irritated.

"Amanda. Welcome." The healer nods to her. "It pleases me to inform you that Drake has been secreted out of the castle and kingdom. His journey to a safer place will be long, but happily he is currently out of reach of the King." The woman bows deeply to her, winking at her. It's Gwendolyn, the same woman who shrank my father. The other females curtsy to mum, all but the last who nods at her and lets out a tired sigh. Nikilaus, Lottie, and Opal. I recognize their faces.

I take a double look at Gwendolyn, her beautiful translucent wings on display. I walk slowly to her and try to push aside the long heavy cape draped around her. My hand passes through it. The woman then turns to me. Startled, I back against the wall. She waggles her fingers at me, shaking her head. She is a small, short, and slender woman compared to the others. Her skin is a deep, rich brown, and she has gentle blue eyes and long ringlets of luscious black hair.

"Seriously! You see me?" I yell at Gwendolyn in case she might not be able to hear me.

A knock bangs against closed doors. All of the women jump, all but the one. Nuala looks bored.

"My Lady, may I enter?"

It is Molag's voice, coming from the other side. The healer of the group jumps and races toward the door. She glances back to my mum—she raises a finger to her lips. My mum nods. She gives a mighty pull upon the door and steps back, ushering in the King.

Molag enters the room, nods to Gwendolyn, then searches the room for my mum. He finds her reclined and surrounded by pillows. His face falls and he flashes her a soulfully sad smile and quickens his pace to reach her side. Mum jumps slightly and pushes back into the cushiony, oversized chair. Molag slows and sits at the edge and reaches for her hand.

"Your Majesty." Gwendolyn is standing right behind him. He examines Mum carefully. "I was able to stop the bleeding. She has only just awakened. I'm sure the creature is very overwhelmed. Would you please allow me more time with her to better prepare her for your presence?" She curtsies low.

"I only wish to bring her a gift." He shows her a small boxed parcel and places it in Amanda's hand.

My mum gazes at it.

"It's warm," Molag whispers to her. She takes a deep breath through her noise. I can smell the unique scent and butter. She opens the box.

"Fresh from the oven! My chef makes these." He fishes one out from the box. "Open." He waits and brings the buttery biscuit to her lips. She takes a small bite. Her eyes light up at the taste.

"You brought me cookies?" mum asks quietly.

"Well, we call them cakes. This is a coconut cake with small chocolate chucks." He smiles at her. She takes the cookie from him and quickly stuffs it in her mouth. Mum sighs with pleasure at the taste and proceeds to grab another.

"Ah, try this." He hands her a glass filled with white liquid. "Coconut milk makes these taste even better." He winks at her as she takes a small sip. Her eyes flash wide and she smiles, clearly confused but shoving another cake into her mouth. Her stomach growls loudly.

"Oh, My Lady, please do not weep. I'm afraid I have frightened you. You have nothing to fear from me." Molag chuckles softly. "I am but an old creature. Are you hungry?" he asks with a soothing voice. It makes my stomach turn but Mum holds her composure better. He strides over to a great hearth lit with a warm fire.

"Come, My Lady, have a seat before the fire with me. I will have more food called for you," he invites.

"Please, Your Majesty, allow her more time with us. A month, perhaps. Let us get her acquainted with her new life, her role here in the palace and the duties required of her. You have only just proclaimed her your new Queen. She is untrained. She hit her head awfully hard, My Lord, I'm sure she is very confused." Gwendolyn is cut off by his growl.

"You have already had long enough, Gwendolyn! No, leave us, all of you. Leave me with my new Queen so that we may become better acquainted." He coos this to them, his eyes locked upon my mum. "I too can teach her! I can show her how to behave as she is expected." Molag's words send a shiver down her spine.

The annoyed-looking Nuala speaks. "Your Highness." She bows. "Might I change your mind? Wasting your time with this pathetic creature, which I know you deeply despise... Why not join me, out on the terrace?" She crosses the room to his side. "We could enjoy each other's company instead, have tea and your favorite kind of cakes." She pauses in disgust at the coconut ones. She snaps her fingers and a servant materializes out of nowhere, bowing and gesturing to usher the King and Nuala out of the room. "You promised you would spend time with me." She looks up, searching for the right words while turning her hands. "Not with this *thing*." Her eyes flash malevolently at the King and he smiles a wicked smile.

"Yes, Nuala. You may try and entertain me for a while." He walks to Amanda. "Those cakes are Drake's favorite." He caresses Amanda's soft bruised cheek, causing her to wince in pain. He shakes his head at the reference to his son, then offers his arm to Nuala. "Gwendolyn, you have a couple hours. I'll be back for her tonight!" And with that he escorts Nuala from the room. She gazes over her shoulder with a satisfied look upon her face, turns her nose up at the other women left behind, and practically dances from the room.

"What a pompous horse's ass, that one!" Nikilaus says aloud once the door closes behind the King and Nuala.

"True, that may be, but if not for her jealous display, Amanda would be in his clutch right now. So, sad to say, you do owe Nuala a thank you later!" Gwendolyn whispers. "And you, Nikilaus! You know better than to speak of another Queen in such a manner!"

"Drake?" Amanda says in hardly a whisper.

Gwendolyn claps her hands. "Now Amanda, I had wished to gain more time, but we do not have it. The remaining Queens and I are going to have to mindshare with you. We will do two at a time." Gwendolyn pauses at the confused look my mother gives her. "It's best just to do and explain the process later. Maybe after we finish, your memories will return to you. You are now Molag's sixth wife. You are to be a Queen alongside us." She waves her hand before the other ladies. "You need years of training in a manner of hours, the knowledge and tips of how we have... how we have been successful at deceiving the King. Yes, unfortunately you'll be very grateful to us for this. We must hurry now—Nikilaus, Lottie, you two first. Opal and I will go next."

"Drake?" my mother questions as Nikilaus and Lottie place the tips of their fingers against her temples.

My mother's eyes dart around in their sockets as visions overtake her. Nikilaus's memories. Her birth, and growing up safe, and held so sacred amongst her pack. She is a shapeshifter, Werewolf of the Crescent Rose Moon pack. Nikilaus becomes her pack's Luna, their Queen, mated to the Alpha. So much love, brotherhood, and happiness amongst the pack. Visions of battles dance by as Amanda watches the werewolves fight against the King's army. Being outnumbered, they try and fail to save their Luna. So much death, so much blood, so many of her brothers and sisters slain as she is dragged from her home. Her mate is chained and beaten with silver. Wolfsbane is injected into his skin. His body violently seizes upon the earth as she is taken away, fighting in vain against her own chains of silver, trying to reach and comfort her mate.

Lottie's visions come next. A vampire and the High Queen of her coven, a thousand years in age, she watches her castle overthrown by the neighboring Giants and army of Goblins. Her people are butchered, their beautiful heads ripped from their bodies and placed upon stakes as trophies, all her precious children... Her maker, lover, and King is burned with heated iron rods.

I watch as the two other women press their palms side by side to my mother's forehead. Amanda's tears stream from her eyes, a sob chokes deep in her throat, gagging her. Opal is the only Elf Princess and Heir to her Kingdom. Amanda watches as Opal climbs down from her high balcony to meet her secret lover. They whisper promises to each other when a sword pierces his back and through his chest. Opal, covered in Conway's blood, warm and dripping from her face when she is wrenched away from him, being gagged and bound. She is ripped away from her home and family, unable to scream, her eyes painfully gazing back to Conway who kneels upon the ground, his shirt in tatters, shredded. The gaping wound where the sword impaled him is already slowly healing, the river of his flowing life force slowing, his pained eyes meeting hers. Opal fights against her restraints as the men drag her. Amanda weeps hard.

"Please, no more," she chokes out.

Gwendolyn smiles sadly and lets her visions flow through Amanda. Young Gwendolyn stands before her people, surrounded by her family and friends as they encourage her to find her wings. Her black hair messy and tangled, eyes shut tight, she feels inside herself as purple and black wings open and flutter against her back, raising her high into the air.

Another vision. Gwendolyn is older and holding the hand of another female in a ceremony of tying hands. Her mate and love, she embraces the woman with a passion-filled kiss as their people cheer their union.

Chaos erupts during that love filled and passionate embrace. Fae are slaughtered and left dead in heaping piles and Gwendolyn watches as her love is hit over the head. She screams and fights. Something hits her hard and the vision goes black.

My mum weeps and looks about the women before her.

"We're not done yet. We must teach you the rules, how you are to behave, what is expected of you," Gwendolyn whispers and wipes a tear away.

"Please, no more," Amanda whimpers.

"I am sorry but we must."

All four women replace their hands and my mum's body tightens and jerks in fits.

I hear a sigh come from beside me, and the vision blurs. The castle room turns to smoking wafts. When I reopen my eyes, I'm standing in a plain room with four small walls, a ceiling, and floor whitewashed in color.

"Hello?" I whisper.

"Merek," my mum's voice whispers back gently.

"Where are you? Where are we?" I question, looking over my shoulder.

"We're in-between. There's more I need you to see." She heaves a heavy sigh.

CHAPTER FOURTEEN

Dreams and Visions (Part Two)

My vision clears, and I am standing somewhere new on a bright and sunny day. I see a woman.

My mother's voice whispers to me, "This is Nuala, the High Queen. Listen to her thoughts, hear her words, and watch our memory of this place in time play before you. This is important for you to know, Merek." I nod and watch quietly.

Nuala is waiting impatiently for the sixth wife her Lord and High King has taken. She sits in a beautiful white sheer gown upon the stone bench near the fountain by the entrance of her garden. She is watching the water cascade when movement catches her eye within the pool. She leans closer. A vision of two young, identical Goblin girls flashes before her eyes. They are dancing and laughing in an overgrown field of wildflowers, mirror images, facing each other, when her sister caresses her cheek. The vision changes; a handsome Goblin of dark emerald skin and amber eyes leans into her to gently kiss her forehead. The birth of their baby girl, beautiful and pure, joyous and light. She watches the two flee, a hooded pair with a bundle secreted away under a traveling cloak.

"Nuala?"

Nuala sits upright and gulps at the air around her, begging that it refill her lungs. Hand pressed to her chest, she gazes up and into the sun. Her eyes find Amanda, the creature she has been waiting for.

"Nuala, are you alright? I truly didn't mean to startle you, forgive me, please," Amanda whispers, and flinches, waiting to be hit by the High Queen and her teacher.

"Yes, um. No. I was not startled just—I was just..." She gazes back into the pool but the images are gone. "I'm fine. Must be this heat." She wipes her brow and realizes she is perspiring.

Amanda cups her hand and dips it into the cool water. "Forgive me, you just look as though you've seen a ghost. Here, drink." She offers her hand.

Nuala glares at Amanda; her offer is absurd. Though her throat *is* dry and tight, and there's a true look of concern upon this creature's face for her wellbeing... She leans toward Amanda's offered hand. The new creature has infuriated her from the beginning and Nuala has made a point to make her new life here a miserable one. Amanda was originally human—human! Only recently turned hybrid. Half human, half Goblin. All due to the King's one and only frustrating, bastard heir, Drake. Sadly, for Amanda, her head was hit so hard that day that she somehow mysteriously forgot all of her memories... even the memory of her only child... Nuala wonders what Amanda will do, how she will react when one day her memories are returned to her. Nuala is running out of time; Molag grows restless and is more vicious than ever. Amanda will be a strong ally and one Nuala desperately needs... but has she taken things too far with the other wives? With Amanda? Will Amanda be willing to listen, will she empathize with her?

She drinks the cool liquid. She has put Amanda through hell and back learning the ways of the Goblins and all other creatures that call this Realm their home. Nuala was forced to marry the King, her life and dreams all stolen, taken ruthlessly from her, along with her freedom. She takes a deep, unsettled breath at the thought of all her daughters. With each day that Amanda takes her abuse, Nuala's heart softens little by little. Even now she thinks of the wretched creature before her as a friend.

"How are you?" Amanda asks gingerly.

"Fine, thank you. Let us go off to the garden now for your teaching. We must begin for the day."

Nuala stops to assess the sun and looks back to Amanda, fully seeing her for what feels like the first time. Her face is badly bruised, her one arm obviously broken as she cradles it with her other arm, dried blood on her mouth. Molag has beaten her again, his vengeance upon his son. Now that Amanda has bonded so strongly to Drake, poor Drake feels every blow that is made upon his beloved. He has been secreted away and is unable to protect her or rescue her. Their mate bond makes him feel it all.

Nuala retrieves a cloth from a small hidden pocket in her gown and dips it into the water.

"*Ree-parr-yaa,*" Nuala whispers, and shoots a glaring, firm look at the lame arm. A bone-crunching *snap* and an agonizingly breathy howl erupts from Amanda.

"Sorry, dearling," Nuala utters under her breath, and begins wiping away the blood from Amanda's lip and chin.

Amanda steps back from her. She takes a sharp breath in and bends at the waist. She obviously is trying to compose herself and when she stands again, "Thank you," she says through gritted teeth. "But I wish not for the High Queen to risk dirtying her hands or gown by helping to clean my face. Dearling? What does that even mean?" Amanda asks, exasperated.

Nuala shrugs. She really had hated this creature when she arrived, but the half breed somehow found a soft spot within her.

"It's a term of endearment," she states flatly.

Nuala wonders if it is Amanda's bravery, her tenacity, her perseverance with all the torment she's been put through. Amanda is still clinging to a false hope of a lie that Molag told her years ago when she first arrived, that she would soon have her memories back, but it has been years now. It was an evil trick he pulled and he has been reprogramming her ever since. Plus, she has dealt with everything Nuala has thrown at her over the years.

Nuala is sure the other Queens are helping Amanda with her studies of the histories because she does not care if she learns her lessons or not. Nuala chuckles to herself. How many times has she whacked the backs of Amanda's hands when she did not get the cutlery correct upon the table? Or the time when the half-breed almost killed one of her most prized flowers when she was being taught how to collect its delicate leaves and to pick the seeds for storing? Or the time she tended the rose bushes and pulled too tightly on the thicket branch loaded with thorns? The branch sent her flying backwards and sprayed her with its thorns, covering her in blood. Gwendolen was pulling thorns out of her for days. Truly, the small slivers of newly grown thorns caused her the most pain. Nuala had not cared; Amanda was something new that one day would be grown tired of. Nuala is the High Queen, the fifth and youngest of the wives, the only pure-bred

Goblin wife who would bare his children. She knows the King holds no true love for the creature that is Amanda, other than for her beauty. He treats her like a beloved grandchild when he is not torturing her. She is a curiosity, something to ponder about, something no one else has and is his ticket to torturing his rebels and his son into submission. Still, this sad little creature is growing on her.

How long has it been? she thinks to herself. Fifteen years? Ha, still a baby compared to her two hundred years. How has Amanda gotten under her skin? Why does Nuala now feel concern over this fragile thing? She smiles.

"Come," Nuala beckons, and Amanda reluctantly inches forward.

Nuala dabs the cloth at Amanda's mouth, then waves her hand in front of her face. "*Sto-ffee-noo*," Nuala whispers. "Better?"

Amanda touches her face and the thrumming pain is gone. "Yes." Amanda tries to smile at Nuala, but she hates it here, this evil world, and desperately wants to be away from it, find her memories, and find her way home. She thinks she died that night only to wake here, her body somehow transformed from what it was once, surrounded by five other women and having to witness their painful memories, forced to serve the most wicked of all, the King and this beautiful but hideous evil Queen.

"Come, I wish to share something with you."

Nuala leaves the cloth by the fountain and turns to the entrance of her garden. Once they are both through the door, Nuala chants under her breath, waves her arms, and pulls her hands to her chest. An enchantment ripples through the air and encircles her favorite place, her sanctuary, her garden. Ghostly figures of Amanda and Nuala engaged in a lesson emerge in the center.

Amanda lets out a soft yelp.

"A secret enchantment, my dearling." Nuala casually glances at the ghostly figures of themselves. "This way."

Amanda follows behind Nuala, still in disbelief of the ghostly version of herself being smacked by Nuala. Her ghostly replica has given Nuala a displeasuring response.

Amanda rubs her cheek at the phantom pain. "Why do you hate me so?" she whispers.

Nuala stops at the base of a large, ancient oak in the middle of the garden, and then gently lays a kiss upon its bark. A small black door materializes and opens slightly. Nuala pushes it open, taking a deep breath, closing her eyes, and smiling as she enters.

Amanda glances back at the ghostly figures. Nuala is making her ghostly double kneel on the small pebbles. She can already see the false blood drawing from her knees.

A hand grabs Amanda, yanking her through the small door.

"Welcome, dearling, to my sanctuary!" Nuala beams.

Amanda gazes slowly around the darkened room. It is much too big to be able to fit inside the trunk of the tree outside. A large hearth sits across from her, unlit, with all sorts of kettles and pots for cooking. A small table sits nearby with a steaming porcelain tea pot and place settings for two. An old looking sparkling silver tray appears with tasty treats. Candles awake and light here and there, giving her a better view. To the left there is a full wall of shelves filled with books and a rolling ladder. A large and plush oversized chair sits before the books, just waiting for its owner to curl up into it and read. Beautiful rugs of vibrant colors in every shade cover a dirt floor but nothing is dirty or stained. To the right, fifteen cradles line the opposite wall, each gently swaying and rocking. A large painting of two young girls hangs over the hearth. They are identical and dancing among overgrown wildflowers. Crowns of poppies halo their beautiful heads.

The tea pot rises into the air and pours hot water into glass cups, the liquid darkening as though the tea is already seeping. White clay plates float out of a cupboard and come to rest upon the small table while tiny desserts fly to fill in empty places among the plates. Nuala has already seated herself at the small table. Amanda makes her feet shuffle forward.

"Dearling, please come sit with me," Nuala says so happily.

Amanda approaches the proffered chair that pulls itself out for her and inhales deeply. The chair hits the back of her knees, causing her to sit down hard, and scoots itself in.

"Th... an... k—" Amanda swallows hard, clears her throat "—you, Nuala."

"Isn't it lovely, dear one? This is my sanctuary, my safe and happy place. I have never once let anyone in here, not once, no one! You should feel very honored indeed." Nuala grins at her.

Amanda nods, eyes wide, still gazing around. She finds an enormous map above the door; studying it, she finds it is a map of all the Realms, even the human world. A violin plays softly at the far end of the row of cradles, a hushed lullaby of a sad and sorrowful tune. The cradles all swing in time to the melody. A glittering of light catches her eye. She sees a small table with a large crystal ball hovering above it, slowly spinning on an invisible axis. From her peripheral vision, a cradle has stopped its gentle swing but soon starts again. Amanda realizes Nuala is speaking to her.

"Amanda?" Nuala snaps.

"Yes, forgive me. I'm very honored, High Queen, I just—" Amanda stops because the same cradle has again stopped.

Nuala follows her gaze and immediately lifts from her chair and races gracefully over to the cradle, cooing and shushing as she goes. She sends the cradle rocking again, bends into the cradle whispering sweet lullabies, and then returns to her seat.

"I no longer hate you, Amanda," Nuala simply states and sips her tea, taking a small bite of something soft and cake-like. "I just realized you have been with us for fifteen years now. Somehow you have, may I say, proven yourself I suppose. You are brave and courageous. No matter what I do to you, you still show me grace. Actually, dearling, I do believe I am proud of you."

Amanda sits shocked still. Even her breath doesn't come. She blinks. The cradle again stops but soon begins to sway again. A blue fire lights within the hearth, its flames dancing slowly. It too seems to dance sadly along to the tune.

Sadness presses and weighs down upon Amanda like a heavy blanket. The two children in the painting above skip in slow motion, hands locked together, prancing around an invisible marked circle, both smiling and laughing to each other. Each candle within the room dims. A crescent moon and twinkling stars appear suspended above the cradles. A ghost echo of cooing ripples from the cradles.

"I was much like you when I first arrived in his Lord's Kingdom. Like you and the other girls, I too was taken from my home." She offers Amanda a small, sad smile. "That's my sister, there." She points above the hearth. "The King did not know of my sister, thank the heavens, or I'm afraid he would have had her too. Luckily, she is safe. Well, I do believe, at least. I'm not so sure that she is as safe as I once believed. Our connection is all but nonexistent now."

Nuala takes a sip of her tea and a deep breath. "I've never shared my tale with anyone, not even the other Queens. It's my secret to keep, you see. It's all that I can call mine." She pauses and looks at Amanda. "I just think you, of all beings, understand. You see, I was out at my village market when the King came through that day and spotted me.

To my great regret, my cloak's hood had fallen from my head while gathering the goods that my mother had sent me to get." She gives a nervous laugh, then bites her lip. "My mother warned me so many, *so many* times not to let my face be seen. She told horrific stories of the past King—he would take anything, anyone he coveted.

"The Old King, Molag's father, was dead. Why should I fear his son? How stupid and careless I was! The new King, his High Lord, just happened around the bend in the dirt road and into the same market and instantly locked eyes upon me." She gives another nervous, almost crazed laugh. "You might say it was destiny, what took hold that moment when he saw me. How cruel fate can be." Again, an almost suppressed laugh on the brink of insanity rips from her lips, but a scream leaps from her eyes. "The next day, my parents were made to hand me over to the soldiers he had sent for me." She sighs a heavy sigh. "I was once a different being, happy and joyous even. I had already chosen my mate and we were happy. I had a loving, strong partner who built our small home and provided for both our newborn daughter and me. A handsome, strong mate." She drifts in her memory to a face Amanda cannot see, but then she can. Her eyes widen in surprise as Nuala's ghostly mate materializes near her shoulder, smiling and whispering something in her ear. Amanda's body freezes as Nuala continues. "We were quite happy. My sister, forlorn." She points again to the portrait of the girls dancing. "As she, too, loved my mate, but he ultimately chose me. He chose me and I chose him." She sips her tea and stares off into the distance.

"Nuala?" Amanda whispers.

"Ah. So, yes. Why, you must be asking, was I in the market that awful day? My mother needed assistance; recently she had fallen ill and was not strong enough yet for the walk to the market. My mother and sister watched my daughter and I go to the market that day. Sometimes when I remember back, it is as if my mother and sister had planned it, knew I would drop my guard, allowed my comfort to overcome me when I should have shown caution and heeded my mother's multiple warnings. Almost like they knew already that the King would come that day, for why could my sister not have gone? Right?" She pauses, a crazed and angry look stuck in her eyes. She continues in an almost insane, possessed, and pained voice.

"I was given a day to prepare, one day to gather my little belongings. Forced to say my goodbyes and leave my home forever. I begged my sister to take my place, choose the palace and King over the impoverished life we had led. Instead she chose to pose as me, so that she could leave with my daughter and mate. My sister refused to help me and eagerly took hold of my LIFE! She told me she feared the King would discover that she was only the sister to the woman he had chosen, that her life would then be in danger if she lied to him. I begged her over and over that I had already taken a mate, that I had given birth to a child. She all but laughed in my face as my family hid my secret from the King.

"My parents decided that my sister would take my mate and claim my daughter as her own. My parents sent for an Elfin witch to place an enchantment over my mate, sister, and my newborn baby daughter and transform them into different beings... a cloaking spell of some kind. They fled that night into the world. My mate and sister left me behind, tossed aside as though they harbored no love for me at all. I lost everything that night, my life... but most important of all, I lost my first-born child." Nuala pauses, breathing heavily after having spilled every horrible truth from her own lips. Why has she done that? This information can surely be used and turned against her. She begins to cry; she can no longer hold the tears back.

"MY CHILD!" She sobs harder. "At least," she gasps, "my daughter is safe. I can feel it in the marrow of my bones that she lives, but my mate and sister, I think they perished," Nuala sobs.

Amanda appears beside her, arms slowly opening. Nuala falls into them as the pain, heartache, and everything she has held back and secreted away comes crashing forth. Amanda holds her while she lets it all flow forth and out of her. Her body succumbs to the violent shudders she cannot contain. Amanda holds her 'til the last of her shaking stops. Amanda lets her go and gently kisses her forehead.

"I'm so sorry, Nuala," Amanda whispers. She leaves Nuala's side and walks to the cradle, the one that once again has stopped rocking. She approaches quietly, reaches for the side of the cradle. A pink bundle of silk lays within. A baby, she thinks, and looks in. A skeletal head, milky swirling pools where eyes should have been, two tiny skeleton fists clenched and shaking, a gaping toothless mouth open in a silent cry... Amanda jumps back as Nuala races to the side of the cradle. Gently lifting the bundle of pink silk and bones, the small creature continuing its silent scream, she bounces and coos at the bundle, bringing the tiny skeleton hand bones to her lips, running the infant's bony hand across them. The bundle slows in its struggle, the milky pools swirling, calmed and turned an iridescent blue. Nuala places a sweet adoring kiss upon the forehead bone. The infant places its bone thumb in its gaping mouth and Nuala lays it back in its cradle, setting it back to rocking.

Everything slows and the room begins to spin. Amanda realizes that Nuala has enchanted the bones of her infant daughters, a tear running down her cheek at the hopeless depression Nuala must feel at losing her children. She keeps them alive the only way she knows how, to keep them close to her, always.

"Amanda!" Nuala whispers, reaching out to her. "I should have never done this."

Nuala bites Amanda's forearm. Amanda screams in pain as Nuala's venom enters her bloodstream. As it does, all of her own life's memories return. Nuala licks the wound. Amanda shakes in anger as her memories flood her. It was Nuala—spiteful, evil Nuala—who kept them from her all these years. She hits Nuala hard in the face and hears the satisfying crunch of her nose breaking. Nuala's head is thrown back from the force of the punch; she wipes a finger beneath her nose while the blood trickles down.

"You!" Amanda seethes. "You took my memories!"

"I am sorry for what I have done to you." She waves her hand at the cradles. "These are my other daughters, the daughters the King and High Lord blessed me with, but also took from me. The daughters he killed, the daughters he did not love or want. They were not the son he so desperately craves to have, my daughters he has murdered out of his frustration at me for not giving him a son. The daughters he took from me to punish me." Tears slide down her cheeks.

"It is not entirely my fault that I cannot give him a son. I was given a curse, you see, preventing me from bearing him a son. It was done so that no son of mine could overthrow his only heir." Nuala takes a ragged breath, seething with anger. "Elgeeva's son," she proclaims, "the witch who transformed my mate, sister, and child, the one who placed this curse upon me of only bearing daughters so that her son could survive and live to be the future King, to bring *peace*, to help bring back the *last* of the *ancient beings*—the Mother of creation!" Nuala screams to Amanda, who has a perplexed look upon her face. Nuala continues, "Once, long, long ago, the creatures who roamed this world were not like us. We are the species now living. Our ancestors were created of the ancients' imaginations and were created to complete a better world. They were Ancient beings of Divine Power, and they created all that is around us. This place, the air we breathe, are because of them. They created the species that we are today.

"Where there is power and love, war always follows. The Divine Powers above and apart from this world bickered and fought amongst themselves as to which of the created species were the purest and highest of the beings. Only one of the Divine Powers loved all of them equally. She left the warring Divine Powers in their Realm and came to our world. She proclaimed herself among us as Mother. She cared for all the creatures, shielding us, protecting us from the wars that waged above. She then began to mate with each of the different species. She guarded her new lineage fiercely, shielding them from the rest of them in fear of an uprising against her newly created offspring.

"Over the millennia, the Divine Powers above all but destroyed themselves, eliminating each other into nothing but energy. Mother survived here, in this Realm, and happily blocked what energies were left above from corrupting the lives below." Nuala tries to read Amanda's features. "Until one day a creature captivated her. Her lineage had not been made from actual love, per se, but the love of all. This one creature had somehow reached a deeper level within her and she fell for him. Sadly, he was evil and wicked, drunk and poisoned from the Divine Powers of her blood and energy after he mated with Mother. He became jealous. He abused the love she had for him. He was able to overcome her and imprison her in another Realm away from this one. He transformed her Goddess being into a new creature, rumored to be a hideous and grotesque bodily form. Rendering her completely helpless in the prison he locked her away in, he then conquered most of the Realms. That wicked creature was Molag's father, the Dead King." Nuala stops to examine Amanda's face for understanding and then continues.

"According to Elgeeva the Elfin Witch, Molag was once a wonderful, loving, and caring soul. He was everything the Old King despised. Having many heirs to choose from, the Old King had finally chosen one male heir who would eventually rule all, though of course that time would only come when the Old King was fit to die. The other, older sons grew crazed with anger, knowing the Old King would never choose to die. They recruited each other and plotted against the Old King. Anger and jealousy between the sons fueled their hatred of the King and each other.

"Somehow his sons succeeded—they were able to fatally wound him, but each died fighting against him. The story I know is that the Old King was inflicted with many, many gaping wounds. He could not heal fast enough for all of them. It was then when he called for Molag, the one and only son who had refused his brothers, who now cared for and sat with the dying Lord and his father, Trenton. He was the one son that Trenton hated the most! Molag was so filled with love and joy," Nuala states condescendingly. "The Old King bit the boy, filling him with the evil poison that had been given to him from the Divine Powers above. It too overpowered and turned Molag evil. That poisonous venom carried the essence of the dying King. He proclaimed to his son that he would take over his body so that he could live on. Insane with rage, Molag destroyed all. That is the supposed story of Molag.

"Molag does not know of a prophesied son, of Molag's bloodline! The prophecy says, *it is his lineage that will find Mother and return her to this world, restore her to her true goddess form, and with the Mother's help will overthrow the evil poison and at last bring peace to our worlds.*" She takes a deep breath. "The other half of this prophecy that Molag *does* know of is of the female of this Realm that will rise up alongside the heir. She will defeat and kill the evil King. It is told of these two children that they conceive a new species, a tribute of peace." Nuala sits back in her chair.

"Molag's bloodline?" Amanda asks. "His only lineage is Drake and—" Amanda gasps. "Merek," she gasps. "My son!"

"Yes, one of the only two male heirs. He honestly believes that the prophecy will never come true, and certainly not now. Drake is no longer a threat to him, and he believes Merek long dead." Nuala takes a breath and races on, "Merek is alive and well."

Amanda stares hard at Nuala. "Why share this?" She waves at the haven of Nuala's surroundings. "Why did you take my memories from me?" Something she has kept hidden all this time, and holds so dear… "Why now? Why? Tell me!" Amanda demands.

"I believe I know the reason I truly hated you. Deep down, I knew but could not convince myself of it 'til now." She gives a small laugh and coughs. "You were the new and shiny thing. I thought just *maybe* Molag would perhaps favor you over me. This is all I have, what little power I wield. It's mine. But now I think I know why you have finally gotten under my skin." Nuala takes a small breath. "He looks so much like you, Amanda. He is growing quickly into a handsome man. Would you like to see your son?"

Nuala smiles and lifts from the chair. She retrieves the large glass ball from the small table. It is suspended above her hands, its axis at a slow spin.

With tears in her eyes, Amanda says, "You play cruel tricks, Nuala…"

Before Amanda can finish, Nuala waves her hand and whispers a few words.

There inside the glass's axis, a boy appears. She looks right into Merek's beautiful eyes. He looks to be about ten years old. Amanda sobs and smiles as she watches her son go about his day. He swims and fishes, walks along paths accompanied by an enormous wolf that protects him, he picks berries and cooks himself a meal. Amanda sits enthralled and watches her son for many hours until Nuala gently pulls her away. They need to return to the castle. Nuala promises that Amanda is welcome here in her haven and she can check on Merek when they can sneak away.

"Why are you doing this?" Amanda weeps as she holds the crystal.

"Because I believe the female in the prophecy is my daughter," Nuala whispers to her, "and the male, I believe is your son." She pauses, licking her lips to moisten them. "I have also finally grasped what was alluding me about you. Now being Goblin-made, you have power of your own. It's time to train you, hone your abilities, and set the path so that our children will meet. Once you are ready, you will find my daughter. You will nudge her toward the path of your son."

Amanda interrupts her. "Why not help me to find my son?" she asks desperately.

"Because no one can truly find him, Amanda," Nuala answers gently. "I have glimpses of him, but not his location. Elgeeva's magic is strong and shields him well. It's an ancient rune magic that cloaks your son, and until he leaves the bubble Drake and Elgeeva made for him, he will remain lost to us.

"Time is also different here. In this Realm of the King, his magic and mist mess with the nature of things. A day to Merek is five days to us here. So, when you saw your son just now, he was about ten years of age, but these five years without you and Drake, on this side of the realm is more like ten years. Time is very distorted in other Realms as well due to Molag and his mist. It corrupts and makes 'timing' a tricky thing. We must begin your training, reach into the well of power building inside you, and bide our time."

CHAPTER FIFTEEN

Difficult Travels

Brice is nuzzling me awake. Images of the past blur and disappear, and I blink against the bright morning's light shining into the cave. I wrap my arms around Brice and bury my face into his fur.

Rowan stirs. She is laying on top of me. She gently whispers my name. My body screams in pain, having Rowan sleeping on me all night. I yearn to move my limbs. I gently lift Rowan away from me and quickly but clumsily lay her upon the floor. She still sleeps. I gingerly lift my body and stretch, grabbing the satchel and digging for food. I'm starving.

"Goodness, I thought you'd never wake! It's afternoon, Merek." Brice huffs at me and I throw him a chunk of the meat. "That was a powerful vision you witnessed. It appeared to me that you were having a bad dream, so I opened the connection between us. I saw everything you saw."

"Good, that'll save time then. So, you understand, we have to leave now." I look to Rowan, still sleeping, her skin already turning a slightly darker hue of emerald just like my mother.

"Rowan said it would be too dangerous to travel today—just look at her!" Brice says. "She's unconscious and still with fever from your venom. Plus, what of the horse and that bloody cow?" Brice glares at me. Bella and Winston look up at us.

"You saw the vision. We cannot wait—we must get Pa's book back, and he *is* alive! Well, at least in the past he was. You set us on this journey a year ago saying you heard my pa, telling us to leave the woods in the first place. It will be slow, and the horse and I can take turns carrying Rowan, but we must try, Brice. I have this feeling that soon I'll get to see him and Mum again." I race about the cave, picking up and stuffing the satchel with our loose things. "I'll carry Rowan. Think you can get the cow and horse to follow you?" I look at the three animals and each one sighs at me in turn. "Right, let's get on with it then, everyone into the water!"

I manage to keep to Rowan bundled in the blanket and her head out of the water, but I nearly drown myself in the process while the animals sit on the shore chuckling at me.

"Thanks for the help!"

I huff and puff and adjust Rowan in my arms to cradle her. I am about to lead our party around the right side of the rock face when something moving and glowing in a thick bush catches my eye.

"Whoa, Brice, did you see that?" I ask, laying Rowan down in the sand.

"No, I didn't see anything."

He follows me to the bush, sniffing the air and scanning behind it. I reach out to part the bush when a gust of wind whips through it, and something leaps out and into another to the left.

"There, just there, did you see it?" I ask, walking over to the next bush.

"I don't like this, Merek! Whatever it is smells strange, like—"

I cut him off. "A lost one does not move like that. Whatever it is, it's definitely very small. Look, see! The bush—it glows!"

I feel so excited, so happy, and it is all due to whatever little tiny thing is hiding in the bush. I point to Brice to circle around the back of the bush and I poke around in the sand of the beach with one foot, pretending to be interested in the sand instead, a distraction from Brice circling behind. Once Brice is in position, having slowly walked toward the glowing and now pulsating bush, I get closer. It looks like a small ball of light bouncing erratically inside the bush from branch to branch. It's so beautiful and the light moves so hypnotically that a smile spreads across my lips.

The dancing light, it feels like it's filling me with so much joy and happiness that I can barely contain myself. I leap unexpectedly, surprising Brice, my arms reached out, trying to cup and trap the ball of fiery light between my hands. Brice howls at my sudden movements. I crash awkwardly into the bush, branches and thorns grabbing at flesh all over my body. I wince against the pain and gasp for a breath. I have knocked the air from my lungs.

Between my hands I can feel something moving, a tiny something slamming into my palms, trying to escape. I gather myself and take in my injuries, which aren't so bad, just a few bleeding puncture wounds. But I no longer feel any pain; all that matters is the catch I have made. I bring my hands to one eye and create an ever so small opening to try to peer in. I pull back in surprise at a blinding flash of light that causes my eye to water. I laugh out loud and practically dance and skip with delight. Brice has come around and is sitting before me, his head cocked to one side, just staring at me.

"Ouch!" I yell, almost dropping the tiny thing between my hands. "No biting!" I look at Brice, completely surprised by such a pain from something so small.

"It smells of old magic, Merek. Release it!" Brice growls.

"Ouch!" It stings so bad that my hands spasm and part from one another just enough for the bouncing ball of light to fly out. It flies so fast away from me.

"Quick, Brice, follow it!" I call over my shoulder, and watch him sigh at me as he curls up next to Rowan on the beach. I scan the woods before me; nothing moves, no floating ball of light. My heart aches at losing it and I run deeper into the woods and stop to scan again. This time I see a faint glow emanating from a tree branch, shielded by leaves. The outline against the leaf looks like that of a small, tiny woman. It is bent over, catching its breath. I tip-toe ever so quietly and reach up to the leaf. Just as my hand is about to encircle it, a tiny face peeks at me from around the leaf.

"Got you!" I laugh and run back to the beach. Again, I feel the tiny thing slam into my palms. "No biting, or else! I cannot promise I will not squish you! *No biting*," I say slowly and loudly at my hands, hoping it will understand. I sit quickly next to Brice and hold my hands before his nose. He raises his head sleepily and looks bored. He sniffs then sneezes. He shakes his head, looks to me, then lays his head back down.

"Release it, Merek, or you'll have trouble!" Brice sneezes again.

"You don't even want to see it?" I tease, and laugh again. Then I feel it trying to separate my fingers. It is crawling and pushing its way through! I squish my fingers tightly together, but it is no use; the tiny thing is about to emerge from the webbing of my first and middle finger. Two tiny hands push up and through to the surface. Next, the tiniest head comes smiling after.

"It's a tiny woman, Brice! Look, see!" I proclaim at the top of my lungs, so full of joy. Brice lifts his head as I shove my hand into his face. Two enormous eyes stare at the tiny hand waving at him. I laugh out loud. His eyes are crossed and so surprised. I fall back in the sand, rolling back and forth in laughter.

I sit up and wipe at my eyes. Brice is still staring at the tiny thing.

"Hello, Merek!" the tiniest shriek yells up to me. Now it is my turn to stare in surprise.

"Um, hello?" I say just above a whisper, and slowly open my fingers to give her more room but not enough to fly away again. I bring her closer to my face so I can examine her better.

"Merek! Can you hear me?" she yells again. I nod. "Oh, good, yes, could you please open your hand and release me so that I might—" I cut her off; I close my hands and push her very gently back down into my palm, sealing her in.

"No," I laugh, "you'll fly away again! How are you so ridiculously small? What is your name? How do you know mine?" I chuckle. "Wait! I know you! From a picture! Where did you come from? Why do you glow? You have the most beautiful little wings! How can you fly? They look much too small to hold you. NO biting! OUCH!"

Her tiny hands reappear at the webbing of my thumb and she pops out her head and takes a large breath.

"I cannot breathe in there! Put me down this instant! Down, down, down!" she demands.

"I'm sorry, I cannot. I honestly have never felt so happy than while holding you! It made my heart break when you flew off. No, I'll just keep holding you!" I smile at her.

"I am a Fae, or, umph… is it Fairy? Do you know those words?" she yells louder. "Fae? Fairy?" she asks, and I nod again. "I've been looking for you! I was sent by your grandmother to find you and bring you to her. My name—" she stops and snaps tiny fingers at my dreamy expression. "Focus, Merek, focus! My name is Sorcha. *Focus*. Merek, did you hear me?"

I giggle. "Sorcha! Yes, that's right! What a pretty name for a pretty lady," I coo.

"Put me down, Merek, down, down! You must! My skin secretes a liquid that is quickly absorbed into the blood stream of any attacker so that I can get away. If you do not put me down soon, you'll be knocked out in a deep sleep for well over a week! You've been holding me much too long!" she screams at me.

This time Brice bites my arm and holds it 'til I finally open my hand fully for her to fly out. A bright blast of light and warmth, and a small woman stands upon the beach. She is dressed in ribbons of silver tied at her neck and intricately wrapped around her torso, belly exposed where the ribbon wraps tightly around her hips. She has thin brown sandals upon her feet. She kneels and carefully looks over Rowan, feeling her forehead, pealing the blanket gently away from her. She checks the bite mark I have made upon her, then gently traces a swirling pattern on her arm. She walks over to me, takes my arm, and traces the mirror image of Rowan's.

She is a lot bigger now, but still small. How did she grow so quickly? She is the size of a small child, much shorter even than Rowan. My mouth hangs open; she gently closes it and searches my face, turning my head this way and that. She is so small, has a beautiful skin tone that makes her look like she was made of the blackest black but at the last moment a swirl of cream was added just to lighten her a hint. Her wings, a golden honey color, stand out against the silver in intricate designs. They flutter every now and then as she checks me over. She passes a hand over my wounds made by the bush and each quickly heals. She has one green eye and one blue, like a rich and luscious green field meeting a calm and gentle sea. Dark black messy hair is piled high upon her head.

"Have you been searching long for me?" I ask in a whisper.

"Yes. You, dear boy, have proven exceedingly difficult to find at times. I had hoped to have reached you at your father's house, but you had already left." She goes back to Rowan. "We knew you'd be gone for a long time before returning to the forest. Three years, yes?" She rubs her chin.

"Wait, what? Three years? I've only been gone less than one year in the human realm," I reply, thinking of the timeline. Of losing Brice at the border, meeting Rowan, and the time I have stayed with her until now.

"One of the *human* years. Time is different there versus here. We were able to regroup, though, build a stronger fortress, gather more and strengthen our numbers. Lots of training, of course. Your grandmother sent me a few days ago to search again for you. I needed to find you before you found your father's house again. You disappeared after crossing the boundary the first time. I was unable to find you even there in the human Realm, but sensed you when you came back through, yes. Still I couldn't find you 'til you reemerged from the protective lines of the boundary. Your father's charm held true—held true," she repeats, smiling brightly at me. She pulls a flask from the wraps of fabric at her hip and lifts Rowan's head to get her to drink.

I stop her. "Is that water?"

"No, it is a special potion brewed by your grandmother to help the child. We need to move, and fast, and she cannot in this condition, no, no. She will slow us down and cause us issues along our path back to your father's, then to meet your grandmother. Many obstacles lay ahead, yes." She becomes nervous now, and tips the drink into Rowan's mouth and helps her swallow by massaging her throat.

She tosses the empty flask into the sand. I retrieve it and give it a sniff, then hold it out before Brice's strong nose. "Citron leaves," we both say between our connection.

"It smells of healing magic." Brice sneezes once more. "It should be safe for Rowan. I sense no evilness from its smell but I'm sure it tastes quite foul," Brice finishes in our connection, his eyes watering from smelling it.

"Alright, time to set off." Sorcha stands but I grab her arm, then remember the secretion she oozes that will made me sick and quickly let go. She laughs.

"Fast learner! Good learner," she laughs again. "I only secrete my protection oil when I am small." She eyes my quickly withdrawing arm.

"You remind me of someone. Well, I think she is of your kind." I pause, swallowing hard, hoping she may know news of my mother. "In a dream and a picture, I saw a female like you. She was helping my mother, trying to protect her. She lives in the palace, her name is... oh, no, um..." I stutter.

"Gwendolyn?" she replies.

"Yes! Do you know her well? Do you know of my mother, Amanda? Is she well? Is she alive?" I shout so fast.

"That tale is not for me to tell. As for Gwendolyn, yes, I know her. She was taken from the village of our people long, long ago, forced to marry and become enslaved by King Molag. He wants, he takes. All in the name of keeping peace. He has taken wives from each of the Realms to ensure no one rises against him. No one will rise against him for fear he would hurt the Queens of the species he took from us." She spits angrily at the ground.

"The other women, wives... Nuala," I remember.

"Nuala is the worst!" Sorcha's face twists in disgust. "I have not seen Gwendolyn or heard from her in many years. One hundred years, I believe." A tear falls from the green eye as she closes it and her body shakes. "She is the reason I fight, she is the reason I risk everything in hopes that one day I might be able to see her beautiful face one more time." She stops walking. "Gwendolyn is my mate," she whispers, "truly mine, only mine. My Gwendolyn, my love belongs with me." She pauses and looks to me, her cheeks flaming red, waiting for me to say something, and when I return her sad look she continues. "When Mother returns, she will fix everything. When her powers return..." Sorcha whispers.

Bella strides alongside Sorcha, licking her hand; the sweet cow is trying to comfort her.

"Mother? You mean the Mother of Creation?" I ask.

"She is of the Old, one of the old and ancient beings that once ruled all of the nothingness. And that nothingness, it saddened the beings of old. So they created this." Sorcha spreads her hands and arms wide, gesturing all around us. "The ancient ones—or the creators—were made up of four different Divine beings. The purest forms of light resembling the first Elves, Goblins, um..." She thinks hard. "You know the word Vampire? Do you know the term?" I nod my head yes and she continues. "And humans. I'm not sure of their proper name. The four of old were gifted with strong magics, very old magic, Divine. One day they noticed their powers dwindling and dying, and desperate to save and preserve themselves, they created birthlings—copies, if you will, of their own Divine selves. So then there were eight instead of four. Their power returned, but their birthlings were dying as their power grew. They decided to try interbreeding with each other, the two male divine powers with the two female divine powers.

"The two couplings created new life within the females' bodies. After the birth of the two new beings, one male and one female, the four divine females traded partners to create two new species so they would then have four younglings and be eight being again. The Divine continued their interbreeding to create more and more, 'til one day three of the deities felt there were too many younglings. The three Divines grew jealous, suspicious of the younglings and their power; they feared that their creations would overthrow them, becoming more powerful. They forbid cross-species breeding. They overruled the Goddess of the Moon, who chose and gave the younglings their mates. Instead they forced their creations to mate with like species, creating less powerful Purebloods." Sorcha pauses to scan the woods, accounting for each member of our traveling party.

"The Mother was powerful and disagreed with the other three, so she left their world and came here to live with us. Her precious children, she loved us more than all, more than her own being. She stayed here and protected us from the raging war the three deities held above, 'til one day Mother's deity sister entered our world, pregnant with child and full of fear. She told Mother how she and their brother teamed up to fight and kill the other deity brother. They were at peace, just the two Divines that remained above, 'til she learned she was carrying a child. The remaining deity brother went mad and was constantly trying to kill her and the child.

"Mother hid her sister 'til the youngling was born but watched as her sister died after the birth. The youngling had evil in it but her love for all the creatures led her to let it live. She hid it away in the Goblin Realm for it to grow. In that time, the younglings of the Realms continued to grow and thrive with new powers and abilities. Mother had to punish the last remaining deity and weakened him and trapped him there." Sorcha points a tiny finger high to the sky above.

"The youngling of her sister grew into a fine creature and she was smitten with it more so than any youngling. The evil she saw in it as a baby was still there. She thought if she just shared a small amount of her blood, she could cure the bad. It did not work—it made it worse and he turned into the evilest creature this world has seen. Then one day Mother disappeared and was gone. She still lived; her proof was all around us.

"The youngling that seduced and tricked Mother was Molag's father, the Old King, Trenton. We need to find where Trenton hid Mother. A prophecy is told of two souls, one male and one female, who will lead the army and help find her. Your grandmother believes you two," she points at Rowan, then me, "are the chosen two souls that need to be united. It is foretold that one of Mother's descendants will return to find her. The two will lead a mighty battle to overthrow the evil and return the world back to Mother's ways, to return the Moon Goddess's power of choosing our mates. It is said the two are immensely powerful. The descendant will plow a new path, a new life, for all to follow, to change our Realms and worlds, to bring back true peace and freedom.

"My own people were disappointed when Gwendolyn chose to pick me as her mate. She knew I was her gift from the Moon Goddess. Our people only agreed to our coupling if we swore to bed the two males of their choosing to impregnate us, to ensure an heir for our people. So, Basil and Dermot were chosen and forced to be our breeding males. We are lucky—the males respected Gwendolyn and I. They were very gentle with us." She sighs heavily. "The Moon Goddess gives us our mates. It is not supposed to be chosen by others. I heard your mother was auctioned off to the highest bidder back in the human Realm, is that true? Was she really auctioned off?"

I nod my head sadly and frown at her.

"Once you find Mother, she will help you. Mother loves all." She stops and scans the woods. Brice too cocks an ear and whispers a warning.

"Something walks nearby," he whispers through our connection.

"Quickly now, gather around the girl. Leave the animals!" she hisses at us and reaches her hand toward a vining plant. That vine quickly grows and forms a wall around us. We are completely covered and enclosed in vines, encircled by wide leaves and thick branches. She places a finger to her lips, and we listen.

I kneel and inch over to the ivy wall and press my eye to a keyhole-sized opening and peer out. A shadow moves but I cannot see the figure. I look back to my companions and point to where the horse and cow still stand. We listen intently to their nervous reactions at whatever stands before them. I peer through the small opening, pressing my face flat and craning my neck to give me a better view. The animals outside have quieted as it moves away from them. Where did it go?

A large dead, grey, and bloodshot eye looks at me from the other side. The eye rolls in a circle within the socket and I freeze, motionless, willing myself not to blink. The dead eye holds my gaze. I can no longer stand keeping my eye open and blink.

A terrifying scream erupts from the thing outside. I stumble back from what feels like a very thin wall of vines, shaking. We all jump when it begins tearing away our shield of vines. I scoop up Rowan and Sorcha turns her palm out to the monster outside. She turns to us.

"Ready to run? Follow my light—do not lose me! It's screaming an alarm. More will descend, more will come, very soon!"

She nods to me and holds her other hand over Rowan. Rowan starts to shrink within my arms. Smaller and smaller she gets 'til she fits perfectly in the palm of my hand. I gently circle my fingers around her in a light grip and look to Sorcha, mystified. She winks.

"Ready? RUN!"

Sorcha screams an encouraging battle cry as she blows a fiery hole into the side of the moving wall and instantly becomes a tiny ball of light again. The cow and horse startle but quickly follow us, trying to match our run, both completely terrified to be left behind. I keep my eyes upon the bobbing light and run for a long time. We crash to a halt when Sorcha returns to normal size. We all bend, sucking in deep breaths. All is quiet, no sound of crashing feet in the underbrush or of our pursuers. Not even of the birds.

"We are nearly there," Sorcha pants, "our grove village hidden in these woods. It is completely surrounded and protected by giant ancient red oaks, yes, red, strong oak."

"How far to my father's house?" I pant.

"Far, too far. A day, maybe two. Too many in company. No, we—" she points at the three animals, Rowan in my arms, and herself "—must go to village first. You will go alone to retrieve the book." Sorcha listens all around. It's too quiet. Why have those things stopped chasing us? "Too open, too dangerous. Must hide, must hide."

She again commands the bushes and trees around us to contort and curve, wrapping their branches around us. "Another way I know, but it will drain me. Must be done. Be careful, Merek. Your father's house is under constant watch! We have been unable to even get close to it. You must be unseen, you must be quiet! Stay unseen! If they find you, they will drag you before the King! Elgeeva!" she screams into the air. "Little power boost, if you will!"

"Wait, what?" I question Sorcha and instantly feel a pressure field flow about me. The hairs on my arms and neck stand on end, my ears pop. Sorcha hiccups, causing a frantic and frightened smile to plaster her face. Her eyebrows raise like she is about to ask a question but instead she blows a large amount of sand in my face.

Sorcha's features dissolve and my pa's stone house stands before me. My head spins. I look left and right. Sorcha, Brice, *everyone* is gone and I'm alone. I stare at the house in dismay. It's nothing but ruins. Crumbling stone walls litter the ground. The door is still on its hinges and held in place with the remaining stone frame. Ivy and vines weave through as though the earth itself is making claim and taking it back.

I approach the door and gently push it open. It swings slowly and with a loud groan. I jump, startled by the sound, and quickly look all around for any trace of movement or sound. All is quiet, eerily quiet. A weighted and heavy oppression bears down on me. Something is off, something not right. Slowly I enter the house.

The last bit of the sun's rays filter through the rubble and vines that are now the roof. Tears fall from my eyes at what is lost, knowing I will never be able to return. My eyes catch the small stand by the bed, completely untouched, completely missed, plain and ordinary. I open the small door and retrieve the books within and smile a sad smile. My pa's book glows bright, its cover springing open in my palm, pages flying. It feels so good to have it back in my hands. I really missed this old book.

"*There you are*," a voice whispers quietly and gently from behind me.

I gulp and gag at the vomit rising in my throat and feel a hand grab my shoulder. Someone has found me!

"Brice!" I scream through our connection.

Smoke and wind swirl around me. I realize I am slowly disappearing into nothingness. I am being transported somewhere else. I'm in trouble!

CHAPTER SIXTEEN

A Fortress Within the Wood

In a smoky haze, my vision clears. A hand still presses against my shoulder. I try to pull away.

"It's okay, Merek, you are safe," a woman's voice calls to me.

I turn and find a cloaked figure. I gaze about and find myself in a small room. A miniature hearth with a low burning flame is at my back, casting warmth over me. Shaking and confused, I realize we are alone in the modest room. Maps paper the walls, small pins marking areas of the forest. A modest table with two chairs is stuffed into the corner, towering and cluttered with books and ancient large volumes. I still hold my father's book and place it in my satchel. Mercifully, it no longer glows. I glance out the petite window to find the tops of enormous tree branches and the horizon almost in twilight, the moon already high, full and massive. I look down to see a wall of tall, thick oaks.

"Where am I?" I ask in a hushed, hoarse tone.

"A safe haven of sorts, one of few strategically placed throughout the forest," the woman answers.

"And you? Who are you and why have you brought me here?"

A tiny tea pot materializes form nowhere along with a chipped teacup and it pours a steaming green liquid.

"Your travel here has you shaken. Please have some tea, it will help calm the nerves." She offers the floating cup to me. It smells sweet and rich, and I feel so cold. The fire to my back is helping. I reach for the cup and warm my hands.

"What of my companions? Where are they?" I ask, sniffing the tea. Again, citron leaves.

"Tell me, my dear one, did you like the images your father and I sent to your photo book? Did the photos bring you joy, ease a bit of your loneliness?" The woman reaches up with emerald green slender hands and pulls back her hood. "I've been very eager to meet you, dear one! How are you feeling? Is the coldness wearing off any?" she asks, and gently places her palm to my forehead, then cradles my face between both palms and gives me a good lookover. "Ah, so much like your handsome father, so much beauty like your mother," she coos.

My mouth drops open in disbelief. Does this creature know my parents? Who is she? This voice, I know this voice... I look closer at her face and eyes. They are the color of my father's. My memories race, trying to remember his features.

"Ah! Smart boy," she beams at me. "My birth name is Elgeeva, but I have many titles. Mostly I am called Lady of the Wood." She caresses my cheek. "I am the High Priestess of the Witches. I am also Princess and next in line of Rule in the Elfin Kingdom. To you, my dear child, I have the highest honor and title." She smiles with pride, still gazing upon my face. "I am your father's mother. It is my deepest and greatest pleasure to finally meet my only grandchild!" Her smile is so big and her eyes are so full of love.

"Grandchild?" I ask out loud. This creature before me is my grandmother?

"Oh dear!" she exclaims. "Come, come with me. Your companions are approaching and I'm afraid it is dire we move with haste." She grabs my arm and drags me through the room and to the door, the cup falling and spilling as I am hurled forward.

The door opens to an enormous fortress, a village within the surrounding structure beyond the modest walls of the room we left behind. Vast walls of extreme height are made of giant oaks grown into each other without any gaps. I gaze down at the lower levels beneath us. I'm standing at the highest level of it all. Looking out past the tall, thick wall of oaks, the treetops of the forest beyond that are only just visible begin violently rustling. Deathly screams surround the fortress, its inhabitants on high alert. Men, women, and creatures of all sorts come running across the crisscrossing wooden suspended bridges, some swinging from thick vines, all racing to the front wall where the ruckus beyond is quickly approaching. They ready themselves at the inside wall of the great ancient oaks, more creatures down below on the different levels throwing open disguised doors and aiming bows and arrows.

"Oh, Mother of Light," Elgeeva sighs. "GIANTS!" she screams.

Every creature within the place that I can see is dressed plainly in earth tones, with painted faces—warriors. Each squarely plants their feet and abandons their bow, choosing instead to fasten and bolt the window doors and hold on to whatever they can.

"READY!" she bellows. She plants her feet, focuses, her hands raising from her waist to her chest, lifting the heavy invisible air around her arms, and forcefully throws her hands away from her chest. A mighty blast ripples from her and knocks me backward and off my feet, sending me flying into the trunk of a tree behind me. The blast waves forward with speed. A loud *thump... thump... thump* shakes the ground. Three?

"AIM!" she bellows again. Everyone takes up their arms. She turns and reaches a hand out to me, helping me to my feet. "Are you alright, dear one?"

I nod my head. I am fine, other than being knocked off my feet. She latches onto my arm once more, lifting me up and throwing me to the side, steering me down a logged path. A box made of wood stands open before us and she shoves me inside, closes the door, and the floor seems to fall out beneath us. We fall to the fortress floor with rapid speed. The box then suspends to a halt just inches above the ground, bouncing slightly. My stomach flops. She opens the door and I fall face first out onto the floor and vomit.

"Sorry dear one, can you manage? I must get to the door!" Elgeeva calls to me over her shoulder, racing away from me. I leap to my feet and do my best to keep up.

At ground level now, I look up to see many bridges, huts, and hammocks swaying in the breeze. Hundreds of huts line the walls. I race behind Elgeeva toward the structure's only gates.

Elgeeva pushes up her sleeves and seems to only touch the trunks of the trees that make up the walls of the fortress. She struggles and then they grow taller. The defensive walls, all four sides, shoot up in growth! She waves a hand and quickly pulls it to her chest. An opening through one tree truck appears. There are no gates at all, no openings but for the narrow hollow she has just created. We stare out, waiting, the chase happening beyond the great oak wall, the ground trembling beneath us.

Arrows begin flying, screams erupt from beyond the wall, men and women above us are hit and stumble backward off the boardwalks, falling to the earth around me. I look up. Long, dark snake-shaped blades fly through the air. A petite woman who resembles Sorcha flies through the air and lands on the level just above me. She rapidly throws her blades through an opening but is then hit by an arrow. She stumbles and falls.

I brace myself and catch her. The black arrow blade disappears into her skin and pools like black ink. Her eyes find mine and with her last breath she lovingly whispers, "Merek."

Elgeeva knocks the woman from my arms and rolls her away from me. Anger flashes through me and I push past her to reach out to the young woman. Elgeeva holds me back, screaming in my ear, but I can hear nothing over the sound that is approaching us on the other side of the wall. All of the screaming and cries make me deaf. I struggle against her, watching the black ink take over the young woman. It dissolves her skin and bones to nothing but a blackened scorch upon the earth.

I vomit instantly. Elgeeva is yelling something to me, but my head swims. She checks me over thoroughly but seems satisfied enough to leave me to vomit alone, squaring herself once again before the open door. Weakly I rise to my feet and stand beside her. A torrent of wind pushes me away from the opening and presses my back flat against a trunk of the oak wall. My breath catches in my chest from the pressure.

"Stay hidden," Elgeeva snaps at me.

I look above me, at all of those creatures fighting. Arrow after arrow shoots outside, only to be matched from the outer wall, making contact, making more and more stumble and fall to the earth below. My heart rips as I am forced to watch these beings fall and die, watch the earth floor become blacker and blacker as bodies melt away into nothing.

I cannot watch anymore; it burns my body as I watch another die. Tears stinging my eyes, I turn my head away and toward the hollow opening as Rowan runs through it followed by Sorcha and Brice. Relief floods my system when I see them all. I twist and pull at my invisible restraints but am unable to free myself. Rowan collapses in a heap upon the floor and I strain harder, pulling at the nothingness that holds me in place. I watch Sorcha grab Rowan's wrists, trying to drag her away from the opening.

The pressure holding me against the ancient wall of oaks releases and I run to them. I pick up Rowan and run behind Sorcha toward the middle of the fortress. I turn to see Elgeeva fling her arms from her sides as three huge bodies slam into the outer wall of the fortress. Everyone stumbles and is violently pitched forward or back. Every creature reaches out to balance themselves. There are three horrifyingly deep, pain-filled screams.

All is eerily quiet. Then a tidal wave of slouching hot, sticky red liquid floods the inside of the fortress. All is deadly silent again as every creature gazes about, taking in the situation. Cheers erupt; a deafening clapping and thumping of feet drowns out the war cries of success. The enemy Giants have been taken out.

After all quiets, there is a knock from the outside wall. A creature runs to Elgeeva.

"My Lady." He bows. "There is a sweet cow and an old horse outside the gate."

"They belong to Rowan!" I yell to the two of them. Rowan is still unconscious. I lay her upon the floor, kiss her forehead, and look up to Sorcha. She begins examining her for injuries. I run to the two animals, who are making their way to the door, splashing through the pool that is knee deep.

"It's Bella and Winston," I explain, catching up to them out of breath.

Elgeeva opens an ornate door again and smiles at me. The two animals enter, then kneel before Elgeeva. She waves her hand over them and their bodies slowly melt away, revealing a naked man, who Brice sniffs intently then lays down beside, and a woman. Two of the warriors approach with thick hide blankets. The man is completely covered, assisted up, and whisked away with Brice following along, tail wagging. I just throw my hands up.

"Brice, where are you going?" I question after him.

The female warrior brings the blanket to the female's shoulders and wraps her as she stands. She smiles at me and approaches.

"Hello, child!" she says softly, caressing my cheek. "Do you know me?"

I shake my head. There is nothing in her features that I recognize. She laughs.

"How about now?"

She brings her hands before her face, hiding behind them. When she pulls her hands away, I gasp in surprise and stumble, falling backwards. I look up at a bony skeletal face, with hollow eye sockets that glow a blueish, purplish hue. A bony hand reaches out and takes my hand to pull me up. She is the skeletal woman from the cave!

"Emira?" I whisper.

She giggles. Her hands flash before her face several times, each pass revealing a different creature, different face, features... a creature of glowing bright light. I hold my breath. It is the woman in my picture book.

"Yes, it is me." She smiles when she returns herself to the form she has taken after the cow.

"You're free? And Rowan's cow?" Confusion is written all over my face.

"After you set me free, I knew where you were headed next. The other met me in the forest when I emerged from the cave and came with me, the man." She points behind me, but he is no longer in sight. "We came to the barn and found that sweet Bella had just died from the complicated birth of her calf. I took her body and became her. Winston, the old horse, surrendered his life and the man took his shape."

Emira approaches Elgeeva. She presses her forehead to hers. Their eyes close but their eyelids flutter fast.

"I am so relieved you are well." Elgeeva bows deep.

Emira kisses the top of her head. "You have done very well, daughter, but there is more to be done. Let us go and prepare. Brice and Rowan need to be caught up." Emira then kisses the top of my head. "Blessings be upon you, my beloved child," she whispers to me, and my body warms instantly. "Bring the female child to my quarters," she calls out.

Rowan is lifted so gently by many hands, and they carry her limp body off and away. They hold her with such care, attention, and love, as though she were their Queen. I turn away from Emira and go to follow them when Sorcha's hand holds my shoulder to stop me.

"Sorcha!" a female screams out. "Sorcha!" The female runs and stops halfway from Sorcha.

"Gwendolyn?" Sorcha whispers.

The two stand there staring at each other, then Sorcha runs as best she can through the red pool that is up to her thighs to the other woman and stops just before her. She slowly reaches out to push a tendril of hair behind her ear.

"Gwendolyn?" Sorcha grabs the other woman who is somehow smaller than her, dips her gracefully, then kisses her lips. Tears erupt into incoherent speech.

"Child." Emira tugs at my shoulder. "Come with me—there are two beings that desperately wish to see you!"

She leads me in the opposite direction that Rowan was taken. Our steps are difficult through the now ankle-deep liquid.

"Forgive me." I pause to find the words. "What is... this..." I wave my hands down and all around at the liquid that has flooded the fortress.

"The blood of three Giants, child," she states simply, and my face pales.

CHAPTER SEVENTEEN

A Transformation

Emira opens a simple wooden door. Her eyes twinkle with happily contained excitement and she smiles at me. She drags her hand through the air, signaling me to enter, and I scan the room beyond. It's small with two overstuffed chairs in the center facing each other. Nothing else adorns the room and it is dimly, darkly lit.

Two creatures turn and look up to me from the sitting chairs as I step through the doorway, and I vaguely hear the soft clink of the door closing behind me. I fall to my knees as the two creatures rise from their seats and rush to me.

"Mum?" I ask in just barely a whisper. Tears run down her cheeks as she nods at me.

"Pa?" I choke out, questioning. "Is this another dream?"

My mother holds her arms out to me and I fall into her embrace, my father encircling the two of us.

This has to be another dream, a cruel twist of fate. My mind cannot believe that my parents are indeed with me, holding me. I feel so wonderful to be able to feel them, feel the tightness of their hold and their solid bodies. Can it be real? Am I truly here, in the present and not the past, or even somehow leaped into the future?

As much as I need my parents, I feel like something is missing. It is painfully absent and should be here with me. Rowan! Where have they taken her?

"How did you escape the castle and Grandfather?" I ask my mum, my voice hoarse.

"Nuala, she helped me... Nuala secreted me to an entrance to an underground tunnel just outside the palace grounds that led me here. Elgeeva, she planned my escape. Many were involved." She sniffles as a tear falls down her cheek. "Some died protecting me and the other refugee women and children to see us safely here, the rebel's fortress. Your father was waiting for me to emerge from the tunnel and we have been here, together, ever since! Training, strategizing, planning." She smiles meekly at me and kisses my forehead. "It has killed me," she sobs, "to not come for you. All these years, the years you were alone, lost to all, safe but hidden by a powerful spell that concealed you. Not even Elgeeva could find you while you tended and maintained the stone cairns that surrounded the house your father had built."

"I am so proud of you, Merek!" Pa says, hoarse, and hugs me tighter.

"So here we have been, training, fighting, waiting, after all the years and the forces of the King. That's when your father channeled Brice, telling you to leave. It was only then we were able to find you, track you, and wait again. And now here you are, my precious boy, all grown, handsome, strong. You did so well, my son." She hugs me again, her grip so tight, crying softly against me.

"I understand, Mum, it's been really hard on all of us, but where is Rowan? I want you to meet her!" I say softly, marveling that my parents are really here, with me.

"Rowan was taken to Emira's rooms. They are checking on her, making sure she doesn't need any medical attention. We can see her soon," Pa answers. "She's safe, Merek, we promise. And we are looking forward to seeing her."

***

Rowan lays slumbering, still unconscious, upon a flat, massive, ancient onyx stone. It is smooth as glass, etched with a long-ago written language. Twenty-eight hooded creatures from seven of the nine Realms enter the room, encircling the stone table, silent and waiting. A large, massive body stands outside the only open window, shrouding the room in darkness at it blocks the full moon's light. Elgeeva enters last, snapping her fingers. Old metal torches pop and hiss in their sconces, illuminating the room with a soft golden glow. She completes the circle, standing by Rowan's head. She examines her sleeping face, feels her skin with the burning fever. Elgeeva then holds up a wooden chalice as Emira enters and closes the door.

Emira slides through the crowd of gathered creatures. She passes Elgeeva an ancient tome. Elgeeva sighs as she lovingly feels its weight and pressure upon her palm.

"Hello, darling." Elgeeva taps its cover. "I've missed you!" she coos to the book.

At her touch and the sound of her voice, the book awakens. Two crescent shapes on the front of the book flutter and blink open. Two black orbs stare at the book's master, the Witch that created its grimoire pages of spells and enchantments, her collected work in this one book. Elgeeva has memorized every spell, all but the one she needs from the book tonight. When she first wrote the spell, it became unstable when her pen left the page. Her words raced about the page and never held still. She guesses that the words are still constantly rearranging themselves.

She handed her beloved grimoire down to her son, who in turn gave it to his son. The book has done well protecting Merek all these years and has taught him the language and histories of this land. She prays silently that the page she needs is now at long last finished and ready for her. The book, sensing its mistress's unspoken words, opens the cover. Pages fly before Elgeeva's eyes until the book reaches the page it knows she needs. Indeed, the words are still racing about the page.

Elgeeva thinks for a moment, then takes Rowan's fingertip and presses it upon the page. The words stop swirling and racing about. Finally they form into a coherent text. Elgeeva studies the inscription intently, then watches as an image forms on the neighboring page. Her head tilts in puzzlement as she examines the image, a perfect representation of Rowan as she is now, but hung suspended before the full moon up in the sky. Elgeeva moves her eyes down and gasps as each creature in the room at present is drawn and depicted as they are now but all looking up at Rowan. Still puzzled and unsure, she rereads the text. At last she nods and places the open book on Rowan's chest.

Emira presses the pad of her right thumb to her canine tooth and breaks the skin. A large, fat, ruby red droplet of blood forms and she draws the shape of a full moon on Rowan's forehead. She dots a certain star constellation beneath her closed eyes, then smears her thumb against the left temple down her jawline, across the chin, and completes its mirror image on the right side, stopping at the temple.

Elgeeva holds the chalice beneath Emira's dripping thumb and collects five droplets.

"I left Merek with Drake and Amanda," Emira says. "He is very aware of Rowan's absence from him. We won't have much time to complete the ceremony. Drake and Amanda are doing their best to keep him distracted." Emira licks her thumb and the bleeding stops.

Elgeeva nods and moves to the first four creatures beside her to begin the ceremony to transform the sleeping creature before her into a completely new and unknown creature.

"Nikilaus, Xander, Lily, and Benjamin of the Crescent Rose Moon pack. Do you willingly give your blood to this creature that is Rowan as your offering and your commitment to her? Will you be loyal, will you follow her into the unknown? Will you give your lives so that above all else this woman can survive for the greater good? So that she may soon destroy the evils that have entered our Realms, vanquish that evil that has corrupted our current King? So she and her mate may bring peace to our lands and unite the species as one?" Elgeeva recites.

"We do, My Lady of the Wood," state four voices proudly, bowing their heads to the chalice, finalizing their part of the spell and binding the magic. Four palms are slit with the Werewolves' sacred dagger so that the chalice can receive their blood offering.

Elgeeva approaches the next four, Emira following behind and bandaging the hands of the first four.

"Rebecca, John, Susannah, and Giles of the Witches Coven. Elements of Earth, Air, Fire, and Water. The winds of the North, South, East, and West. Do you willingly give your blood to this creature that is Rowan?"

"We do, My Lady of the Wood," state four voices proudly, and bow their heads to the chalice. A whispered spell opens the skin of their palms, and Elgeeva completes the bloodletting and moves on.

"Gwendolyn, Sorcha, Basil, and Dermot, the Queens and Kings of the Whispering Wind, land of Fae. Do you willingly give your blood to this creature that is Rowan?"

"We do, My Lady of the Wood," state four voices proudly as they bow their heads to the chalice. Four marble stone blades are kissed by each, then used to open their palms. Sorcha swirls her fingers and the pooled blood of the four palms rises into the air and pours a combined offering into the chalice.

"Brigid, Cormac, Grainne, and Oisin, Lords and Ladies of the Human Lands, Paladins of the history of Old. Do you willingly give your blood to this creature that is Rowan?" Elgeeva holds the chalice before them.

"We do, My Lady of the Wood," state four voices proudly, bowing their heads to the chalice. Emira extends her sharp nail and slices each. They each squeeze a fist over the chalice then allow Emira to bandage their hands and step aside so that Elgeeva can reach the open window.

"Esurg, Agrok, Tozir, and Borog, Giants of Old!" she speaks loudly, hanging out the window so that they can hear her. "Do you willingly give your blood to this creature that is Rowan as your offering and your commitment to her? Will you be loyal, will you follow her into the unknown? Will you give your lives so that above all else this child can survive for the greater good? So that she may soon destroy the evils that have entered our Realms, vanquish that evil that has corrupted our current King? So that she and her mate may bring peace to our lands and unite the species as one?"

"We do, My Lady of the Wood," state loud voices from outside the window. Elgeeva steps back as the first Giant's finger is pushed through the window frame. She pulls a pin from her hair and pokes the first enormous finger, 'til all four drops are combined in the chalice.

"Lottie, Vampire Queen," Elgeeva bows. "King of Old, Vladimir." Elgeeva bows her head to him then continues, "Dawn and Lothous of the Ice Mountain Range Coven. Do you willingly give your blood to this creature that is Rowan?"

"We do, My Lady of the Wood," state four voices proudly, and bow their heads to the chalice. Each extends a claw and lets their blood run into the chalice. Emira offers Lottie a bandage. Lottie smiles and winks at her, showing her palm has already healed.

"Queen Opal, King Conway, Aerin, and Lucious of the Elfin Kingdom. Descendants of the First Beings, the Keepers of Time. Do you willingly give your blood to this creature that is Rowan?" Emira asks the last group.

"We do, My Lady of the Wood," state four voices proudly, bowing their heads to the chalice. Each bites their thumb and holds it over the chalice.

"I, Elgeeva, High Priestess of the Witches Wood, Elfin Princess of the Crown and Pureblood daughter of Emira, give my blood and promise to this child." She pauses, holds the chalice higher, and takes a large breath. "We all gather before you, Rowan, and with the Goddess of the Moon as witness do freely give the knowledge of our powers, the blood histories of our people, to transform you, to empower you with all we have known to become a Mighty Warrior and a New Breed for that of Love and Light. You will be the first creature of your kind, a salvation to the Realms to lead us to the light and out of the darkness."

Elgeeva whispers the spell. Her skin opens at the wrist and she collects the drops, and with a twist of her fingers stirs the blood offering within the chalice. A warm torrent of wind whips through the room; an amber glow rises from the chalice.

Emira goes to the top of Rowan's head and brings her lips to the full moon drawn in her blood and kisses it gently. Rowan's eyelids flutter. Elgeeva places a feathered pillow under Rowan's knees as Emira places a pillow down along her back and underneath her head. Once they are confident that she is comfortably reclined, they go to either side of her and sit upon the ancient stone, watching her face and waiting for her eyelids to open. A collective breath is held and when Rowan opens her eyes to the soft lighting, thirty pairs of eyes look at her.

"Hello, Rowan. I am Elgeeva." She bows her head to her. "I am Merek's grandmother."

"Hello, child. I am known as Mother, creator of all." Emira bows her head to honor the child before her. "Drink this, dear one, a warm brew to help return your strength." She lifts the chalice to Rowan's pink lips.

"Thank you," Rowan whispers, her voice hoarse from lack of use and her mouth dry.

"You must drink it all down at once. It's best to take large gulps. I warn you, it will not be sweet. You must not spit it out. It is indeed a potent medicine that needs to be drained, understand, child?" Emira speaks with soft eyes searching Rowan's face.

"I understand. Is Merek here?" She gazes about the room, searching the many eyes for him.

"He's just next door, dear one, close by. You can see him soon, but you need rest and strength." Elgeeva calms her and pushes a tendril of falling curls behind Rowan's ear.

A large eye comes to the open window. "Elgeeva, may I see the child?" Agrok whispers. Rowan shrieks but Emira places a hand on her shoulder to hold her still as a dizzy spell makes Rowan's head loll violently.

"Agrok, you'll frighten the girl," Elgeeva snaps, but Emira cuts her off and nods for Elgeeva to move down the table a bit.

"Hello, pretty little lady!" Agrok whispers in a voice that still sounds like loud, beating drums. Rowan's head turns to the voice and she tries to give a small wave, but her uneasiness of the crowded room will not let her own arm rise. She smiles at the large iris and pupil at the window frame instead.

"Well done, child," Emira whispers into her ear. "Ready to drink now?"

Rowan nods to her. Emira tips the chalice and Rowan takes a small sip. Once it bathes her tongue, she coughs desperately, trying to swallow the liquid and not to spill, but her throat will not follow the command. She forces it down then hiccups.

"I am sorry!" Rowan winces. "It is quite warm and thick."

"Oh, I am sorry, dear one, but you must finish it." Emira rubs the back of her hand. Rowan takes the cup from her and begins to try and chug the liquid. Her face contorts as she forces the thick liquid down her throat, tipping the cup for the last of it. She swallows hard then hiccups again.

"Well done indeed, child, well done!" Emira claps.

"May I see Merek now, please?" Rowan hiccups again.

Before Emira can respond, a small tornado of wind begins spinning at Rowan's chest until it grows large and fierce. Elgeeva and Emira are thrown from the table. The creatures' backs are slammed against the four walls. Rowan's body shoots straight up. A blast of wind shatters the ceiling as her body is thrown up and out of the room. Her body slows and is suspended before the full moon, centered. Her head snaps backwards and a horrifying scream pierces the night.

"Elgeeva!" Susannah yells against the violent winds. "Silence her! Her screams will draw unwanted attention from the Realms."

Susannah and the rest fall to their knees as Rowan's scream continues and grows louder. Elgeeva flicks a wrist at the creature above and all is silent. The raging winds die, and the creatures begin to stand.

"Merek heard. He's running this way," Emira snaps at Elgeeva.

Every creature looks up at Rowan's body still suspended before the moon, looks at her gaping mouth, and still hears her silent scream.

***

I hear Rowan's scream while Mum is still embracing me. My animal instincts kick in and I start pulling away from my mother. She hangs onto me. Pa tries to hold me back but I struggle against them until free, throwing the door open and tearing through the halls, tracking the sound of her screams until suddenly all goes quiet, and I'm left chasing an echo. I desperately sniff the air for her scent... *there!* I catch the trail and I'm off again, turning quickly to my left and slamming into the wall. My father is on my heels, calling me back, but I quickly lose him, my feet pounding harder than his, my need to protect my mate greater. His voice is long behind me, nothing but a distant cry now, as I navigate a labyrinth of halls that are unknown to me.

I bang with a loud thud into the small door separating me from my mate. "Rowan!" I yell. I draw back and charge at the door again, breaking through. I stare at the gathered creatures in shock.

"Emira! Where is Rowan?" I yell at her.

All eyes stare up and into the night, locked on and entranced by whatever is happening above them. Emira never takes her eyes away but simply points up. I slowly look up to find Rowan's body suspended before the moon in a seizing fit. Her body jerks left to right, up and down violently.

I climb upon the large platform beneath her and leap into the sky. Arms outstretched, I embrace her body, gently pulling her to me as her body continues to twitch and jerk. Her eyes open wide, two large black orbs. Her mouth hangs open in a silent, painful scream. My body is then pressed against hers, stuck, suspended there with her, unable to fall back to the platform below. Rowan's body bends backward and in half. I desperately look below me. The room is crowded, every pair of eyes staring at us. Four tall Giants outside the wall of the room also look upon us. I do not know what to do or how to stop her pain.

My hand traces up her back to bring her face back to me, and what I see makes my own body freeze with fear. Her skin grows black as midnight, as though the universe itself has reached out and touched her skin. Her markings of our mating disappear, then flash in silver. I am examining her arm when I see it move; her hand holds my shoulder firmly. I feel her other hand trace my opposite shoulder, up my neck, then her small hand fists tight at the back of my head, gripping my hair. All I can discern of her blackened face are the pointed, sharp rows of her pearl teeth as she latches onto my neck and bites me hard.

Pain courses through my body and I lose my grip upon her. She holds me against her and shakes me. I scream as the pain hits in a second wave and my body jerks and spasms in her hold. My scream is stolen from my lips; nothing comes from me. Slowly I feel a warming in my body followed by extreme pleasure. I reach for her shoulder as I feel my body wet from my own blood and bite her back. Her blood pours into my mouth too fast to swallow. It pools in my mouth and drips from my lips. Our bodies spin slowly around and around each other. An odd suspended dance, twirling before the moon. Our blood runs from our bodies in heavy rain, soaking the creatures below. I feel our bodies falling, gently lowered to the ground below. Our backs are laid against cold stone, and then all is dark.

***

Thirty pairs of eyes stare at the unconscious bodies that are laid upon the ancient stone. The small room is overcrowded by creatures soaked head to toe in blood, mouths agape. Silent.

"Was that not the most beautiful transformation of love you have ever witnessed?" Emira yells excitedly, bouncing on her toes. Covered and dripping with blood, she laughs out loud, filled with pure joy, ecstasy, and love. The creatures about the room let out a collective held breath as blood drips from their faces and fingers. They lean forward to examine the two pristine and clean creatures before them. Elgeeva slowly moves toward Merek and places a hand upon his chest, then Rowan's.

"They live," Elgeeva whispers.

Every creature sighs with relief and wipes away the blood from their faces, their eyes darting around the small room at the amount of blood covering everyone and every surface. Emira continues to bounce excitedly upon her toes and licks her arms clean.

Amanda and Drake reach the door. A scream erupts from Amanda's lips as she takes in the blood-soaked creatures.

"What happened?" Drake demands as he and Amanda run to the children's sides.

"They live," Elgeeva pants. "They are slumbering. They are with the Goddess of the Moon now. It is now her time to have with them."

Amanda examines her son's new silver skin tone. She traces the midnight black ribboning pattern upon his forearm then traces its mirror image of silver iridescent on Rowan's. Her son's body has tripled in size. No longer is he a tall, gangly boy, but he is even taller, his shoulders and chest wide and massive. He has long jet-black hair that reaches his waist, tangled and wrapped about him and Rowan.

Amanda saw Rowan when she entered the fortress, and her body and features too have changed. Her once bronze-emerald skin tone has become the deep black of night. She has kept her short height and small and slender frame. Long silver hair tangles about them just as Merek's does. Pure white full lips pout as her forehead creases, as though confused in her slumber.

"Keep them safe. Let my children return to me, Goddess," Amanda prays, looking up to hold the moon's gaze.

Emira catches a small light reflected from the glow of the moon. She pushes back the shards of debris and strips of clothing that once covered Merek and Rowan. She secretly lifts the small glass stone from Merek and hides it away in her pocket.

"Elgeeva, what have Merek and Rowan become?" Amanda asks quietly.

"I do not know, my dear," Elgeeva answers, short of breath. "Their genetic makeup has been transformed into each and every one of us in this room. I do not know what traits will be dominant, which will be recessive. I have no idea what powers they will possess. It is as the prophecy says: they are new, unknown beings."

Drake wraps his arm around his mate and holds her tight as she cries, fearful of what awaits her son and his mate. Emira and Elgeeva murmur together as the rest of the creatures in the room pace, anxious to greet Merek and Rowan, whose slumbering bodies lay still upon the ancient stone.

Emira claps. "Clean yourselves, children, and be back here posthaste for the preparing of the bodies. We have work to do."

After the room has been cleansed of blood, Basil and Dermot busy themselves by placing silken fabric and ribbons about Merek's body, clothing his manhood. They twist and loop the long ribbons, covering him in new clothing, wrapping his muscled legs in a crisscross pattern. Sorcha and Gwendolyn work on Rowan's body, wrapping her breasts and womanhood to match Merek's in the chosen clothing of the Fae. Elgeeva and Emira brush and comb their long hair. Elgeeva has decided to leave Merek's hair long, but ties the hair from his temples back behind his head in a small but complicated knot shaped like a rose. Elgeeva then assists Emira in braiding and knotting, loosely pulling the braids into multiple rose knot ties that flow long and will hang, beautiful and delicate, along Rowan's back and front.

Once Rowan and Merek are dressed and their hair is finished, Basil, Dermot, John, and Giles work hard together to gently roll Merek's body to face Rowan, to free up his massive feathered wings. They flutter, flap, and stretch upon being freed, then settle. Sorcha and Gwendolyn also roll Rowan to face Merek so that her downy feather wings can stretch themselves. Amanda places Rowan's left hand against Merek's chest and takes Merek's right hand and places it upon her hip, so that even in their slumber they can have the comfort of the touch of their mate.

***

Rowan and I awake upon soft, plush purple moss. Small white flowers with red centers stretch all around us. Large mushrooms hold massive frogs that sing along with a symphony of crickets. We examine ourselves and each other: Rowan's dark skin, long silver hair, white lips; my silver skin tone, black hair as long as Rowan's, with full red lips. I examine my naked body that sits upon the purple moss, with its huge muscled arms, wide and thick shoulders. I stand and help Rowan up.

Rowan pulls on my hand and stands before me. Her eyes widen at my size and bulk. The top of her head reaches my breastbone and she places her temple against my chest and hears my heart still beating. I wrap my arms about her and hold her.

"Merek? Please tell me it's you. What happened? Why do I look different—*again*? Why are *you* different? What the... Where are we now?" Rowan studies herself, twisting her arms this way and that, pulling at her silver hair.

"I am not sure." I gaze about, examining my own arms, chest... We are at the top of a tall mountain range. I reach out a hand. The moon is so big and full, so close. I wonder if my fingertips will be able to touch it.

"*Hello, children*," a musical voice says softly behind us. "*Welcome to my home, Land of the Moon.*"

CHAPTER EIGHTEEN

The Moon Goddess

Two dragons circle above us underneath an infinite universe of blending and bending colors of black, purple, blue, and gold. The dragons coo lovingly down at us below. Millions of stars twinkle, pulse, and glisten in welcome. The dragons land softly beside a bright glowing light in female shape.

"I am the Goddess of the Moon, and these magnificent beasts are Midgard—" she points to the larger, the female "—and Fafnir." She rubs the snout of the slightly smaller male that has brought his face to the woman of light at hearing his name. "They are my most beloved friends and now I give them to you." She smiles at us and at the dragons before her.

Midgard strides with grace and beauty over to Rowan and nuzzles her side gently. Fafnir prances proudly to me. He circles my body and bounces on his front feet, one to the other, extending his long serpent forked tongue to lick my chest.

I let out a mighty laugh then rub down the dragon's neck.

The creature of light that is the Goddess of the Moon slowly brings her hands held out wide together, and when her palms touch, Midgard and Fafnir disappear into a hazy smoke. I sprout massive feathered black wings; a long heavy tail sways behind me. Rowan grows wings of iridescent white. Tiny down feathers with intricate designs flutter against her, then wrap themselves around her front in a silken hug. A long, slender tail of silver with a black tip curls around her. The woman of light smiles and approaches us.

"You are now fully transformed, recreated and made of every essence of the creatures that were made in love by Mother," she whispers to us, placing gentle kisses on each of our heads. The Goddess, bathed and glowing in moonlight, kneels before Rowan. She waves her hand before Rowan's belly and places her hand upon it, then gently places a kiss upon Rowan's skin. She rises to her feet and embraces Rowan.

"You are with child, dear one. Congratulations to you both," she whispers to me.

The Goddess steps away and I take Rowan's hand. I smile at my beautiful mate and gently caress her cheek as Rowan rubs her hands over her belly. I add my hand to hers and kiss her gently.

"It's time to return. Three more gifts will arrive for you soon."

She winks and blows a kiss. Rowan and I, hand in hand, gently lift into the air and disappear.

***

The first thing I feel as I come to is Rowan's warm hand on my chest, and the softness of fabric against my palm. Instantly upon feeling my mate, my tail sways and bounces happily.

I hear the door open quickly.

"My Lady," a voice breathes heavily, "there are three deer outside the southern wall."

My eyes flutter open.

"They are gifts from the Moon Goddess."

My voice is deeper and hoarse. My throat is so dry, and it burns. Rowan grips her throat with a slender hand and uses the other to push off my chest to sit up. As we detangle ourselves from each other, Rowan's hair waves and flows in delicate knotted braids, swaying about her as she rubs her throat and adjusts her sitting position. Her new clothing is soft and lush, unlike anything I've felt before, and I notice the feel of my own new clothing against my skin, lifting my foot to inspect the sandal tied there.

"I'm so thirsty," she whispers.

A feeling pulls at my heart as I help Rowan stand. I'm still in awe that she carries a small life inside her, a life we both created, and I'm scared. Being within the safety of the fortress and all its warriors and guards is one thing, but what if my grandfather crumbles this structure to the ground with his evil magic? Rowan and I will forever be on the run, always hiding, alone and isolated—it's a hellacious life for a small child. Rowan and I know all too well what that isolation can do.

What of my parents, will they even come with us? Will any of us even survive the wrath and retribution of the Goblin King? What of the baby? If my grandfather learns of this pregnancy, Rowan will have a target on her, she'll be hunted. By the Mother of Light, what if he finds out about Rowan being my mate, let alone the new child she carries! I take Rowan into my arms and shiver with fear, trying to be so very gentle with her as I lift her to my chest. My new strength courses through me, and I marvel at it. I am taller, my chest wider, with large rippling arms.

Rowan feels like the weight of a down feather, and as she snuggles into me, somehow I know that I need to fly us to the southern wall. Our flight gives me time to think.

This war that these rebels rage against the King—it was never mine or Rowan's but now we've been pulled into it by a prophecy written long ago, and even then we had a choice to walk away, but no more. With this baby inside my mate, I must join this war. Otherwise my mate, my *child*, will never be free and will live a life of fear.

The tip of Rowan's tail caresses my cheek and she looks at me full of concern, her brows pinched, trying to read my shift in mood. My beautiful mate, undergone so many changes. First when we crossed the border and the mystery of her dead family, who were clearly Goblin, suddenly made sense as her humanness melted away, revealing the Goblin hidden within. And now, she and I are genetically changed by the blood of the creatures surrounding us. We weren't asked, we weren't told, but because of a stupid prophecy Rowan was forced into changing. She was scared, and so as my mate she bit me, taking me along with her, and all the while Emira knew.

I'm angry, scared, yet I'm grateful for my new strength, so much stronger than ever I've been. My senses are heightened, strong wings adorn my back, I have sharp teeth, my claws are more like daggers that I can sheathe and unsheathe at will, and I've gained a tail with such agility... I wrap it around Rowan, encircling her. How easily and efficiently I could strangle an enemy.

I smile at her and pinch my own brows together in mock, then lean my forehead to hers and whisper, "I will protect you both, 'til my dying breath." Rowan's breath hitches with alarm, her hand still gripping her throat, desperate to quench this new thirst. "Be calm, my mate, I have you now. Let us see what the Moon Goddess sends."

I wave my hand as we land and a small door opens. In walks an albino doe followed by a black and then a golden stag. The stags have beautiful large, crowning horns. The female kneels then lays upon her side before Rowan, who kneels and runs her fingers through its beautiful white fur. Rowan bows her head to the creature before her then lowers her lips to its neck, bites, and drinks all the blood. She lifts her lips, whispers a prayer of thanks as her thirst is quenched, and runs her fingers through its fur until its body disappears. It leaves behind a beautiful white cape and a few bones. Rowan glances at me, confused.

The black stag lowers its body before me. I drink from the creature and whisper my thanks to it as it also disappears, leaving behind a large cape and its golden honey-colored horns.

The golden stag places its body between the two of us and together we drink. It leaves behind its horns of black and silver. Every creature within the fortress has come out and watches in silence. The bones and horns lift into the air and spin, each piece knitting together, creating two beautiful matching crowns that gently place themselves atop our heads. The capes drape against our backs between the wings and flare out at the bottom behind our heels. Rowan's is the white, mine the black. Slender strips tie them around our shoulders.

Two long tables appear, then wooden chairs. Golden linens drape the tables, and large platters filled with cooked and raw venison are placed down along each table. Platters of steaming vegetables and fruit and baskets of warm bread fill the empty spaces. Crystal glass goblets appear by the plates. A luminescent woman appears, bright, hovering above the tables. The glasses fill with amber liquid.

"*My blessings to you—eat.*"

The Moon Goddess bows before the people then dissolves.

It is a feast, just for us, lovingly given. The creatures cheer and take to the empty seats that wait for them. Once everyone is seated, a familiar man stands from his seat beside Elgeeva and clinks his glass to gather everyone's attention—it's Azlocke, the man from my father's picture book, my grandmother Elgeeva's mate. He helped Gwendolyn free my pa from my evil grandfather all those years ago.

"Blessings be from the Moon Goddess herself. Dear friends, may we accept and be nourished by her offering." Azlocke bows his head to the gathered mass. "Before we begin our meal, may I use this time as we are gathered to update all? Our scouts have informed me that Molag has split his remaining armies into four groups. Each group contains a formidable number of thousands that are now traveling here to our main fortress, coming at us from each of the compass points. The Western group will arrive first." He pauses as he sees each worried face staring intently at him. "It's reported they are aided by ten Giants and they should arrive at midnight, the witching hour, this evening."

Agrok and Tozir peek up over the defensive wall. "Leave the Giants to us, Azlocke. The Four of Old should be able to sway them without loss," Agrok gently whispers, but even the whisper is thunderous, and the crystal orbs vibrate and everyone at the table covers their ears, trying to muffle the loud voice. Tozir shakes her head.

"Agrok," Tozir sighs, "you know that the Wicked King's evil has spread across our Mountain Range. It was seeing that evil take root in our people that brought us here. You and I both know and can feel it deep down that our own youngest son is one of the ten Giants that marches here."

Azlocke nods to the two Giants of Old. "We are blessed to have you, friends. Thank you for aiding our cause. Battles are rarely won by discussing and listening, but the armies that approach will be our own brothers, sisters, family members." He sighs sadly. "Our own people are coming to slaughter us. It is my deepest hope that they at least let us speak before they engage. I fear we are outnumbered—we are only one thousand strong. We will most definitely lose many of our brothers and sisters who sit beside us now, including the family we will be fighting. Molag's evil has manipulated, twisted, and reprogrammed their minds. They are coming to our door loyal to their King, not us, their family." He looks out at the sad faces. "May this meal give us the strength we need to stand strong together. May we fight with love in our hearts. May we find the energy needed in our quest for peace. I am honored to be your trusted and loved leader. I humbly offer my life to you, with you, for our cause." Azlocke bows deeply to all, then takes the hand of Elgeeva and places a small passionate kiss upon it.

"Warrior Azlocke," one of the vampires, I believe Lothous, speaks up, "what of the whereabouts of the King? Will he be approaching with the Western army?"

"As his loyal and most trusted guard—" Azlocke sighs in disgust at his own title "—he last updated me that he and Nuala are staying and have locked themselves within his castle. He will not be joining the fight. He feels his army's numbers are substantial enough to wipe us out without dirtying his own hands."

"Azlocke—the Western army, how many men of the King's guard in addition to the Giants?" Grainne, the small but fierce human warrior, questions.

"One thousand," he calls out. "The combined total of the compass points that are marching toward us are four thousand strong," Azlocke yells over the anxious crowd.

"How has he gathered such numbers?" Basil yells out.

"Two thousand are his guards, soldiers, and those loyal to him. We already accounted for that number. The other half is the lost ones he collected from the forest," Azlocke answers. "We did not account for so many lost ones from the forest." He sighs heavily then continues. "I suggest we dig into this wonderful meal before it gets cold, then begin preparing to leave. Take only what is necessary and take the underground tunnel to the Dark Hallow Lands of the Satyrs and Centaurs. There we will be in a better position, closer to and ready for a strike against the Goblin Castle. The Western army will be disappointed when they find our fortress empty. From there the Satyrs and Centaurs have agreed to join our cause. They have offered us sanctuary in their land and will add to our numbers, fighting alongside us when we attack the castle. My hope is now that Molag has his armies spread out and away from the castle, we can overtake him by surprise," Azlocke finishes.

King Conway speaks up. "The theory of that plan's almost too good to be true. That underground tunnel has long been known to have collapsed at the bordering edge of the forest to the Dark Hallow Lands and is unpassable. Forgive me, Azlocke, for bringing up loyalties, but you are Molag's Head Guard and Knight. Tell me, why should I trust my beloved people in your care and guidance?"

He sneers this at Azlocke, and Azlocke sneers back, "King Conway, you question my loyalties. I have never expected you and your people to bow to my command. You need not follow me. One of the many reasons I fight for this cause is so that no one is ruled so that we might be able to live in peace. We corrupted beings might look to Merek and Rowan for guidance in love and light and begin anew where we are all one people. I am simply sharing my knowledge with our numbers so all may be better informed, each having a better chance of survival. By all means, I will gracefully step aside, and you can take the burden of this position that was just heaved upon me."

Conway shakes his head and flicks his hand. "Forgive me, Azlocke, I just want what is best for my people."

"Please let us eat." Azlocke takes a large, warm roll and breaks it and takes a bite as he takes his seat. Everyone heaps large amounts of food upon their plates and we begin our meal.

I stand and speak. "Azlocke, an idea came to me." He nods that I should continue. "What if we split our numbers in half? Half take to the underground tunnel toward Dark Hallow, half make the journey through the forest? I would suggest any of the flying creatures stay above with perhaps half of the Elven and Vampiric warriors so that if we were to encounter an army, we would have fights in the skies, trees, and forest floor. I do not wish to volunteer those who would rather try the tunnel, but it might ensure at least half of us arriving in Dark Hallow to then be able to advance upon the castle."

"We Giants will stay with those that travel the journey through the forest," Borog says. "I honestly don't think we of Old will fit in a tiny tunnel. If the earth has indeed collapsed, perhaps we will stay behind while the others move forward to Dark Hallow. We could help dig it out from above."

"That is a very insightful plan, Merek." Azlocke rubs his chin and watches our small army of people nod in agreement. "Those of you that wish to proceed by tunnel, raise your hand." Roughly half of the audience before us raises their hands. "Those who would wish to travel through the forest and sky?" Every winged creature stands, four large hands emerge from over the wall, and half the Elven and Goblin warriors stand. "It's settled. We will proceed with Merek's plan and hopefully we will all arrive and see each other once more in Dark Hallow. Barcella?" He scans the crowd. A small female Centaur raises her arm up high and waves. "Barcella, would you send a raven now with a message to your High Lord to brief him on the changes and to be watching and ready? Please let him know of the armies coming!"

Barcella whistles into the breeze and a large black raven shrieks above her then lands on the table. She whispers to the bird, and her eyes turn milky white as the raven's eyes swirls with white and black. It caws loudly in understanding and takes to the air. It banks hard westward and is gone.

Our group finishes our meal, trying to enjoy the last of the quiet and togetherness before the impending storm that is to come and the split of our defenses. There is laughter and stories, music and dancing, 'til Esurg bellows for silence. She kneels and places her ear to the forest floor. Agrok, Tozir, and Borog do the same.

"There isn't much time. An army approaches from the East. Azlocke, it's time," Esurg states plainly. "Two hours' time, and they will descend upon the fortress."

CHAPTER NINETEEN

The Eastern Army

Chaos and shouting erupt but Borog claps his mighty hands to silence the hysteria, while Azlocke begins barking out orders.

"Those who wish to proceed by tunnel, go now! Those who will remain above—we leave in one hour to begin our march to meet the army head on. Do not panic!" Azlocke calls to the small crowd of those who are ready to enter the tunnel. "Stay calm and, for the Mother of Light, watch your footing and your heads in the tunnels!"

A ground floor door is opened. "Emira! Elgeeva!" Azlocke yells over the hysterical cries of goodbyes of lovers, of children being separated from parents. The two step forward. "Elgeeva, take the lead. Lead our people through the tunnels." He lowers his head to his mate's, cups her face, and his eyes flutter closed as he grips her face tighter, his voice hoarse and wobbling. "Stay alive, stay alert, get to Dark Hallow. I will, *I will* meet you there, my love."

Elgeeva reaches out with tears in her eyes and gives him a long passion-filled kiss. "I will see you again, my love, in Dark Hallow!" she whispers urgently to Azlocke.

Emira is lowered down into the tunnel first. She reaches up as the children are handed down next. There are twenty small children in her guard and they set off down the tunnel.

"Come, dear ones! Come with Mother and follow the bouncing light!" A bright glowing orb pulses forward from her hand, lighting the way, and makes the children laugh as they race after the ball. "Goddess, hear me! Help me keep these younglings safe," Emira calls out, racing behind to keep up with the children, while releasing a second ball of light for the adults.

The humans enter the tunnel next. "Stay together, watch out for one another," Azlocke says, wishing them well on their journey.

The she-wolves and female goblin mothers come next. "Nikilaus! Safe journey, my friend." Azlocke helps lower her down into the tunnel and she steps to the side, looking up at him. The rest of the non-fighters enter the tunnel next.

The warlocks John and Giles lead half the witches and warlocks, along with Basil and Dermot with half of the Fairies, and they enter second to last. Azlocke kisses Elgeeva one last time and lowers her into the tunnel.

"Travel well," Nikilaus says as she helps Elgeeva down, the last to enter the tunnel. "We will see you in Dark Hallow, Azlocke!"

From below, Elgeeva seals the door. She watches as Azlocke's face disappears, dirt and roots taking the opening's place, and heaves a heavy breath. She links arms with Nikilaus and they run to catch up with the group.

The rest of the Fairies, Goblins, Elves, Witches, Wolves, Vampires, and Centaurs alongside Azlocke, myself, and Rowan prepare to depart. Rowan opens the massive fortress doors and everyone begins spilling out beyond the secure walls into the darkness-filled night to gather before the Giants.

Brice rubs his large head against my hip, making my hand rest between his ears. I give him a nervous scratch, eyeing him.

"I feel your unease, my friend," Brice whispers in my mind. "I'm wary of the situation also."

"Everyone is counting on me and Rowan. They seem to have known us all our lives, but we... we are just meeting them. Their hopes and dreams weigh so heavy on me when all I want to do is secret away the three of us, live like we used to."

Azlocke calls our attention. "Wolves, Giants, Witches, Centaurs, Merek, and Brice will take the forest floor. Elves and Goblins, the forest canopy. The Fae folk, Rowan, and I will take the skies. Giants of Old," he yells, "could two of you please take the lead and scout ahead and two stay behind to watch our rear?"

Fear drops into the pit of my stomach as Rowan's eyes grow large and she grips my hand tighter. Brice growls. "Why is he splitting us?" I scream within my mind. Brice snaps his jaws.

"As you wish, Azlocke." Agrok nods and he and his mate Esurg head East before the others.

"Tozir and I will watch to the West," Borog says quietly into the night to Azlocke. "We will give you a head start before we follow."

"Blessings, my friends—keep safe!" Azlocke shouts. "Let's move."

"Azlocke!" I yell and race with Rowan and Brice to stand before him, desperation written all over my face.

"Sorcha!" Azlocke calls to the sky above him and the sweet Fae creature lands whisper soft beside Rowan. "Take her!" Azlocke orders.

Sorcha gently links her arm with Rowan's, giving her a reassuring, sad smile.

"Come, my lovely, I'll help get you lifted up and I'll steady you 'til you're ready to fly on your own," she says softly.

A raging growl erupts from my throat and my body begins to morph. Pain shoots through me as my bones lengthen, I grow taller, my wings flare out, canines descend and thicken, my eyes change to jet black. Razor claws painfully tear through my skin. A lethal roar of warning erupts from my throat as my eyes lock on Sorcha. She pales, my rageful gaze landing on Azlocke.

"Excellent, Merek! We need fighters, warriors. I cannot have you two near each other; you'll only be a distraction!" He has to stand on his toes to shout in my face.

"This isn't even our fight!" I bellow down at him.

"This has always been your fight, since the day you were both born! *This* is where you have to be!" he urgently shouts at me. "You think I want Elgeeva in those tunnels? You think I don't want her by my side?" His voice breaks and he pauses to pull himself together. "We all do what we have to, to win the fucking war so one day we might know peace! I'll be damned if the prophesied couple gets squeamish about wanting to end all this oppression. Too many have died for you!" I blink at him, lost for words. "Kiss her, Merek," he breathes. "Hold her in your heart and protect her there and let her go!"

Tears run down his cheeks. Brice and I breathe hard, erratic, as Rowan's eyes scan over me. She grabs my arm, pulling me flush to her. She reaches up and, not able to reach me, flaps her wings to bring her forehead against mine.

"Please!" I whisper to her.

She claims my mouth affectionately, sucking the air from my lungs. For a second in time, where it all seems to stop, her eyes find mine and they say goodbye. She rips herself from me, hovering and moving awkwardly to Sorcha who is beaming with a bright smile at her.

"For the Mother of Light, she still can't really fly yet!" Brice whimpers as Rowan grabs at Sorcha for balance and together they lift higher into the sky. Rowan turns, blowing a kiss to the wolf that whines beside me.

The Elves and Goblins leap high into the trunks, taking their cue to begin the ascent up into the trees to travel by the camouflage of the canopy. The rest of us shift our attention to the forest before us, one step, second step, into a jog and then a hard run, a chorus of battle cries erupting from our months. Brice sprints to my left, Azlocke to my right, and we are surrounded by warriors, covered by darkness. Forest floor, canopy, and sky begin the long journey.

After the battle cries have long gone quiet, we intently listen for movement or danger ahead. I make out Rowan through the canopy every few moments, so high above me, haloed by the moon.

"Please let the path be clear," I pray to the Goddess of the Moon. "Keep her safe."

***

Emira holds up the group to rest. They have been travelling for over two hours. She presses her finger to her lips, encouraging everyone to stay silent, catch their breath, rest their bones, but no talking.

That's when everyone hears it, soft at first, barely a sound. A humming of sorts that begins to grow just a bit louder. Then the sickening realization that it is the footsteps of the army coming from above. Emira flashes the balls of light to get everyone's attention then dims them low, scattering everyone in shadows. She's fearful of any holes that could alert the army above to the light in the tunnels below.

Thunderous rumbling begins to shake the ground. Dirt rains down upon them. The children whine softly, tears streaming down their faces. Emira waves them over to her, her voice cheery, as two new, reassuring balls of light split into embers resembling fireflies. While their eyes are wide, watching, transfixed on the dancing embers, the children are cloistered in an alcove just a hair's breadth away from the adults. Emira encourages the younglings to remain calm, quiet, and watch the dancing lights as she backtracks down the tunnel to the adults, looking over her shoulder once back at the hypnotized babes. We will wait here, Emira thinks, 'til the army passes overhead, and then we will resume our journey to Dark Hallow. She converses quickly and softly with her daughter, trying to gage Elgeeva's memory of the tunnels. She judges how long they have already traveled, she estimates they have reached or are about to reach the halfway point from their empty fortress to the Dark Hallow tunnel exit.

John and Giles race forward past the quiet children. They're supposed to be miles ahead of the party, scouting, and Emira's heart thunders a heavy beat.

"Emira, Elgeeva," John pants, "The tunnels ahead have collapsed! Years of disuse and lack of tending... it's impenetrable! And soldiers are filing into the tunnel!" John breathes hard as Nikilaus shouts a warning, racing toward them.

"The tunnel collapsed behind us," she screams, running hard toward them as arrows soar past, flying through the tight tunnel aimed at her exposed back.

Emira's hand flies up and a blast of artic, rushing air caresses Nikilaus as she jumps for Elgeeva in an embrace, safe. Arrows slow midflight, dropping to the earthen floor as a chorus of charging voices echoes, screaming and groaning against the wind. The wind spell will only hold for a few brief moments. She needs more time to think.

The way back no longer an option, the way forward impenetrable, and with soldiers entering both ends of the tunnel, she breathes a long breath out as time slows, earth groans, crunches, then breaks. The tunnel is collapsing faster than she can hold it back.

Emira's eyes are glued to the younglings. She struggles, holding the spell. A small girl no more than four gazes back at her, her small hands outstretched for her as Emira watches a new section of earth above them crumble violently, ruthlessly fast, crushing the younglings that she thought she had placed in a safe, protected area. The girl is there and in the blink of her eye she is gone.

Emira falls to her knees, crying out in pain. She crawls toward the collapse, her hands and knees now coated in thick, warm, muddy wetness. Her breath heaves, her heart splinters. Power erupts from her at the echo of unsheathing swords and the sounds of bows being pulled tight. A silver, pulsating shield expands past her, surrounding her party. John slides forward, grabbing her, stopping her from digging helplessly at the rubble.

"Stop!" John roars at her. "They are gone! You don't want to uncover that rock to expose the proof, Emira!" He grips her hard, his face close to hers.

"The younglings" she chokes out. "*The younglings!*" she roars, her body shaking with pure rage.

"I know, Emira! I know." He swallows the bile in his throat hard. "But we need a new plan." He places her hands against his beating heart. "Giles and I can open a portal from here to the exit tunnel door in Dark Hallow. Giles has seen the door so the portal should take everyone safely there." Elgeeva cuts him off.

"Won't that be a death sentence? You said it's dangerous, *perilous* in confined areas," she hisses sharply. "I believe you explained it to me as a bomb going off, an implosion!" she growls.

"Well, if Giles doesn't remember the door exactly as it is, we won't end up in Dark Hallow," he explains. "We could end up anywhere, and technically speaking—" he wrings his fingers "—with the tight enclosed tunnel, the closing of the portal would... cause a rather large implosion due to the air pressure changes."

"Giles!" Barcella whispers. "That door has changed since you were visiting our kind! The earthen magic is always changing it. I know the new door. Could you use my memory of it to open the portal?"

"Yes!" Giles rushes to stand beside Barcella and places his finger-tips against her temples. "Visualize the door, Barcella," he urges, and her eyes close. "See it, every detail, color, and texture," he whispers. A slow smile spreads across her face and her body relaxes into the image in her mind's eye.

Giles pauses as he listens to the growing sound of approaching feet. "Everyone will enter as we keep the portal open. Once everyone has entered, when the portal closes..." He pauses for the right words, using his hands to show the space around them erupting. "Essentially the closing of our portal causes a powerful burst of energy. This section of the tunnel would indeed implode, so we need to be absolutely certain that everyone is through the portal and not lingering behind!" He realizes something and his face lights up with thought. "Depending on our depth, it will cause a large crater. Due to the tightness of the tunnel, an explosion!" He slaps John on the back, bouncing up and down.

Emira's face lights up and she turns vicious, purring almost seductively with menace, "Do it!"

Giles holds Barcella's hand. "Keep the image of the door in your mind. Don't let that vision go 'til we close the portal!" Giles takes John's hand and together they whisper the spell to open the portal door, their power combining.

The door of the spell opens and stretches in the tight confines of the tunnel then holds its shape. The exit door opens on the other side. Elgeeva and Emira usher everyone inside, then enter themselves. Barcella goes next, still holding Giles's hand as he follows her within. John strains to hold the portal by himself as the last enter and Emira turns, reaching out her hand to pull him in. She stares at him, her shields giving way now that she is surrounded by the portal, her magic failing as her body is pulled through it to the other side. Her eyes widen as John roars to her, "Tell my wife I love her, and I await her in the next life!" And he lets his magic fall.

The door of the portal wobbles with the last of his strength and he turns from her, kneeling on the earthen tunnel, arms spreading wide and his face thrown back, looking for the stars he cannot see as the cataclysmic explosion pounds the walls, ceiling, and floor of the earthen tunnel. The portal closes and Emira's body is flung through time and space.

The pressure builds in the tight confines of the tunnel. A loud rumble, an ungodly sound, shuddering, shaking... Earth is blasted up and wide, halving the earth violently. Trees and boulders are thrown into the air, debris racing for the skies, gravity pulling back at them, then a rain of soil, splinters of rock and wood. A scar tears through the earth, deep and vast where the tunnel once was. Soldiers of the King's army scream as debris rains upon them, piercing, crushing them, the earth swallowing them as the ground begins to settle.

***

Esurg and Agrok are scouting out front, peeking up over a wall of a mountainous range, watching the army approach. Susanna and Rebecca perch up high upon their shoulders. Giants and Witches watch and wait for the rest to catch up.

A loud rumbling sounds begins to shake the ground. A powerful blast ripples out. Esurg and Agrok are knocked from their feet by the mighty explosion. Susanna and Rebecca are flown backward as the Giants fall. Their screams pierce the night as their bodies plummet to the ground below. Esurg desperately reaches up to catch and cradle the tiny women falling above her. Agrok catches them gently and places them on the ground below.

"MOTHER OF LIGHT! John and Giles must have created a portal to the Dark Hallow door," Susanna yells.

Rebecca screams in agony, her body trembling, her hands reaching out to nothingness. "John! Something has gone wrong! They're insane! Why would they risk such a ludicrous idea? He's—" she labors for air in her lungs "—he's—" hysterical now, she tips her head back and screams to the blanket of stars. Finally she whimpers aloud, "He's sacrificed himself."

"It looks as though a third of the army was taken out by the blast," Agrok says with intrigue and sorrow as he scans the army front and the confusion that has wreaked havoc against their ranks and lines. "They must have been directly under the army in the tunnel. Do you believe that all—" he pauses, realizing that not all could have made it. "The others that entered the tunnel," he gently whispers to Susanna, "are they safe in Dark Hallow?"

Susanna closes her eyes, breathes deep. Her eyes are milky when they open and she stares at Rebecca, who is curled into a ball and whose eyes have also gone white.

A deep baritone emanates from a tranced Rebecca. "We are here, we are safe. We have not all made it through the portal. Susanna, my love," the voice pauses and Rebecca's eyes flick up to her, "the children were crushed prior to our opening the portal and John..." the voice pauses, and a female voice speaks through Susanne now. "Rebecca, John says he loves you very much and," the voice wobbles in a distant throat, "he awaits you in the life after."

A sob tears through Rebecca as Susanna falls to her knees before her friend, scooping her trembling body into her arms, holding her tight.

A male voice speaks through her again. "I hope we took a chunk of them out for you!" Rebecca's eyes flutter and her fellow witch lets the tears run down their cheeks. She calls up to Agrok.

"Let's go find the others."

***

Rowan and the rest of the Fae creatures quickly land before our group and she smiles, briskly walking to me. "Did you see me?" She winks. "I'm getting better!" She is radiant.

Elves and Goblins swing down from the tree line. Azlocke and the others on foot emerge from the brush. Coming together, we are whole again.

"What the bloody hell was that?" Azlocke yells.

Susanna, heavily supporting a weeping Rebecca, appears through the darkness. My ears are still ringing from the explosion. The werewolves in their wolf forms paw at their heads in pain, Brice shaking his.

"A pretty lucky aftereffect of a spell," Agrok says. "It took out a third of the army, Azlocke!"

"There is no movement from the west, north, or south!" Tozir says as she and Borog emerge from the woods. "We felt a mighty shake of the earth. What did we miss?"

"Are there any Giants with this Eastern army, Agrok?" Borog says as he embraces his other companions, giving a forced smile as he reads the somber faces.

"None that I can see, but they have a lot of winged creatures with them," he describes in a whisper. "From what I can see, in the sky they are a hundred wide, roughly fifty deep. We are outnumbered when it comes to wings."

The Giants continue to scout over the tops of the mountainous rock ledge. It is a well-concealed gathering area and we have the advantage of being able to look down at the open field below and at the army.

"*Ssshhh*, everyone *ssshhh*!" Susanna whispers. "Do hear that?" Everyone goes quiet. "Is that... drums?"

The ground begins trembling beneath us. I scale up the rocks like a huge spider and peer down over the top, Susanna shivering at my spidery image. I re-emerge on the side of the rock wall.

"There is an enormous cave below us!" I shout. "Something is marching out of it." I look back to the opening in the mouth of the mountain. Loud drums beat out a war chant, and the rhythmic beating of metal against metal echoes out of the cavernous cave.

"It cannot be!" Conway's eyes grow wide. "Azlocke, where's the map? In what section of the forest are we located?"

Azlocke begins to pull a folded map from his pocket, but Conway is too impatient and scales the rocks to me. He gazes below. "I cannot believe that old, stubborn creature has surfaced!" he yells to me, shaking his head in disbelief.

Below us, creatures emerge and march, drums beating. An army comes forth from underground, beating their weapons against their metal clothes, headed straight toward the chaotic front line of the King's army.

"The Dwarves!" Conway screams out. Conway, the Elves, and the Goblins leap up over the stone wall and begin dropping with a terrifying plummet to the ground below, landing hard with grace, but they get in line alongside the marching Dwarves. Conway runs to the front and stops the leader.

"What are Dwarves?" Rowan asks, unsure of the word.

Agrok speaks up. "They are short, stout, husky, spitfire creatures. They are known to be miserable, truthful, but blunt things. They drink heavy amounts of ale and usually keep to themselves. Much like us Giants, they rarely get involved in other creatures' disagreements and never choose a side but their own. Another lucky chance that they just so happen to appear to be angry with Molag and not us. You would not want to upset a Dwarf, little miss! An aggravating and specky enemy those are!"

"Gavor!" Conway blocks the Dwarf King and yells over the chorus of drums and clanging metal against chests. "What brings you above ground, old friend?"

"Molag took our women, children, and slaughtered our elderly and some of the men! Out of our way, Conway!" Gavor beats his sword's pommel against his chest then heaves his heavy sledgehammer high above his head.

"Join us!" Conway stops him again. "Let us fight this army together. Come with us to Dark Hallow to regroup before taking the castle."

Conway makes eyes at me as I descend with Brice to the ground below, my hand reaching up to a fluttery Rowan to help her land softly, my sensitive ears hearing their conversation.

"Battles first, discussions later!" Gavor grunts out and begins the rhythmic beat with his weapons against his chest as his men follow.

The Giants lower the Wolves, Witches, and Azlocke to the field below and they take places alongside the Dwarf army, the Fae creatures flying above. The Giants step carefully over the creatures below and form a line up ahead of the others.

The enemy line is divided and split, but so much closer. The impending slaughter and death are just mere steps in front of us. I pull back on Rowan.

"Please, stay behind me," I whisper, placing her there as she begins her confident stride, heading straight for that horrific line. I rest my hand on her small round belly. She nods.

"You better leave me something to kill, Giants!" Gavor yells, but the Giants cannot hear him over the war cries from behind them and the frantic shouting of orders being given by the enemy front ahead of them.

The enemy rustles and shifts. My stomach turns as I stare ahead and watch the soldiers part, making way for the lost ones.

We knew the King would have lost ones amongst his armies. My heart pounds hard and loud in my ears as my eyes track their impatient swaying. Within the breath of a blink, the creatures race, charging at us, ready to attack, running on all fours. The Giants stop abruptly, confused by creatures they are not familiar with, and hold our advancing line back. The Giants begin reaching out and scooping up dozens of the frantic, crazed demons in each of their hands. They tighten their fists to squish the lost ones they manage to catch. Black oozing blood pops from between fingers, flying in all directions. Ribbons of entrails, organs and rotting tissue dangle from the hands. The rotten sticky blood splashes us, gagging the second and third of our lines as they realize what they are covered in. Death, rotting and pure liquefied evil.

"Yuck!" Esurg yells, "I hate the feeling when the bones pop!" Agrok laughs at her and scoops up more.

"Watch your second line," Tozir thunders back to us. "Some are getting through!"

Gavor grins and readies his sword and sledgehammer, but a wolf leaps up and over him, tackling the first of the breaching lost ones.

"That one was mine to kill, Wolf!" he shouts, cursing the shaggy beast that claimed his foe and snapped its neck.

The wolf shifts and takes human form. "You snooze, you lose, old man!" the she-wolf taunts him, laughing. "You've grown sluggish being underground all these years! Are you even ready for this war?"

He splutters at her as she shifts back into her wolf and takes off for the Giants, leaping into the air again, taking out another lost one. Gavor puffs out his chest at the slandering, disrespecting mutt of a wolf. He rolls his eyes and growls loudly, running for the Giants.

The Giants hold back the first line on their knees, making an almost impenetrable fortress of a wall. Esurg spins on her knees to face the creatures behind her and the other Giants. "Lost ones eliminated! Ew! Ew! Ew!" She wipes her Giantess palms along the earth, trying to scrape off the sticky gore of the putridness of the lost ones' guts that seeps between her fingers. "Ugh, it won't come off!" she yells in frustration, grabbing the edge of her partner's shirt to wipe her hands clean.

"Esurg!" Agrok scowls at her, shaking his head in disgust. "Did you have to? No use, it's not worth saving now." He carefully pulls the shirt up over his head then he too wipes his hands clean, handing it to Tozir and Borog.

There is a pause in the battle. I smell them first as a whistle sounds from the enemy lines along with clanging chains and the scratch of heavy metal scraping. My ears ring, and all other sounds disappear as the King's next line marches forward, the ones in front peeling back to reveal hideous, grotesque beasts. Glistening, razor-pointed canines fill their over-stretched mouths. Overly large eyes, black as onyx, hold a red glowing pupil at the center. Their hunched backs heave with ragged breaths. The creatures slowly begin walking on all fours. They are bulky with muscled limbs, shining claws splitting forward, digging into the earth.

Shock ripples through the rebel party, everyone staring at the beasts the King bred from mist and evil. Then a second line rises into the air, wings booming, lifting a second nightmare from behind the first. These are gangly, bones elongated and lithe. There are talons upon the clawed, disformed feet and hands. The first line lumbers at us, the second taking to the skies, soaring forward.

Gavor's battle cry has them all moving, racing to clash with the enemy line. I push Rowan behind me; an ancient instinct has my heart pounding for war. Brice and I as one run forward. In this new form I will slaughter them, but with Brice. His eyes find mine, betraying the same thought. I reach for my companion, his soft fur beneath my fingers. I feel the blending begin, our bodies becoming one, stronger, faster, larger, a roar lashing through our throat as our body leaps into the air, our maw open and clamping down on the throat, bones, wind pipes of the beastly creatures. We see red, furious as black, purplish blood sprays. Our head jerks, the creature's body going one way, the enormous head the other. We watch as the Dwarf king jumps into the air, spinning with graceful accuracy as he brings his sword down, down through the top of a head, his sledgehammer swinging into the side of the head. A twist of his sword wrist drags it through and the head cracks loud, its skull splitting open.

The Giants reach on their toes, grabbing for the flying things overhead. More blackish purple blood begins to rain, our fur soaked in it. Rowan flies above us, a soft moonlight glow indicating her dragon hard at work helping her to fly, balance, and fight. Brice howls a warning as she battles a creature in the skies. Sorcha races at the attacker coming at Rowan's side. Slamming into it, she sends the creature spinning, falling. It hasn't noticed Sorcha, her blade now aimed at its chest as she dives for the disoriented thing. Rowan hisses with her free hand around the throat of the creature, its talons scraping and grabbing at her hands, Rowan's dagger falling to the earth below, impaling a creature prowling for Azlocke. Rowan thrusts her sword through the dangling creature's center. She watches the light leave its eyes, releases her hand, and it plummets to the earth below. She pivots in the air, racing for another flying beast.

A female werewolf in the middle of the field desperately paces then lays herself by her companion, its dead body morphing back to its human form, revealing a gaping wound from throat to groin. The female howls up to the skies. Her pain-filled song grates against our bones, our ears lowering and falling back. Brice and I as one swallow hard against the bile rising in our throat as a stench of death lures us toward the female, still howling her pain to the Moon Goddess.

One of the enemy creatures slinks toward the werewolf and her companion. We race, our claws digging, gripping the earth, propelling our body forward. Our head down, we charge, plowing into the creature and knocking it to the ground so it rolls away from the mourning werewolf. Our enormous paw steps hard upon the grotesque creature, and it pants. Its eyes find ours. They are full of pleading, like the creature it once was has pushed to the surface and now begs with its too big eyes. With a heavy heart, we realize while looking past the nightmarish mutation of the King's mist that it was once human.

Its hoarse voice pleads within our mind, "End... me... please, free... me!"

The female werewolf is there now, while we have it pinned down at its throat. She tears into the beast with her claws, slashing chest to groin, its innards spilling to the ground, staining it. She bows her head, thanking us for allowing her to take the kill, having the blood revenge. We blink at her and she is gone, lost in the bodies.

We watch as Susanna and Rebecca stand back to back, wielding their magics, battling. That fouling blood has matted their long hair, freckles of it splattered on their faces, beading and dripping from them. The creatures keep coming for us, so we battle, all of us fighting, as our teeth and claws rip and tear through beast after beast, our brains registering the armored humans now fighting against us, draped in colors of the evil King, my grandfather, his colors plastered to their armor, his signet on their helms. Rage empowers our body as we shred and tear through his soldiers while he sits comfortably in the safety of his castle. He willingly sacrificed his people, his grotesque creatures, and that knowledge enrages our body more, powering us through the battle.

Hours pass and the battle ebbs. Warriors and magic users alike are spent and exhausted. The enemy army completely falters, order lost in the ranks as creatures scream out their final death. The small herd of the human men goes running, throwing their weapons down and fleeing to the cover and protection of the forest's tree line.

"They're running away!" Gavor screams in frustration. "This is why we never fight alongside Giants! You take all the glory out of it!"

Agrok and Borog let out a chuckle that shakes the ground, causing our party to stumble with fatigue. Swords and shields lower as what little numbers that remain of the King's army retreat, falling back to the cover of the thickly wooded forest, and then there is silence, and emptiness.

Suddenly Azlocke breaks that horrible silence with hysterical, crazed laughter. Brice and I sit, resting gingerly with pain shooting through our muscles to our belly. Our bodies separate, cleaving apart from one another. I gulp down air, now lying in my own body, rock digging into my back as I look up. My heart hammers in my chest as I let everything sink in. I wait, my senses hyper aware, but the tension turns to fatigue and pain. Rowan flitters down and she bucks against her wings as her body limply lowers itself next to me. Her breathing is as labored as mine. Brice, barely picking up his body, his limbs wobbling, limps to her exposed back as she faces me. He drops, curling his body against her back.

The four Giants lay down, couples head to head, the women feet to feet, creating a wall with their bodies. Agrok whispers to the rebel army safely ensconced behind them, the mountain range and sheer cliffs at our back.

"We rest." His fingers entwine with his lover's. "Our bodies will guard the unprotected field while we all rest."

I let loose a heavy breath and scooch my body closer to Rowan's, wrapping my arms around her, breathing in the scent of her. Tears run down her face. Her hand presses against my chest, feeling its thumping rhythm, as she closes her eyes. I wait while she cries and, when the exhaustion takes her, and Brice is gently snoring behind her, the field around us turns quiet. I let my eyes close and fitfully find a deep sleep.

***

Hidden and unseen, Gabriel watches, hiding like a wretch within the forest. He watches as the King's army weakens, slaughtered at the hands of the rebels. He watches the rebels, head cocked to the side, as they gather their dead and injured. He strains his ears, listening for the direction they are heading next and when he has it, he turns and begins northward, thinking happily to himself. It is time to update and truly upset the Mighty King.

A wicked grin takes over his face. So much for Azlocke being his beloved Head Guard, the traitor! He grins further. Surely with this information, the King will make Gabriel his new Head Guard.

No longer will I be a lowly footman, he thinks to himself. He envisions his new high position and the luxuries it will bring him—the attention that he rightfully deserves, the females he knows will finally throw themselves at him instead of turning away in disgust.

I am so looking forward to seeing Azlocke come back to the castle to update his King thinking no one knows his secret, he thinks. *An ambush will be ready when he arrives. I will throw him into the dungeons personally.* Gabriel smiles to himself. *Maybe I will even have some time alone with him and punish him.*

He stops, chants a spell. A fearful-looking ancient oak door opens in the middle of the forest. He looks back over his shoulder at the small pathetic army and steps through, chuckling. The door closes and vanishes behind him.

***

Gabriel kneels, head bowed before the fuming, raging King as he roars out through the pain against the deception of his best warrior, his beloved Head Guard. Nuala sheds a single tear and wipes it away before anyone can notice. She places her small hand over the King's fisted, shaking hand.

"My Lord, may I suggest..." She pauses and cautiously glances at the King.

"What is it, Nuala?" He lets out his held, angry breath.

"What if My Lord opens the portal doors to his Southern and Western armies and repositions them at the Dark Hallow Lands' boundary? If Gabriel is speaking truthfully, the rebels will not see an attack there happening. Make it at the dead of night, while the rebels sleep—it perhaps will ensure his King's victory." She pauses, knowing he will brush off her next statement, not thinking it necessary. "Since they are aided by four Giants, perhaps now would be the time to bring the dispatched Northern army back here and send them with the rest of your mighty army. It would make an unbreachable, strong, and solid front."

"You have always proven most useful for strategic planning, wife. I do so appreciate how your mind works." He kisses her cheek. "For your peace of mind, I will bring the dispatched Northern army back here," he says gently, then caresses the back of her hand. Nuala suppresses a disgusted shudder, forcing herself to give him a feline grin.

Molag twists his wrist and three doors appear within the throne room. Gabriel watches in awe at his King's power, to open portal doors out of thin air. The King nods to his three heavily chained slaves and they each take a separate door and reemerge with the King's army generals. The slaves move away and disappear in the darkness of the pillars of the throne room. The Generals kneel before the king.

"Gabriel will now be honored as Head Guard to the King," says Molag. "The Southern, Western, and Northern armies will go with him, leading an attack in the Dark Hallow Lands where we believe all the rebels are hiding and regrouping before coming here. You, my brave armies, will hit them there first. Leave no survivors. Except," the King pauses, "Azlocke. I want him alive and brought before me."

Gabriel acts surprised by his new position. "Your Highness, it would be my utmost honor to lead your men. I promise to you here and now, I myself will bring the traitor before you." He bows deeply.

Nuala snickers at the foul creature that is Gabriel. She has never trusted him. His gaze only ever sends a shiver down her spine. Nuala stands with grace, cunning, and beauty, and claps thrice. "To our esteemed generals, welcome to my home." Three ornate seats are carried by servants and placed behind the warriors. They are heavy, decorative and grotesque ornamented things that Nuala thinks are so very ugly, but to these creatures she knows the chairs will be seen as elaborate, *smaller* thrones. Molag shifts, irritated, beside her.

"Please, my Lords, sit and let me welcome you properly." Nuala snaps her fingers at three of the most delicate beauties of the King's concubines. These three men are the most sadistic, feral, and lethal of the King's men and that is why they are generals. Nausea rises in her gut, up her throat, threatening to choke her. She shoves her fear back down, deep down. She swallows and flicks her slender wrist and three large bowls appear, filled with steaming liquid. It rises in gentle swaying plumes. The three concubines kneel and settle before the men and bowls, each beginning to undo their boots.

"I welcome you and invite you to sit and take your ease. Your time away from this palace has been long, your journeys hard." The women begin soaking the men's feet and washing. "Tonight you will be given comfortable and warm beds to sleep in. Tomorrow we will have a feast, each soldier eating his fill, a ball to celebrate these mighty men's victory, and on the third day the kingdom will surround these men as they take to their steads and ready for war."

Nuala is met with a chorus of stamping feet. The three generals give a slight bow of the head to the gracious Queen as Molag stands beside her. Taking her hand, he brings it to his lips.

"Your Queen is a gracious Queen," he calls out, not looking away from her eyes as she gives a shallow curtsy to the king. "Tonight we rest, tomorrow we feast, and on the third day my Generals will parade through the streets and," he takes a deep breath, his eyes glistening at Nuala, a wicked, malicious grin corrupting his face, "We go to war!" he bellows, and the ominous beating of feet begins anew.

Nuala casually glances to the side and behind at the black raven that sits listening on the windowsill. She winks at it, and the bird tips back out the window and falls. Falling then banking hard, it flies as strong and as fast as it can toward the Dark Hallow Lands to warn Amanda.

CHAPTER TWENTY

The Dark Hallow Lands

We arrive early morning in the Dark Hallow Lands with the help of the centaur guards along the border who spot our troop coming. The sun has just barely risen, the sky filling with hues of pink and orange kissing the horizon, and we are escorted to a large canopy tent. Azlocke smiles and sighs at the sight of the Chief Centaur's tent.

The large centaur exits the tent to welcome the last of the rebels to his lands. He walks slowly to me and introduces himself. "I am Brynzin, the ruler of the Dark Hallow Lands." His satyr wife—I flip through my memory—*Ryanna*, I believe her name to be, follows behind him, smiling at the creatures before her. "Welcome, fellow creatures. It is a relief and blessing to have you here. How went the battle against the Eastern army?" Brynzin's voice is rough and loud.

"You mean lack of battle!" Gavor grumbles. Brynzin tilts his head, puzzled at the Dwarf's comment.

"We have tents and beds ready for you. Just there," the Chief points along a narrow path, "in those two canopied huts."

Ryanna bows her head to the group. "You'll find your other companions there resting. You all seem to have arrived untouched, so for that we thank the Goddess."

"We have our losses," Rebecca barks out, more unshed tears glistening in her eyes. Brynzin softens and approaches her, gently bowing his head to place his forehead to hers, acknowledging the loss of her husband.

"I urge those of you who would like to take rest to head towards the designated huts. Those that wish to start discussions about what happened along your journey and how best to approach the castle, enter my hut." Brynzin then nods to his wife to escort the group that wants to rest to the huts. He pulls back the flap, allowing creatures to enter around the large log table in the middle of the room.

Barcella approaches her mother, Ryanna, and rubs her nose against hers. "I am most happy to see you well, daughter," Ryanna says. "Join your father, I will return shortly."

I kiss Rowan and urge her to go rest. She follows the Chieftess reluctantly. Before letting my fingers go, she whispers, "I will find Drake and Amanda." I nod over to Brice, a gesture that tells him to follow her and keep guard of my mate. He trots beside her slowly once he reaches her side. Her fingers caress the fur atop his head.

I enter the Chief's hut along with Azlocke, Gavor, and the others. Brynzin lays out a large map that stretches across the table and clears his throat to begin introductions.

"You all know of myself and my daughter Barcella. There are faces I know well, but there are new faces also." Brynzin nods toward King Conway but his eyes dart to me, assessing, puzzling. I feel Fafnir pulse within me at the unwanted attention and my wings erupt from my back. I stretch them a bit, bone tired. Everything is heavy and sore. I gaze about the tent and the faces within. When a scroll appears atop the large table, I lean forward to see it.

The New Realm Order of the Rebel Alliances
King Conway, of the Elven Kingdom
King Gavor, High Dwarf of the Caves
Vladimir, Vampire King of the Ice Mountains
Azlocke, Goblin, Head Guard to King Molag
Drake and Amanda, Goblin Prince and Goblin-made
Xander, Alpha Werewolf of the Crescent Rose Moon Pack
Benjamin, Beta Werewolf of the Crescent Rose Moon Pack
Brynzin and Ryanna, Centaur and Satyr, Chief and Chieftess of The Dark Hallow Lands
Sorcha and Gwendolyn, Fairies, Queens of the Fairy Lands
Elgeeva, High Priestess of the Witches, Princess and Daughter of Conway
Susanna and Rebecca, second and third Priestesses
Cormac and Oisin, Warriors of the Human Realm
Agrok and Esurg, Giants
Emira, The Mother

"Please, sign the treaty of the rebels for the promise of a new realm, the hopes and dreams of the common creatures, the promise of a better future," says Brynzin. I notice all the names, titles, and lands, and I am absent. "Merek, state the species of yourself and your mate. Pledge to the treaty as the others have and sign," Brynzin adds as a quill feather pen rises in the air, readying to write.

I shift on my feet. "I am Merek, son of Drake and Amanda, mate of Rowan. I am... um..." I pause and look down at myself, unsure how to answer for my species. "Honestly, we have no idea what I've become, my mate included," I shrug. "Elgeeva, Emira, and the Goddess of the Moon preformed a ritual and transformed my mate Rowan. She in turn transformed me. The blood of every known creature was mixed and given to Rowan and I. The Moon Goddess blessed us each with a dragon." I close my eyes and Fafnir's eyes appear and scan the room, and he speaks through me.

"My mate Midgard and I are creatures of Old, the last two of our kind. The Goddess blessed me with this vessel. His body and blood make me stronger." Fafnir closes one eye and it reopens with mine. Every creature surrounding the table stares at my one eye and Fafnir's one eye as I exhale a gentle mist of smoke.

"Ah, the prophecy children! Fafnir, Dragon of Old," Brynzin greets him, bowing. "Merek, I would very much like to meet your mate Rowan after our meeting. Welcome, my unique friend!"

I watch the feather pen ink into the document,

Merek and Rowan, The Prophecy Children
Fafnir and Midgard, Dragon Guardians of the Prophecy

"Excellent!" Brynzin claps and gestures toward the map. "We are here." He places a wooden female figurine of the Goddess of the Moon on top of Dark Hallow. "The Goblin Castle, here." He places a small carved wooden throne, marking the castle on the map.

A frantic crowing raven pierces the day as it enters Dark Hallow. The bird screams. Everyone exits the hut and looks up.

It caws frantically to the creatures below, scanning each of the upturned faces. Brynzin reaches out his arm and calls to the bird. "Raven! Here! Who do you seek to relay your message?" he bellows to the creature in the sky.

The raven swoops down and lands on Brynzin's outstretched arm. Nuala's voice comes from the bird as it opens its mouth in a silent caw to let its sender speak. "Amanda," it whispers.

Brynzin clears his throat. His voice booms loud as he calls out for the name requested. "AMANDA!" He pauses to listen for a reply. "Is there an AMANDA within the camp?" he calls out again.

"Here!" my mother shouts and runs forward, my father at her heels. Mum approaches and stares warily at the raven. She knows that bird. "It is Nuala's personal raven," Mum whispers to us. The bird tilts its head to her and once it recognizes her features, it nuzzles its small face to Mum's cheek, pulls back, and opens its mouth again.

"The Southern, Western, and Northern armies will be outside the boundary of Dark Hallow soon. Gabriel, the new Head Guard to the King, will be leading them. All are to be slaughtered, no survivors are to be left in Dark Hallow, that is all but one survivor—Azlocke. The traitor to the King will be brought before him and executed." Nuala's voice pauses. The raven tilts its head, listening to something. "I am delaying as best I can. READY yourselves! On the thrice dead of night they will come!" Nuala's voice urgently whispers.

Sober expressions are exchanged. Mum gently strokes the raven's iridescent feathers and whispers to it.

"Thank you for this, my brave friend. Stay safe, stay alive. I will see you again." She kisses the bird's beak. It blinks at my mother and then she throws the bird high into the air. It caws shrilly as it circles us before racing back to whence it came.

"It's time for rest. Nuala has given us a mighty gift—let's not waste it," Amanda commands.

***

Everyone is on edge. I'm on guard and it's the dead of night. All the lands of Dark Hallow are still and quiet, waiting, listening. My breath plumes in front of me, wafting heavily. The air is too still.

Brice's eyes glow silver in the moonlight, reflecting the light as his gaze searches the deep, dark woods. The silence is oppressive and it clenches my jaw, my teeth aching. Brice's head rotates sharply to the left, his nose scenting the air. A distant *thawk* sounds, reverberating through the eerie stillness, like something big has been launched into the sky.

Agrok whispers from my left, soon after the strange sound, "They are here." His voice is strained and gargled; blood drips from his mouth. Everyone looks up to the Giant and blood rains down upon them. A tree trunk sized spear is pierced through his heart. He stumbles back and falls. Esurg screams as she tries to catch her mate before he falls. She kneels beside him and sobs.

"I am sorry, My Love," he whispers and touches her cheek. Tears run down the Giantess's face as his body slowly turns to stone. A mountain formed of a Giant, who has just turned to stone and rock, lays slain near the war room hut of Brynzin. Esurg weeps as she pulls the tree trunk of a spear from his chest. His gaze is still upon her, frozen in stone. His outreached finger stills, forever frozen in stone, trying to caress the cheek of his mate.

"I cannot continue without my Mate," she cries out. Her voice shakes the ground. She aims the spear—

"Esurg! NO!" King Conway yells up to her but she has already pierced her own heart. The Giantess gulps down the blood rising in her throat. Her body buckles. She pulls the spear from her bosom and lays it gently down. She lowers her head upon Agrok's chest and curls her body into her stone mate. She lifts her one leg, placing it on top of his, and curls her foot around his.

"Forever together, forever frozen, My Love. I will stay with you, always!" she whispers and rests her hand upon his chest next to her face. She closes her eyes and as I gaze upon her she too slowly turns to stone and all goes quiet.

I frantically search the area where the enormous arrow has come from. There's nothing. Brice growls so low, I know I'm only hearing it within my mind as he is fifty yards ahead of me, hidden in the thicket at the edge of the forest before us. I watch patches of movement, his nose protruding from the cover surrounding him as he scents the air. I catch a new, strange scent and switch to my Goblin sight. This lull in attack—where... where the *fuck* are the King's forces? The smell registers in my brain as something's large shadow filters through the trees. The only sound is Tozir's weeping.

"Where is everyone?" I ask, agitated, through my mind to Brice. "Where the hell has the Giant who threw the spear gone?"

Crickets chirp, and I bristle with pent up adrenaline, anxious from the nothingness. Tozir and Borog approach gingerly, their large eyes darting about, searching, looking. They kneel before the stone couple. Tozir holds onto Borog as they both weep with grief. Tozir reaches out and places her hand upon the stone shoulder of Esurg, while she still clings tightly to her mate. Borog reaches out his free hand and rests it atop Esurg's hand upon Agrok's chest. Together they cry and say their goodbyes to the frozen Giants that lay before them, forever tangled in a loving embrace of rock that will last for the remainder of time.

From far to my right comes the sound of wind. My eyes locate the source of the sound in a large vortex of swirling blue mist. Enlarging, its surface calms to a rippling vertical pool of water. It ripples as an onslaught of arrows breaks through the portal door.

They soar through the village of Dark Hallow. Susanna and Rebecca quickly form a wide magic umbrella shield, protecting everyone underneath. Those who are not under the magical shield begin running, screaming. Panic and chaos erupt in the small village.

I tunnel down into myself, eyes closed, concentrating, and tap into Fafnir within me. I open myself to him wholly, tunneling deeper and deeper, down and down into that ancient, wild power. Screaming his name, my body arches, stretches and grows. I let him morph my body into that of his, my legs lengthening, growing wide, my arms growing scales and talons that plummet to the ground, shaking it. I feel Fafnir draw in a deep breath as he places our massive body before the rippling mirror of a door, then he releases a torrent of fire into the portal. My throat is warmed by the purplish heat of the flame as we continue vaulting the fire. From the periphery of my conscious, I notice too late the second portal pool opening to our left. Our own fire erupts from this smaller door, condensing the flame. A chorus of screaming flames fires at us. Its tight confinement plows into our flank and blasts our side, throwing us from our feet, hurtling us into the tree line. Our body blasts through the old strong growth of the trees, splintering them, a boulder of rock crushed beneath our massive body, knocking the breath from our lungs.

"Giles!" Susanna screams over the chorus of death drums, the noise leaking loudly from multiple new shimmering and rippling portal doors. They cast everything in an unholy bluish tint. Giles casts a large, wide shield that races from him, plowing into the first of the foot soldiers to emerge through the two portals before them.

My head throbbing, my lungs wheezing, I race back in my own body to the forming line of rebels. Coming to stand beside my father, "Where is Rowan? Where is Mum?" I ask urgently.

"Together." Drake gazes out at the chaos unfolding.

"Go back! Protect them," I bark at him. He nods to me, turns, and runs off to protect the two women and the children cloistered within a tent where I left Rowan resting.

I watch as lost ones spill into the village, attacking anything that moves. The chorus of their detached voices screams in my head.

"Kills everything! Kill! Attack! Eats them, eats, food, food, food! Tear, rip, shreds them. Annihilate!"

Brice, Fafnir, and I instantly morph into one. My body grows as the wolf, the dragon, and I shift into a new, larger, more powerful being. Our back arching, I can feel the echo of pain as bones and sinew reshape, remake, as we let the power take over, let it fill us, transform us, unleashing its potential fully.

Our new eyes watch the werewolf warriors leap into the battle, clothes ripping from their muscled, strong bodies as their wolf forms come erupting forth, a flurry of fur, teeth, and claws, maws dripping.

Dwarfs charge at the advancing enemy army, their swords swinging in one hand while they bring down sledgehammers with the other. Borog stands and turns toward the approaching line of lost ones, stomping his feet hard on top of them. A female satyr screams. The Chieftess is in a struggle with a lost one; she holds its wrists back but its mouth snaps at her face. She desperately tries holding back the decaying wild creature, but her hooves keep slipping against the clay dirt. Brynzin snaps the neck of the lost one he is battling and runs to aid his Chieftess. He grabs it away from his wife by the back of its head. Brynzin snarls in its face then twists his hand. The neck snaps and the body crumples to the ground.

"Are you alright?" Our ears ring with Brynzin's voice yelling to his wife over the clang and discord of the battle beginning to rage. His Chieftess shudders. Our senses heightened, we see her regain control, her body pulsing. She lets loose a shrill war cry and charges, forming a line with her husband and daughter by her side, their glinting swords shimmering in the blueish purple hue that radiates from the portal doors.

"Ryanna!" I yell to her while gripping an enemy soldier's arms. "Find my father, Drake! He will help guard!" My tail materializes and swishes behind me then shoots out around my side to pierce through the lost one, killing it. Our tail snaps, jagged razors protruding from the tip of it, skewering a second lost one with bloodlust, our eyes on Ryanna while she shoves her blade quickly and fiercely through the chin and up, crunching the soft of the skull of her opponent. She twists and the creature before her crumples. She nods to me, breath heaving, then spins gracefully on her hooves and rushes to another section of the village.

"Fafnir!" I yell out loud and shut my eyes. Haze and smoke swirl around me as Fafnir's form leaves my body and materializes beside me. Yet my new form stays true, his magic and power still mine to wield, our power growing and ever changing with new abilities.

"Brice!" His form leaves me as well. My form holds true, dragon and wolf magics still pounding through my veins.

Fafnir roars; fire erupts from his mouth, igniting twenty creatures that advance toward us. He flicks his tail and jagged spades push through the tip of his tail. Fafnir spins his massive body around, his tail whipping out and felling forty more enemy soldiers.

Susanna and Rebecca let down their casted shields and run for the hut that contains the children. Giles shifts his casted shield and repositions it against the raining arrows that continue to fall.

"Drake!" Ryanna calls out.

"Here! My Lady, here, in here!" Drake waves his hands high in the air, directing the satyr. Susanna and Rebecca chant a spell, casting a protective barrier around the hut.

"Here!" screams a female Centaur with an infant cradled in her arms.

Tozir lowers her hand and the Centaur climbs up onto her palm.

"Hold onto my thumb!" Tozir speaks to her and as quickly and gently as possible lifts the small creature within her hand to the hut with the other non-warriors. Twenty human warriors and Drake encircle the hut. Susanna and Rebecca guard the entrance, their shield spell encircling the fighters that guard at ground level and rippling up into a dome bubble.

Susanna projects her voice out over the battle. "King's Guard are approaching the children's hut! Merek! We need HELP!" she roars as a sword comes slashing at her.

Brice howls to me then races for the hut. A Guard points the tip of his sword, poised to pierce Susanna's belly. The sword deflects against the casted invisible barrier shield; the steal cannot pass through!

Emira storms out of the hut and approaches the advancing soldiers. She throws her arms away from her chest. A blast of wind throws the soldiers thirty feet back, knocking them from their feet.

The rebel Elves begin firing their own arrows at them, killing each soldier that approaches the hut. The Elves form a circle, creating a second barrier around the hut, fighting with grace and speed as they fire arrow after arrow. Emira casts her own domed shield to protect the Elves who continue to draw their arrows.

Two male enemy Giants of the King emerge from the woods and enter the village. Tozir and Borog carefully step over their fellow fighting warriors, but make sure their feet land on the lost ones and King's Guard that are now pouring out from the tree line of the forest. Tozir watches, enraged, as one of the King's Giants reaches for the quiver on his back, grabbing for another spear and aiming it toward her mate.

"You will not kill another of my kin!" she screams with a war cry, reaching for him and wrestling the spear from his grasp. The Giant backs deeper into the woods with the struggle.

Borog kicks out in a swing hard and fast at the charging opponent. Connecting hard to the chest, bones snap and echo about the trees, sending the enemy Giant flying backward, crashing and causing a storm of falling trees about the forest. Tozir grabs the back of her opponent's head and slams his face into the newly formed rock that was once her dear friends' legs. Its face crunches, the Giant's skull and face sunken in, and she lifts its body with all her strength and throws it into the woods to fall atop the other Giant foe that Borog is dealing with. Its solid rock form quickly entraps the other one beneath it. Borog stomps through the forest and rips the other Giant's head from its shoulders. He holds the rock-forming head and rolls it along the forest floor. As it rolls, it takes out lost ones and soldiers who cannot get out of its path. It continues rolling straight through the village, finally stopping at the opposite end of the village at the tree line. Trees topple in every direction from the impact of the boulder. The rock head has gouged a trench through the middle of the village. Borog continues to step upon soldiers and lost ones as Tozir reaches, swatting for the new portal forming high above in the dark night, winged creatures flying from it into the Dark Hallow skies.

The King's army of Fae creatures takes to the sky and the hordes of wings group up, forming lines, banking for the children's hut. Emira adjusts her stance and holds her focus on her casted shield. Twenty flying Fae dive hard in an attempt to rip open the top of hut. Twenty long fingers of bright white streaks of lightning zap out and reach their flying targets. The bodies disintegrate in ash.

"I'm injured!" screams a female Fae who runs toward Emira. The poor woman is disheveled and limping badly; her left wing looks bent at a painful angle. Emira allows her to pass through the shield, her eyes darting about the fairy, trying to place her, to recall her name. Rebecca and Susanna let their shield drop for her to cross and then recast it.

The fairy limps into the hut. Children are huddled closely together. The injured Fae surveys her surroundings and approaches a female Centaur that holds tight an infant.

The Fairy coos at the baby and smiles. "May I hold it?" the injured fairy asks its mother.

The female Centaur steps back warily. The mother, also not recognizing the strange Fae woman, feels something is wrong or not quite right in those eyes that stare at the infant. The Centaur backs away further, pulling her baby closer to her chest.

Drake stands up and places himself between the mother and injured fairy that he too does not recognize.

"Excuse me, miss." He extends his hand to her. "I am Drake." But the injured fairy interrupts him.

"Yes, everyone knows who you are," she gets out between clenched teeth.

"Forgive me, but I take pride in knowing every creature that is in our rebel army. I do not know you, and I can see no visible injury to your leg or your wing, so why do you limp?" Drake asks softly, but before he can continue the fairy spins him fast by his shoulder, flutters her wings, and grips Drake's head hard and places a dagger against his throat.

"Alright kiddos, listen up! This here is your beloved Prince." She spits on Drake's face. "I'm going to make this real simple like. I know the prophesied female is in the hut." The fairy pauses, scenting the air. "I can *smell* her." Her eyes blacken, growing too large for her face.

The children stand. The older, taller children grab and push the small children behind them.. The standing crowd obscures the intruder's sight so she cannot see Rowan and Amanda at the back of the hut, Rowan laying with her head in Amanda's lap. Amanda tries to calmly play with Rowan's hair, the girl still asleep. She tries hard not to tense up and wake Rowan. She bites her lip hard, praying that Rowan is in a deep slumber and unaware of what is happening.

"You give me the female that I am looking for and I'll return Drake here unharmed. I'll just slowly back out of this hut with the girl and will leave you all alone." She gazes about at the eyes staring back at her, but no one moves.

"Come, come. Surely the girl isn't worth the risk to your beloved Prince, the risk to your own lives?" She grins wickedly at them.

Amanda gasps softly as a gust of wind whips her hair. Rowan is no longer laying where she was. Amanda jumps up and stands on tiptoes to see over the others. There is Rowan, standing behind the intruder unseen. Gone are Rowan's bright steel gray eyes speckled with blue. Large black orbs stare at the back of the head of the fairy holding Drake. Rowan's head tilts to one side. Amanda shivers as Rowan's appearance changes, her body becoming more of a black buzzing haze, a shadowy form. Her facial features gone, a black slate, a smoky haze remains. What is now Rowan's form hovers behind the Fairy that holds the dagger to Drake's neck. A gasp escapes every mouth when the only thing that is visible on Rowan's face is her smile of razor-sharp teeth. She is positively frightening.

"Looking for me?" Rowan whispers, causing the Fairy to lose her grip on Drake but grip the dagger tighter. Drake staggers forward and Rowan sinks her pearly razor smile into the neck of the creature that she holds tight against her. The body buckles and jerks as Rowan's tail wraps around the torso, squishing and crushing it. Rib bones pop loudly out of place; within seconds Rowan drains it of blood and lets the body fall crumpled and withered to the floor.

Rowan takes a deep breath and relaxes her wings, slowly stretching them. Amanda blinks and when she opens her eyes, Rowan is gone.

Rowan flies out and through the barriers cast by the witches and Emira that guard the hut. She flies unbelievably fast as she captures the first flying creature she sees. Lightning fast, she latches onto her prey and drains their blood. Bodies begin raining down. A horrid sound ripples throughout the village as Rowan drops their bodies and they hit the earth below.

I look up as her black, hazy, speeding blur catches my attention while the bodies continue to fall.

"Rowan!" I call out in fear. I watch as she takes the last of the creatures that are in the sky. I then notice Emira standing near the hut. She has changed her appearance and appears like a bright glowing shape that pulses like the sun.

"Come to me, my dear child. Rowan, come to Mother!" she sings out and coaxes to Rowan. An agitated Rowan is drawn to the glowing figure like a moth to a flame. Emira holds her arms out wide and pulses her glowing light brighter. Rowan flutters on weakening wings down and into Emira's embrace. Emira quickly walks Rowan back into the hut.

Through Brice, I listen.

"I don't feel well, Emira," Rowan whispers with a hiccup. Emira lays the girl on a cot and fetches for two wooden buckets as Amanda runs to my mate.

"She's burning up, Emira," Amanda says, feeling her face. She sees the nausea contort Rowan's sweet face. Amanda holds a bucket as Rowan turns. She vomits hard and fast into the bucket, covering Amanda's face in a hot sticky red fluid. Rowan's body heaves and erupts more liquid from her mouth and nose. Blood drips from her nostrils and chin as she moans in discomfort.

The adults surrounding the cot back far away from Rowan. Emira turns on them, furious as she smells their collective scent of fear.

"Don't you dare fear this child!" she screams at them. "Don't you dare! She only did what came to her instinctively, to PROTECT all of you! That fear is what started all this nonsense in the first place! FEAR of an unknown creature!" She shakes with anger. "The fear of a known creature, that is different! She is a CHILD! She is no trained warrior! She acted on instinct! Instead of fearing her, get to know the poor girl, teach her your ways, learn from her in return. That child was transformed just like the prophecy said, into a new creature we all prayed for to save us, formed of blood given freely from each of your species. Don't you dare fear her!" Emira huffs. Amanda grabs the second bucket as Rowan leans forward again, emptying her stomach of blood.

"Emira!" Elgeeva calls. "I need your assistance, now!"

Emira glares at the people that gather near the children's hut one last time before stomping out of the tent.

"MATE! MINE!" I snap at Elgeeva as she bars my way. I can hear Rowan vomiting again. "The baby?" I demand.

"Calm yourself, Merek!" Elgeeva growls at me. "You may see your mate, but you must calm yourself! You cannot enter that tent as you are now! Go back to fighting, use that energy. We have your mate, she is safe!" Elgeeva speaks firmly.

"You're blocking me!" I roar at Elgeeva. "MINE! MY MATE! Let me through!"

"Merek!" Emira places herself between myself and Elgeeva. "The children are scared as all hell at what they witnessed your mate just do inside that tent. I cannot have them fearing you as well. Calm yourself and I will take you to see your mate!" Emira smacks me hard on the face, stunning me, Brice whining against the pain we both feel. My dragon roars somewhere above us, rattling the hut. I shake my head, shoulders heaving, and slowly calm myself. My black orb eyes slowly return to normal.

I glare at Brice. He's already laying beside her and I nod to him and Rowan. Both nod back then she vomits hard. Her small frame shivers heavily. I resist running to her as she gasps for breath, but the vomit comes forward instead of air. I search the sky, finding my dragon, and spread my wings. I push off the ground, my wings spreading and carrying me into the air. I hear Rowan's hiccups, the wind whispering to me that her breathing is calming.

"She is not injured, Merek," Emira says to Brice, her words clear in my mind with the connection. "It is not her blood that is coming up. It's the blood from the creatures she drained dry. She drank too fast and from too many. Her belly cannot hold it all," Emira whispers and I see her caress Rowan's cheek as Rowan falls back, passing out, exhausted.

"Amanda, watch over her. Drake, come with me. We may be needed outside," Emira whispers.

I glance down, watching Emira, Elgeeva, and my father emerge from the hut to find the battle looming beyond.

The night waxes and wanes, the battle rages. It ebbs and flows, a dance of wild chaos. My brain is fused with three sets of eyes, three different positions of battling, our three bloodlines flowing, surging, strengthening. Brice and the wolves battle wretched four-legged teethy creatures of onyx, tricky shadow things that move like spilled ink. Fafnir is in the skies, wrestling, biting, clawing creatures half his size with twice his speed. Winged beasts emerge, bred to resemble dragons, but they are a terrifying combination of snouts, of iron teeth, lithe slithering bodies that seem to not house bones with five clawed, pronged talons. They were made by a mad breeder to birth forth nightmares.

I engage with the soldiers of the King's Guard, these ruined men. Every species has been brought together to fight the horrors of the mad king. What had these creatures once been? Fathers, brothers, husbands, bakers, groomsmen, blacksmiths? What were they before the King corrupted them, what lives did they lead? My heart tears as another life is winked out by my blade, my claws, my own razor-sharp teeth. Their blood, rotten and black, drips from my mouth, the foulness that invaded these bodies so long ago. My body hums with strength and what seems like a bottomless well of energy and motion, but my heart and mind mourn, wail against the act of it all. Watching the blasphemy of all this life gone to waste, these creatures that fight and fight, by the Mother of Light! They just keep coming throughout the night, while my grandfather the Goblin King sits safely upon his throne, no doubt somehow watching this wretched nonsense unfold, sitting on his cushioned throne, the coward, the pompous ass, the insufferable King of the land who uses all to do his bidding.

Rage and anger boil through my veins, pumping harder, feeding the fight in me. I think of the female lost one back in the forest that became my friend, in her own way, greeting me, smiling her toothless smile with berry stained lips. I think of the way she was devoured before my eyes, her skull cracked open, brains spilled on the ground and pooling into a melting, oozy liquid—it's burned into my memory.

Everything smells of death and blood. Bile rises up in my throat, choking me as I hastily swallow it down. It burns as I dance with a King's Guard, our bodies spinning. He hammers a blow with his sword arm. I deflect this and slide my blade down his, my free hand fisting his hair and sword arm contouring in. I bring his neck to my blade, shoving his head back as the blade slices forward. His blood sprays in time with his pulse—he staggers, his neck a spewing, pulsing geyser.

Falling face first to the ground before my feet, I heave. Our three sets of eyes gaze about the battling village. I watch as Rebecca and Susanna fling out a powerful white blinding spell at a mirrored portal door. We hear the cracking, the splintering of glass as the door implodes upon itself. The impact knocks into friend and foe alike. Cheers erupt loud and echoing from the rebels as Rebecca and Susanna take out one mirror portal after the other. Together they change the tides. The women have strategically bottlenecked the remaining portals, forcing what remains of the emerging King's armies that continue to pour from the rippling, shimmering surfaces into our regrouped front lines.

Tozir hoists herself up onto Borog's shoulders, the massive Giant rising to his toes as his mate reaches up into the sky, grasping, pulling, and ripping the sky portal. It shatters, the spent magical pieces raining down upon the Giants, slicing and nicking their skin deep. The shards jut out, plunged deep into their bones, as the two howl in pain and victory. I watch Tozir cup her left eye; before her palm covers it, I see a shard of glass the size of my head protruding from her eye socket. Borog scoops his injured mate into his arms, taking massive unthinking steps toward the warded hut. The ground bounces and trembles as his racing feet slip, he and his mate sliding, his body gliding across the coarse earth through and into the warded magical wall that Emira still holds. Elgeeva runs for the injured Giantess.

Fafnir lets loose another fire breath of searing white, the heat prickling my neck, against the creature above me. Sweat drips down my back, my sword parrying as I continue my dance, dipping right, sliding forward, chest arching inward, evading the oncoming slicing swords, stepping back twice. Bodies fall hard, a deafening crunch of bones meeting earth, vacant eyes staring heavenward. Blow after blow of my sword deflects the enemies' weapons, the sweat dripping as another searing white light illuminates the sky above.

Brice's maw drips in a rainbow hue of reds, blues, and inky black. I feel his body leap, so graceful, so powerful, as he collides in the air with a nightmarish creature, his teeth buried deep in the creature's ribs. I feel the reverberations of teeth crunching through ribs and organs, the body limp in his mouth, the shake of his mighty head, the body flung away to the right. A goosebump-eliciting howl breaks from my companion as he howls to the full moon appearing from its hidden place in the thick, voluptuous clouds. The other wolves howl as the Moon Goddess shines bright and strong upon her beloved children, filling them with strength and valor to continue the fight.

A man leaps out from behind a hut and grabs tightly onto Elgeeva's neck.

"Gabriel!" Azlocke roars.

"You're coming with me!" Gabriel yells into her ear, looking out at the battlefield. He watches as the rebel warriors engage with the last of the King's Guard, the last of the flying soldiers. I dive back to the earth, landing hidden beyond the barrier of the hut. How the hell did he get through the shields? Gabriel wrests Elgeeva backward toward the forest.

Azlocke screams, racing for the hut. I reach out, grabbing his arm, hauling him behind the oak, pressing my finger to my lips. He pulls against me, trying to fight me off, wanting to race to Elgeeva, but I grip him tighter as a black streak whips through the air along the outer edge of the village and grabs hold of Gabriel from behind. Rowan sinks her teeth into him. Vlad and Lottie appear instantly on either side of Rowan.

"Rowan, take a long, deep breath through your nose, darling," Vladimir gently tells her. "Slow your drinking. Good, good." Vladimir continues to speak softly to Rowan. "Your catch is your own, no one will take it from you. Relax—calm, deep breaths in and out. Well done, Rowan!" he coos to her as she releases the bloodless Gabriel.

Lottie moves fast and is nothing but a blurred shadow as she embraces Rowan. She holds Rowan tight then begins rubbing and patting her back. Rowan hiccups then burps.

"Well done, child." Lottie smiles at Rowan, but soon Rowan's face twists in discomfort and she launches forward, vomiting. Lottie, having been shoved aside, stands beside a hunched over Rowan, rubbing her back. "You must learn to slow down when drinking. Don't let the blood just run down your throat. You must remember to swallow slowly," Lottie says as Rowan continues to hiccup and burp. Rowan relaxes further into Lottie's embrace.

"It seems Rowan's new being is more vampiric. With a lack of knowledge about what species' blood is most prominent in her..." Lottie pauses to collect her phrasing. "The child's feeding and killing habits are that of an untrained Vampire." Lottie makes this observation out loud to no one in particular. Azlocke appears and holds out his hands to Rowan.

"Thank you for coming to Elgeeva's aid." He hugs her tight.

"I feel my Alpha blood in Merek," says Xander, approaching me. "Perhaps he's more inclined to be a Werewolf?" Xander scratches his chin. "Brice is your Beta!" He winks at me.

I rub Brice's head and pounce on top of him. We roll over each other and fortify our bond, exhaustion setting in as we roll, finally laying next to each other on our backs, heaving breaths and feeling spent.

"What should we do with this one?" Azlocke holds up Gabriel's dead, withered, and limp body.

A loud, shrill caw calls in the night.

My eyes travel up, finding the large raven riding a wind current. It banks and dives, barreling to the earth below. It slows its descent, cawing out and circling our group. Mum races out of the hut toward us, reaching out for the creature.

"Nuala!" Mum shrieks, coming to a stop just a few steps away. I see the sleek black raven arch backwards. Its body morphs, turning into a female Goblin, her feet landing hard upon the earth, her legs giving out from underneath her. Mum slides along the dirt, embracing the woman who is taking heaving breaths, blood running down her temple, a large bruise blooming to encircle her swollen left eye.

The battered woman embraces Mum, clutching her, holding tightly to her.

"Amanda," she whispers, tears freely running down her cheek. Mum pulls back, taking her friend's face gently between her hands.

"Nuala, what happened?" Mum gently touches her face. The woman's eyes travel to Azlocke still holding up the limp, dead Gabriel.

"I have an idea." Nuala's voice is hoarse, strained, and so very weak, like someone has tried crushing her throat.

"Do you have enough magic left, Nuala?" Azlocke quietly asks.

I'm dazed and confused. The raven transforming into a woman, Mum holding her ferociously, Azlocke's pained features...

"Are you sure you... want to open that door?"

Nuala shifts in my mother's arms, straightens her spine, and steels herself. "Let it be the last gift—of my soul—to give that bastard—" her voice being pushed to the max, she whispers to us "—but first..." She looks into Mum's eyes with yearning. "My daughter," Nuala squeaks. "Where is Rowan?"

***

The King sneers from his Throne, watching a foreign signature of a portal beginning to open within his Throne Room. He hesitantly rises, his breath deep and heavy with apprehension.

A blast of wind rushes into room. He stares into the turning, swirling center of the portal door. A metal spear flies through the opening, its pointed end embedding itself in his marble floor. The spear splinters the marble. It stands tall in the middle of the room.

Blood drips down the shaft of the spear, pooling, staining the cracked white marble. The King shakes with fury at Gabriel's head and its clouded, dead eyes that look back at him.

"*Nuala!*" the King grunts through clenched teeth, and then roars out in anger.

CHAPTER TWENTY-ONE

The Throne Room

Azlocke enters the throne room through the portal first and emerges smiling at the raging and seething King. I enter close behind him. Azlocke gives a lavish, overly enthusiastic bow to the King, then steps aside and we let our fellow companions emerge through the magic portal door.

Elgeeva spins her body around once she is through the portal door powered by Nuala, whispering an enchanted spell. Her spell slams closed all the doors of the throne room. The furniture of the room is thrown about to barricade the doors. Two Guards standing transfixed and stupid next to the King brace themselves to protect him. Nuala, held up by my mother, hobbles through the portal door.

Emira emerges blowing a powder of blue from her hand; it swirls about all of us harmlessly but goes straight and true to the guards. Each breathes the powder in and sneezes. The guards fall over snoring and Emira chuckles.

"Molag!" Emira approaches the unguarded King, but the King smiles at her.

"Am I, woman? Perhaps you should take a closer look." Molag's face smiles a wicked grin, then begins to dissolve. Emira gasps and recognizes the face of the old wicked King, Molag's father Trenton. But that is impossible. Emira glares at the face that died so long ago.

"Surprised, aren't you?" King Trenton laughs.

"How?" Emira spits.

"I did it just as you do, darling, when your host body eventually grows too old and begins to die. You, Emira, transfer your life essences into that of another creature. When my four older sons came to brutally murder me, I was able to end them—but my body was finished. My pathetic youngest son took pity on me and cared for my failing body. I turned it to my advantage and bit Molag, transferring myself into him. I have almost complete control of his will. Molag occasionally takes control and pops up here and there to annoy the hell out of me. Molag has become weak over the centuries and I easily overpower him."

"I do not force myself upon any creature!" Emira yells at him, shaking with anger. "I create an entirely new form to inhabit. I do not take the life of another to continue my own! You are sadistic, Trenton. Look around you at how you have destroyed the lives of your people, sickened our lands with your evil mist. I should have killed you long ago!" she screams.

Trenton's face moves and changes again, resembling a weak, hollow face with shadowed eyes.

"But you could never harm him. He was precious to you and you loved him! You could not stand the thought of ending him. You couldn't end the life of your lover," a defeated Molag croaks out to Emira, blaming her. Molag's face contorts abruptly in pain. A battle ensues for control over the body of the King. Molag maintains control, resisting Trenton's thrall, and his voice pushes through his clouded eyes, becoming brighter.

"End me, Emira! End his madness. Kill me!" Molag's voice is hoarse and strained as he pleads. His face contorts again.

"Silence!" Trenton's face reemerges, his voice shaking in anger, and takes back control. I pull Rowan closer to me. Seeing two people war over control of one body is unnerving and my gut is begging me to take Rowan from this room.

Trenton's eyes snap to Rowan then me and he scans the crowd before him until he spots her, long raven hair and emerald green eyes. Mum jumps a little and hisses as she gazes at the changing face of the King. She stares at his newly loving face and he stares back at her. The face of the King is now her mate, Drake. Mum looks down at the arm that holds her own. Her eyes slowly look up and into the eyes of her mate, her beloved Drake beside her. Confusion knits her face as she covers her mouth and begins to sob. Rowan holds me back with a painful yank. I want nothing more than to race to my parents.

"Confused, my love?" Drake's voice comes from the body of the King. Drake pushes his mate behind him and glares into his own face, teeth bared. My father seethes. "I overheard you, Drake, telling Azlocke of the beautiful woman in your dreams. I listened as you admitted to him that you had gone out and searched for the girl. You found her in the human Realm. Angered, I gave you a tonic that night. You slept heavy. I took your blood and your visions of the girl flooded my mind. I altered my appearance to yours. It was I that went to Amanda that night, breaking my own laws, but what a delicious creature I had found!" He pauses and gazes at Amanda.

"It was you that night!" she croaks as the tears stream down her face. "I sensed something was different," she whispers.

"Ah yes, Amanda, it was I you gave yourself to that night!" He pauses, closing his eyes and focusing. The false Drake shoves his sleeve up, exposing his skin. The shading of his skin dims and changes, revealing the mate bond that mirrors Amanda's. Tears run down her face. She grabs Drake's arm and drags him before the King, placing his arm beside the King's arm. Three arms, three mirrored ribbon mate markings, identical. Both Drake and Trenton's mate bonds are much dimmer than Amanda's glistening arms. Drake and Trenton's mate bonds pulse dimly while Amanda's shines bright. Through the tears, Amanda glares at the King.

"It was my purpose to find you out and kill you that night. It was my goal to prevent Drake from mating with you. He'd be going against my law that no mixed species mate. But alas, my dear, you, your beauty and infectious, fiery soul captured my icy heart. I made love to you that night and claimed you with the blood I had taken from Drake to take his form. You are indeed MINE!" The false Drake roars, then sneers. "Once I returned here to the castle, Molag gained control in a moment of my own weakness. He transferred my memories of what happened between us—OUR MATING—to Drake's mind! Transferred my memory so that Drake would believe it was his own. When he woke, Drake had no idea it was me, thinking it was himself that mated with you, but our bond was made through my blood. Our markings aren't whole because each of us—Drake and I—has taken our claim of you." He laughs out loud hysterically and Drake pulls Amanda away from the mentally insane King.

My mind reels at the realization. I think I'm going to be sick to my stomach. Falling to my knees, I slip through Rowan's arm, heaving, bile lodging in my throat. Vomit erupts, covering the throne room floor. I wipe my mouth with the back of my hand. My body heaves once again. Drake's eyes lock on me, horror written across his face.

A scream tears through my throat, the sound piercing into my heart, slicing it in two. I am not the son of the man who I so desperately have wanted. I am the son of a monster.

"No!" Drake screams.

"Yes!" Trenton laughs. "Why do you think I let you all live?"

Drake's fist smashes the King in the face. He roars, staggering back as he changes his appearance back to himself, Trenton. "When I returned and found you two with her dead betrothed human, already pregnant with *MY* child, it was all too easy to keep my secret hidden, putting the blame on you." His gaze falls upon me. "His blood is mine! He is my son! And now I do believe *yet again* two of *my sons* will try and murder me," he laughs hysterically. "I will continue, I will live on through you both! MY BLOOD lives in you both!" he says wildly, laughing. He lashes out then, grabbing Rowan, his teeth sinking into her neck.

"Get your fucking fangs away from my daughter!" Nuala shrieks from behind the King, gripping the back of his head. Her fingers tangled in his hair, she yanks his head back and places her small dagger to his throat. Trenton releases Rowan, hissing at Nuala, and something flies in a blur out from his hand as Nuala slits his throat.

"Your current sons, the people of the fucking Realms may not have the stomach to end you, but your *WIFE*, the *MOTHER* of the daughters you slaughter, will!" she screams at Trenton.

He softly laughs, black blood trickling down his chest. She kicks his body to the floor, his face crunching horribly as it hits the marble stone. Black bubbling ooze pools about his face.

The moment his dead body hits the floor, a rushing gust of wind shoots out from his body and through the room. All of the evil the King had used to corrupt the lands comes rippling in from all over. Thick ribbons of slug enter the room. They scream like a siren, twisting into a funnel above his body. The angry storm cloud of slugs thunders. Lightning streaks out of the pointed center and back into the body of the King. The storm is sucked up into the creature laying on the floor, then all is quiet.

Drake's body then glows brightly, his mate bond to Amanda brightens and shines, pulsing before it settles, as vibrant as Amanda's.

Nuala looks up and into the eyes of her only living long lost daughter. Rowan's eyes are wide and full of fear. Her eyes then shut against pain, her small mouth drops open as she looks down. Nuala follows her gaze. Her daughter's hand wraps around the hilt of a dagger that has plunged into her belly just above her pubic bone.

She pulls it out, blood dripping and covering her hands. She drops the blade and stumbles. I catch her before she falls. Panic shoots through my body like a red-hot iron. I desperately reach for my pocket, the one that contains the glass stone, but I no longer wear my old clothing.

"Save her!" I scream at Emira, trying to hand Rowan's body to her. "Heal her, save her! I lost the stone, please take her! SAVE HER!" I roar, my body shaking.

"Merek, calm down, you do not need the stone," she gently whispers.

Nuala shakes with rage and screams out and grabs the dagger that has struck her daughter. She plunges the blade in and deep, ripping it out and back in again, over and over, screaming as she stabs the body of the King, "YOU HAVE TAKEN EVERYTHING FROM ME! How many cradles do I have, how many! How many hold my skeletal children, the daughters you slaughtered? My first born stolen from me, taken in the night because of you! Every piece of my soul devoured by you, everything was taken, my babies, my babies." She rages and sobs, plunging the dagger once more, twice, thrice, then lodging it deep within an eye socket where she leaves it.

Nuala crawls up and over the body, covered in his blood. All is silent as she crawls away from the body. I watch the King—no, Molag—as he raises his hand, whispers something inaudible, and then I feel the last of his magic leaving him. He ages like wildfire; molten ash chunks fall from his raised hand into a grey sooty pile. A soft wind, no larger than a sigh, blows the ash away. A black scorch mark stains the marble floor where the body had once been.

Nuala crawls, crying and sobbing, slowly and pained. Amanda runs to her and drops beside her, trying to comfort her.

"Don't touch me! Get away!" she screams, shoving Amanda back, and continues to crawl until she finds the feet she searches for. She places each of her palms to my feet.

"Please," she heaves out through her tears, "let me hold my daughter, let me embrace her. Let me hold her while she leaves this world." Nuala can hardly breathe as she forces her words out, her heart constricted. I gently lower Rowan into Nuala's arms.

"Rowan will be okay, look!" Emira says, pulling back Rowan's hair and a strip of cloth that is covering the wound. The wound is already healing itself. "Molag healed her," she whispers in a choked cry, "and Midgard, her dragon, shielded her womb. The babies are fine."

A black hazy smoke lifts from Rowan and Midgard materializes. Amanda runs her fingers through Nuala's hair as she gazes upon Rowan's face. Amanda leans her face to Nuala's shoulder and wraps her arms around her. I walk over to Midgard, her eyes bright and longing, and lift my arms and close my eyes as I continue to walk toward the dragon. Fafnir releases from within me and materializes beside his mate. Fafnir gently nuzzles his mate then licks at her wound.

I hug her snout and whisper my thanks for protecting my mate and babies. My eyes flash wide open and stare at Emira.

"Babies? Not baby?" I ask in a whisper of shock.

Emira nods to me and smiles. She lowers herself to the floor to speak to Nuala, who continues to sob.

"Nuala, your daughter lives. Rowan is fine. Look at the wound, it is healed already. She just fainted, Nuala. I'm sure the dagger, the babies, the King's confession just overwhelmed her!" Emira traces a finger across Nuala's cheek to comfort her. "Watch your daughter take breath!" She pulls the glass stone from the pocket of her dress and weaves a spell of twine. The string encircles the stone. She stands and places the woven rope over my head, resting it against my chest.

"Keep it close," she whispers to me and smiles. I place my hand over it, feeling its weight. Relief to have it back washes over me.

Nuala looks at her daughter's face as Rowan's eyes flutter and open. Nuala takes in a deep breath and cradles her daughter to her, hugging her tight, tears erupting again.

Drake slowly approaches me.

"Merek," he sobs, his voice breaking. He grabs me, pulling me into his embrace, his hand cradling the back of my head. "My... brother?" His tears soak our cheeks. "My... *son*," he gets out, holding me tighter.

Mum crumples to the floor behind him, a shrieking sob shaking her. Instead of a father, he's my brother. I pull back from Drake and pull him toward Mum, the two of us sinking down on either side, each of us desperately holding her sobbing frame, a tightly tangled knot of limbs. A mother and son, mate and mate, brother and brother. Brice curls in front of us, whimpering softly. An utter sense of being lost fills the air.

"You ARE my son, Merek! Nothing is going to change that." His voice is deep and gruff, and he pulls away from us, gently placing his palms to my cheeks, holding my face within his strong hands. "You are my son, understand?"

"Yes." A hoarse whisper makes its way past my lips. His eyes bear into mine. I nod, not taking my eyes from his.

CHAPTER TWENTY-TWO

The Crowning

A ceremony is held in Dark Hallow. Creatures from all the Realms gather there. The mist that once plagued the Forest of Wedgemore is gone, and a mass grave is dug at the base of the Agrok and Esurg mountain range. Every creature who lost their lives in the battle are laid to rest there. Including a plaque for Molag.

Emira blesses the ground and the two bodies of stone that create the new, beautiful mountain range. With her eyes closed and concentrating, Emira whispers spells to the winds. Luscious, thick green moss covers the Giants of stone here and there. Small sapling trees sprout and grow into massive oaks. Birch and maple trees follow. Lupines of purples and blues, pink and yellow daisies sprout. Orange citron flowers and white yarrow, buttercups and bloodred poppies, thistle, lavender and pink bergamots. Columbines of royal blue and bloodroot sprout, swaying in a gentle breath. The crowd applauds at the new growth and color. It is truly a beautiful memorial to honor the lives lost.

Once Emira is satisfied with the mountain range and burial area, a large onyx and marble stone materializes and is lowered into place atop a regular granite stone. Markings appear in gold writing upon the onyx-marble:

FIFTH FULL MOON OF YEAR 1684
MEMROIAL TO THOSE FALLEN
IN THE DARK HALLOW LANDS
MOUNTAIN RANGE FORMED
OF AGROK & HIS MATE ESURG

Beneath the date and description, five columns appear listing each and every name of the lives lost, even the missing, those souls claimed by the mist. Emira takes a deep, cleansing breath. She nods to honor the memorial and work she has done to make it into a beautiful, new, inviting, and welcoming area.

"At this time," Emira calls out so all can hear, "let us all take seats for the Coronation of the Realms' new Rulers!"

Emira twirls her fingers. A tall platform forms in the middle of the Dark Hallow village. Long rows of benches materialize facing the central stage. Creatures clap and begin taking seats.

Emira gazes out at the seated creatures. The once separated creatures are coming back together, rediscovering themselves and soon redefining how the Realms ought to be. No more wars, no more mist, no more oppression. No more fear, no more pain of servitude, a new beginning will be. Creatures of every Realm are assembled here to witness a rebirth.

Emira clears her throat. "Hear me now! Dear creatures, let go your prejudice, let go your knowledge of other creatures. That knowledge was told you to make you fear one another. Let go of this fear. All gathered here today are here to witness the coming together of a whole, to embrace a new way, a new path for peace and love to rule. We come here to celebrate and recognize a new creature." She pauses, her elegant wrist turning, her hand presenting Rowan and I. "Please, find it in your hearts to reach out, feel one another's presence and the life within them. We all want peace, but that will never come to pass if you continue to hold onto the old ways that were ingrained in you with fear."

Slowly creatures begin to rise and move about, rearranging themselves next to creatures they do not know, greeting and speaking. Emira smiles when hands are shaken and introductions are given. She sighs deeply and her eyes tear at watching the creatures she holds so dear begin to embrace one another as equals.

"The creatures that are now before you were voted on by the peoples of the Realms, chosen by those peoples to be Rulers and the Enforcers of Peace throughout the lands. Those that stand before you will Rule in grace and empathy. Gone are the ways of enslaving and the fear of ruling crowns. Peace will endure from this moment forward!" She takes a breath and turns her attention away from the gathered to creatures to Drake, Amanda, King Conway, and Queen Opal.

Her hands swirl and twirl; four crowns made of a vining plant fuse together, glistening bright with onyx stones. She places them gently upon the four.

"I give you your Kings and Queens of the Goblin and Elven Realms." The crowd cheers and Emira kisses each of them and blesses them. "May you rule in love and grace!"

Emira beckons to Brynzin and Ryanna. Two headdresses are formed of elegant feathers and thin branches. Onyx stones twinkle at the centers and Emira places them upon their heads.

"I give you your High Chief and Chieftess of Dark Hallow," Emira calls out and presents the two to the crowd. Cheers erupt and hooves pound the ground as Brynzin and Ryanna take their seats beside Opal.

Xander and Nikilaus rise next to stand before Emira. A strong breeze blows, and two crowns of white gold speckled with onyx stones appear.

"I give to you your Alpha and Luna of the Crescent Rose Moon Lands," Emira loudly proclaims, beaming. Howling erupts through the crowd. The Alpha and Luna bow to the crowd and take their seats.

Elgeeva and Azlocke rise next. Two crowns formed of bones glisten with gold; four large onyx stones are embedded in the bones.

"I give to you your High Priestess of the Witches and her King," Emira calls out. Tiny fireworks of fire, water, earth, and air collide and explode beautifully above their heads as cheers and clapping ring out.

Sorcha and Gwendolyn stand and approach to kneel before Emira. Two crowns of woven reeds, flowers, and dangling tear-shaped onyx stones adorn their heads.

"I present to you your Queens of the Fae Realm." Emira smiles and kisses them.

Cormac and Brigid stand and bow to Emira. White silver crowns with flower-shaped onyx stones are placed atop their heads.

"I give you your King and Queen of the Human Realm." Emira kisses and blesses them.

Vladimir and Lottie stand. Bright onyx crowns with studded rubies are placed upon their heads. Vladimir gently kisses Emira's cheek, followed by Lottie, then they kiss each other.

"I give you your High Priestess and her King of the Vampiric Ice Lands." Emira claps as they are seated.

"And now," Emira says as her hand flies and twirls. Two enormous crowns take shape of solid onyx stone. Tozir gently picks up one of the intended crowns but places it on her middle finger instead. Borog places his on his smallest finger. The crowd laughs heartily and cheers to the Giants of Old, the last remaining pair.

"I give you Tozir and Borog." Emira gives a small, sad smile and bows deeply to them.

Borog helps Tozir stand. She winces and wobbles. Where her eye once was, now an ornately bandaged patch reminds us all what was endured to get here.

"I give you," Emira bows to the Dwarf King, "Gavor of the Underground Mountains!" I cough to cover my laugh as I watch Gavor's cheeks redden at the many eyes upon him. Grumpy old Dwarf, indeed.

Midgard and Fafnir rise from within me and Rowan, materializing off the side of the platform stage. Fafnir and Midgard bow their mighty heads as Emira forms two crowns identical to the ones that the Moon Goddess has given myself and Rowan. Emira lifts the crowns from the ground slowly, careful of the small children that moments ago rushed to climb and play between the elaborate swirls and loops. She crowns the Giants with the use of strange magic to lift them upon their heads.

"I give you Midgard and Fafnir, Dragons, protectors of the prophecy children," she says and bows deeply to them. They in turn gently nuzzle against her sides, each of her arms rubbing beneath their chins.

"One more Ruling will be established and acknowledged before all today! Merek, Rowan, please rise and join me!" She smiles to us. We look at each other in confusion. I rise and gently pull Rowan to her feet. We place ourselves before Emira, and she speaks.

"I give you the new Guardians of the Forest of Wedgemore. Merek and Rowan will rule and ensure the peace within the forest!" She kisses our foreheads and bows to us.

The crowd cheers and claps for all the new leaders. I turn to face my mate, kissing her ferociously, dipping her back. A laugh bubbles past her lips. I pull her back up and spin her away from me. I marvel at her smiling face.

As she spins away, our arms taught, her smile slips. Horrified, I watch as her eyes roll up and white glassy orbs stare blankly, her body limp. I quickly pull her back into my arms. As her chest caresses mine, power erupts from Rowan. It barrels into me, sending me flying away from her, flipping me head over heels. I heave, my body arching, righting myself so the world is right-side up and my feet hit earth in a crouch. I slide through the dirt.

Everything is blown back. Creatures and benches topple, some of their mouths open in silent screams of pain, all broken limbs and bleeding faces. My ears are ringing, the only thing I can hear. The platform is in splinters, and I frantically search the sea of faces for my mate. Screams pierce through the ringing and I look up, up into the sky. Rowan hangs suspended, her head thrown back. The sky darkens as deep storm clouds block out the sun. Night descends and lightning erupts throughout the heavens. Rowan's hair stands on end about her head, static charged. It sways and floats about her as if underwater. Her arms spread wide. A seductive, musical laugh comes from her lips as her head slowly tilts down, her face coming into view. Black orbs stare down at me. Blinding light flashes behind her, eerily illuminating her.

A musical, heated voice comes from Rowan. "Power!" Her body shudders with pleasure and she purrs, "Such delicious power!"

"Rowan!" I call to her, my wings materializing. I leap from the earth, beating my wings to come before her.

"Fools," she coos to me, her eyes blinking and hooded. "I rise, I rise," she sings.

Sorcha races to me, grabbing me, dragging me back to the earth below. Numb, I let her pull me back and away from my mate, my eyes never leaving her.

Rowan examines her body, every inch of herself, her hands caressing her face, her fingers trailing down her neck, her chest, and seductively her hands trace down, cupping her breasts. Her hands trail down to her swollen belly, swirling against her stomach. Her hands come back to her face and her eyes focus, finally seeing through them. She laughs musically again.

"NO!" I say. "No, no..." But the proof is there. Even from here I can see the jagged marks that mar her neck. "He—he *bit* her. *He bit her!*" I scream in agony, falling to my knees, burying my face in my hands.

"This body, oh this marvelous body, so much power," she sultry whispers within my mind. Looking around me, I see that we can all hear her within our minds. "Bow before me! Your Queen!" She laughs. "The prophesied children indeed could not kill me, but *my wife*," she hisses, "my *wife* stabbed my old body to death, but yet—I live! Bow, bow!"

Azlocke is slowly maneuvering toward me, as is Drake. Azlocke places an arrow beside my kneeling form, Drake a bow. My heart cleaves and I pant, teeth clenched against the pain of understanding. The prophesied child, we thought it may have been Rowan, but Mother of Light! It was always me, me from the start. But my mate—is she gone, or has she been pushed aside somewhere deep within her body as Molag had been?

My breathing is labored as the day turns black as night where not even shadows can exist. My eyes dart about, taking in the creatures surrounding me, the monster above us. I choke on a sob as I desperately try to find my mate bond, and nothing but inky smoke answers me. Rowan's head is thrown back again, drunk with the lust for power.

I grab the bow, nocking the arrow. The stone necklace is a heavy weight upon my chest. Let her be in there, let her be okay, by the gods help me! I take aim.

Excruciating pain flares throughout my body as the arrowhead seeks its target, the heart of my mate. My body buckles, my breath knocked from my lungs, eyes squeezed tight. I settle, blowing out the last of my air. Eyes flying open, the arrow releases and I crumple to the ground.

A whizzing pierces the night, a wet *thunk*, and a horrific scream. Rowan's head snaps back staring at me, tears running down my face. I can't breathe. She looks down to her chest.

Wind blows. The clouds churn, light erupting. A cyclone forms. Creatures shriek, the wind howling, throwing us back, purple haze erupting from the screaming, shrieking Rowan, her body plummeting to the earth below. Howling screams come deep from within my body.

The clouds part, sunrays streaming through. A ray of it shines upon Rowan's still form. I scoop her into my arms and race for the beach. I run, run... Creatures frozen about us blur by, her body curled in my arms, her head bouncing against my chest. The stone necklace bounces off me and I grab it between my teeth, my fangs shredding the cord about my neck. I spit, propelling the stone from my mouth, hearing the *pluck* as it sinks into the water. The lake before me disappears and a fountain forms in its place. A wide base of sculpted stone rises up. I grunt, leaping over it, my body and Rowan falling feet first. My boots touch the water and we are sucked down hard and fast. I tighten my grip on Rowan—*I will not lose her.*

I adjust her in my arms, wrapping my legs arounds hers, an arm around her waist, my free hand cupping the back of her head as an invisible force hauls my feet downward. We speed through the cold and dark water. I tilt my head up. A pinprick of light is all that remains of the world above.

Sucked further and further down, my lungs burn. I pull her head and hair gently back and gaze upon her lifeless face, the rest of her hair whipping above her head. I bring my lips to hers, our embraced limbs tightening with my hold on her. I kiss her deeply, with all my love, with all my soul. Let it be, then. Here we will stay, suspended in these watery depths, plummeting, speeding down. Here we will be.

CHAPTER TWENTY-THREE

A Beautiful Beginning

My back slams into something hard and dry.

Air rips into my lungs as heavy, labored breaths force air into me. Pain ripples about my bones. Rowan's body is still against my front, protected from the impact. Our bodies bounce. We come to a sliding stop, and gently I roll Rowan off me, the air knocked from my lungs. I climb to my knees gulping like a fish. I can't breathe. I will my body to calm.

I can hear Brice whining for me within my mind. It's so dark here. I blink my eyes, using my Goblin vision.

"Brice," I whisper to myself, and feel his relief flood through me.

"Where are you, Merek?"

"I don't know, it's so dark. Wait."

I open my eyes and see soft glowing slugs against rock. A faint blueish light pulses, darkens, pulses with a soft blue glow, darkens, then blue light illuminates.

"Can you see this, Brice?"

"Yes." I hear his awe.

"It looks like a cavern."

I rise, walking in a slow circle, and notice a shimmering wall of water. I slowly step towards it, trace my fingers over it, gently pushing my hand threw it, twirling my fingers. My hand comes back dripping wet. My brows pinch together.

"Rowan?" I barely hear Brice, his voice rippling through water.

I turn and kneel beside her. I feel her wrist as it gives a weak pulse, her breaths hardly visible. The feathered end of the arrow is buried deep within her chest. I roll her to the side and grip the arrowhead, panting, my eyes closed tight. I pull, ripping the weapon from her body. Red blood coats my hand, pooling around her.

"Shit! Rowan?"

The blue light pulses again. My eyes snap up and to the wall of water as a yellow glow passes through the water and a bright flare of light momentarily blinds me. I blink.

A skeletal being with sharp pointed teeth smiles harshly at me. I suppress a shudder.

"Mother," I whisper.

"Hello, dear one," she whispers back. The skeleton moves to Rowan's other side. A bony hand hovers over Rowan's heart. Warm muted light leaks from the hand and into my mate. The creature bites a bone in its wrist and a silver liquid drips onto Rowan.

"Open her mouth, Merek," the creature whispers.

I lift Rowan's head and torso, gently sliding my leg under her, propping her up and using my thumb to press it to her bottom lip and push down. The Mother holds the dripping wrist over Rowan's mouth, the liquid splashing into her mouth, then dissolving into her.

More warm glowing light emanates from Rowan. I watch mesmerized as the wound to her chest heals and knits back together—a thin sliver of pale white skin marks her. The skeletal hand reaches for mine, giving my fingers a tight squeeze. I feel Rowan's body jolt. I suck in a breath as her chest rises and falls. Silent, grateful tears stream down my face. I pull her into me, rocking us.

"*Merek*..." Rowan's voice is hers as she blinks up at me.

"Want to see something so very special, dear ones?" the Mother's voice whispers to us.

I laugh as Rowan's brows knit together in confusion, then her face clears in awe at the skeletal being. I nod and her bony fingers point toward the water wall.

The wall ripples and a room appears before us, our friends and family rushing in and out. Rowan lies in a beautiful poster bed, and I kneel beside her. She's sweating, teeth clenched together, and her grip on my hand tightens as we both suck in a breath. Her hand isn't holding me here in this cave, but the phantom pain of her crushing my hand is there. Her eyes widen on mine.

Our bodies are violently pulled into the water wall image, defying time and space. Our souls are thrown into the image before us.

***

"You must push, Rowan!" Elgeeva yells over the raging thunderstorm outside.

Lightning flashes, illuminating the room brightly. Candles are placed about the room. Amanda hums loudly to help soothe Rowan as she dips the cloth back into the cold water and dabs at Rowan's sweaty face.

"It hurts too much! I hate this stool!" she screams out. The stool is made of a hard wood, the middle of the seat hollowed out, the rim of it digging into her butt and thigh bones.

"Push through the pain, dear, visually push out that pain!" Emira encourages her.

"Ah! Keep pushing, Rowan, I can see the top of your baby's head!" Elgeeva calls out to her.

Rowan pants for breath and looks down between her thighs and the seat of the torturous stool at Elgeeva's excited face resting on the floor beneath her.

Rowan yells down at her, "Get me off this seat!" then cries out in pain. She grips my hands as another excruciating contraction seizes her abdomen and back. When it passes, I assist her and lift her to a standing position. Rowan wraps her arms around my neck, leaning her face into my chest and rocking her pelvis back and forth.

Elgeeva moves to the front of her legs. Nuala kneels behind her daughter and readies a blanket to catch her grandchild. Rowan inhales deep and fast, squats slightly, and bears down and pushes with all her might, desperately drawing on my strength and energy like a magical siphon. It fuels her as she yells out through it.

A baby cries out into the night, taking its first breath. Nuala quickly wraps it in a blanket, kisses its beautiful face, and stands to place it in the arms of its mother. I sit Rowan back on the stool as she takes the baby from her mother.

"It is a boy, Rowan!" she exclaims with tears in her eyes.

"Hello, my love." Rowan kisses his head then cradles him to her as another contraction shatters through her body. Trembling, she hands our son to me but quickly changes her mind, handing the baby back to her mother Nuala and gripping my shoulders as I try to catch a glimpse of the baby's face. I pout at her but wrap my arm under her and support her as she squats again and inhales deeply and pushes.

"Good work, Rowan, push again!" Elgeeva calls out to her over the storm and thunder.

"I am *trying*," she gets out through clenched teeth. Amanda grabs more blankets and positions herself to help Elgeeva catch the next infant.

"PUSH, PUSH, PUSH!" Elgeeva chants. It is beautiful as it emerges from within its mother. "Wonderful, Rowan. ONE MORE PUSH!"

Rowan bears down and screams as the baby's shoulders finally pass. Her legs crumple. I lower her onto the stool, but Rowan pushes herself back up and tries waddling toward the bed. I scoop her up then lay her down. Rowan pants heavily, eyes closed as she tries to catch and slow her breathing.

"At least," she gulps down air, "the second baby came quicker." She blows out her breath. The women about the room chuckle.

Amanda hands her a bundle of blanket and baby. "It is a girl," she whispers and kisses Rowan, holding her granddaughter to her mother. Nuala places her son in her other arm. I sit next to her and gaze down at our beautiful babies and then at my sweaty, hair disheveled, exhausted mate and kiss her passionately.

"Mother of Light, you are so beautiful!" I whisper into her ear. Rowan laughs softly and groans one last time.

"Oh good, the afterbirth has come forth!" Emira exclaims. "May I take it, Rowan? I will bury it and have two trees planted in honor of your younglings!" She bounces on the balls of her feet, filled with so much joy and excitement.

"Uh-huh," Rowan whispers, and she continues to stare at her babies. I take the baby girl and hold her, then Rowan and I pull back the blankets to see both of our babies.

Their skin is a swirling marbling of black and silver. Our son has bright blue eyes while our daughter's are emerald, bright green. The boy has soft white peach fuzz hair like Rowan's and the girl has jet-black fuzz like me. Each has full pouty lips with chubby cheeks. The babies find each other's tiny hands and pull each other closer.

"Do you have names for the younglings?" Emira has returned to the birthing room after leaving with the afterbirth. She gazes at the babies and instantly falls in love with their perfect faces.

"I think Aspen sounds nice for the boy." Rowan looks to me, and I nod in agreement.

"How about Willow?" I ask and Rowan laughs.

"I love it." Rowan continues to giggle at me. "Say hello to Aspen and Willow," she sighs contentedly.

Rowan is bathed and changed and reclines back in the bed with new clean linen. Creatures soon gather in a procession to see and greet the babies.

Sorcha and Gwendolyn push themselves to the front, then place two small woven flowered crowns upon their heads. So many faces push forward to catch a glimpse of the babes. Willow cries out.

"Alright, feeding time!" Emira yells out. "Back, all of you, back. Come on, back with you and out, give the new mother room to breathe." The gathered crowed complains.

"But I didn't get to see them!" Susanna cries out and pouts her lip.

"Let the younglings eat, let the storm die down! It's too crowded and loud in here!" Emira shoos all of the creatures out along with herself to calm the hordes that continue to complain.

Amanda approaches and lifts Willow and repositions her in Rowan's arm. Amanda points to me to do the same with Aspen.

"Alright, my darling, now time to try feeding. Just bring their faces to your breast and let them nuzzle you as they root about to latch on," Amanda advises her.

Rowan takes both infants' heads into her palms and brings their faces to her. "What do I do n—OW!" She shrieks as the infants latch in unison and begin to suck hard. "Ow, ow, ow!"

"Okay, relax your body, do not tense! Try a deep breath in through the nose and blow out slowly. That's it, darling, just relax. The discomfort of feeding should pass in a day or two. I have a cream for you once you finish feeding to rub on to help with the redness and soreness." Amanda strokes her hair gently. Nuala, Elgeeva, Amanda, and I watch as the babies fill their bellies and Rowan drifts off to sleep.

Emira pokes her head in and enters, softly closing the door behind. She approaches the others and looks down at the babes.

"These two will be the most loved and cherished creatures to have walked this life. The castle is completely full of expectant creatures wanting to see these two!" Emira laughs softly.

"At long last, we finally have found Peace." Elgeeva hugs her mother, Emira.

I place a soft kiss upon Rowan's lips. My eyes shine when I gaze upon her beauty, her strength, and just how wonderful and completely perfect she is.

Chapter Twenty-Four

Epilogue

I'm sitting before a warm, crackling fire. The chair is high back, carved by my hand, made from the trunk of my favorite oak by the pond near the old shack of a house Brice and I grew up in. Three years ago that giant oak toppled over and crashed to the ground.

Drake and I harvested the wood together and at its widest section we counted together the many rings of life of that old tree. I carved two chairs, one for Rowan and one for myself to have in our new home. The two wooden thrones are placed before the stone hearth.

Drake and I worked the land where once my mother's house stood, a home gone long ago, consumed by fire, and in its place a stone mansion was erected. The house rests on the old border of the human Realm and the once haunted and feared forest. It was built purposefully on that border, a solid stone structure of beauty to replace the old wicked oppression. Drake's stone knowledge and craft came to life before our eyes. I laughed and called it a castle. Drake huffed, stating it was a *mansion*, a masterpiece of architecture with its four wings and many rooms, its gorgeous stone pillars. But the entryway staircase is everyone's favorite.

Brice sits beside my chair and I stroke his soft fur and turn my gaze to my mate. She is curled up on a chaise lounge chair, Nuala tucked behind her, holding her sleeping daughter. Naula twirls her fingers through Rowan's long hair, gently rubbing Rowan's swollen belly. Nuala whispers to the life within her daughter while Rowan dozes. I grin mischievously as I watch the smallest bit of drool drip from the corner of her lips. My poor sweet mate, the babe is due any day now.

Brice purrs to the white wolf that also lays dozing on a plush throw blanket on the floor beneath Rowan. The lovely female wolf is panting, restlessly shifting her position to accommodate a belly full of pups. The white wolf makes a noise in her sleep and I feel Brice's pride, love, and the joy toward his pregnant mate radiate through me. Brice leans into my hand and I absently rub his chin, his eyes closing.

I look past Nuala and Rowan to Emira telling an epic tale of Giants, Dwarfs, witches, Goblins, the Goddess of the Moon, and the Mother of Light to two twin four year old children. My daughter and my son listen at her feet, hypnotized and entranced to the story she regales them with.

My attention drifts to my mum, to the puttering noise as she works her new sewing machine, while my father—because that's what Drake has always been and what I need him to be—while he stares at his mate, the book in his lap long forgotten. His feet are propped on mum's table, the small section where his slippers rest the only space upon the table that's not covered in patterns and fabrics. The love and admiration are clear on his face as he watches her work, her top teeth biting into her lower lip, teeth and said lip full of pins, her eyebrows knitted together in concentration as a beautiful gown of emerald green begins to form.

Willow jumps from her seat on the floor before Emira, a small wooden sword brandished. She artfully dances about, parrying an invisible foe. Aspen gives a big yawn but his eyes still glisten from the story. My daughter is a spitting image of her fierce grandmother, Elgeeva, and when I look upon my son, my heart tells me this is what Molag must have looked like as a small child.

"My Lord," a tall, spindly old man calls softly to me, pulling me out of my reverie. "This has just arrived."

"Is it from Gwendolyn, Bernard? Give it here." Nuala beckons the creature to give the letter to her. "Ah! It is! A letter from Gwendolyn," she calls out.

Rowan gives a loud snort and jolts awake, her eyes finding mine. I mime wiping my mouth. She glares at me, scowling, wiping away the wetness. She stands, the white wolf beneath her yelping.

Rowan falls back into the chaise, Nuala desperately trying to help right her daughter as Rowan hisses out, "Mother of Light, Zion! You're always underfoot. Are you alright?" Rowan leans forward, her belly obstructing her wishes. The white wolf stands and shoves her face into Rowan's. She chatters at her, the wolf's head bobbing angrily until Rowan takes her face between her hands and nuzzles her nose to the wolf's.

"I'm sorry, but you know how uncoordinated I am these days! Are you okay? I'm sorry for stepping on her paw."

Brice shakes his head. Rising, he walks to his mate and maneuvers her back toward the hearth. Rowan stands again and stretches her back deeply; she rubs her belly. She waddles over to me, sinking into my lap, and I curl my arms around her as Nuala clears her throat and reads.

My Dearest Nuala,

I was so delighted to receive your letter updating us on all your happy news. It is with great joy I share what I have learned of the others and the happiness of Sorcha and I.

The orphans that Sorcha and I adopted after the war are adjusting beautifully, although some nightmares still surface every now and again. Our three daughters and our two sons are growing strong, healthy, and are so very loved by all of our Fairy Land.

Our eldest son surprised us all two mornings ago around a chaotic breakfast table when Sorcha flipped a flapjack high in the air for me to catch on a plate for our youngest, when out of nowhere, brilliant blue transparent wings fluttered out of my son's back and he zoomed through the air to catch said flapjack in his teeth. All the children squealed with delight and Sorcha and I both gave nervous laughs. We are still bubble wrapping the chandeliers and the antler horns decorating the high walls and ceilings.

Elgeeva wrote me, sharing her joy of promoting Rebecca to High Witch and Susanna to High Priestess as Elgeeva steps down from her Coven to take up the role of Queen with Azlocke, her new King. King Conway and Queen Opal have stepped down from their crowns, anointing Elgeeva and Az. Tell Drake he'll be having a baby sister any day now to spoil very soon. The poor dear has all these things to arrange while she's about to deliver a child. Bless her.

Conway and Opal are traveling to visit Vlad and Lottie in their Ice palace, then they are off to visit with Borog and Tozir. Did you hear? Tozir gave birth to a healthy, ("small," reports Tozir) plump, chubby-cheeked baby boy weighing in at 30 pounds. Mother of Light! Small for a Giant. Can you even imagine?

Gavor recently wed his beautiful bride and I do believe they will be traveling near you shortly. Hope a reunion might take place between you. I hear his bride is quite the beauty. Give him our love if your paths cross.

Nikilaus and Xander are also expecting another round of pups themselves. They believe she's carrying triplets.

So much joy, wonderful peace. I pray to the light Rowan's delivery is an easy one. Give little Willow and Aspen kisses from their aunties for us.

So much love to my dear friend, Nuala. We miss you. Promise you'll visit us soon.

All our love,

~Gwen

Character Page

Drake: Hybrid of Goblin and Elf called Gelfin. Bastard son and only heir to Goblin King Molag. Son of Elfin Witch Elgeeva. Mate of Amanda. Father to Merek.

Amanda: Human. Betrothed to a human man Caylen. Mate of Drake and turned into a new type of Hybrid Creature. First of her breed. Mother to Merek.

Caelen: Human. Betrothed to Amanda.

Merek: Son of Prince Drake and Amanda. Hybrid, second of the breed. Prophesized male that will free the Mother and bring peace to the Realms. Mate of Rowan and turned by her into a new unknown species, one of only two.

Brice: Purebred wolf. Blessed with magics by Prince Drake. Companion of Merek.

The Lost Ones: Creatures of all species that wandered too deep into the Forest of Wedgemore. Unable to find their way home. Mutated and transformed by the Evil Mist created by the Wicked King of Old, Trenton, into zombified, decaying forms. Unthinking and sickly-looking beings. They survive on the flesh of others and animals. Left to continuously wander the forest.

Molag: Pureblood Goblin. King and High Ruler of all Realms. Turned wicked and evil by his father the Old Wicked King Trenton. His only true lover is Elgeeva. Grandfather of Merek.

Elgeeva: Pureblood Elf. High Priestess of her coven in the Witches Wood. Princess to King Conway and daughter of Emira. Next in line to rule the Elfin Realm. Mother of Molag's only heir, Prince Drake. Mate of Azlocke. Grandmother to Merek.

Rowan: Was thought to be human. Pureblood Goblin. Mate of Merek. Prophesized female to bring peace to the Realms. True daughter of Nuala and her mate. Transformed into a new, unknown species by Elgeeva and Emira, one of two creatures. Most powerful of all known creatures, second to the Mother.

Emira: The Mother of Creation, Oldest and last known species of the Old Divine Powers. Mother to Elgeeva, great grandmother of Merek. Ashamed mate of the Wicked King Trenton.

King Trenton: Pureblood Goblin. The King of Old. Poisoned the Realms with his Evil. Son of Emira's deceased Sister and Brother of Divine Power. Manipulated his mate Emira, taking her blood and becoming more powerful. Transferred his life force into that of his youngest son Molag when his four older sons tried to kill him.

Azlocke: Pureblood Elf. Warrior and King Molag's highest ranking guard. Mate to Elgeeva. Best friend of Drake.

Gwendolyn: Half breed Fairy and Witch. Second Queen of the Fae. First to be made wife of Molag. Healer. Mate to Sorcha.

Nikilaus: Shapeshifter, Werewolf. Luna of her Crescent Rose Moon pack. The second to be made wife of Molag. Mate of Xander, Alpha.

Lottie: Vampire. High Queen of her Coven in the Ice Lands. Third to be made wife of Molag. Mate to Vladimir, King of the Ice Lands. Vampire Mother of Dawn and Lothous.

Opal: Pureblood Elf. Mate of King Conway. Fourth to be made wife of Molag.

Nuala: Pureblood Goblin, born a peasant. Rumored to be the most beautiful of all Goblins. True mate was Rowan's father. Mother to Rowan. Fifth to be made wife of Molag. Molag's favorite wife. Only wife allowed to engage in mating with the King for a possible heir. Mother of fifteen daughters that Molag slaughtered in annoyance at not having a son born of her.

Sorcha: Pureblood Fairy. First Crowned Queen of the Fae. Mate to Gwendolyn.

Xander: Shapeshifter, Werewolf. Warrior and Alpha of Crescent Rose Moon Pack. Mate of Nikilaus.

Benjamin and Lily: Shapeshifters, Werewolves. Warriors and Betas of Crescent Rose Moon Pack. Mates.

Rebecca: Witch. Second High Priestess of the Witches Wood Coven. Elgeeva's trusted right hand. Gifted in magics of Earth and the Winds of the North. Wife of John.

Susanna: Witch. Third High Priestess of the Witches Wood Coven. Elgeeva's trusted left hand. Gifted in magics of Fire and the Winds of the South. Wife of Giles.

John: Warlock. Husband of Rebecca. Gifted in magics of Air and the Winds of the East.

Giles: Warlock. Husband of Susanna. Gifted in magics of Water and the Winds of the West.

Basil and Dermot: Pureblood Fairies. Mates to each other. Reproductive mates of Sorcha and Gwendolyn of the Fae Realm.

THE KINGDOM OF MIST AND BLOOD

Brigid and Cormac: Humans. Husband and wife. Warriors. Council members of the creatures for the human species. Appointed by Molag.

Grainne and Oisin: Humans. Husband and wife. Warriors. Council members of the creatures for the human species. Appointed by Molag.

Esurg and Agrok: Pureblood Giants, two of four Giants of Old. First coupling born of their kind. First of many creatures created by the Mother.

Tozir and Borog: Pureblood Giants, two of four Giants of Old. Second coupling born of their kind. First of many creatures created by the Mother.

Vladimir: First known Pureblood Vampire. King of the Ice Lands. Mate to Lottie. Vampire Father of Dawn and Lothous.

Dawn and Lothous: Vampires. Skilled Warriors. Daughter and son of Lottie and Vladimir.

King Conway: Pureblood Elf. Elven King of Old. Life Partner to Opal. Father of Elgeeva.

Aerin and Lucious: Pureblood Elves. Warriors. Life Partners.

Midgard and Fafnir: Dragons. Keepers and Guardians of Merek and Rowan.

Barcella: Half breed of Centaur and Satyr. Warrior. Daughter of Chief Brynzin and Chieftess Ryanna.

King Gavor: Pureblood Dwarf. Warrior King. Arrogant and proud. Undergrown dweller.

Brynzin: Pureblood Centaur. Warrior. Chief of the Dark Hallow Lands. Mate to Ryanna.

Ryanna: Pureblood Satyr. Healer. Chieftess of the Dark Hallow Lands. Mate to Brynzin.

Play List

~**Fancy Hagood**
"Forest"

~**Forest Blakk:**
*"I Saw Love
Where I First Found You*

~**Ava Max:**
Kings and Queens

~**Imagine Dragons:**
Believe

~**Josh Turner:**
Will You Go With Me

~**Sam Smith:**
To Die For

~**George Ezra:**
Hold My Girl

~**Nate Ruess:**
Nothing Without Love

THE KINGDOM OF MIST AND BLOOD

~Niall Horan:

Slow Hands

~Ed Sheeran:

Nancy Mulligan,

The Joker and The Queen

~David Bowie:

As The World Falls Down

~Lord Huron

Love Like Ghosts

~Hozier

Work Song

~Taylor Swift

Timeless

Acknowledgements

Thank you, yes you, holding this book, my Darling reader. Thank you!

A huge Thank You to my very first readers: Rose Padin, Sarah Quinby and Andrew Wood. You have no idea how much your words of praise and critiques meant and means to me. I am so very grateful!

The biggest Thank you of all, is for my wonderful, encouraging, re-assuring, gorgeous and beautiful cousin and editor! Melly, this book won't be what it is without you. I cherish our collaborations, our wine nights, the million texts, calls and emails. I am so proud of you and all the work we've done! I love you my dearling, how lucky am I that you are in my life!

About the Author

Amanda J. Stevens grew up in Hopkinton, NH. She is a Licensed Massage Therapist by day and a novice writer by night. She is an insatiable reader and a collector of books, a lover of Greek mythology, dark fantasy romance, and of course the classics of "old." She loves plants—annuals, perennials, and house plants. Her home is a jungle of said plants inside and out with her books sprinkled here, there, precariously placed, piled and prized 'til her dream library can be built. Her sour dough starter is named "Soura" (a nod to TLOR) and most everything she makes is from scratch with a satisfying pastime of milling her own flour. She lives in Wolfeboro, NH with her husband and their four beautiful children on a slice of land she named Cricket Hallow.